SUNRISE, SUNFALL

ASTRAL KINGDOMS BOOK 2

SPENCER STEEVES

Sunrise, Sunfall

Astral Kingdoms Book 2

A novel by Spencer Steeves

SECRETIVE HOMECOMING

The black horse trotted slowly down the dirt path, dust flying up from its hooves, which churned the loose ground underneath. The wheels of the cart the animal pulled dug furrows in the road, but the rider didn't care. He'd traveled long, bearing his burden, and now he finally neared his destination. In the distance, across the grey grass, he saw the small, walled community. In this place, even the smallest villages had tall walls. They had to, or else they risked destruction. The windows of many of the houses glowed with lantern light, like beacons of hope for the traveler.

His heart beating fast with anticipation of what awaited him in one of those houses, the man leaned down into the horse's mane, urging it with a word to go faster. With a quiet whicker, the horse complied, moving into a canter. The traveler glanced back at the wagon to ensure that his cargo was still safe. The studded leather straps still held the long crate secure, the buckles jingling as the rumbling cart passed over ridges and burrs on the path.

It wasn't long before the wall was close enough for the man to make out the individual cobblestones of the structure. A sense of relief spread through his chest, seeing no sign of damage to the wall or the gate. Such an occurrence was commonplace here, and often the man feared he would return home to see the iron gate twisted and the houses ransacked.

But not today, thank the Divines. The man stopped his horse just outside the gate. Already, someone was standing at the top, the yellow light of his lantern illuminating his face in the grey evening. Though a new layer of stubble coated the boy's lower jaw, the traveler instantly recognized the unwavering blue eyes and somewhat crooked nose.

"Who goes there?" the boy called down, his voice deeper than the traveler remembered. *I've been gone for quite some time,* he admitted to himself.

"I don't think you need to ask that question, Kravex," the traveler replied. "I know that you recognize the horse, if not the rider. You were always fond of them. I remember the night that you got your first beast; you slept in the stable alongside her. Your mother was furious, but you were happier than could be. How is Siara doing? Has she borne you well?"

"Sir!" the young guard exclaimed in surprise. "We thought you weren't coming back!"

"Ye of little faith, Kravex," the traveler chided. "Now why don't you open that gate, so that I may see to my personal business."

"O-of course," Kravex stammered, clomping down the steps set behind the stone wall. A few moments later, the gate creaked and slowly swung open, admitting the man into the village. As soon as his horse and cart had passed safely through, the creaking sound started again. With a clatter and boom, the metal bars closed off the village again.

A few people glanced fearfully out of the windows as the man trotted his horse down the road, relief taking over their features as they recognized the rider. Visitors were rare here, and when they came, it was usually one bearing grim news.

While this traveler did bear grim news, it was not meant for them, and for that, the villagers were thankful.

The man came to a stop in front of one of the houses. A small wooden abode, with folded shutters, painted green, though you could barely tell, with the overcast sky. A window, recently cleaned, shone with comforting light. The man swung down from his horse, running a hand through its mane. "Thank you, friend, you've served me faithfully." The horse snuffled softly as if to say it was no issue, and the traveler nodded. He quickly unhitched the wagon from the animal, allowing it to rest its weary muscles, then led the animal back to the stable at the side of the house. He scooped fresh grains into the feedbag and drew up a bucket of water. "I will return in a little while to take off the saddle and rub you down." The man rubbed the horse's nose appreciatively, then circled back around to the front of the house, glancing quickly at the wagon, and then down the road. The village was eerily empty, a deep silence seeming to have a hold over the entire place. It was a familiar silence, he decided. Only rarely did anybody leave their homes or shops, so he had little worry about leaving the cart unattended. *We keep our own in this village,* the man thought. *Because if you can't trust your neighbors, then who can you trust?"*

Banishing that sobering thought, the man strode up to the door of the little house and knocked. A few moments passed in agonizing silence. Then he heard the shifting of the locking apparatus, and the door opened slightly.

A woman stood there, her dull brown hair streaked with faint hints of grey. Her careworn grey eyes looked out from the crack curiously, but, like all the others, with a twinge of fear. That fear melted a moment later, dripping into shock, and the door was thrown open.

The woman collapsed into the man's arms, trying her best to suppress tears. "Ignis," she murmured into his shoulder. "You've returned!"

Ignis brought a pale hand up to stroke his wife's brown hair. "Yes, Naomi. I've returned."

Naomi drew back to scrutinize Ignis's pale face. "It's been months! We thought that somebody had managed to kill you."

Ignis hated seeing those tears in her eyes. He wiped one away with his thumb. "I know," he replied. "I never wanted to stay away for so long."

"But you had no choice, I'm sure." Ignis was glad his wife understood. Naomi always understood. "At least tell me that you have a few days before you have to go again."

"A few," Ignis agreed. "I have to go to the Keep at week's end to deliver... that." He gestured vaguely towards the cart, unsuccessfully trying to keep the tension from his voice.

"What is it this time?" Naomi asked. Her voice was nearly a whisper. Ignis was just about to reply when a gasp from the other side of the room grabbed his attention. Ignis stepped inside the house, closing the door behind him. He stepped away from his wife, and tears filled his eyes. A watery smile splashed onto his face. "Lumi." He couldn't keep the quiver from his lip, and it reflected in his voice.

"Daddy!" The blonde-haired little girl broke into a run and threw herself into Ignis's arms. Father wrapped daughter in comfort and love. Ignis had been so long away from his family, and he felt it keenly now, as he held his beautiful daughter in his arms. She cried into his leather armor, the tears running down the oiled surface to splash on the floor. His knives were stowed in his saddlebags; he knew he wouldn't need them in here, but he rarely went anywhere without the armor. It had been crafted by masters, perfectly fitted to his form, making it suited for getting around quietly, as was his job, while also having some measure of protection.

"Lumi," he whispered into the girl's ear. "I missed you so much." Ignis gave Lumi a final squeeze and let her back down to the floor. The dust of travel had stained her previously white blouse, but the girl didn't care. Her father was back home, and that was all that mattered.

Being with Naomi and Lumiira was pure bliss, and Ignis stayed for as long as he possibly could, but it would never be long enough. He always had to leave his uncomplaining wife and beautiful child, for the Lords ever had a new task for him. *No rest for the weary soul,* Ignis said mournfully to himself. *Not to mention the body. I'm not getting any younger.*

So it was that only a scant few days later, Ignis was back on his horse, riding through the morbid field of grey grass. After spending so many months in Sun's Reach, where the dew in the green waves of grass shimmered in the sun, this bleak landscape was a shock. And though this place was home, had been for some time, Ignis felt a wistful pang for the Sunlit Land.

A day's travel took him within sight of the Keep, where he was headed with his cargo. The massive stone building rose ominously out of the color leached field, five towers reaching high into the sky, like fingers of some giant hand, grasping eternally at something hidden beyond the clouds. Ignis stirred as he saw it. This was the place where he'd been ordered to head to Sun's Reach, the place where the Lords lived. The Lords who kept him away from his wife and daughter. Ignis felt incredibly blessed that his long-suffering wife was patient and understanding. Any lesser woman, he knew, would have split from the stress and his absence. But the two of them had an agreement, one sealed by the presence of Lumiira. Naomi would never blame Ignis for not being around and would teach Lumi the same thing. They simply relished every moment they had with each other, however few they were.

Ignis galloped up to the towering walls. Forty feet tall and twenty thick, the Keep was an impressive and imposing structure. But unlike the first time he'd seen it, Ignis was not afraid. He'd been called into the Keep many a time and seen the inside. The towers commanded awe and wonderment, but no fear. "Ignis Duskwalker," he proclaimed to the silent walls. "I have something that the Lords desire!" There wasn't anyone on the battlements of the Keep, and no voice answered him, but all the same, the doors of the Keep swung open, and Ignis trotted into the court-yard. He left his horse at the stable yard, knowing that the animal would be taken care of, despite the emptiness of the place. Ignis unhitched the wagon, a small cart, light enough for him to pull, as it only held one thing— the covered crate.

He was met at the entrance, same as always, by a mute giant of a man, with alabaster skin too smooth to be human, and features too stocky to belong to an elf. The mute nodded curtly and led him down the hall. They passed endless corridors and rooms, none of which Ignis had ever seen into. He wanted with all of his curious heart to investigate, to see what mysteries the Keep held. But the giant man never allowed him to explore, stopping him with a sharp gesture. And Ignis doubted that the huge ax on his back was for show. As the Secretkeeper back in Sun's Reach, he was meant to see things that the public eye shouldn't, but here, Ignis knew that the punishment for unwarranted snooping would be severe.

The mute led Ignis to an innately carved door, the same door that Ignis was always brought to. He pushed it open, and the Secretkeeper entered, his wagon behind him. As usual, a large, multi-seated podium stood at the front of the room, its five chairs occupied. All the occupants wore hooded robes, each a different color and embroidered with different designs. Though Ignis didn't know much about the Keep, he knew about the Lords. A myriad of races: They were, Human, Elf, Dwarf, Khindre, and Gnome, and each was mighty. Ignis bowed deeply, ignoring the pain in his normally limber joints. Many days of hard riding to reach the Keep had strained them, he knew.

The robed man in the middle spoke to him, his voice cracked and cackling, but still powerful. "Duskwalker, you have finally returned. And just on schedule!"

"You ordered that I be here today, my Lord," Ignis said, not rising from his bow. "It would have been foolish to wait any longer anyway." He cleared his throat. "I have the thing you have asked of me, though the task was not a simple one."

"That makes good hearing, Duskwalker," another figure said. By the morbid yet musical tone of the voice, Ignis suspected it was the elf. "You have much wisdom in your mind. But never-mind that. Show us the prize!"

"My, my," cackled the first figure. "Aren't we impatient today!"

"With all due respect, Greatlord, we didn't expect everything to fall into line so quickly, and we don't know when things might turn in our competitors' favor." The others at the table burst out in accordance. The central figure waved a hand to calm them down.

"Fair enough," he agreed once they were quiet. "I suppose the time we have waited has been sufficient." The center-most robed man leaned over and stared down at Ignis, who felt his very soul being peered into without consent. "As my other Lords' decree, open the crate, so that we may assure that you have brought us what was requested."

Ignis nodded obligingly and circled around to the back of the wagon. Recalling that the Lords liked a bit of drama, he pulled the black cover off with a flourish, revealing the long wooden box. It was carved with runes that Ignis couldn't read, which almost seemed to glow in the dim light of the Hearing Chamber.

Ignis unclasped the straps and pushed them aside to clatter to the floor. Then he turned the wagon around so that the open back was facing the Lords. Every one of them was leaning over the table in anticipation, a couple even rubbing their gloved hands together.

Gulping down a lump of anxiety, Ignis braced his hands on the cover and pulled up. The container opened with a quiet groaning creak as the old hinges protested movement. Inside was indeed the prize the Lords had been looking for; Ignis could hear the utterances of joy that they tried to quash. He couldn't bring himself to look at the chilling contents, so instead, he turned away, while waiting for the Lords to address him. He stifled any reaction that tried to appear on his face, as he doubted the Lords would take kindly to him being upset. Not when they were so visibly excited.

"The day we have awaited has indeed come, my brothers," the center most Lord said. "With this, we can make our plans come to fruition," he gestured vaguely to the crate and Ignis tried not to flinch. "As Erendreth has said, we don't know how long we have to work. We already know that *Her* agents are still active in the world, despite our schemes to be rid of them." The creature turned to Ignis. "Thank you, Secretkeeper, for all you have done. You shall have a reward, unlike any you have already received." His laugh was just as Ignis recalled, a dry, rattling death knell. "You have always wished to know more about the workings of the Keep, our workings. Now you shall! Come, brothers, let us get to work!"

Ignis sighed. He had hoped to be allowed to return home, but no, it seemed that the Lords had other plans for him. Shivering once as the five undead mages slowly levitated from their seats and down to the ground, the leader beckoning him to join, Ignis Duskwalker looked once into the crate, and sighed again. "I'm sorry," he said to nobody in particular. Then he closed the lid, settled the handles on his shoulders, and followed Qrakzt, the Mad Mage, and his fellow liches to a door he'd never noticed before. Deeper into the Keep, to learn its mysteries at last.

PART I
SHADOWS OF THE MIND

TARUS

THE WIDOWER PRINCE

It was a bright, beautiful day in Sun's Reach, and Tarus Gardstar stood in the garden, listening to the birdsong carried on the wind. Tarus smiled; he'd come to love the sound of those birds in his time here. They represented a pure-hearted beauty that Sun's Reach held, something very much unlike anything Tarus had seen before this.

Another creature also lifted its voice in song, the sweet melody drifting into Tarus's ears. *Speaking of beauty.* The boy followed the music to the source and was gladdened to see the one he'd hoped for. The gorgeous red-haired girl sat in an alcove of the wall, her eyes closed, and sweet mouth opened in song. Fiery hair hung down around her shoulders loosely, limned by sunlight. Emery Redwyn was, without a doubt, the most beautiful woman Tarus had ever seen in his life.

A hint of doubt stirred in the back of his mind; something didn't seem right about this, but he couldn't quite place it. Had he ever heard Emery sing before? Tarus hadn't a clue that the princess enjoyed singing, but there she was, belting out a lovely song. They hadn't known each other long, and she could have hidden it from him until now. That must be it, he decided, and with a shrug, he continued on.

He strolled up to the alcove where she was sitting and placed a hand on hers. Her singing stopped abruptly, and she whirled around, her expression all surprise and worry. But when Emery saw Tarus, the worry all melted into a sweet smile; the smile that sent Tarus's heart beating wildly and made him glad to be alive.

"Emery, I am no man's poet, but today, you look like...," he thought for a moment, trying to think of something the princess would understand. The land Tarus came from was different from Sun's Reach, and the analogies he would usually use would have little meaning here. "A single sunlit flower, among all the grass of the world," he decided on.

Emery blushed a deep crimson at the compliment. "Come." Emery shifted to the side, allowing her shapely legs to swing in the open air, and making room for Tarus to join her in the alcove. The stone of the wall was warm beneath his hands, but Emery was warmer. "I'm glad that you came to Sun's Reach, Tarus Gardstar," she said, leaning back to rest her head against his shoulder.

"As am I, Emy," Tarus breathed. Emery tilted her head back to look into the young Lord's eyes. Tarus's heart skipped a beat. She looked so inviting and pleasing. The young lord couldn't wait to have a taste of her fiery sweetness. He leaned down, but before he could kiss Emery, it seemed to Tarus that they'd been flung into the air. The ground looked far away as if the alcove they were sitting in had been raised to a higher position on the wall. Hoping for some sort of answer, Tarus looked down at his lovable princess.

But she had changed as well. Tarus didn't find himself staring into the soft brown eyes he loved, nor the full lips awaiting a kiss.

Emery's face was contorted in pain, and her eyes were filled with tears.

Tarus gasped in alarm. "Emery! What happened?" The young Lord let his eyes wander over Emery's body, as they had many times before. But this time, he saw it. The cold, white knife protruding from her belly! He reached down to remove it, but though he pulled with all his might, fueled by frantic desperation, the blade was stuck fast.

"Why, Tarus?" Emery whimpered pitifully. Tarus felt his heart shatter, staring at the beautiful lady in pain. He was too horrified to speak, frozen in fear, unable to act. Her next question slammed into his heart like a ton of stone. "Why did you kill me, Tarus?" The words echoed inside his skull, the awful din leaving a flaring pain each time they repeated. His grip on the princess slackened, and without the strength to hold herself up, the dying girl slipped. She slid down over the lip of the alcove and fell into the darkness enclosing what was once the courtyard. Tarus barely noticed; all he could see was the shock and pain on Emery's face. He didn't pay any attention to the tendrils of shadow that reached out to grab at him, hoping to drag him under. At long last, the darkness filled his view, blotting out the picture of dying Emery.

But his ordeal wasn't finished yet. As he sat there, stunned, in the darkness, a voice filled his head. Though the call of his beloved princess was familiar, it wasn't pleasant this time. Her tone was cold and steely, rather unlike her natural warmth. "Your father is a vile man." If Emery's words before had been a cacophony, this was a maelstrom in Tarus's head. He clenched his teeth, for he knew now what was coming, and it didn't excite the Lord at all. He wished above all that he could block his ears, stop the hurtful words from coming.

"And it seems you're no different!"

Tarus Gardstar sat bolt upright in bed, his skin drenched with cold sweat. Breath came to him laboriously, and his stomach roiled with grief and pain. Tears burned in his eyes as if Emery's words had been fire, coursing through his veins.

It was a beautiful, warm day in Sun's Reach, but the room in which Tarus awoke was dark and cold. The young Lord's shiver had little to do with the chill, though. It was his heart that felt the cold keenly. The chill of love lost. Tarus braced his hand on one poster of the bed, which held up the canopy. This bed, this large, comfortable, ornamented bed; the bed he should have shared with Emery Redwyn. But Emery was dead, *murdered.* As if that wasn't bad enough, *Tarus* had killed her! Grief wracked his heart and mind, his every thought hounded by that pained expression on Emery's face when the dagger slid into her soft belly.

The young Lord buried his face in his pillow, hoping to muffle the scream that bubbled up into his throat, but it came out as only a hoarse whimper.

He felt weak and exhausted, though he'd just woken from sleep. His legs and arms ached as he pushed himself out of bed. Stumbling his way over to the window, he gently pushed aside one of the curtains. A low hiss escaped his mouth as the bright sunlight burned his eyes. But he didn't flinch away; he deserved this pain, a fitting penance for everything he had done.

Hadn't he known that his father's intentions were impure? Hadn't he, Velara, and their parents come here with the sole aim of taking the throne? But for all of Lord Geurus's planning, he'd never once mentioned slaying the princess, or the queen, for that matter!

And there'd certainly not been any discussion about doing so in public!

Tarus thought of the dagger that his father had given him on the wedding day, wincing painfully as the ghastly image of the white blade stabbing Emery. *Divines,* would he never be free of this guilt, these haunting images?

What had been Geurus's purpose in giving his son that dagger? In the giving, he'd said: *"You know what must be done."* But Tarus wasn't quite sure that he did! He reflected deep into his mind, trying to recall other things that his father had told him, clues as to the purpose of the dagger's gift. Something else did come to him then, something he didn't remember hearing on the day, but came clearly to him now.

"You are about to make Emery Redwyn a woman wed, my son," Geurus had said right before the princess had come up the stairs. "You will soon be called upon to perform, Tarus." The soon-to-be king had braced his hands on Tarus's shoulders and pulled him close, dropping his voice to a harsh whisper. "No woman is more vibrant than on her wedding night, boy. But caught up in the moment, she is also quite vulnerable." He must have seen the question in his son's eyes then, for he smiled his cruel, thin smile—a murderer's smile, Tarus realized. "You know what must be done." He wanted Tarus to... no! No, that couldn't be the case! The boy couldn't believe it! But couldn't he? Lord Geurus had proved himself to be a terrible man already. For all his son could tell, that had been his plan—the new king's plan the whole time.

Tarus had to know, had to consult his father this instant! Force him to tell the truth. But as he stormed towards the door, his stomach clenched in awful pain. A wave of weakness ran through him, and Tarus felt suddenly faint. "Perhaps I should grab something to eat first," he said with a pained, humorless chuckle.

He staggered out of the room, using the wall to support himself, as sharp pangs of hunger continually stabbed into him. How long had it been since he ate last? He couldn't remember, so caught up in grief and confusion. Tarus straightened himself up and smoothed his wrinkled tunic as best as he could. Tarus knew that his long, curly hair was an absolute mess, but there wasn't much he could do about it. Taking a deep breath, the prince opened the door of his chambers, only flinching slightly as light flooded his vision again.

A well-dressed man with close-cropped brown hair was leaning back with one foot on the wall, his arms crossed over his chest. He started awake when the door swung open and looked around, alarmed. Tarus studied his face; he wasn't anyone familiar, but by the cold snarl he admitted, the servant recognized him.

"So the Widower Prince finally wakes," he growled. Well, that answered that question at the very least. He must have been one of the Redwyn's servants, still working for King Geurus. At first, Tarus wondered why any man would stay in the service of their master's murderer, but then he answered the question for himself. *If I were a Lord or Lady and a servant of the dead Royal Family came to me looking for a job, would I take them in? No, I suppose not. I wouldn't want to relate my reputation to the Redwyns, not when their killers rule the city.* He didn't know whether any of the servants had thought to leave yet. *Any that don't are still on the Kingdom's bankroll. Perhaps the payment is sufficient to keep them from defecting.*

Suddenly Tarus seemed to notice what the man had said, and he choked back an enraged retort. Was this what the people of the castle called him now? The Widower Prince. Divines, the name was fitting, and it felt like a hammer to the chest.

Tarus refused to favor the servant with a reply, ignoring the less than discreet chuckle at his disheveled appearance. Running his hand along the smooth stone of the wall, Tarus walked down the well-lit hallway, focusing his attention on navigating his way to the smaller dining room, where he hoped there would be some remnants of breakfast left.

Much to his chagrin, when he arrived, he found he wasn't alone.

His sister, Velara Gardstar, was lounging at the table, her pale legs supported on a cushioned stool that Tarus was positive belonged in one of the solars; specifically the one a few stories up, if he remembered correctly. Tarus winced, feeling sorry for whichever servant Velara had sent to retrieve it, sure that it was one of Redwyn's.

"By the Divines," Velara gasped, looking up at her brother from the book she was leafing through. "Would you look at what the bobcat dragged in!" Tarus wasn't sure if they even had bobcats here in Sun's Reach. "We were beginning to worry whether you were still alive, brother," she said with a smirk on her face. "I don't think that Father would have taken kindly to you turning up dead, after all."

"Nice to see you too, sister," Tarus crossed to the table and plucked an apple from the bowl in the center. He'd grown rather fond of the sweet, crunchy fruit since coming here. Back home, few edible plants actually grew; around this time, the 'warm' season would be almost finished, meaning the last of the berries and other miscellaneous foliage was being gathered and stored to supplement the primarily carnivorous diet throughout the rest of the year.

Velara sniffed the air and wrinkled her nose. "Ew, you stink, Tarus. Divines! It's been three days since the wedding. Have you even changed, or bathed for that matter?" No, in fact, he hadn't, Tarus thought. He'd been a little busy. Had it already been three days? Three whole days that he'd spent in his room. *And I might have stayed longer if it wasn't for the hunger.* Tarus recalled that the servants had brought meals to him for a time.

As if Velara heard his thoughts, she watched him ravenously chomp on the apple. "Father ordered the servants to stop feeding you. Said it would draw you out, eventually."

"And if it didn't?"

"Then I imagine he would either storm in there himself or let you starve. I couldn't tell from his reaction." Velara giggled. "Oh, don't look so shocked. I doubt King Geurus would let his heir die of starvation!"

That wasn't what had Tarus's eyes widened and brimming again with tears. The prince had just noticed what his sister was wearing. A dress, which wasn't unusual for her. But it was made of silk—Velara didn't own any silk clothing! Nobody back home did! It was too damn cold to even think about wearing something so light. The silken dress was dyed orange, and Tarus's jaw nearly unhinged and hit the floor. That was Emery's favorite dress!

The piece, tailored to fit the previous princess, was far too tight on the more amply endowed Velara Gardstar. That fact didn't seem to bother his sister very much. "Oh, this?" she said, gesturing to her outfit and giggling at his gaping mouth. "Your precious little princess seemed to really like this dress, and most of my clothes needed a wash anyway, so I figured I'd try it on. I must admit, it's surprisingly comfortable!" Velara pulled at a strand of her blond hair absently. "Did you know that she doesn't even have a single dark outfit in her wardrobe? It's crazy, so many reds, yellows, and lighter shades of blue and green, but besides brown riding leathers, nothing!" Tarus didn't hear her, still unable to get over the fact that his sister was wearing the dress of the dead princess. The princess he had hoped to marry. Who he would have married if...

"Hey!" Velara snapped her fingers a couple times to get his attention. "Are you even listening?" Trying to keep from sputtering or crying again, Tarus could only shake his head in reply. "Well, listen to this, if nothing else. You should go bathe and change now before Father finds out you're awake. I imagine he'll call you to the audience hall to speak about the wedding, which, if I may say, went perfectly. A perfectly symbolic death for Emery; quite literally the fall of House Redwyn! But you don't want to be seen like *that* in front of the king."

Tarus shivered at the thought. Emery had once told him of a

time when she'd come back from a visit to town wearing the equivalent of commoners clothes. Her father had been apoplectic. Geurus Gardstar, on the other hand, would likely flay him alive if he appeared at an official summons with anything akin to his current outfit. Nodding mutely, Tarus took another apple from the bowl and turned to leave. Deciding that he would ask the servants to whip up something more substantial as he bathed, the Widower Prince shuffled off to the private bath near Grayson's room. He needed to get clean but also clear his head and think.

As he walked down the corridor, he saw Grayson Redwyn, the last living member of the Redwyn royal family. Tarus wasn't quite sure why Geurus — at the moment, with the doubts and thoughts raging in his head, the prince was having difficulty thinking of King Gardstar as his father — had allowed Grayson to live. It seemed wrong to him. Wouldn't Emery have been the more valuable hostage? If his entire plan was to take the throne, why not kill the King, Queen, and lesser prince, and hold on to the crown princess? If he'd meant to demoralize the people of Searstar by showing that he had more power, Tarus would have expected Geurus to kill every member of the family, rather than leaving even one alive.

Whatever Lord Gardstar's reasoning was, he now had the throne.

Though Grayson Redwyn was alive, he didn't look pleased about it. Tarus recalled the younger prince always had issues with keeping his anger in check, and right now, he was obviously having a bad time of it. His decently handsome face — nowhere near as handsome as his sister had been beautiful — was contorted in rage: teeth grinding, eyes flashing, chin quivering. Tarus quickly scanned him for weapons, wishing he'd had the foresight to strap on his sword. Luckily, Geurus had thought of that for him. Grayson wasn't allowed to carry a weapon unless he was in the training field, where he spent a fair amount of his time. The king was obviously afraid that the volatile prince would try to slay him or one of his children to avenge Emery.

From the look on Grayson's face, Tarus didn't blame Geurus for his worry.

"Good morrow, my prince," Grayson bowed stiffly to Tarus, his expression not changing in the slightest.

"Morning," Tarus replied, not sure whether the modifier *good* applied in this situation.

"You don't understand just how *pleased* I am to see you up and about this morning." Tarus glanced about, hoping to see a guard or servant. Tarus was slightly taller than Grayson, and his shoulders were broad and robust, but the prince had a mean look in his eye, and Tarus didn't want to wager on his chances. *And that's besides the fact that if I killed Father's last playing piece, he'd have me flayed alive.*

"I'm afraid I don't understand," Tarus said in an attempt to defuse the situation. "I don't see why you would be happy to see me, after everything that's happened."

Grayson arched an eyebrow. "The hell?" Then he shook his head irritably. "No, I won't be tricked by your fancy words, Widower Prince!" Tarus tried to hide his flinch at the nickname, but by the glint in Grayson's eye, he'd failed. The young Lord Gardstar really wished that people would stop bringing Emery's death up. Couldn't they understand it hurt him just as much as it did them? No, of course, they couldn't see that. "I came here to get my aggression out, and I'll be damned if I let you take that from me." Grayson removed the glove he was wearing and thrust it through the air onto Tarus's shoulder, a formal challenge, a request for a duel!

"You can't be serious about that!" Tarus protested

"And why not?" Grayson countered. "You killed her, my

Lord." The respectful moniker did not mix well with Grayson's seething tone.

"With that in mind," Tarus replied coldly. "You would be stupid to think I'd actually accept your challenge. Giving you a chance to kill me would do nobody any good."

"I wasn't planning to kill you, my Lord," Grayson drawled. "I know that doing that would forfeit my life. But I have little freedom to do anything but fight since our King won't let me outside the gates." Tarus could hear a longing in the princeling's voice. He flashed back painfully to the Rothsster-Leygrain wedding when Emery had practically abandoned him in favor of her recently returned knight Leonidas Braveheart, whom, as she'd said before her death, she'd been entirely in love with. As Tarus had danced with myriad partners that evening, the young Lord had observed the other couples in the halls wistfully. Not least among them had been Prince Grayson Redwyn and Reyna Rainclaw, one of the commoner sisters. Did Grayson truly miss his Khindre love so dearly?

Tarus could understand just how awful it must be: trapped in the castle where your family had been slain. "Perhaps that situation could change," he mumbled vaguely, pushing past the red-haired boy and letting the glove drop from his shoulder, challenge unacknowledged. He was aware that Grayson was staring at him queerly, but Tarus dismissed the young Redwyn out of mind for the time being. He had much to stew over this day.

CAITRIAL

WORKING THROUGH GRIEF

Geurus Gardstar had promised to be a graceful king, a good king, or at least those few supporters who heard his post-murder speech believed. Within his first month of his rule, he proved this to be false. Geurus was quick to stamp down any foolish enough to attempt outright rebellion, and rumors drifted down from the castle that his family were demanding masters, and cruel, not in the least amenable about his methods of lordship. Emery had been benevolent and effervescent in life, and Grayson dour but a staunch friend and ally, but the new royal heirs were of a totally different class. Servants claimed that Velara Gardstar was more demanding on her best day than Geurus on his worst. And Tarus was apparently disconsolate, though over what, the servants had mixed reports. It left him locked in his own head, and dismissive of those who tried to aid him.

Despite these tales, and the ineffable experience of seeing most of their royal family extirpated, allies of Geurus's just kept appearing, quicker than daring rebels could snuff them out.

Whether disgruntled nobles, or grudging commoners, or that obsequious bunch that didn't care who sat the Highsun Seat, they provided enough support that the usurper king saw no reason to change his ways. Before the Redwyn's blood had dried on the stones, security around the city had tightened significantly. Those less than careful dissenters soon learned that the streets had eyes and ears. They all disappeared without a trace, and those brave fools who tried to speak out were slaughtered silently in back alleys or castle dungeons. Despite this quick action, a few cautious revolutionaries, wiser than those left rotting in unmarked graves established secret codes and organized meetings. Managing to find times and places out of the earshot of the seemingly ever-present Enforcers, these few coalesced in order to rally support, to plan, to *survive*.

Among these faithful supporters were the children of the Rainclaw family. Under the raw red light of the sun, which seemed to weep for the tragedy that had occurred less than a full turn of a month ago, Caitrial, Reyna, and Arcadia held their nightly vigil for Emery's soul alongside Berdur Longshield, the respected dwarven herbalist of the town. Nobody cried; their tears had long been worn out, as made evident by their red-rimmed eyes and bleak, drawn expressions. Three candles burned in the center of the room, one for each member of the Redwyn family.

Berdur's blind eyes stared blankly at the flames for a few moments longer before rising from his squat stool, bones creaking and protesting. "Not to cause any offense, ladies," Berdur said apologetically. "But it would do me well to get some sleep. Unfortunate though it may be, in this world, losing a royal family doesn't stop business. In all likeliness, there may be a line at my door when I return to work on the morrow."

The two Khindre twins nodded vaguely and said their

farewells to old Berdur, who had allowed them to practice their magic behind his shop many a time of Emery..

Caitrial finally shook herself out of her own trance and stood, guiding Berdur to the rack and helping him put on his cloak. Then she turned to her two younger sisters. "Berdur speaks wisely, you two. We all ought to get some rest. These coming days will doubtlessly be long enough as it is." Caitrial gently patted her two siblings on the back, preparing to whisk them off to their beds.

"You know," Berdur, who had one hand on the open door, said. "I know that the elder Mistress Rainclaw has a job, but if the two of you twins wanted something to do, and perhaps a way to earn a few radiants while you're at it, my shop is open to you."

Both Reyna and Arcadia looked up in surprise at that. "Would you actually hire us, Master Berdur?" Reyna asked. Her musical voice tinkled with hope.

"Why, of course, dear ones," Berdur replied. "I know just how hard it can be to sit around and do nothing with dark thoughts on your mind. Not to mention, I could use the help. With my blindness and my shaking hands, it's difficult to get much done quickly." The old dwarf chuckled. "Besides, I'm not much of a dwarf's dwarf, so to speak, so chafing against the grain isn't much of an issue with me." Berdur was not incorrect in his statement. Caitrial only knew a few dwarves, but she knew that by giving up his hammer and living among the humans, he'd broken the expectations of his people, most of which had retreated underground following the Eclipse. Though Dwarves had very few official mages among them, the spells running the forges on which they made many of their peerless weapons and contraptions had been broken. To lose their life's work was trying on all dwarves, and few examples of dwarven kind made their appearance among the cities of Sun's Reach. Even the tribalistic Hill Dwarves had become less active.

But Berdur had lived in Searstar so long that most of his tell-tale dwarven accent had been buried! It wouldn't be much of a stretch for Berdur to hire a couple of Khindre. "I agree with our respected apothecary," Caitrial said, smiling despite herself. "A job is just what you two need. You can start in the morning after you've both had a good rest. Now shoo, off to bed with you!" Their mood somewhat improved from only a few moments before, Arcadia and Reyna did as their sister bade. Caitrial mouthed her thanks to Berdur, almost forgetting that the dwarf was blind in her satisfaction. She audibly thanked him and helped the old man down the step in front of her house, before heading to bed herself.

The next morning, all three of the Rainclaw sisters went off to their jobs, if not with smiles on their faces, then at least with some manner of light in their souls. With all the backlogged orders that Berdur and Caitrial found themselves with, all three sisters had plenty of work to do. They often came home too exhausted to do anything more complex than eat dinner and hold cursory conversation before heading to bed.

Life went on like this until the first month under Geurus's shroud was complete, and a few days into the second. Caitrial was tucking in her sisters, and one night, she saw a distinct sadness in Reyna's eyes. She knew that Arcadia and Reyna were both too old for being tucked in, but perhaps it was just Caitrial trying to be motherly and supportive, giving the girls what they deserved, but rarely received due to their race.

"What's wrong, Reyna?" Caitrial smoothed the dark hair from her sister's sunset orange forehead. "You look troubled."

For a moment, Reyna didn't answer the question, busy soaking in the affection Caitrial was granting her. Even though Cos and Sardan treated Reyna far better than they had Arcadia, the twins could tell that the two commoners were more than a little embarrassed to have Khindre, devil-kin, for children. Never had their love been unconditional, as one would expect between mother and child—as Caitrial had received growing up. Everything had been based on whether Reyna and Arcadia acted 'human.' It hadn't been easy for either of the twins, and Reyna had worked hard to remain resolute no matter what.

When Reyna opened her eyes, those marvelous golden orbs, Caitrial again saw the dolor welling deep within them. Emotion wasn't easy to discern within a Khindre's eyes, seeing as they were usually monochromatic spheres. But a trained eye, usually of a close friend or relative, could read the clues in the small glints of light or nearly imperceptible flecks that appeared with intense emotion. For the twins, it had only ever been Emery, Caitrial, and each other who could understand them so well. An unimaginably lonely life to lead, Caitrial pondered.

Now, those golden spheres were flecked with deep, melancholy blue. It broke Caitrial's heart to see that.

"Father came into the store today," Reyna finally answered.

"Oh?" Caitrial wondered what Sardan would need to come to the apothecary for. She got the answer soon enough, and it wasn't pleasant.

"I overheard Father talking to Berdur. He was looking for a few specific herbs; apparently, he is looking to replicate a beverage that Geurus is very fond of. Most of the ingredients for making the drink aren't found here, in the Kingdom, I mean, and the King wouldn't tell him where they could be found."

"So he's trying everything in his power to make some sort of imitation, using Berdur's herbs," Caitrial swore under her breath. "I have a bad feeling that our father is going too far out of his way to please our new king."

"That's why I left; why I came to live with you. I know I never explained before. I didn't see the harm in it, but now..." Reyna shuddered briefly. Caitrial gingerly sat on the edge of the mattress Arcadia had once slept on, continuing to pour comfort towards her sister. Arcadia was snoring softly in Caitrial's old bed. The twins were set up in what had once been the smith's room. She'd dismantled and rebuilt Arcadia's bed in here, so they could be together. The darker Khindre had quickly claimed Cait's mattress for her own. All for her sister's comfort, Caitrial slept on the lumpy, threadbare couch in the sitting room. "Geurus used to frequent the tavern, but he rarely ever drank, except out of courtesy to his hosts, or the occasional toast to King Godfrey." It didn't go unnoticed by Caitrial that Reyna refused to acknowledge the man who now sat in the Highsun Seat as her ruler. "I could never hear what they were talking about, but I fear that Lord Gardstar may have been charming our parents slowly but surely." Reyna cleared her throat nervously, and her voice came out as little more than a whisper. "And I never liked the looks that he gave me. I could almost feel the malevolence in his glare."

I wonder what information our parents gave Geurus? Caitrial wondered to herself.

"It turns my stomach to think, but it's possible that they might have let something slip that facilitated the Redwyn's deaths. If so, do they know, and does it bother them?" By siding with Arcadia, and taking her in, Caitrial had fallen out of favor with her parents. They hadn't spoken in years. Given how friendly Emery was with the daughter they barely cared to acknowledge, Caitrial wouldn't put it past them.

The beautiful Khindre shook her head sadly. "I want nothing more than to know that secret, but all I know was that Mother and Father started to grow somewhat less...fond of me, shall we say. Like I said, it's why I came here. I feared that Gardstar's honeyed tongue was winning them both over. I do know that Father has already resigned his deal to provide drinks to the Crown, and at a reduced price from Emery's proposition earlier this year. The price of drinks inside the bar has increased, though. The regulars call it the 'the grief silvers,'" Reyna added helpfully.

Again Caitrial muttered a colorful oath. That Sardan Rainclaw had so quickly agreed to supply the Crown with alcohol, and at capital rates too, was not a good sign. Sardan and Godfrey had spent much time at each other's throats. Caitrial reflected it was ironic how, despite their heated rivalry, Emery had still become the twins' best friend. Sardan and Godfrey had little common ground, except for alcohol. Caitrial was sure that if Godfrey hadn't been mollified by Sardan's booze, and Sardan by Godfrey's gold, their feud could have torn apart both families. Caitrial had always assumed that it was part of the typical relationship between the Crown and their drink provider. But now, her father was willing to go along with Geurus Gardstar without any confrontation!

The room was silent for a few moments as the two sisters sorted through their own thoughts. Caitrial laid another kiss on Reyna's head and began to leave. She barely gained a few steps before the Khindre spoke up again, and now Caitrial knew they had reached the underlying cause of her sadness. "Do you miss him?" Reyna asked quietly.

Caitrial was about to admonish her sister; as a family, they'd sworn not to talk about Emery's death anymore, though it carved its way into their thoughts. They realized that to give their sadness such imagery, would be to provide it with power and thus grant Gardstars yet more leverage.

This they would not do.

But then the last word came to Caitrial, and the smith realized that Reyna was not talking about Emery. She'd said *him*, not *her!*

"Do I miss whom, dear one?" Caitrial asked, already forming hunches in her mind.

"Sir Leonidas," Reyna mumbled nervously. "It's been over a

month since we saw him, and everything seems to go much slower. At least it does for me. Sir Leonidas used to come around almost every day to spar with you so his absence... it's pretty noticeable."

Caitrial realized Reyna was right. The day before the wedding was the last time any of the Rainclaw family had seen Leonidas. In the time between the Rothsster-Leygrain marriage, and that catastrophic wedding, Leonidas had become part of the family, it seemed. Not having him here, it left a hole in Caitrial's heart, one she couldn't reconcile, no matter how hard she tried.

Caitrial crossed the room again and squeezed Reyna's shoulder. "I'm sure that he's busy inside the castle. I can't imagine that... what happened is easy on Leo, either. Don't worry, we'll see him again before long." She cocked her head to the side. "But why are you wondering after him?"

"Well, I guess..." Reyna seemed suddenly unsure of herself. "As you said, he's probably dealing with a lot right now. I was wondering if he needed support after his loss, and if so, whether he could get it inside the castle..." The Khindre cleared her throat and sighed in reluctance. "I was also thinking about Grayson," she admitted after a pause.

Caitrial nodded in understanding. She should have figured that Grayson would come up eventually. The former Prince of Sun's Reach had fallen for the commoner Khindre, much to his father's chagrin. The two hadn't had much time together, and Caitrial wasn't entirely sure that it was anything more than young infatuation, but that was a facet that didn't need exploring at this very moment. "I doubt that Geurus Gardstar is going to let Grayson out of his cage," she answered apologetically. *I know I sure wouldn't if I were in his situation. I'm almost surprised that the new King didn't butcher Grayson too.* Of course, Galbraith Severesse, one of the Lightstriders, had been standing right next to the prince. To put his life in danger would have been suicide! But hadn't

Casinius Brightblade been up on the balcony with the King, Queen, and Princess? How then had Lysaria and Emery been killed? Questions for another time. Seeing the tears brimming in Reyna's eyes, she smiled wryly. "Or at the very least, not for a time. I'm sure that eventually, the King will grow tired of having Grayson skulking around the castle and open the gates to let him out. And when that happens, I'm sure that your prince will come running. Now go to sleep, my darling."

Caitrial quietly closed the door and paced down the hall, back to her couch. As she crawled underneath a blanket and settled down on a pillow, the smith found herself wondering about Leonidas as well. She couldn't imagine what it was like to be the knight at this moment. Shortly before the fateful ceremony, Leonidas Braveheart had returned from imprisonment by Venomsting operatives in the Scorched Waste. As Emery's appointed retainer, the knight shouldn't have left her side. That point was one on which Caitrial could agree with Godfrey's detractors. What kind of King — or father, for that matter — would send the prime protector of their daughter and heir on a dangerous mission? For Leo to return and then have his employer and charge murdered right in front of him — Caitrial felt only the deepest sympathy for the man. She hoped he wasn't taking it too hard on himself. It wasn't his fault that Godfrey had sent him out to the Scorched Waste! And when Galbraith, who'd been *born in the desert,* was right there! The smith grumbled and shook her head irritably; she'd never fall asleep if she let these thoughts rule her mind. Focusing instead on happier thoughts of Leonidas and her sparring, Caitrial drifted off into sleep.

Briskelthiar Xilpharys and Thraedan Ingrottigen worked wonders in their workshop, which had expanded dramatically since its foundation many years prior. Caitrial strode to the door of the wooden building, glancing up at the sign, which swung almost imperceptibly in the breeze, suspended on chains above the door. Made of iron, another of the master smiths' creations, the crest bore a crossed Dwarven war hammer and Elven scimitar, with a horseshoe frame. *Sunwright Artisans* was carved into the wooden door in multiple languages: Elven, Dwarven, Common (of course), but these were also joined by Fyran, Gnomish, and even Khelvaish, the tongue of Khindre. The two master smiths with whom Caitrial was taking her apprenticeship had long ago learned to put aside personal reservations when it came to their work, which proved just how much they loved their craft. Caitrial knew that in general, Briskelthiar and Thraedan weren't the biggest fans of Khindre, and yet they still ornamented their door with their language, and if any came for the sake of buying, they would receive the same courtesy as another customer.

The door swung inward and admitted Caitrial into a comfy storefront. Oil lanterns hung from the rafters, casting a warm, friendly glow over the entire room. Tables and racks were arranged around the room, displaying the wares that the shop produced. In terms of display, the room was divided in twain, one half sporting farming tools, and building supplies, while the other had racks stocked with weapons as well as other, more specialized tools.

When Caitrial opened the door, a dull *plunk* sound resounded, signaling that somebody had entered. That design was one of Briskelthiar's ideas. When the portal was opened, the pressure on a small hammer perched on the top would be removed, allowing the piece to fall and hit a shaped metal plate on the door itself. As the customer closed the door again, a chain connected to the hammer would draw it back to its original position. Once introduced to the community of shopkeepers, the idea spread like wildfire, and Briskelthiar had come up with a variety of shapes and thicknesses which caused the metal plate to make different sounds upon impact.

"Mornin' Lady Caitrial!" a jovial voice called from the corner of the room. Caitrial saw Skierys, a half-elf that worked the retail side of the business. The son of one of Briskelthiar's kin, Skierys had a head for numbers that the two artisans counted on daily. The half-elf kept Briskelthiar and Thraedan on schedule, as well as handling the financials, and was a genius at selling products to people. "You look positively lovely this morning."

"Good morning, Skierys," she replied politely. The half-elf was one of the shapely smith's many suitors and believed himself quite fortunate to be able to work in the same establishment as she. Though truth be told, they saw each other very infrequently, with Skierys trapped in front, and Caitrial busy at work at the forge. That was perfectly fine with Caitrial; she had plenty enough to deal with, considering her two sisters and her job. Trying to throw a relationship in the mix would just make every-thing that much more complicated. Besides, even if she were looking for a partner, glib-tongued Skierys would *not* be her first choice. The half-elf wasn't unattractive by any means, but Caitrial couldn't help wanting to shear off that ridiculous beard on his slim, elf-like face. To someone who worked near flames all day, the scraggly nest of hair just screamed fire hazard. Beyond that, though Skierys's ice-blue eyes might wander over her body pleasurably, her sisters were another matter entirely. Caitrial knew that if there had been more Khindre in the city, had the majority of them not been consigned to the wilderness, or shipped off to Carrion Cove, the half-elf would never have been hired. The poor, pale-skinned boy was deeply prejudiced against the devil-kin.

Caitrial maneuvered around the tables and in between two racks, sporting several varying sizes of hammers. A wooden stair-case in the back led down to a stone landing, actually the ceiling of the shop's basement, which hosted the blacksmith's workshop. Caitrial unhooked one of many hammers from her belt and tapped lightly on the wooden trapdoor to indicate that she was coming down. A few moments later came a clattering sound, signifying that the locking mechanism had been removed. The smiths didn't want anyone getting down into their workshop, so they had multiple prevention methods set in place. Briskelthiar said that he'd once used magical means to do so before the Eclipse, but Thraedan had introduced him to the surprisingly effective methods of mundane protection. Briefly, Caitrial wondered what it would be like to live in a world with magic. When she was a child, her parents used to read her fantastical stories, and she had done the same with Reyna and Arcadia on occasion. Because of that, a small part of her longed to see what the world was like back when wizards had towers on street corners, and street shows had mummers playing with fire, or pulling exotic animals out of hats. Caitrial shook the wistful thoughts out of her head. She didn't live in a magical land; she lived in magic bereft Sun's Reach, and she was decently content with life here. With those thoughts, she reached for the handle, lifted the trapdoor, and spryly climbed down the ladder into the hot forge room below.

TARUS

A PRINCE'S ADVICE

A little less than an hour later, Tarus Gardstar was clean, shaved, and dressed in a black doublet with gray hose, which one of the servants, Tarus wasn't sure from which family, had pressed and laid out on the end of his bed. He wore a courtier's rapier by his side, the typical blade that nobles wore for protection. But after seeing the sort of swords that Casinius Brightblade and even Grayson, when he'd still been able to carry a weapon, had strapped to their sides, Tarus honestly thought that the thin, needle-like blade was a bit silly. Of course, he amended, a long, thin blade can do just as much damage as a short, wide one. Tarus cringed as he recalled the design of the weapon that had ended Emery's life. A sharp, cruelly curved dagger made of white metal. His father would be wroth about the loss of that weapon.

Heaving a long sigh, young Lord Gardstar walked down the tiled hall towards the massive double doors to the audience chamber. Two guards flanked the entrance, both Geurus's black armored troops. Tarus noticed several Redwyn servants that passed by shooting hostile glances at the men. Tarus didn't know why he was surprised. The warriors followed Lord Geurus's orders without question, but when left to their own devices, they tended to get themselves into all sorts of atrocities.

His father was angry, Tarus could tell. The yelling echoed out into the hallway, though it was indistinct through the thick doors. Seeing the young man approaching, one of the guards solemnly raised a mailed fist and rapped twice on the stone door. The yelling from inside stopped, and the door scraped open slightly. Another guard poked his head out, only his eyes visible beneath the heavy helmet. Tarus wondered, not for the first time, why the guards never seemed to take off their armor. It must be stifling to wear all day. During those precious days when Emery was still alive, Tarus had seen Leonidas walking around the castle corridors in ill-fitting chain mail, even when he wasn't with Emery. But at least Leonidas Braveheart hadn't worn his helmet, and his gauntlets often hung on his belt. Geurus's troops, on the other hand, never seemed to go anywhere without their full suits and a spear, if not their long lances.

The guard from inside the audience chamber looked at Tarus for a long moment and then made a gesture for him to enter.

"Lord Tarus Gardstar!" he announced to the room in his heavily accented voice.

Tarus, standing in the doorframe, saw his father nod and smile down at the quivering, weedy man at the foot of the throne. He wore the colors of Redwyn's administrative staff. "Remember who is king here, Chelak. Servants like yourself are easy enough to find. So you'd best get out there and tell your men to keep their eyes peeled. I don't care how many doors you have to break down, or people you have to push around. Just find me what I am looking for, or else the consequences will not be pretty! You are dismissed." Though Geurus's voice never rose above his normal speaking tones, it might as well have been delivered at full scream, with how quickly Chelak scurried out of the room.

Then the king turned towards the door. "So it seems my son has finally managed to extirpate himself from his chambers. You had me worried for a while there. Servants like Chelak are simple to replace, an heir is not."

"You still have Velara," Tarus mumbled, not meaning to be heard. Geurus waggled his finger sternly.

"Now, boy," he said warningly. "Speak clearly to your King."

"My apologies Father, I had no intention to disrespect you," Tarus replied, louder this time, though he couldn't figure out quite how Geurus had noticed his lips moving from all the way across the room. "I've had a rough couple of days." Tarus approached the throne.

"So I've noticed," Geurus said. "Would you care to explain what has kept you confined in your room until this morning?"

Tarus didn't. In fact, he would rather have not talked to his father at all this morning, but he figured that avoiding Geurus would have been worse for his health than the emotional toll this meeting was sure to impose upon him. As Geurus stared pene-tratingly at him, Tarus felt a painful headache develop. Repressing the urge to press his hands against his temples, he put on his most impassive face. Showing any sign of weakness in front of his father would be a grave mistake.

When Tarus did not respond, Geurus leaned back deeper into his throne and grunted. "Very well." He picked up a glass of white wine from the table next to him and sipped it. "I'm sure that you would be very interested in hearing how things are progressing in our new kingdom, but I shall save you the boring drivel for now. Just looking at you, I can tell that you have plenty of questions. Go ahead, ask."

Tarus blinked; he wasn't used to Geurus allowing him to ask questions. It seemed off from the man's usual stern disposition.

But Tarus wasn't going to let this rare opportunity go to waste. "What happened with that man, Chelak? He scurried out of here like a scared rabbit."

"Oh, him," Geurus waved dismissively. "He is one of many people searching for something of great importance that seems to have gone missing."

"And what is this item?"

"Something that should pique your interest," Geurus glared down his nose at Tarus. "The body of a certain princess cannot be located." Tarus's heart jumped into his throat. It took an extreme force of will to not react outwardly. "That was a delightful little stunt you pulled; you should have seen the looks on her subjects' faces! However, as I said, her corpse is nowhere to be found. There was quite a mess of blood left on the stones, but we cannot dismiss the possibility that she somehow managed to live and be rescued. If you have endangered my seat on the throne, you will certainly regret it, Tarus."

"What I did..." Tarus steeled his nerves. "What you say makes sense, Father, but she fell six stories onto cobblestone with a dagger embedded in her stomach. It would take a feat of magic for Emery to survive. Besides," Tarus knew he was risking his neck with these next words, but they had to be. "What I have done is...better than your original plan." Geurus's eyebrows shot up, and his icy blue eyes grew harder and colder than usual. Tarus hurried on heatedly. "You would have had me kill Emery while we were..." His face grew hot. "You wanted me to stick that dagger in her stomach while I consummated the marriage!"

"Yes, a tidy little plan. It would have been much easier to just claim that the royal family had died of poison. Some peasants didn't approve of our houses being matched, so they took matters into their own hands. We dispose of the bodies, burn the sheets, slay a few cooks for added evidence. Nobody's any the wiser."

Tarus couldn't believe what he was hearing. "How did you

plan to pass off the blood flowing from the balcony as death by poison?"

A thin smile spread across Geurus's face; it sent a flash of white rage through Tarus's mind. "Boy, you understand nothing." He jabbed a finger at his son. "The knife was a test, Tarus. I wanted to see if you would actually do it. If you had enough guts to kill a woman while you pleasured her. I saw in your eyes that you were going to fail me, so I had to take drastic action. Luckily, I had a few fail-safes in place." Geurus shook his head in disappointment. "That being said, I'm quite proud that you managed to step up when it came time to deal the final blow to House Redwyn." He let out a short bark of laughter. "Honestly, after watching both of her parents die right in front of her eyes, one could easily argue that you gave Princess Emery mercy."

Tarus's gut roiled at the thought. Emery's life cut short on her wedding day, and King Geurus had the gall to call it mercy! *Breathe,* he told himself. *Just breathe. No need to get into an argument with the King.* "As you say, Father... Milord," he hastily amended. The pressure in the back of his head wouldn't go away. It was really distracting, but Tarus would not grimace, not now. "Milord, you earlier said that I may have endangered your place on the throne. But if you will permit me to speak frankly, haven't you done the same by allowing Grayson Redwyn to walk freely in the castle?"

Geurus actually blinked in surprise at that. Then he gave another dismissive wave. "The boy? He's harmless, and he knows there are eyes on him at all times. Grayson wouldn't dare try anything stupid."

"With all due respect, Milord, you are wrong to underestimate Grayson Redwyn. His anger at us may lead him to take some rash action. One must question why you let him live at all."

"I think that should be obvious, even to you," Geurus sneered. "If I'd simply butchered the lot of them, I would have seemed like a monster, and only earned the city's ire. By allowing one of the children to live, I've proved not only that I can show mercy, but I get leverage over the people."

Tarus saw more than a few holes in that explanation. "I suppose that makes some sense. But, I'm still not sure why you let *Grayson* live," Tarus knew he was walking a thin line insulting the King's choices again, but he had to get his words out. "He was the youngest son of the family, *not* in line for the throne. And when compared to Emery, far less popular. I feel you could have gained far more leverage by keeping the beloved crown princess alive and from her throne, rather than her rage-prone drunkard of a younger brother."

"Don't let your heart speak in your mind's place!" Geurus snapped angrily. Did Tarus imagine the trepidation in his voice? Perhaps, the King realized his son was correct in this situation. "On the way here, I told you specifically not to get too attached to the princess. But by your reaction when I gave you the knife and the way you speak about her now, I can see that you have failed me once again. I will ensure that Grayson Redwyn is unable to do anything against me. I am planning to wed him to Velara. He may not be a prince anymore, but he does have royal blood." Geurus nodded. "Yes, that ought to placate him. He'll be able to spend the nights with your beautiful sister."

While I have to live the rest of my life without his, Tarus thought sourly. "It won't work."

"What was that, boy?"

"I said it won't work," Tarus repeated. "A wedding, Father; so soon after the first? Nobody in the city is going to believe you. They'll be expecting another murder."

"And when it doesn't happen..." Geurus started.

"Then they'll be waiting for it, Milord. The moment you show any sign of hostility towards the last remaining member of their royal family, you'll lose them. I don't know much about

Lordship yet, but I doubt it will be easy to run a city when all of your people want you dead."

"You may be right," Geurus admitted, much to Tarus's surprise. He'd expected the king to fight him on that. "So then, my Widower Prince," he sounded exceptionally proud of the moniker, "what would you suggest."

Tarus thought of Emery, how on the day they'd first met, she'd denied the comforts of a carriage to walk through the city instead. She'd chosen to see her people, and that had really inflamed the citizens' trust and love for her. *Not to mention mine.* "Let the people of Searstar see him. For all they know, Grayson is dead, just like Emery. Perhaps he was slain silently. If you want the people to not hate you totally, you need to prove to them that you hold trust in them."

"That shouldn't be too difficult." Geurus scratched at his full blond beard. "I can hold an assembly and display him, alive and well on the balcony, so his people can..."

"No!" Tarus said sharply. "Displaying him like a prisoner will not work. Remember what I said, *make* them trust you. Let Grayson Redwyn walk the city streets. Let him go to his people, speak with them. Undoubtedly he won't have very kind words to say about you or any of us for that matter, but that much you can expect. If you keep the castle well-guarded, you won't have to worry about any retaliation. Besides, if you let Grayson free, you might solve two problems at once."

"Oh?" Geurus cocked an eyebrow.

"Grayson has a lover out in the city," Tarus explained, recalling that much from his conversations with Emery. "If you let him go see her, then you may mollify him for a time. And if the citizens see their former prince, you might stop their anger from reaching you. But whatever you do, don't let any of your guards be seen with him."

Geurus pondered for a moment. "What do you think, my advisors?"

It was only then that Tarus noticed that two others were flanking the throne. The two contrasted each other to striking effect. On the King's right side stood Tarus's cousin, Tavindre. He was clad in the ornate black armor with white star patterns that marked him as an officer in the Gardstar's Enforcers. Tarus felt a small spark of rage that the broad-faced man had the position of honor, which *he* should have held. He shook that off quickly, surprised by the thought. Why did he want the right-hand spot beside his father? He would never agree with the decisions Geurus made, and he doubted he had the stomach to handle the easy conversations the King enjoyed holding about his most recent exploits in torture or killing. If Tarus were in that position, he would undoubtedly have to keep hearing about the deaths of the Redwyn family. *Or the girls back home.* A few years before the family had left for Sun's Reach, Tarus had gotten romantically involved with a serving wench in their employ.

Sina had been the daughter of Geurus's personal butler. She'd been a bit plain in the face, but not ugly by any means. She was sweet and very eager to please. They'd had several secret trysts underneath the stairs, or in Tarus's room. But when Lord Geurus had found out... Tarus shivered. Geurus had taken her and forced him and her father to watch as his torturer branded the word 'whore' onto her forehead, and then let the man and his three assistants have their way with the poor girl, before finally giving her the sweet release of death. Less than a week later, Geurus had a new butler, and the old one wasn't ever seen again.

Tarus dismissed the anger at Tavindre as nothing more than jealousy at the fact that Geurus wasn't willing to take his suggestions at face value. Him, the king's advisor? Not if he could avoid it.

To the King's left stood Casinius Brightblade, the Captain of the Lightstriders, the legendary heroes of Sun's Reach. The great hero who had succeeded at such laudable acts as slaying entire bandit camps, stopping attempts on his king's life, and using his ancient, enchanted sword to slice off the head of his own Queen, Lysaria Redwyn. If Tarus hadn't seen it himself, he would never believe that the man had the capacity in him to do such a thing. All the stories Emery had told him signified Brightblade as an honorable hero, who came from a long line of noble and worthy knights.

"I must admit, milord," Tavindre said, attempting to stroke at his chin, a task made impossible by the gauntlets he wore. His thin lips were creased into a thoughtful frown, but his grey-blue eyes were anything but ponderous. "The plan has some merit. Of course, there is the chance that it could all backfire, and we'll have a full-blooded rebellion on our hands." Tavindre shifted his eyes to stare pointedly at his cousin. "One might wonder why young Tarus seems so insistent that the princeling not be guarded." There was no masking the hostile flash in Tavindre's eyes this time. The man seemed almost threatened by Tarus, though young Lord Gardstar couldn't think of any reason why he should be.

"Simple logic, really," Tarus countered. "Remember that those self-same guards slaughtered these people's neighbors and friends after Emery was slain."

"Because, they went mad."

"As should be expected from people who just saw someone they cared deeply about killed! If your guards are seen around him, your people might take it to mean Grayson is your prisoner. You want them to feel comfortable in viewing the former Prince, not the opposite." Tarus held up a finger to forestall any arguments. "By no means should he be unguarded. I would not be so stupid as to entertain that notion. But he should be attended by someone whom people trust, but is wise enough to keep Grayson from doing anything too foolish."

"Hmm," Geurus nodded while he thought. "You might just make a worthwhile heir yet, boy. What do you think, Casinius?"

"It's as you say, my Lord," Casinius said stiffly. "He is quite skilled in this matter of courtly business and dealing with the common folk." Tarus thanked Emery for showing him her manner in the latter.

"And who do you believe should guard him? If not one of my own guards, perhaps yourself?"

"No," Casinius said flatly. "I fear that servants tend to talk, milord. Even if no word of my actions on the balcony has reached the public's ears, there is little doubt that Grayson knows. Especially since he has been spending much of his time around Sir Leonidas." Nobody in the room missed the blatant hostility in Casinius's voice when he mentioned the knight. Tarus remembered that on that fateful day, Emery's retainer had called the Captain of the Lightstriders out and openly challenged him. Apparently, Casinius still hadn't gotten over the fact. "Grayson would not willingly go with me."

"Then perhaps we should give dear Leo a chance to get some fresh air. I don't think he's left the Drill Yard much since the wedding," Geurus suggested. "I didn't get much of an opportunity to converse with him, but I sense that he may have a sage soul in his warlike frame."

"Yes, and I do recall that Emery was quite *fond* of Sir Leonidas Braveheart," Tavindre pointed out, directly it seemed, for Tarus to hear. The devilish grin he flashed at his cousin proved it. "Who else better than to temper the hot-headed young prince?" Tarus really did not need to be reminded of that little fact. Emery hadn't even cared about Tarus, as she did in his dreams. She'd been in love with her retainer.

"None better, Sir," Casinius agreed. "But if I may make one

suggestion. Perhaps give the people a bit of time. Let's not send Leonidas and Grayson out while the wound is too fresh. That *would* incite their rage."

"A wise thought, my trusted advisor" Geurus clapped his hands once, the sound reverberating through the chamber. "I shall let the lot of you know when I plan to send our emissaries into the city." The King turned his icy eyes on his son. "You have done well today, Tarus. You are dismissed." Tarus turned and began to walk away, but as the Enforcer at the door raised his fist to knock, Tarus heard his father's voice again. He turned, but nobody else in the room seemed to have heard Geurus. The words chilled Tarus to the core. "You have done well *today*, Tarus. But you disappointed me at your wedding. You were too enamored of the Redwyn family. Fail me again, and you will *not* be fond of the consequences."

LEONIDAS

LIMITED FREEDOM

Sweat dripped down his sides and back, and his muscles felt like they were on fire. His breath came in ragged, labored gasps as he leaned back against a stone partition. Leonidas hung his head, forcing his body to relax, and his inhales and exhales to come slowly. As the pounding in his head finally subsided, Leonidas allowed his eyes to open. In front of him lay the Drill Yard, where the King's men would train to keep their skills honed and sharp. To look at the field, one would undoubtedly say that at least one knight was in perfect condition, if not a score. In the last week and a half, the count of training dummies standing at attention in the field had dropped dramatically. Leonidas stared hard at the most recent victim. The oak post, secured to the ground to form the 'body,' was split in half, pummeled by many fierce blows. Sword and shield arms were scattered in pieces around the field, barely left functioning; its strength treated wooden shield had a long crack running up its length, and the metal pole that counted for a weapon was bent into a grotesque

'L.' As Leonidas stood there, the makeshift head rolled, coming to a stop at his feet, as one of the many dents in the helmet found solid ground and stopped its revolutions. Leonidas stared at it for a long moment before stepping out from the structure that was buttressing him. His heavy hammer whistled through the air in an upward arc, connecting with the head with a solid *crack*. The projectile soared across the field and bounced along the ground, clanging each time it impacted.

"Very well done, Sir Leonidas," Grayson called, strolling over from the arch he'd been leaning against. "Think, perhaps you could save a few for me? I don't think making replacement dummies is going to be on any of the servants' minds any time soon."

"If they all break, I can make my own," Leonidas said gruffly.

"No offense meant, Sir, but though you are undeniably skilled at breaking them, I would wonder how you would fare at actually building one." Grayson's voice took on a dark tone. "My father, when he was still alive, told me of his days of glory before he became the lump of lard sitting on the throne." Leonidas raised his eyebrows in shock. Many times, the knight had been surprised by the former prince's inconsiderate words, but until now, Grayson had never openly insulted his father. Of course, Leonidas knew well that Godfrey's children hadn't held too high of an opinion of him, Emery had told him so on multiple occasions.

"I think he must have been well in his cups when he said: *"Be careful with where you wag your sword. It's much easier to chop somebody to pieces than put him back together, and usually, even if you do put them together, they just won't work quite the same as they used to"*

That brought a brief smile to the big knight's face. "Your father did tend to say some interesting things when he was drunk." Shaking his head, Leonidas took a long look over the Drill Yard. He was currently standing in a separate yard of the sprawling grounds, a broad, circular field, surrounded by tall arches, each with a flat, metal sword and shield combo ornamenting the keystone. One of the few ornamental pieces that Jorjen, the utilitarian castle smith, had ever made. A small regiment of dummies was posted here regularly, but many of the 'soldiers' had fallen in combat recently, evident by the splinters of wood and bent pieces of metal that littered the field. Exhausted from his day's efforts, fully three dummies reduced to firewood, Leonidas walked over to a stone longhouse directly to the east of the circle. Leo hung his borrowed shield, battered from many practice sessions against various opponents, on a peg near the door, and leaned the hammer, more a small block of iron than a real replica of the knight's favored weapon, in the corner against the wall. He stood a moment longer in the hall, taking in the dusty scents that mingled in the air. The rich, earthy smell of oiled leather, the metallic aroma from a multitude of weapons, and the unsavory odor of human sweat, much contributed to by Leonidas and Grayson over the past week and a half, lingered, soaked into every nook and cranny.

"I have received some exciting news, Sir," Grayson informed him. "Something that I'm sure will interest both of us. But I would suggest that you take a bath first; I doubt the citizens want to smell that."

"What are you on about, Grayson?"

"King Geurus, in all his remarkable generosity, is allowing us outside the castle walls. He didn't say it in so many words, but he wants to prove to the people that he didn't give us the same treatment he gave my sister." Even underneath the sarcasm, Leonidas could hear the relief in Grayson's tone.

The former prince let out a ragged sigh and motioned for Leo to follow him. With one last look at the weapons in the room, the knight did as he was bid. He might not have his royal title anymore, but as far as Leo was concerned, Grayson was as much his Lord as Emery had been his Lady. "Leonidas," Grayson said shakily, sounding much less like a gruff man, and more like the sixteen-year-old he still was. "Did you know that Emery loved to watch you practice out here?" He pointed to a man-made escarpment concealed behind some bushes. "She told me once, while you were off in the Scorched Waste. My dear sister would change into clothes that my father would say more befit some servant, and creep out here to hide in the bushes and watch." Leonidas felt a sharp pang through his heart. That sounded exactly like something his Princess would do. The last remaining Redwyn pointed out several well-concealed places around the various locations in the yard. "She had many different hiding spots. She could get a good view of every activity around here, except maybe the circuit-riding and running, but those are somewhat less exciting to watch." Then he pointed across the jousting lanes, where all the knights would practice both for skill improvement and leisure. "She said that was her favorite place to watch. From everything she told me, you were quite the jouster."

"I suppose I was a fair hand," Leo said modestly. "Certes, there were those far more skilled than I."

"Emery's tales would disagree," Grayson chuckled hollowly, as he indicated the wall of ivy beyond the lanes. "That leads straight into the castle gardens. She said she would slip through the tunnel there after you finished so that when you came to attend her, she would be in the garden."

"I wondered how those stray leaves seemed to find their way into her hair." Leonidas furrowed his brow. "I always thought that the gardens were her favorite place on the castle grounds. She was always reading when I came to her out there."

"There was a little alcove that had a couple of loose stones," Grayson explained. "Emery took out one of the stones and slid her book inside there so that she would have one readily available."

Leo whistled under his breath. "The princess had me hood-winked." He rubbed a hand through his hair. "I never would have guessed that my little bookworm had such a taste for swordplay."

"I'm not sure that she did," Grayson said, causing Leo to arch an eyebrow. "Did you hear me? She didn't just come to watch any knight. When I discovered her out here once, she told me she was waiting for you." He stopped abruptly. "Did you care for Emery, Leonidas?"

"She was like family to me," the knight answered truthfully.

Grayson nodded slowly and let out a long breath. "I miss her, Leo. I thought her an awful nuisance, constantly upbraiding me about my time at Cynderstone, and my courtly manners. But now that she's gone..."

"I understand, my Lord," Leonidas patted the boy on the shoulder. "What happened will leave a hole in your heart, just as it has mine."

Grayson nodded solemnly. Then he chuckled. "Listen to the two of us. We are about to be let free from the castle for the first time since that day, and yet our thoughts are still morbid!." Grayson sniffled and then wrinkled his nose. "Go take a bath, Sir Knight, shake off that foul mood, then change into something presentable; we have a day on the town ahead of us."

Leonidas bowed to Grayson Redwyn and headed off to the bathhouse. He'd never really taken the chance to get to know Grayson Redwyn. The princeling had always just been his princess's younger brother. A moody and temperamental one, like most boys his age. But it seemed that under his anger, there was a hint of virtue. Though he looked and drank like Godfrey, Grayson Redwyn was not at all similar to his jovial, yet nervous, father.

As he walked away, a spectator let out a relieved breath, coming out of hiding from the first bush the prince had pointed to. Tarus surveyed the mechanical carnage on the field in front of him. The Widower Prince recalled what the mighty knight had said after he'd thrown Emery over the balcony. *"You are damned lucky I follow Emery's orders. Elsewise I might not leave here alive, but rest assured, you wouldn't either."* Considering what he saw before him, Tarus did indeed count himself lucky. If rage could drive Sir Leonidas Braveheart to do so much... Tarus doubted even his cousin Tavindre could have matched him. Had Emery not ordered him otherwise, all of the members of House Gardstar on that balcony might have died, and Leonidas could have walked away with nothing more than a few new scars. Tarus shivered, he definitely didn't want to find himself on Leonidas's bad side. He'd begged his father to act soon, and finally, Geurus had listened. Tarus wondered if the King knew something he didn't. *Many things, I'm sure.* Taking one last glance at the training field, Tarus hoped that being allowed outside the gates would be enough to stop Leonidas's anger from boiling over completely.

Leonidas slowly submerged his aching body into the steaming water, sighing in contentment as relief spread through his muscles. These baths, taken after his long training sessions, had quickly become the only things the knight still looked forward to. The servants in the halls were quiet and avoided conversation even more than they used to. Leonidas was sure that had something to do with King Geurus. The man was none too kind to Godfrey Redwyn's old staff. Many of them looked much worse for wear, ragged and exhausted. Leonidas ate his meals alone, refusing to share a table with the Gardstar's troops, least of all Casinius and Tavindre. And worst for Leonidas, all the Redwyn's Royal Guard, save himself, and much of the city's standing army (small though it was in these times of relative peace) had been marched off to the Scorched Waste on Geurus's orders. *The result I'd hoped for, but the king is wrong, and something about this mass expulsion seems dubious.* Those few who remained had found new favorite abodes in various ale shops and brothels around the city, without a care or financial worry in the world.

Leo could train with Grayson, but even though the boy was powerfully built for his age, the knight could not go all out without risking Grayson's health. With nobody to spar or talk with, Leonidas had little to do besides train on his own or think. And Leonidas hated where his thoughts went when allowed to run free. With the new information he'd received today, the knight was unsurprised when Princess Emery's image flashed in his head.

Emery had loved to watch the knights hard at work training. But, Grayson had said, it wasn't just any knight that she had come to watch. Emery Redwyn had snuck out of the castle, away from proper activities such as needlework or reading, to watch her retainer, to watch *him practice*. In any other circumstance, Leo would have thought little of it. It made sense that a member of the nobility would want to ensure a competent warrior protected them. However, after everything Leonidas had experienced since returning to Searstar, the thought lent itself to a different coloring.

On that day, Leonidas had failed his King; he failed to do the one job he was hired to do. His princess was dead now. Emery had been trapped in deep limerence for her knight, and as punishment, her life was ended.

Tarus Gardstar had stabbed Emery because she rejected him in marriage. *And for a good reason.* But Leonidas had frozen in place with her final words, used not to revile Tarus Gardstar, but to confess love to Leonidas Braveheart. If he'd run over to her, slain Tarus, and sheltered his princess, Emery could have been saved. A medic could have been called; perhaps she could have survived! But no, Leonidas had foundered in a crucial moment.

Salty tears began to drip into the hot water, mingling with the suds as Leo washed. *"Don't get yourself killed, Leonidas; my soul couldn't take it."* Emery's terminal order to him. He would never disobey that mandate, but rest assured, he would avenge her, even if it took him the rest of his life.

Returning to his quarters, Leonidas looked through his wardrobe. He was set up in a modestly sized chamber, close to Emery's old room; that way, he would have been close if ever she'd needed help. The flagstones were chill despite the relentless sunshine outside. Leonidas refused to place a rug on the ground. In the rare chance that a fight broke out here, or he had to act quickly to save a life, he didn't want to be tripped up by any loose objects that could send him sprawling, leaving either himself or another in a dangerous position. The hearth was stocked with wood, waiting to be lit, though Leo had left it unused recently. A simple bed, with covers and cushions in Redwyn colors, took up most of the floor space, though there was a writing desk—stocked with quills, parchment, ink, and candles—in one corner, and a ladder leading up to the rookery in the other. Next to the bed, an oil lamp hung on a ring, right over a bedside table upon which Leonidas kept several trinkets and gifts from Emery over the years. His favorite was a wooden carving of a phoenix she'd made for him many years past. The simple craft reminded Leo of the halcyon days when his worst issue was Emery trying to climb down the ivy hanging below her window, or making sure she remembered to eat. On top of the small table, Leo kept two new items. The first was a book, the same book that Emery had received from the Rainclaw twins as a wedding gift. His princess had always desired to travel, to see things beyond the walls of the castle she lived in. Whenever a traveling musician had come to court, Emery had begged the performer to play something from beyond her borders. But hysterical Godfrey never even allowed Emery to see what her own kingdom beheld. Leonidas wasn't sure how the old King had justified that to himself. Hadn't his father taken him around the land to meet the citizens and see the area he'd be tasked with ruling? If Leo recalled correctly, that was how Godfrey had met his wife, Lysaria. If Emery had been allowed to travel her kingdom, she might have met a suitable husband and fell in love. *Maybe that would have shaken her infatuation with me,* Leonidas thought ruefully. *And then not only would Emery be alive now, but she'd be happy in marriage. I would have been content to protect Emery and her husband until the end of my days.*

Leo sighed and picked up the second object. A silver and gold brooch shaped like a feather, and a crown hung off of a necklace of interlocking rings. Caitrial Rainclaw had made the piece to go along with the replacement armor he'd commissioned. *"That piece is free of charge, Sir Knight. I figured since the Crown is already paying a substantial sum for your new steel suit, I could afford to throw in this little trinket as a charity."*

Leonidas smiled when he thought of the ingenious smith who had persuaded him to pay her business some patronage, rather than giving another job to old Jorjen. With Caitrial in mind, Leonidas glanced again at the brooch, and then back to the closet, where the magnificent armor was displayed. He needed something presentable to wear, something to prove to the people that he and Grayson were still there for them. The 'steel suit,' as Caitrial called it, would do nicely.

Two hours later, Leonidas waited attentively at the guard-house past the courtyard, where he'd been greeted and embraced by Emery upon his return. Two of Geurus's Enforcers stood on the wooden walkways flush with the stone walls, one watching the outer gate, the other's eye on the courtyard. The portcullis leading outside was still shut, to deter any hopeful quarrelers Leonidas could hardly believe that it had already been over a month since his royal family had been slain. The pain still felt just as fresh as if it had only been three days. And by the suffering he saw in Grayson's eyes, the same was true for the prince.

Leo could feel the Gardstar Enforcer's eyes on his back, his skin crawling in revulsion. Geurus's men were strange, silent warriors all, except for Tavindre and a few of the other commanders. Leonidas had seen the officers in the wine cellar a few times taking inventory, but never before had he seen the Enforcers performing any manner of leisure. They almost seemed inhuman, unlike any race that Leonidas had ever encountered. His first supposition was that they were Khindre, taken from Carrion Cove, but though the devil-kin were a sullen lot, they still fell to the vices of alcohol, and of course, talked.

An odd thought, but one not out of the realm of possibility occurred to him then. After finishing the deed on the bell tower, Tarus had told Tavindre to send a message across the Eclipse. To Leonidas, protector of the kingdom, that brought Moonwatch, the enemy kingdom of Sun's Reach to mind. Hadn't Amaru Sunbrand, the apparent daughter of Yamaria, whom he'd met in the desert claimed the Chillfang, creatures from that fell land had already made it within our borders? *Not just their monsters, then. It would seem their people have managed to cross the barrier too. I should have realized it earlier. Gardstar, the name relates to the points of light in the night sky, and what once came out at night? The moon! The Gardstars are nothing more than the second part of the Moonwatch incursion.* That thought terrified the big knight, who'd been raised on stories of the disastrous war a little over a century ago. It seemed they were heading towards yet another battle. *And this time, we won't have a brave King or Queen to lead us to anything more than our deaths.*

Seeing that Grayson was coming down the path, Leonidas shook those dark thoughts from his mind. His prince had told him to shake off his foul mood, and this occasion deserved no less.

Grayson was dressed in a paltock patterned in Redwyn colors, the colors of fire. He wore a light mantle, lined with soft brown fur, over the doublet, with silky doeskin stockings for his legs. His red-brown hair was combed back neatly, and the signet ring of house Redwyn sat heavily on his right hand.

The prince took in Leonidas's armor, silver steel with gold tooling, pauldrons shaped like lion heads, and claw-like designs on the gauntlets. A cape of white and red fluttered in the breeze, in place of the hammer normally mounted on his back. The garment, while not the flaming red cape emblazoned with the sun and sword symbol of the Lightstriders that Emery had promised him, marked Leo as part of the royal guard of Sun's Reach. Or at least it had when the Redwyns ruled.

Grayson smiled. "Fitting choice of garments." He glanced up at the Enforcer on the wall, who no longer seemed to be paying attention to the two of them. He lowered his voice. "Anything we can do to remind the people will help."

Leonidas took up his position behind Grayson Redwyn quietly, standing tall and stately, a stolid expression on his face. Grayson put on an expression of contentment. Despite his words, Grayson wasn't foolish enough to speak out publicly against the man who held him captive within his own home. That would be a death sentence.

Leo heard a grinding, creaking sound as the portcullis was dragged open, and he and the former prince marched down the tunnel, towards the other open gate. Outside, a gaggle of people looked on with stunned expressions, as the gates of Searstar's castle opened for the first time since the throne had been usurped.

Grayson and Leonidas walked down the broad flagstone steps, greeting the knot of noblemen and women. The sun, sagging in the sky, indicated that it was nearing evening, and it would soon begin sunfall. Nobles and trade folk alike were heading home by this point of the day. This pleased both of the sojourners since they both had business in the Trade Ward. But first, they had to get through this crowd. They withstood a barrage of questions about the state of things within the castle, most of which they answered evasively or not at all. Leonidas, keeping his eyes peeled for any sign of danger as he always had before, spotted the simpering looks on some faces and, mostly from members of the more powerful noble houses, disgusted stares. Leo couldn't tell whether the glares were directed at Grayson or the Gardstars.

Finally, as their stomachs called for dinner, the crowd of nobles broke off, some heading home, and others to Cynderstone. Though he'd seen the anger in a few of the pairs of eyes that watched the two, Leo saw nothing but pure hostility in one pair. Lord Sardan Rainclaw gave Grayson—this time, there was no ambiguity about the intended recipient—the most malicious stare that Leonidas had ever seen in any human eye. The knight reflexively stood closer to Grayson, and tapped him twice on the back, indicating that it was time to move on. As they walked down the street towards the Trade Ward, Leo could feel the fiery glare following them, until at long last, they moved around the corner, out of sight from Cynderstone.

Leo wished for his sword or hammer. Hadn't Sardan and Cos been good friends to Emery? If so, why the hatred? This time, the knight would not dismiss his feelings, stowing them in a folio at the back of his mind instead. If ever he passed through the area again, Leonidas Braveheart would keep an eye on the proprietor of Cynderstone Brewery and Bar.

CAITRIAL

EFFORT REWARDED

Caitrial wiped soot-stained hands on her jacket, stepping back from the heat of the forge, examining the malformed lump of metal she'd been trying to beat into proper shape for two hours now. The metal did not seem to want to set correctly, no matter what she tried. Grunting in frustration, Caitrial pushed aside the hunk of metal and stepped back from the forge, running her soot-covered gloves through her cinnamon-colored hair.

"Let's take a look, Caitrial," Briskelthiar's cool, crisp voice came from behind her. The smith reflexively moved over to cover the disappointing display, but the elf was much faster. The master smith nodded as he studied her work. What had once been an ingot was now a long, hardening smear, covered with bubbles and pits. "Caitrial?" he asked. "Tell me what you are thinking."

"As I'm sure you can tell, esteemed master, I am growing increasingly frustrated with my inability to work this material you have given me," she replied respectfully, trying to contain her anger.

"Ah," Briskelthiar waggled his finger reprovingly. "Did you hear yourself there, dear girl? You immediately leaped to the conclusion that the fault in your failure comes from your inexperience or lack of skill."

"If I had the proper skill, I wouldn't be failing to make this simple curve that you've instructed me to form the ingot into," Caitrial argued.

"Tell me, Caitrial," Briskelthiar said abruptly, not answering his apprentice's thought. "What metal were you working with just now?"

Caitrial opened her mouth to reply, but then hesitated. It hadn't acted like iron, bronze, gold, or silver, all of which she'd worked with many times before. It looked very similar to steel if tinged with a hint of blue. "I don't know, sir," she admitted with a sigh.

Much to her surprise, Briskelthiar just smiled. "Correct, Caitrial Rainclaw. You didn't know what metal you were using, so you couldn't have any knowledge of how to properly work it. The pale elf took his apprentice by the shoulder and forced her to look into his unnerving silver-red eyes. "You are too quick to take the blame upon yourself when it was our lack of teaching that led you astray. I presume that you understand now."

"Was this a teaching moment?"

"Why yes, Caitrial, it was," Briskelthiar replied, pleased. He took the sorry excuse of a project and tossed it in an empty melting pot. Then the elf moved over to the worktable, bent down, and opened a safe that ran underneath. The door opened with a hiss of air, and Briskelthiar selected another ingot from within. It was another of the same metal she'd tried to work before. "This ingot comes from an ore commonly used by elves from Kindol forest. Tell me, what are some things that you noticed about the metal?"

"It was much softer than other metals I've worked with

before, and it started to bubble only minutes after it had been placed near the flames. That and the bluish tint, of course."

"Given what I've told you thus far, can you come up with a reason why?"

Caitrial thought for a moment, considering what Briskelthiar had said very carefully. Suddenly, it came to her. "The metal is used in the forest," she started slowly. "With the trees all around you, you wouldn't want to use a metal that needed a lot of heat." Now Caitrial had it, and her momentum took her through the rest of the explanation. "The elves didn't want to turn the Kindol Woods into Kindling Woods," Briskelthiar blinked at the unexpected joke, but the smile that stretched across his face showed that the Elven master approved. "So they would likely use a different, more mechanical method of creating their weapons, meaning they'd need a softer, more compliant metal that could be worked with such primitive technology. Or at least, primitive compared to modern forging."

Briskelthiar clapped his hands together and bowed his head. "Very well done, m'lady! Yes, as you have figured out, the wood elves use a stone wheel and hammer contraptions, as well as a variety of other methods to forge their weapons and tools. Back when magic was still widespread, they had arcane means of creation, but they've adapted quite well. This," the elf tapped the ingot in his hand. "is called Suulsurr Iron." Briskelthiar lead Caitrial to a separate room of the workshop that she'd never been in before. Within were several contraptions, like those that her master had spoken of.

A thick stone wheel set on a wooden pole rigged to rotate, positioned over a wide, smooth stone bowl that the apprentice smith couldn't figure out the purpose of for the life of her. Briskelthiar moved over to the stone wheel and attached it to a rod connected to a crank. "Come over, Caitrial, and spin this wheel for me." She did as she was instructed. "Now, in Kindol

Woods, there is a coven of consummate druids, so they have a much easier time working the Suulsurr than you or I." Caitrial watched as she turned, and marveled at how, as her master told her of the difficulties, he seemed to have a stunningly easy time with it. With fluid grace, Briskelthiar took the Suulsurr ingot, sprinkled it with some sort of liquid from a flask hanging on his side, and then, with the help of the stone wheel, began to mold the ingot like clay. The elf kneaded and rolled the piece underneath the stone until he had a thin, flat piece. Finishing that, he carefully bent and shaped the part into the curve he'd been trying to get Caitrial to make. Finally, he pulled another flask from his belt and liberally drizzled the contents onto the finished curve.

"You see, Caitrial, you are a wonderfully talented smith. Were it in your mind, you could start your own shop, and prosper with ease."

"I would not dream of doing that, Master Briskelthiar."

"Caitrial, dear, you can drop the 'Master,'" Briskelthiar ordered. "As far as Thraedan and I are concerned, we are peers."

Caitrial felt her face grow hot. Briskelthiar and Thraedan were masters at their craft, perhaps the best smiths in all of Sun's Reach, if not further. That they would consider her a peer, an equal, was more of an honor than she deserved. "Yes, Mas...Briskelthiar," she answered, still blushing profusely.

The Elven artisan reached back and picked up the piece of Suulsurr steel, which, to Caitrial's surprise, had solidified and hardened. Seeing her wonderment, Briskelthiar handed it to Caitrial, who rapped on the crescent with her knuckles. It was just as hard as steel, if not harder!

"Suulsurr metal holds an edge decently well, but it's mostly used to make tools for maintaining the gardens and orchards within Kindol. The elves there might train with weapons for the sake of having something to do, but save for frenzied wild beasts, they don't find themselves with many things to engage in battle."

"Briskelthiar," the tradeswoman asked. "Why have you shown me this today?"

The elf smiled. "Recall that you are our peer, lady. You can shape steel and silver as well, if not better than either of us could when we were equivalent to your age." That was a surprise to hear. She'd never actually learned her masters' ages, though she figured they had to be ancient, with the skill they showed. She'd even noticed streaks of grey in Thraedan's red beard, and the oldest dwarves live up to three centuries! But to think that a human could ever match an Elf or a Dwarf in metallurgy sounded absurd. Both races were gifted in the arts of Creation, where Humans and Khindre were mostly skilled at Destruction. "It would be a waste of your talents to have you making horse-shoes and nails for the rest of your life. Thus, Thraedan and I have decided to start importing some rarer metals from the wider kingdom, to test and school you in some of our secret tech-niques." Briskelthiar paused for a moment. "This may be some-what difficult to hear, Caitrial, but you very well might outlive the both of us."

The woman smith drew in a shocked breath. "What are you talking about?"

There was a palpable sadness in the pale elf's silver-red eyes. "We are quite old, Caitrial," he admitted. "I met my partner nearly one hundred years ago, and—what's that expression you humans always use?" Briskelthiar fingered his chin for a moment. "I was no skirling chickadee back then," he said finally. "It is time that the secrets of our trade were passed along to a worthy apprentice. In our lifetimes, we've had a great many apprentices, but it is the way of our profession that we only pass our deepest secrets onto the most promising pupil. We both waited for quite some time, and passed up a number of hopefuls, but we believe that our choice is sound. You, Caitrial Rainclaw, are the best apprentice we've ever had." Briskelthiar smiled and clasped Cait's shoulder.. "Go and take a rest, dear Caitrial. The next few weeks will be trying. There are things we will be teaching you that have caused extremely skilled Elven and dwarven smiths to founder. But Thraedan and I have the utmost faith in you."

Caitrial walked home that evening in a near stupor. Her mind was racing, as one might expect. A relatively short-lived human learning the secrets of a Dwarven or Elven artisan was nearly unheard of. Perhaps, if Caitrial knew the whole history of Sun's Reach, she could find some examples, and had she thought about it, the woman might have recalled that the Lightstriders borrowed combat skills from each race in the kingdom. But even given that, it was still insane to think that simple Caitrial Rain-claw would ever be considered suited for such an honor.

That night, when the smith returned home and shared the news with her sisters, the three threw their own little celebration. Caitrial even opened a bottle of wine that she had on reserve for a special occasion. She wasn't quite sure what she'd had in mind when she'd put away the expensive bottle of Tharminder Vine, but Reyna and Arcadia were able to convince her. Especially persuasive was the fact that dour Arcadia had a smile on her face, too, even before the wine started flowing. Arcadia, for her own part, had seen just how hard Caitrial had worked to keep her fed. It certainly wasn't easy to support both herself and a growing Khindre, even one who didn't eat all that much, on just an apprentice's salary. And now that Reyna had joined them, Caitri-al's budget was sorely pressed. So when the day came for wages to be given to the workers, the family was pleasantly surprised.

Thraedan, the dwarf half of the Sunwright Artisans, came over to Caitrial and pressed a hefty bag of clinking coins into her bronzed hand.

The woman smith looked on in confusion, thinking that the dwarf had given her the wrong pouch. "Master Thraeden?"

"Aye?" the dwarf asked, half-turning to peer up at his fellow smith. "How can I help 'ee?" His dwarvish accent was thick, and all of his consonants were hard and pronounced.

"What is this?" she jingled the coins.

"Yer weekly wages, girl. I though' that much'd be obvious."

"This is far more than I usually receive," Caitrial protested.

Thraedan glanced up at Caitrial, confusion evident in his eyes. "Did Briskelthiar ferget t' tell ye? I coulda swore he let ye know o' yer new position. If th' daft elf fergot, I'm gon smack 'im upside th' head, Divines be me witness!"

She furrowed her brow. "He told me I was going to be learning more about your techniques, but I'm still an apprentice. Are you positive you didn't mistakenly give me Master Briskelthiar's payment."

"I dern't make mistakes," he said flatly. "Yes, yer gonna learn our techniques. I was suren ye were aware of th' whole deal, but it'd be seeming not!" Thraedan turned fully around and looked straight up into her eyes. "Were ye fer thinkin' we'd give th' honor we're givin' yerself to any' run o' th' mill apprentice? If so, get th' fool notion outa yer head! Ye ain't an apprentice no more! Yer a fully-fledged member o' the company now! And that there coin pouch is all th' proof ye should be needin'. Oh, an' cut th' 'Master' hogwash already! I was suren that Briskelthiar told ye that much if nuthin' else! Yer one of us now, an' ye durned well better start actin' like it!"

Stunned for the second time that week, Caitrial could barely manage a simple reply beyond a nod.

"G'day t' ye then," Thraedan began to storm off. "Now I'm off t' knock some sense into that fool elf partner o' mine!"

"Thraedan?"

"What?" The dwarf sounded marginally irritated about being stopped.

Caitrial couldn't resist. "How are you planning to hit

Briskelthiar upside the head? I'm afraid his chin might be a bit above your reach."

Thraedan glared at her for a moment, before a smile broke out over his thick lips, and a rumbling chuckle resounded from his barrel chest. "Tha's a good one, lass!" But ye have never been subjected t' a dwarf's kick!" he mimed a foot thrust into the air in front of him. "It'll bring tha' elf's face right down t' me level, just ye wait!" They both shared a hardy laugh at that, and Thraedan went off to fulfill his promise, advising Caitrial not to spend her whole wage in one place. The newest member of the Sunwright Artisans wasn't quite sure how she could imagine, looking at the pouch filled with jingling radiants, using that much money in any one place. She found herself thinking of Leonidas. Though knights weren't exactly what someone could call rich, he was under the employ of the Crown itself, and his job protecting the princess had been quite vital. She could only imagine that he had some fair sum stored up. The Royal Protector didn't seem the type to waste radiants on wanton pleasures, so what did he do with it? Caitrial decided if she ever had the chance to see Leo again, she'd find out.

As the smith walked down the street towards home, feeling lighter than air, she noticed that there seemed to be some strange energy about the city. *It's more likely than not my imagination,* she thought practically. *I'm just so giddy about this huge honor that everything seems brighter.* Caitrial was glad to see the brightness again after these past weeks.

But when she returned home, she realized that it wasn't just her imagination after all. Reyna was in the sitting room, a glowing excitement in her golden eyes, and her foot tapping nervously while her tail futilely tried to curl around it. Suppressing a giggle, Caitrial looked keenly at her sister. "What has you all in a tizzy?"

"You might want to go take a quick bath and get changed," Reyna peeped excitedly. "We're going to have guests very soon!"

Caitrial put her hands on her hips, assuming a stern, motherly stance. "What are you on about, Reyna?"

Reyna sighed. "Just trust me, sis, you don't want to smell like sweat for this visitor. I used a bit of magic to keep your bath warm. You don't have long, so no prolonged soaking. The nobles can only keep someone for so long." The last part almost seemed to have some hopeful pleading in it. Caitrial was curious as to who could make Reyna act like this. Perhaps Arteni Galare, whose books the Khindre was fond of reading, had come back to Searstar for a visit. Anyone would be excited about the chance to meet their favorite author, and they would want their families clean and presentable. It would also explain why Reyna had chosen such a cute tunic to wear. No disrespect meant to Berdur, but it wouldn't do to smell like herbs and potions, few of which had a pleasant odor, to meet such a famous personage.

Shrugging, Caitrial followed her sister's orders, taking a quick, but rejuvenating dip in the warm tub, and changing into one of her own handsome tunics and leather armor coats. After what had happened to her today, she could afford to go along with one of Reyna's dalliances. The family was gathered in the sitting room, even Arcadia, who sat quietly on a hard wooden chair. Caitrial was perplexed. "Dear, shouldn't we go out to meet your visitor?" The smith was beginning to doubt her previous belief. But who could this visitor be? Thraedan and Briskelthiar hadn't spoken of anyone coming into the city. "What reason would someone who was waylaid by nobles have to come down to this quarter of the city?"

"Oh, trust me, sis," Reyna said, assuredly. "They'll come. I'm sure they wouldn't miss us for all the world." Caitrial gave up trying to figure out who was coming. She'd rarely ever seen Reyna so sure in all their time together.

Imagine her surprise as a little less than a score of minutes later, there came the long-awaited knock at the door. Reyna clapped once gleefully and stepped back to let her older sister answer the door. Caitrial had always been the one who answered the door here, just on the off chance that the caller was someone who didn't take kindly to Khindre. Imagine the smith's undeniable shock as she opened the door to see a man wearing silver and gold armor. Very familiar silver and gold armor. "By Yamaria," she gasped. "Sir Leonidas!"

The knight bowed courteously. "The Ladies Rainclaw. How fare thee today?"

"Cut the damned chivalry, Leonidas!" Caitrial scolded. "You're alive!"

"That could be inferred by my arrival on your doorstep," Leo smiled warmly at the smith. "How are you, Caitrial?"

Caitrial stepped back and motioned for him to enter the house. "Please, Sir, the doorstep is no place for chatter. Come in, make yourself comfortable. You have much explaining to do."

Leonidas nodded, but instead of moving inside, he sidestepped. "After you, my Lord." Then Caitrial saw the reason why Reyna had been acting up.

"My prince," she bowed to Grayson Redwyn, with all the respect she could muster, despite her aching limbs. As exciting and enlightening as working the Suulsurr ore had been, it had indeed been grueling work. Both of Caitrial's arms, and her back, were sore and throbbing.

"It's not safe to call me that in these streets, Lady Caitrial," he said gruffly.

"And it's not safe for you to be calling a tradeswoman Lady, my prince," Caitrial answered instantly, turning the situation back around on him. "But as you say, the streets have ears. The hospitality of my home, meager though it might be, is yours. Come in, that we may use whichever titles we please."

Grayson cracked a smile and nodded. "I can see why Sir Leonidas enjoys spending time with you." He entered, walked a few steps forward, and then stopped, blinking and staring ahead. Right in front of him, looking fit to burst with joy, was Reyna Rainclaw, and the princeling threw himself into his lover's arms.

Leonidas entered, closing the door behind him. Caitrial moved towards the icebox in the corner. "I was about to cook dinner. I wish I'd known you were coming, Sir Leonidas," she lamented. "I'd have stopped by the market."

Leo shook his head and pulled a satchel from his shoulder. "I figured that our stint outside the castle walls would come as a surprise to you, much as it did for me. I stopped by the kitchen and procured some food for us to sup on. The knight opened the satchel and pulled out two cool pies and a selection of fresh produce from the palace gardens. "Since we are imposing on you, I thought it wouldn't be right to force you to spend your money or cook for us."

"The gesture is greatly appreciated," Caitrial said sincerely. "But though I don't live in so lavish a house as you," Leo chuckled at the relation of the castle to a simple house, "us Rainclaws are plenty well off!" As Leonidas set the pies on the sunny windowsill to warm and divvied up the fruits, Caitrial explained all that had happened since they'd seen each other last.

"I am glad to hear that you are doing so well," Leo said, patting the smith fondly on the arm. "And I might as well say, I never doubted for a moment that you would be afforded such an honor. After you made this armor for me, I knew your skill was the genuine artifact."

Beneath her tan, Caitrial's face blushed deeply. "Ah, thank you, Leo. I owe it all to Brisklethiar and Thraedan though, if not for them, I couldn't so much as make a nail."

"I know what you mean. It's always helpful to have a master to train you in your field. I was trained by Sir Vedalken of the

Lightstriders after he discovered my talent for combat. If not for *him*, I would likely still be working construction in Morndale. Or fighting bandits as a mercenary, if I'd been lucky enough," Leo admitted, a grateful smile creeping onto his face.

Caitrial was intrigued to hear about Leonidas's past, even if it was only one little tidbit. The chivalrous knight rarely talked about where he came from, and it was only through rumors around the court that anybody who still lived knew anything about Leonidas Braveheart. As far as the smith knew, only Emery, Godfrey, and perhaps Vedalken Nairvebyen knew his whole story. If Caitrial had ever expected to see Leo again, she never expected him to be in such a good mood. Then the smith thought for a moment. She knew little about what happened at the tower, but from their conversations, she knew Leo had been very fond of the Redwyns. Taking a keen look at the knight's face, she saw it then. The man was wearing a mask. Not a physical one, to disguise his features, but an emotional one, meant to hide his true feelings. The protruding dysphoria his eyes held proved it. Caitrial wished she knew how to comfort the knight who had been so kind to her and her sisters, though they hadn't known each other long. The good-humor was a facade, crafted and wielded, just as Caitrial might craft and use a shield. The woman hated what she had to do next.

"Leo," she gently pressured the arm next to her. "I know this will be hard for you, but we are curious to know what happened on that balcony." The dolor radiated out from his eyes, and Caitrial watched as the handsome, robust knight's face suddenly took on a haggard look.

When Leo gave no indication of starting, to everyone's surprise, Arcadia spoke up. "I know you were up there with her. She would not have let you leave her presence. As her closest friends, we have a right to know how she and her family died."

"We were rather far back in the audience," Reyna chimed in.

"Luckily, not at the edge of the ring, or we may have found ourselves on the receiving end of those spears." The girl shuddered as she pictured the bleeding bodies hanging off of the shafts of those cruel spears, and their stoic wielders. "We barely heard Godfrey's speech, and only saw him shot by the quarrel and then Emery's fall." Tears were lining Reyna's luminous golden eyes. "Sir knight, did Emery at least die with dignity?"

Leonidas looked the Khindre girl in the eyes. "With absolute dignity and grace, Reyna. The courage on her face as she reviled Tarus Gardstar was stunning and inspiring. How she held strong the way she did after taking that dagger to the stomach, I'll never understand, nor forget for the rest of my days." The story seemed to serve as an anchor for the knight, who was able to crawl far enough from despair to answer their questions.

"I never trusted that swine," Arcadia growled. "Always knew he was going to do something. I expected him perhaps to take an unwilling Emery by force. Murder is further than I imagined he'd go."

"He deceived us all by the passion and care in his eyes," Reyna followed. "When I saw him looking at Emery, it seemed to me that he'd give up anything in the world, even for a girl he barely knew."

Arcadia snorted rudely. "He is a snake, just like Geurus. A vile manipulator and trickster!" Leonidas was shocked by the parallel between Arcadia's words and what his own princess said to her killer.

Caitrial, who still hadn't taken her hand off of Leo's arm, squeezed it a bit. "Sir Leo, we saw King Godfrey and Emery's death, and Grayson's removal from the throne," At that, Reyna hugged closer to the deposed prince, who had an enraged look on his face. "But what of Queen Lysaria? It was a surprise to see her outside the Roost's walls, but we've seen and heard nothing of her since."

"Grayson is the only living member of the Redwyn family," Leo explained, holding up his hand to prevent the expected outburst. "The one who struck Lysaria's death blow is_."

"Casinius Brightblade," Grayson finished for him, his voice dull and angry. Leonidas had confirmed as much for him during their practice sessions.

The gasp that ran through the sisters was one of abject horror. "Yamaria," Caitrial said, stunned. "Even the honorable Brightblades?"

"Geurus captured Casinius's loyalty somehow," Grayson growled.

"Galbraith Severesse is adequately bitter about her leader's actions, to make up for the members of the Lightstriders not present at this dire time."

"Someone ought to tell them," Caitrial murmured.

Leo stood and moved to the window, taking one of the pies from the windowsill and cutting it with a knife from the block. He pulled out small dishes, somewhat chipped but still usable, and set a slice on each plate, carrying the food over to everyone, serving Grayson and Reyna first, then Arcadia, and finally Caitrial and himself. The smith smiled and nodded secretly in approval. Precisely the order she would have chosen. It was comforting to know Leonidas didn't blame the Khindre for the assassination. Arcadia had spoken of many whispers in the streets from people convinced the Rainclaw twins, or other Khindre in the walls, had brought this horrendous event upon the city, by their mere presence. Though knights of the kingdom were supposed to listen to the people, Braveheart followed his own guiding principles, which meant he was not led astray by the prejudice of others. It was this facet of the knight's being that had captured Caitrial's fancy in the first place, long before she had actually met Leonidas. And once she saw how far that compassion could go for herself, she'd been gladly drawn into fellowship with him.

By the time the five had finished their sun-warmed meat pie and shared small slices of the second pie, this one filled with succulent berries and fruits, Sunfall had taken full effect, and the streets were bathed in orange radiance, similar in color to Reyna's skin.

"We can't stay for too much longer," Leonidas said, somewhat sadly. "I'm sure that King Geurus will be expecting us back." Caitrial's heart nearly broke at the sound of pain in the knight's voice. It was clear that the man didn't want to return to those halls, where undoubtedly ghosts of his previous Lords and Ladies roamed. She spared a glance at Reyna, unable to stand the broken look of those normally calm gray eyes. Caitrial's sister and Emery's brother were holding tight to each other, neither one wanting to be separated, the affection and anguish in their eyes almost as painful as Leonidas's.

Though their next words were supposed to be private, their strained passion made them speak louder than they expected, and all in the room heard them.

"I feel like I've lost everything," Grayson mourned. "Emery, my parents, my freedom."

"I understand that it's awful," Reyna cooed, sweeping her dark hair behind her tiara-like horns, a hot rush of crimson taking over her sunset features. "But...you haven't lost everything." Grayson's brown eyes shot up and were drawn into the entrancing Khindre's soft golden orbs. "I'm still here, my prince," she muttered. "I'm here, and I swear I won't ever leave you."

Thinking that their words had been private, and with everyone's stoic faces giving them no indication otherwise, they turned their blushing faces up to Caitrial and Leo. "We would enjoy a little time alone...if you don't mind," Reyna muttered.

The two shared an amused glance, already sure they knew what the two lovers were up to. They nodded in unison and waved for the two to go off. Leonidas didn't know when they would be allowed to see each other again. "Ah, young love," he sighed wistfully as the sound of their feet disappeared up the stairs.

"If I weren't still so surprised that the former prince of Sun's Reach was in love with my commoner sister, I might have it in my heart to stop them," Caitrial said. "But for all I know, Geurus might have Grayson killed next, and I've seen what happens to a woman when their love dies before they have a chance to express it in full." She looked at Leonidas and saw that he was hunched over, running a hand through his long hair. The distress in his eyes had multiplied a hundredfold. Caitrial turned around to dismiss Arcadia, but to her surprise, the second Khindre was nowhere to be found. Caitrial hadn't even heard her move! Shrugging, she turned back to Leonidas.

"Emery loved me, you know," Leonidas said plaintively.

"Well, that makes sense," Caitrial said, not quite understanding. "I'm sure you were like family to her."

"No," Leo's voice cracked painfully. "Not like that, Cait. Emery's love for me was more than just familial. I never told you before, but remember the evening when we had our first dance? When Emery asked me to go outside with her…," a ragged sob escaped his throat, "as we sat out there, she...she kissed me and proposed marriage!"

"Divines," Caitrial gasped. "And what did you say?"

"Of course I said no. I'm only a knight, after all, no proper consort for a queen. Besides the fact that I didn't feel that way for her. I loved Emery as a younger sister. Guarding her was like protecting my own family back in Morndale." Leonidas's face was a pitiful sight, and again Caitrial wished she knew how to ease his pain. She'd never imagined something so horrid as this. To have to deny the advances of your liege lady, and then cope with her death only weeks later! The pain of that loss had to be nearly unbearable. But Caitrial wasn't prepared for what came next. "Cait, I think I killed her," Leonidas muttered weakly.

"What are you talking about, Leonidas?"

"Emery's last words, Caitrial. Up on that balcony, after Tarus stabbed her," he shuddered at the awful memory. "She confessed her love for me to everyone on that balcony. It was only after she finished saying that, that Tarus… She could have gotten healing, they could have saved her. My refusal killed Emery, Caitrial." Caitrial put her arm over Leo's shoulder, bidding him not to continue.

The powerful flame that always burned bright within Leonidas like a guiding torch had been dampened, as the grief ran its rampant course upon his spirit and body.

Suddenly, as if in response, a strange fire lit inside of her own heart. "Stop talking like that!" The knight looked woefully up from his hands to stare at Caitrial in shock. "Tell me something, Leonidas. Do you regret being Emery Redwyn's knight?"

"No, why would I?" Leonidas looked hurt that she would even suggest such a notion, but Caitrial pushed on.

"With how you're talking now, I would think you were ashamed of your job." She softened her voice a touch. "Look, Leonidas. You're feeling sorry for yourself for something that you can't change. You served as Emery's knight and was kind and helpful to her, I'm sure of it; gave her the companionship she so desired when my sisters weren't around to give it. Nobody should be surprised that she fell in love with you. Hells, I don't blame her." Leonidas looked at her queerly. "You should hear the talk at the trading halls," she said in explanation. "I'll spare your honor by not telling you about the conversations they have." Leonidas blushed, and Caitrial couldn't help but smile. "And Leonidas, none of them even knew you. You cannot blame yourself for Emery's falling, neither in her heart nor from the tower. They are things you can't change, and though it's right to mourn Emery's death, wasting your life thinking about it is doing a horrid dishonor to her name."

Leo, seeing where Caitrial was coming from, looked appalled, but nodded. The smith was glad to know she'd made her way through to him. "What can I do?" The knight's voice had firmed up, some of his old sturdiness returning.

"How do you feel about the Gardstars, Leo?"

"That should be obvious, Caitrial. I hate them. I've no desire to work under my Lady's killers."

The smith locked eyes with the knight. "Then don't. You are a knight and a grown man." Caitrial shook him gently. "Leave them, Leo. Find yourself a project worth devoting yourself to." Caitrial tiptoed lightly around the subject. If Geurus Gardstar had spies in the area, then all of them would be in jail with what they had said already, but getting herself and Leonidas beheaded would only be a detriment to her ultimate goal, of which she hoped to plant the seeds in Leonidas's head. "Only by taking some sort of action can you honor Emery Redwyn's memory."

The knight nodded, rubbing the tears from his eyes. "Thank you, Caitrial. Your words are wise as ever."

Caitrial smiled at him, laying her hand on his shoulder. She could tell that he'd caught on. "Whatever you do, I'm sure you will succeed. I believe in you, Leonidas Braveheart, and if we could contact her from beyond the grave, I'm sure that we would find Emery with the same faith." The knight grinned in return.

And unseen by both, concealed by a spell of invisibility, Arcadia too felt a grim smile stretch over her face. Emery would be avenged, and that made the Khindre quite glad.

ARCADIA

A SHADOW'S RECONNAISSANCE

There were many things that Caitrial didn't know. Her sister was smart and generally sensible, but...there were just some things Arcadia wasn't going to tell her. Even siblings needed to keep secrets. For example, Grayson had kissed Mia Rothsster shortly before her matching with Leygrain, though he'd been interested in Reyna even then. Emery had told her, but Arcadia judged her twin didn't need to know. Besides, they wanted to keep as far from the topic of Emery as they could. With their eyes wet with remembering tears, nothing would ever get done, and there was much to do.

If Caitrial knew everything her two magical sisters could do, and the things they did with that power, she'd have a conniption. So, Arcadia did as she'd done many a time before. Stuffing a pillow underneath the sheets to simulate her form, Arcadia nodded to Reyna, and her twin silently wished her luck. The purple-skinned Khindre sucked in a deep breath and concentrated on her magic. Orange-gold shafts of light pierced through the window-panes, blocked by her body. Then slowly, more light splashed onto the floor behind her as the edges of her form grew fuzzy and blurred. The blur slowly crawled inwards towards her chest, before, suddenly, the room was empty save for two beds and one orange-skinned Khindre, already falling back into the rhythmic breathing cycle of sleep—Arcadia was gone.

The young woman climbed out of her window, using the ivy Caitrial allowed to grow on this side of the house to reach the street below. She hoped her sister wouldn't notice the bare patches; ivy ripped away by her unseen climb. Even from here, in the Trade Ward, Arcadia could see her destination, looming high and mighty above the city, like the usurpers that lived within. The Khindre had always hated that notion. Why did the person who killed the king get rewarded with possession of their home and finery? Arcadia shook the thought from her head; right now, she needed to focus. Even being invisible, this mission wouldn't be easy. Her previous excursions had taken her to several key places: markets, barracks where soldiers loyal to the late King Godfrey resided. A few times, she'd even provided reconnaissance on the manors of noble families, several of which had declared for Geurus shortly after he'd stolen the throne. *Bloody lickspittles, the lot of them.* But now, Arcadia meant to breach the castle walls, to uncover whatever information she could about these new royals. The Rebels of Searstar needed this information, and soon, if they were to stand any chance against Geurus Gardstar.

Arcadia planned to make sure that the treacherous bastard and his son, Tarus, had a rough time of their rule.

At this hour, the drawbridge spanning Qrakzt's moat would be raised, so Arcadia would need to find a different entry part. That suited the khindre sorceress just fine; she hated the feel of that moat, seeming to grasp at her, like one of the royal kennel master's catch collars, attempting to drag her down to its whipping, singing depths. Why it did, she couldn't fathom, but she'd gladly avoid it, given this opportunity.

Shifting her gaze up the wall, Arcadia saw several Enforcers, encased in their black armor-shells, lance points glinting cruelly in the sunlight. The Khindre resisted the urge to blast them off of the walls. *Had we been much further back in the ring in the plaza when Emery died, they would have skewered us without remorse.* Both Khindre had felt the inescapable press of the crowd that day. Arcadia swore to this day that she'd felt the cold scrape of a metal edge on her back before the Enforcers raised their weapons. *What sort of soldiers could slay fellow men and women running in fear, and seem entirely unimpacted by it?*

She reflected on how glad she was that the sun never set. Girt in their darksome armor, Arcadia would have no chance of seeing them.

"More's the pity for them. I don't need darkness to remain unseen," she muttered to herself.

There was a small copse of honeybark trees situated near the outer castle wall. *Get over that, and I'm in the bailey, where I can get to the gardens. With any luck, one of the new royals will enjoy walking in the gardens as much as Em did.* The stand was owned by a merchant who sold perfumes crafted from flowers that curled up the trunks like desirous lovers. Arcadia knew from days wandering through the markets, suspicious of everyone as they were of her, that these trees were watched. The owner didn't want rival merchants coming in to steal his goods, so he stationed a man atop the house nearest the trees—which the wealthy merchant owned, of course—from sun up to sunfall, and back to sun up again. Squinting into the sun, Arcadia could just make out the figure of the bored guard, chin resting in his hands. His crossbow was laid to the side, strung but unloaded.

"Let's give him a little excitement, shall we?" Under normal circumstances, Arcadia would conjure some phantoms to spook and distract the man, but she couldn't cast any other spells without losing her invisibility. The sorceress had learned that the hard way. She feared the scar on her tail from the lucky guardsman with the crossbow would never heal.

Arcadia dug into a belt-pouch at her side and produced a gem-studded bauble. The tiny pink flower earring was one of a pair gifted to her by Emery. Arcadia, never one to care much about jewelry, hadn't ever worn them. A fact for which she felt guilty about whenever she saw them. She felt nearly as guilty using Em's gift as a distraction. *More use than I'll get out of them. Can you forgive me?* One way or another, Arcadia didn't have much choice; she'd come all this way, after all. With all the strength in her arm, she hurled the jewel into the air. It sparkled in the sunlight for a moment before knocking into one of the crenellations. The piece clattered down to the street, and Arcadia winced, hoping it hadn't broken. The guard, glad for any source of excitement during his shift, peered over the wall, catching sight of the gleaming object. "Whazzat?" Surveying the street below, and seeing nothing, he crossed to a ladder and disappeared from the roof. Before the man could even cry out, "Egads! Me lady'll love this darling thing. Thankee, Yamaria!" Arcadia scrambled up the tree nearest the wall.

Arcadia had ample time to pick her way to a limb hanging over the moat with the man making his way back to his post and imagining his reward when his mistress saw his gift. From there, she could see her intended breach point.

Once during a great storm, a bough from this very tree broke off and slammed into the wall, breaking the barrier and the gargoyle atop it. The statue had lost a wing and part of its sneering face. *Who thought a gargoyle could be made even uglier?*

Emery had begged her father not to replace the statue, saying it gave the wall a bit of character. Godfrey had acquiesced. He could rarely resist his daughter's pleas. *Except when it mattered,*

Arcadia thought bitterly. Emery had promptly named it Ol' Lopjaw.

"Lopjaw, don't fail me now," the Khindre muttered, sweat dripping down her back. The moat whistled just below her, unconcerned and yet threatening. *Reyna and Sir Leonidas aren't here this time. If I fall in now, I'll be dead, for sure.* She took a deep breath, banishing the worry from her mind. It would just cause her to fall to her painful, searing death.

All she had to do was spring off and land just—

—right, catch the gargoyle around the neck, and scramble atop the wall. Arcadia sank back against the shattered stone, catching her breath. She looked at her hands, seeing the blood on them, and their visible tremble. Wait—she could see her hands! The sorceress cussed to herself; she was running out of time! Becoming invisible like that was a relatively new skill, and she could only do it once in a given day. She probably should have waited to cast the spell, but it was behind her now. Across the bailey, Arcadia could see the hedges where she hoped to spy. The Enforcers on the wall hadn't seen her. Their attention seemed to be focused outside the walls anyway, so maybe she'd be fine. *Over-confident idiots, those Enforcers are. Though there's something not quite right about them. I can't place it, but the way they just stand there, stock still. It doesn't seem human.*

And what else would they be? Her conscience retorted. *Demons? Read your history, Khindre. The demonkin haven't been seen since the Black Dawn, hundreds of years before the Eclipse!*

That was true, but was it so outlandish a theory? After all, mages hadn't been around for a century, but here she stood! Even then, it wasn't solid proof, and Arcadia *never* went to her contacts with baseless conjecture.

While her invisibility remained spotty though it was, Arcadia dropped down lightly from the wall, and sprinted across the courtyard, slipping into the bushes with nary a sound.

As she quietly picked her way through the hedge, cursing every snapping twig and the branches that plucked at her sheer garment, Arcadia could hear voices. One sounded like Geurus himself—the sorceress thanked her good fortune—while the other was unlike any voice she'd ever heard before: flat, cold, and raspy, like the sound of a dying man's rattle.

Deadvoice was talking now, as Arcadia edged as far as she dared towards the gardens. "But yes, your family has done quite well for itself, if I'm not mistaken. I'm pleasantly surprised. My colleagues and I all expected another failed coup. No offense, of course, but the people of Moonwatch don't have the best record concerning this matter."

Geurus chuckled. "Looking at our history, I can't blame you for your worries. Rats often disappoint those whose feet they scurry under. But I assure you, my lord, that I will not disappoint."

"See that you don't," Deadvoice said. "We have much riding on your success here. You may have eliminated the royals, but there are still influential nobles, some of whom were close to the previous crown."

"Fear not. Godfrey was notoriously greedy with his wealth. I have plenty of coin to ensure that these upstart nobles don't get any foolish ideas."

"What of the Redwyn armsmen? You say you sent a battalion out to the Scorched Waste to deal with the Chillfang threat, but didn't you request me to transport the Chillfang into Sun's Reach? The Sun Wench hasn't yet been captured. Their goal is not yet complete."

"As the Redwyn armsmen's mission shall not be completed." Arcadia could almost see the venomous smile on the king's face. "Shortly after they left, I mobilized a sizeable force to, shall we say, intercept them. What few manage to escape will be of no concern to me." This sort of evil act was precisely what Arcadia expected from Geurus, but it was a shock to hear nonetheless. Despite that, even Arcadia—no master of tactics and strategy—could see the flaw in that plan. If any of Emery's soldiers escaped the slaughter, they would go running with the tale to the influential lords of Sun's Reach. Of course, she wasn't in any hurry to correct him, not with her wall of fury at Geurus's treachery. Neither, it seemed, was Deadvoice.

"Very well, I suppose I should trust you to complete the rest of your task," he said, if Deadvoice even *was* a he. "With the magic we've taught your wife, and the allies we have contacted on your behalf, you should be more than prepared to lead the people of Sun's Reach into submission...and slaughter any who don't go willingly."

That made Arcadia rock back on her heels. *Other* mages? Arcadia didn't like the odds if Queen Cereos had magic, and Deadvoice and whoever his compatriots were had taught it to her. Sun's Reach had two mages—well, two and a half, if you counted Lightstrider Vedalken—who were both young women, barely out of their flowering. Besides that not so small detail, she had to wonder what Geurus and this ghastly voiced figure were after if they were so willing to kill anyone who got in their way. *Like they killed Emery.* Her tail flicked in annoyance and rage, causing the bushes to rustle.

"Who goes there?" Deadvoice called out, his words sounding all the more horrifying for the increase in volume. "Show yourself! Is it you, Widower Prince? I know you have a fondness for skulking!"

Arcadia froze in place, feeling a cold sweat drip down her spine. It dripped all the faster as the voice rasped, "If you don't come out, then I'll just have to reveal you!" Moments later, Arcadia's world was devoured in a flash of blue-white heat.

"You may want to invest in a few cats, Geurus; it seems you have little rats scurrying about." The voice sounded like it came from a league away. "But it doesn't matter what that one heard, my little spell will have left its mind fried." Arcadia had only a moment to marvel that she was still alive. *Probably my devil blood. Reyna and I always had a higher tolerance for heat than most others.* She had to get up now, before Deadvoice and Geurus came to investigate. Her body felt like hastily hammered together chunks of iron, clunky and awkward, and the ashes— all that remained of the section of hedge she'd hidden in— were slippery beneath her feet as she dragged herself back to a standing position. She stumbled forward, cursing at the pain. Below the rising smoke, she saw a few charred splinters of branches. *That should be me.* Arcadia felt the sting of various cuts and scrapes on her body, but strangely, no aching burns. *No time to worry about that, focus on surviving, foolish girl.*

Gathering all her strength, she crept forward, hoping that the smoke would cover her escape, for she knew, without knowing quite how, that her invisibility was long gone. Her eyes stung something awful from the acrid fumes, and before long, she had to close them, her arms groping blindly for the next section of branches. *How big was that explosion?*

If she could find the rest of the bush, Arcadia would be safe. She remembered her contact, Barnibus Boome's words. *Head along the planted wall until you reach the stone gate. Four paces to the right, three stones up, you should find a small portway. Servants used that entrance to bring amorous guests into the castle under Godfrey's nose almost every night. Make sure to close it up behind yourself. It would be a shame for Geurus to find out and leave those good maids and butlers wanting."*

Finally, Arcadia found what she was searching for, as a thorny constrictor vine, rudely deprived of its victim—and half of its body—stabbed her in the palm. Sucking in her breath, the Khindre gathered her legs underneath her. Like a gazelle from the Sulfaari Expanse, she darted out of the smoke and along the bush. From behind her, the sorceress heard a cry of alarm,

Geurus, like as not. *I need to go faster; I must reach the wall. I can't die here!* Deadvoice rasped something, but Arcadia was far beyond listening to their words, so intent was she on escaping.

Thwap, thwap, thwap. Shoots and leaves slapped at Arcadia as if they too were trying to catch her. Ahead, she could see the reddish-brown stone of the wall, with its crenelated square watch-posts, thankfully unoccupied. The Khindre didn't feel like sprouting a black spear through her chest. Already breathing hard, Arcadia pushed herself faster, and several ragged breaths later, she was there. *One, two, three, four. Hand on the wall. One, two, three, and push!* A sigh of pure relief rushed from her throat as the wall opened up, revealing a roughly hewn rectangular tunnel. The walls pulled at whatever scraps of clothing remained on her bony form, as she crawled through, pulling the panel closed with her tail. *I'm safe,* she thought, nearly giddy with adrenaline. Arcadia was so caught up in the incredible luck of her escape, and reinforcing what information she'd learned, it took a moment before she noticed she couldn't move. Not only that, but there was a shadow over her. Her mismatched eyes saw the hem of a stark grey robe, with thick white fur trimmings. Slowly, Arcadia's eyes traveled upwards, seeing chapped white hands, bonier than hers. Above that, partially shrouded by a cloak hood, was a face that seemed nearly fleshless, its eyes the same smoldering blue of the flames that had nearly cost Arcadia her life. They even flickered like little embers. Her mind, acting out of sheer, reflexive terror, reached for the surrounding shadows, commanding them to reach out and grab at this strange creature. The creature, for surely this thing couldn't be human, nor any of the other known races that inhabited Sun's Reach rattled out a laugh. *Deadvoice.*

"Hello, little sorceress," it said, one desiccated finger inching towards Arcadia's forehead. Several angry retorts jumped into the Khindre's head, but all she did was swear, as colorful as any drunken merchant. *Caitrial would frown and shake that reproving finger at me if she heard that.* Arcadia thought it very fitting that her last thought was of Caitrial, who'd protected her all these many years. "Pity, she's not here to save you now." Deadvoice grated. Before Arcadia had a chance to wonder how it had read her mind, the finger pressed into the flesh of her brow, and everything went black.

She woke the next morning to hear Reyna's light breathing in the bed across the room. Arcadia wondered if it was all a dream for a moment. But when she moved, she felt the burning ache from the various scrapes on her arms and legs, and the splitting headache originating from where Deadvoice had touched her. Arcadia shuddered. For some reason, she was alive, and Arcadia swore she would never step inside those castle walls again, not until the day the Gardstars, and whatever horrid monsters they kept in there, were well and truly gone.

TARUS

FINDING FAITH

As Tarus walked around the courtyard of the castle, he could feel eyes on him, watching him. For just a moment, the prince regretted his decision, telling his father that it would be smart to increase security to forestall a possible rebellion. Geurus had listened to his son, nearly emptying his barracks of every Enforcer that wasn't on duty in the city streets. Now they lined the wall like so many silent statues, spears in hand, and short bows within reach. For a moment, Tarus wondered what orders his father had given the Enforcers. Would they attack any man or woman who came up to the castle gates? He hoped his father wasn't so foolish; an unprovoked murder by the castle gates would, without a doubt, spark retaliation against the Gardstars. Tarus shivered at the thought; it didn't matter how resilient and skilled the Enforcers were if the entire city of Searstar stood against them.

The unnerving sense of being watched was too much for him, even though he knew the Enforcers wouldn't attack him unless given direct orders to do so. Tarus turned from the court-yard, wishing the best of luck to Grayson and Sir Leonidas. He walked past the drum-like tower, the Roost, with its golden Phoenix statue gleaming magnificently on top. Tarus knew that statue wouldn't last much longer. Geurus wanted to erase every sign of the Redwyn family he possibly could. That didn't bode well for Grayson. But Geurus had said it himself; he didn't want to come off as a monster, which is why the princeling still lived. At this very moment, a team of silversmiths was building a statue shaped like the Astral Knight on the Gardstar standard. The phoenix would either be destroyed, melted down, and sold for more coin to refill the Crown's coffers. The preparations for the two recent weddings, including the colossal feast Godfrey had planned for his daughter's wedding, which had fed to Geurus, his men, and his dogs, had depleted the coinage significantly.

Eventually, Tarus could see three of the five towers that radiated around the Roost like rays of a great Sun. Looking behind his shoulder, Tarus could see the Lightstrider's barracks, where Emery said the armor of past Lightstriders stood on display. The order had been established thousands of years ago, during the first wars between the newly born kingdoms of Sun's Reach and Moonwatch.

He couldn't imagine just how many suits of armor stood sentinel down in that crypt. How many levels did the tower descend to fit all of those armaments?

To his right, the sound of metal clanging resonated from the smith, Jorjen's workshop. A steady flow of weapons had been coming from this tower since Geurus took the throne. Tarus didn't know why his father felt the need to make new weapons, but the notion disturbed him. The Enforcers were already equipped with cold-worked armaments from home. Perhaps Geurus was just keeping the castle's workers busy. All of Godfrey's garrison had been sent out towards the Scorched Waste before the wedding, taking armor and weapons with them. But somehow, Tarus doubted that. His father was cruelly efficient. If weapons were forged, they would be used. Despite Geurus's speech about enemies entering the kingdom, Tarus would bet his entire inheritance that the arms weren't going to be distributed to the citizens for their protection.

To his left stood a squat, square tower, with a tall minaret to make it even with the others. This extensive, multi-sectioned building contained the stables, kennel, and rookery, as well as the barracks where Godfrey's soldiers, and now Geurus's slept. Tarus thought that seemed like a serious insult, forcing your men to sleep in the same building as the animals, but he supposed Godfrey had his reasons. *Probably to save space and upkeep money for his lavish parties.* The furthest tower and the least ornate were dedicated to Yamaria, the goddess of Sun's Reach. The dull brown stone of the split tower was limned with the fiery glow from above. Tarus had to shield his eyes as the setting sun shone partially through the missing section, focusing the sun's light on the castle. No matter what Geurus did, save blocking that gap, the sunlight would always serve as a reminder to the people of Searstar that this kingdom was the domain of the sun. The priests left their doors open to those remaining servants of Godfrey who needed some solace in the wake of the changes life had sent upon them.

Not knowing quite why, Tarus found himself moving towards the tower. With the jumble of emotions he'd experienced recently, Tarus felt the need to talk with someone. Someone who understood what he was going through, as his parents and Velara never could. Perhaps the priests would be able to soothe his soul. Holding out this hope, Tarus crossed beneath the arch in front, illuminated by two torches. Engraved in the stone was a saying that he could only imagine came from the holy book of their religion. *"Very few things in this world are eternal. The light of the sun, the love, and mercy of Yamaria, and the hope, however feeble, that times will be better."* By the look of the arch, it was a relatively new passage, likely written shortly after the Eclipse, when the light of the sun became truly eternal for these folk. *Emery was right,* Tarus thought morosely. *Constant sunlight is far better than the alternative.*

Tarus exhaled in wonder as he entered the narthex. Tall windows poured sunlight into the room at every angle. Any shadow that the sunshine didn't illuminate was affixed with a torch, leaving a space whereas few shadows existed as possible. A few monks sat at desks around the pentagonal room, dressed in shabby red robes, their heads shaved. None of them even spared a glance at him, busy at work writing on the scrolls in front of them. Quiet music drifted through the temple, seemingly flowing out of the walls themselves. Two of the walls were lit with books large and small, and two with scroll cubbies. The fifth wall had an opening, likely into the main church, covered by a curtain of beads rattling softly as the breeze from the open doors pushed it about.

Just walking in lifted Tarus's spirit, and he took a deep breath, drawing in the lightly incensed air. He stared around for a long moment, just taking it all in. How different this temple was from everything he knew from home. Back in Moonwatch, a temple to the god of the moon, Gaarhowl, was cold and severe, like most things within the kingdom. Carved from pillars of dull grey stone, they were caked with ice and snow, with only one lantern lit on a hook over the door, to guide people to the entrance. The temples were silent and cold, unlike the warm, cheery atmosphere within Yamaria's place of worship. Tarus felt like he could stand there, absorbing the waves of comfort forever, as he'd been discouraged from ever doing in Moonwatch. *Gaarhowl has little use for prayers. Prayers are merely words, and words get little accomplished. If you want to pray to your god, then take up a spear and go hunt.* The priests never directly specified what was supposed to be hunted, but only a few of the weapons on the wall were made for slaying boar. Tarus never minded the short stays, since the rooms somehow managed to be colder than the outside air, as if an invisible winter storm raged inside at all times. The priests had always terrified him as a kid, shrouded in numerous pelts and furs, all with the heads still attached, looking for all the world like some sort of nightmare beast. It may have only been a dream, but Tarus was sure that he'd seen one wearing a hooded cape with a man's face on the cowl. He shivered and banished the evil thoughts which had no place here in this beautiful holy house.

Suddenly, the Widower Prince was acutely aware of eyes on him. He turned around slowly, as a finger of dread scraped down his spine; the malice entrenched within the glare was palpable. A monk stood at the main desk, his bald head gleaming in the sunlight.

"I'm quite sorry, sir," the monk drawled. "But I believe you are lost."

"N-no, sir," Tarus stammered. "I came here on purpose."

The man narrowed his eyes. "That doesn't make you any less lost." He sighed. "I thought I made this clear to your broad-faced relative. *People of Moonwatch aren't welcome within the Sun Mother's halls!*"

"With all due respect, Master..."

"Balvrich."

"Master Balvrich. I understand why you don't want us here. But you have to believe me. I don't mean you or your temple any harm. If it were my goal to destroy the Redwyn servants' final refuge, I wouldn't be so foolish as to come alone. Please, Balvrich, I only wish to speak to a priest."

"Your words make sense, Widower Prince," Balvrich hissed. "But that doesn't mean I trust you."

"Only an idiot would take my words at face value," Tarus said. "Holding onto doubt proves you're thinking." He saw the monk backing up towards a small block upon which two bells sat, one gold, one silver. Doubtless, one of them would call a priest, but the other... "Do whatever you believe best, Master Balvrich. Whether it's getting a priest as I've asked, or having your guards arrest me. I will accept either option." He chuckled dully and patted his waist for the monk to see. "Not that I'm in any state to deny your choice." Not knowing quite why, Tarus had left his weapon in his chambers, but now he was glad for the instinct.

Balvrich raised an eyebrow somewhat suspiciously and moved back without turning around as if he expected Tarus to pull some hidden weapon from behind his back. His hand hovered over the bell block for a moment, before grabbing and ringing the gold bell, the melodic tone reverberating in the air. Tarus held his breath, waiting for doors to open and admit armed guards. Then he heard a clattering sweep, as the bead curtain was pushed aside, revealing a middle-aged man with olive-colored skin, and somewhat pointed ears, showing some Elven heritage. Despite his relative youth, the man leaned heavily on a staff carved from gilded silver with a spherical sun emblem wrought in gold on the top, and multiple rubies inlaid into the shaft. He wore a simple habit, white with a red sash. Calm, blue eyes, like gently rippling ponds, searched the room and came to rest on Balvrich.

"You called, Master Balvrich?" he said in a quiet voice, nearly as melodic as the bell that summoned him.

The monk's face blanched. "I apologize for disturbing your rest, Patriarch." He bowed. "I hoped one of the others would be free."

"The other priests are in the middle of Mid-morning devotions. But I wouldn't dare leave a call unanswered."

"You could have left this one," Balvrich murmured under his breath.

"What was that, Master Balvrich?" The Patriarch looked sharply at the monk, who rubbed the back of his head sheepishly, looking supremely embarrassed, though the Patriarch hadn't raised his voice. "Have you not learned anything from your training? Even if we don't like a supplicant, they deserve the same deference that all do in the eyes of Yamaria." The priest shifted his gaze to Tarus. "That includes the son of Geurus Gardstar."

Balvrich bowed his head, muttering an inaudible answer, and shuffled back to the wall, busying himself with the scrolls on the wall. The Patriarch chuckled under his breath. "He makes a good monk, but I doubt that my good friend Balvrich will ever be priest material. Ah, well, what can I do for you, my son?"

"It's an honor, Milord," Tarus bowed to the Patriarch.

"Considering rank, it should be I who is bowing to you, Prince of Sun's Reach. However, there is little need for such lofty titles here. Yamaria's sanctuaries are neutral ground. Please, just call me Vail."

"As you request, Father Vail."

The Patriarch chuckled again. "I ask again, what can I do for you, Tarus Gardstar?" There was no hostility in his voice, his tone even and neutral.

Tarus wasn't sure why he'd come here. The prince had found himself at the door before he could question himself. Father Vail waited patiently, and suddenly his heart took control of his mouth. "I come seeking confession."

The Patriarch nodded slowly. He swept his free hand up towards a staircase in between two bookshelves. "Follow me, my son. These are private matters which deserve a place far away from prying ears." Vail led Tarus up the stairs, a slow winding journey, which seemed to take a toll on the man.

The second floor of the temple had as many doors as it did windows, each one with a candle sitting unlit in a sconce outside. Not a single door was adorned to differentiate it from the others. Shaped from smooth, expensive wood, the staff in the Patriarch's hand seemed to be the most ornate thing in the building. Tarus brought up this matter with Vail, earning himself another laugh.

"Yes, if you compared this temple with its decorations before the Eclipse, it would be nearly unrecognizable. The Temples to Yamaria used to be filled with gilt and glamor. It was only after I reached a high order within the clergy that I convinced my fellow priests to sell the wealth and use the money to remediate what wounds of war we still could. The positive impact of that decision earned me my current rank. However, they wouldn't allow me to get rid of the staff. 'Twas passed through generations of Patriarchs, and to be rid of it, would be an insult to our ancestors, they said. So I have the staff."

"You've been around since the Eclipse?" Tarus asked. The story made sense, and he applauded the Patriarch's generosity. "You don't look a day over forty!"

"Elven blood does wonders for a man," Vail said in reply. "But enough about me, this is not why you came." He lightly rapped on the first door with his staff. Satisfied that nobody was inside, he reached inside his sleeve and pulled out flint and steel. Vail leaned back against the wall, taking the staff in the crook of his arm. Hands shaking, he reached up and tried to light the candle. Despite multiple tries, he only managed to create sparks. Tarus thought it strange that Vail was having difficulty, despite his apparent age.

Placing a hand on the Patriarch's shoulder, Tarus took the starters from him. "Allow me, Father." With the deftness of experience, Tarus struck the steel against the flint, and the wick caught, the flame leaping up to greet the air.

"Thank you, my son." He rebalanced himself on the staff. "Come in."

The confession room was small and cozy. A square table dominated most of the space, surrounded by cushioned chairs. A small bookshelf stood against one wall. The walls were sparsely decorated, just a few pieces of parchment, written with phrases in a language Tarus couldn't read. Vail moved around the room, directing Tarus to light a lantern for light and a portable brazier for tea. The lamp must have had disks of incense placed in it, for a pleasant aroma filled the room. Tarus didn't recognize the scent, but it put him at ease, and so he took multiple whiffs of it before sitting. Father Vail was already mixing herbs into a small pot of water, setting it above the fire to stew.

"The tea will take some time to brew and steep, so while we wait, I must ask you a few questions." An apologetic look came into the man's eyes. "You seem quite genuine, but I must ask you this question all the same. It is for the sake of the people within these walls, I hope you understand." Tarus nodded, allowing Vail to continue. "Why did your father send you here, Tarus Gardstar?"

"He didn't," Tarus answered brusquely. "He hasn't told me about his plans, but I don't think this temple holds any interest for him."

"I'm not surprised," Vail said. "His Enforcers refuse to come in here, for one reason or another. His disinterest shows Geurus's a wise man. Any sensible king would fear something his soldiers can't search.

Tarus looked into Vail's eyes. Why was the Patriarch telling him this? He had to have an agenda of one sort, but what it was, the prince couldn't tell. But before he could question it, the man shook his head. "But that's enough about him, let's talk about you. I believe that the king didn't send you. So tell me, my son, why have you come." Tarus started to speak, but the words caught in his throat. His eyes welled with unbidden tears, and the prince's breathing became ragged. Father Vail looked at him with sympathy. "I cannot help you if you refuse to speak, son. I know whatever you have to say, it will hurt. But the simple fact it hurts proves you are human."

Tarus still couldn't meet his eyes, but slowly, trying to hold back the awful tears that he couldn't shake even weeks after the event, he told the Patriarch the entire story. He started with his arrival in Sun's Reach, landing on the boat, excited to see the new land, and dealing with the strange heat and light of the sun for the first time in his life. How bizarre to cross the Eclipse on the sea, where the magic curtain ended and suddenly go from utter darkness to blinding light. Had it not been for the skill and luck of the sailors Geurus had hired, they would all have died right then, crushed upon the rocks. Then his journey with his father and his army straight through the Kingdom. Tarus had wanted to see the sights, experience this miraculous and strange place, but Geurus had insisted that they move quickly to the capital. Then, he explained the day he'd first met Princess Emery. Here, it became hard to speak again. He choked over descriptions of Emery's beauty and her generosity. The Roost was a fascinating sight, a simple, clean complex, rather than the ostentatious palace in Enoch, the Capital which Tarus had seen a few times in his past. A sudden epiphany came to him as he spoke. "I think, though I didn't know it then, I decided right there, I loved Sun's Reach. With Emery's arm in mine, the warm sun on my face and scents of summertime in Searstar filling the air, there was nothing more I could ask for. But now, that's all lost." Though Tarus couldn't finish, his throat closing up too tightly to speak, he could sense the understanding in Father Vail's eyes, which hadn't lost an ounce of their compassion through his tale.

As Tarus sat quivering in his chair, a steaming mug was pushed into his clammy hands. "Drink, my son. You deserve it. There is guilt in you, which is a good thing. That you cared for Emery is obvious, even to an ascetic like me. Just then, a bell rang, signaling that it was nearly time for mass. "I must go, Tarus, but please feel free to stay here as long as you need to. Far be it from me to deny a man any comforts that I can provide." The

Patriarch began to walk out but stopped in the door. "And Tarus?"

"Yes, Father Vail?"

"Admitting our sins and having guilt about them is only the first step to receiving Yamaria's forgiveness. You still have much work to do. Please, feel free to come back sometime, if you are interested in the redemption the Sun Goddess offers." With that, Vail left Tarus alone with just the pot of tea and burning lantern. Tarus sighed. "I will, Father Vail. I will return, indeed."

LEONIDAS

A MISSION AND A VOW

"Sir Leonidas Braveheart, to what do I owe this unexpected pleasure?"

"Lightstrider Galbraith." Leonidas bowed deeply. "I require wise guidance, and I think you may be the only person within Searstar I can turn to."

The tall, dark-skinned woman chuckled. She replaced the sword she'd been cleaning onto the rack and turned to face him. "Flattery, though appreciated, is unnecessary to borrow the ear of the Lightstrider." Galbraith gave the knight a keen glance. "Besides, you've visited the Scorched Waste not too long ago. You should know that the brain boiling sun doesn't promote much more than instinctual survival."

Leo shook his head. "On the contrary, m'lady. Some of the wisest people I ever had the pleasure of meeting were in the desert." He hid a smile, recalling his saviors in the Scorched Waste. Faithful Amaru, the daughter of Yamaria, and a magical healer, the likes of which hadn't been seen in Sun's Reach in a century. The Fyroxi girl had refused to join him on his journey back home. He wondered what would have happened had Amaru accepted the invitation. Would Geurus, upon learning of her origin, have slain her too? A true daughter of the prime goddess of the region would, without doubt, be a threat to his seat on the throne. Or perhaps, could her story have convinced Godfrey Redwyn that trouble was brewing? If so, Godfrey could have easily ordered Lord Gardstar to send his own army out to deal with the issue as a show of faith to the Crown. That would have left Geurus vulnerable and perhaps saved Emery's life. But despite his personal feelings on the matter, Leonidas knew Amaru made a wise choice. It was better that she stayed in the Scorched Waste, with utterly besotted Alaric, brave Dalphamair, and experienced Celwyn. *Better she tries to stop, or at least delay, the Chillfang threatening to overrun Sun's Reach. Better we don't have enemies coming from both sides.* No matter what Geurus Gardstar might say, Leonidas had a niggling suspicion that the new king didn't plan to stop his killing with the royal family of Sun's Reach. In the years before coming to court, the knight had seen his fair share of bloodthirsty men, and Geurus had all the qualifications. "In the heat of the day, the desert folk's bodies may not be active, but that only gives their brains more time to work."

Galbraith chuckled. "Fair point, Leonidas," she conceded. "However, I'm sure you came here to converse about something besides my homeland. So I ask again, how can I help you, Leonidas Braveheart?"

"Coincidently, that's what I came here to ask *you,* Lady Severesse. To put it plainly, I've been far too idle since the Gardstars so rudely ripped my duty out from under me." He tried, with limited success, to keep the seething rage out of his voice, and saw a gleam of approval in the Lightstrider's eyes. "I figured that if there was anyone still devoted to the people, it would be the

Lightstriders. Or at least," he amended, "you and the three others out on their missions."

Now, a wave of smoldering anger took over Galbraith's face and voice. "Yes, I am doing whatever I can to end the unrest in Searstar. I want to send missives out to Raerizen, Tinco Anar, and Vedalken, but all mail from official offices goes through our king's new favorite puppet." Galbraith spat onto the stone floor. The dark-skinned Lightstrider went quiet for a moment, so Leonidas took the chance to look around. The two were meeting inside the Lightstrider's tower, where only the heroes, their servants, squires, and invited guests of the order itself were allowed. Not even the King or his advisors were permitted without express permission, granted only by consensus from all present members of the team. Thus, Galbraith had denied any advances by King Geurus to enter the tower. The room the two warriors conferred in was comfortable, yet sparsely furnished.

A fire crackled in the hearth, illuminating the red stone of the walls and floors. A simple cot, like those used by the Water Callers in the Scorched Waste, stood folded against the wall, a wooden chest with iron bands sitting next to it. On the opposite wall, a shield hung, emblazoned with the Sun and Sword symbol of the Lightstriders. Underneath it sat a wooden shelf, on which two books were displayed. The first was a dull leather-bound tome, engraved with a picture that Leonidas recognized as the sunlit fox head of Yamaria, the holy book of the Sun Goddess then. Most houses had this somewhere in their libraries, though whether it was actually read or even opened was questionable. The second book was a thick volume ornately bound with red leather and gilded in gold. Gold wrought sun and sword stood out on the cover, identifying it as the Lightstrider Codex, the book kept the rules and basic history of the Lightstriders. Between those covers were in-depth descriptions of all the wars and significant battles since the founding of the order. Leonidas was surprised. The Codex was supposed to be kept in the Captain's office!

"As far as I am concerned," Galbraith said, as if she'd read his mind. "Casinius is no true leader of the Lightstriders. In all things, members of this order are supposed to act in the best interest of the realm. By slaying Lysaria, and helping Geurus gain the throne, Casinius has broken all the tenets of Lightstrider code, defamed himself, and became a blemish upon this proud order. According to the laws in that book, a Captain can be removed from office in only four ways: retirement, death, official decree by the King or Queen, or by a unanimous vote by the four other Lightstriders, officiated by a personage of religious office. Damned formalities," she swore. "I'm sure this fact has influenced the nature of Casinius's counsel to the king. Geurus has closed the main gates; nobody enters or leaves without his permission, so even if the others were to come striding up to the walls, they'd merely be turned away, be it by words or arrows. Naught but an army or a skilled smuggler could get them in. With the veritable infestation of Enforcers in the city, and the disappearance of the Royal Secretkeeper, no sane man is willing to try his luck. Can't say I blame them. As for the army, I've managed to get my hands on several letters Casinius was hiding; fool should have burned them, but I'm not complaining. It seems like Geurus' fingers reach farther than just the capital. Several cities have turned their banners to Geurus's side, including Redhawk and, most notably, Fyrestone.

Leonidas blinked, recalling something Emery had told him about. A slaughter of Fyroxi in Fyrestone, and Godfrey would do nothing about it. She'd cried hard into his shoulder relating that news. Emery had always been willing to cry for the suffering of those she scarcely knew. Leo wondered whether Geurus ever cried, or whether he was just as heartless as he seemed. The signs had all been there—Chillfang in the Scorched Waste, slaughter in

Fyrestone; market prices on food and other commodities had even been higher than when Leonidas had left for his mission—they'd all just been too blind to make the connection.

Leonidas growled at the injustice of it all. "How did an unscrupulous wretch such as Casinius ever reach the office of Lightstrider Captain?"

Galbraith gave him an appraising look, then nodded and stood. "Follow me, Sir Leonidas." With long, quick strides, the desert warrior exited the room, Leo just behind her.

Galbraith led them down the staircase to the bottom of the tower. Once there, she moved to the wall, drew a short axe from a ring on her belt, and snagged an inconspicuous chain hanging from the wall. Galbraith grunted as she pulled down, and shortly after, the wall recessed and slid sideways, revealing a long, dark passageway. "What you are about to see has never been shown to any person save Lightstriders and Royals." Without waiting for Leonidas to reply, Galbraith took a torch from the wall and entered the hallway. "Come on, Sir. That door won't stay open forever." Leonidas shook off the shock at the deep trust and honor the Lightstrider had just granted him, following.

His footsteps echoed off the walls of the dark corridor as they walked for many long minutes. *Clang! Clang! Clang! Clang!* Leonidas got the strange sensation he was disturbing the dead. His premonition proved correct a moment later, as Galbraith stopped and turned to the left. At this point in the tunnel, the stone brick walls turned into a series of alcoves, running down just as far as the eye could see. Turning around, Leonidas could see that the nooks continued on the right side as well. Standing inside each alcove was a stone statue, meticulously carved to look like the person whose grave it stood over. The detail was astounding. The stonemasons captured every facet of their subjects: every hair in their mustache, every wrinkle on their face, every scar. Leonidas didn't recognize any faces, and when Galbraith lowered her torch down to one of the stylized stones in front of the cairn, he understood why.

Cialsin Brightblade, 50 A.F. Founded the Lightstriders. Died fighting valiantly against the Orc King Grazzaki.

Several things here caught the knight's eye. "50 A.F " Leonidas started.

"Fifty years after the founding of the kingdoms of Sun's Reach and Moonwatch. A long, long time past. According to the histories, we were still peaceful with our neighbors back then. Around that time, orcs and other vile creatures were rising up, hoping to destroy our fragile peace. With bands of rogue mages and fell creatures roaming about causing wanton destruction, Cialsin felt the people needed something to boost their morale, keep their faith in the fledgling kingdom. To that end, the Lightstriders were founded, with Cialsin as their first leader, and four Fyroxi taking the other positions."

"So Lord Vedalken *wasn't* around for the founding of the order," Leonidas exclaimed in mock surprise.

That elicited a chuckle from Galbraith. "Far from it, though I imagine he'd be flattered that you think him skilled enough to have been around since the Founding." She continued on down the hall, periodically leaning down to illuminate a nameplate. *Caeser Brightblade, Cicero Brightblade, Cynwyn Brightblade, Cibrix Brightblade, Caelex Brightblade,* on and on and on, until at last, they reached some more familiar figures. *Cassian Brightblade, 20 A.E. Died in his sleep following a successful career serving Algrith and Solanya Firstqueen.* "After the Eclipse, the Lightstriders, accurately predicting the changes that would come over the kingdom after the Eclipse, decided it was the signal of a new age. After Algrith Redwyn died, his son, Prince Friedrich, should have taken over, but the grief over his father's death was too much; he was driven to nearly suicidal hysterics. Had it not been for his sister, Solanya, who became Firstqueen of the new age, the transition would have been far more catastrophic." They walked a short while longer, passing a few other groups of statues until, at last, they came to the furthest yet prepared alcove. The bases here were empty, but Leonidas could guess the names and figures they were meant to carry. "From the beginning of the order, there has always been a Brightblade among the Lightstriders. We were fools, allowing our preconceived notions of the family's honor to overrule our common sense. To answer your second question, Leonidas Braveheart, Casinius Brightblade came to his position as Captain of the Lightstriders because we, as an Order, took the Brightblade family for granted."

"And now, he has betrayed your trust and the most sacred tenets which he swore to uphold," Leonidas said tightly. "I ask you again, what do you need me to do, Galbraith?"

"I can see it in your eyes, Leo," she said warningly. "You want to kill him, and I understand." Her hands gripped the handles of her twin axes. "I want that honor for myself. But I must beg you not to be rash. He is older and slower than his prime days, but Casinius is still a dangerous warrior, and he fears you."

Those last words stopped Leonidas in his tracks. "What reason does he have to fear me?"

"I'm sure that Princess Emery, may Yamaria grant her soul respite, told you she wanted to make you a Lightstrider." Leonidas nodded gravely, recalling the second-to-last oath he'd made to Emery, and the last verbal one. "Then you understand that she would have named you such at the first moment she could." Galbraith looked into Leo's eye. "It was no secret to us that Emery loved you and wished to see you named either Lightstrider or her consort. She'd have had both were the choice hers. For a Lightstrider to be named, there must be an open spot in the five, or a current one must be released from service." She paused for emphasis. "Casinius is old and growing slower, with children of his own at home, and no shortage of enemies at court, while you are young, strong, and well-liked."

It dawned on Leonidas that, "Emery would have dismissed Casinius, naming me in his place!"

"If you were in his position, how would that make *you* feel?" Galbraith prompted.

Leonidas thought for a moment. "I suppose I'd feel that this young, upstart knight was in place to steal my family's legacy and everything I've worked for. But," Leonidas said, interrupting Galbraith, who'd tried to speak again, "now that Emery is dead, how do I pose a threat to Casinius?

"Because you are still alive, and we haven't been replaced by men and women suitable to King Geurus. He knows that he's committed high treason and fears our retaliation. So to answer the first question, what I need you to do, it's relatively simple. If you stay here in Searstar and Casinius climbs higher in Geurus's favor, you might find yourself at the end of an assassin's blade before long. Like I said before, the other Lightstriders are being kept away, and only with all convened can we depose Casinius, thus robbing Geurus of one of his most potent weapons, and perhaps even decapitate this problem at its head. Leonidas, we need someone on the outside, who knows as much as possible about what has transpired. Someone with honor, skill at arms, and the favor of the people. There are monsters both in the capital and without. There's nothing we can do about the monsters within, until some of the monsters without are gone. Can I count on you?"

Leonidas nodded. "By my troth, I am yours to command, Galbraith. I've been wondering about what's happening outside the walls as it is. A close friend of mine advised I find a project worth devoting myself to, and I can't think of anything more fitting."

Galbraith sighed in relief. "Good. Remember, it is of utmost importance that you not share your plans with anyone you don't trust with your very life. If Geurus or Casinius hears about this, we'll all be executed."

"I think I can handle that much," Leonidas said. "But now, I must start preparing, so I will bid you farewell, Lady Galbraith. And thank you for everything you have shown and told me today. On my honor as a knight, I will complete this task." Leo turned around to return the way he'd come.

"Leonidas?" The knight glanced back quizzically at the desert-born woman. "If you'd been assigned to the Lightstriders, you would be the best of us." Leo blushed at the high praise, bowed, and exited.

In an effort to not seem suspicious, Leonidas made no haste to act on Galbraith's orders, though, in truth, the knight was champing at the bit to be gone. Geurus, seeing how the last outing hadn't done any damage to his reputation, had allowed Leonidas and Grayson into the city proper again. Both were sure the King had eyes on them, but with any luck, they would be ignored after a while. They only ever visited the Rainclaws' abode, Leo enjoying conversations with Caitrial and Arcadia, and Grayson enjoying a bit more than talk with Reyna. Leonidas savored every moment he could get with the smith since he'd miss Caitrial dearly when he left. Even so, he told nobody about his plans; the knight wasn't going to risk a damned thing. There was too great a risk that Geurus might harm Grayson or Caitrial if he thought they knew anything. Leonidas couldn't abide that happening. Only in the dark of night did he pack and plan.

Thus, when the day for him to leave came, all the packing was done. All Leo needed was a horse and permission to go outside of the walls. And as he'd told Galbraith, there was a plan of how he was going to do that.

Clad in Caitrial's armor, Braveheart approached the audience chamber, where he knew he'd find Geurus Gardstar. The new king sat in the Highsun Seat for all of his business, as a child greedily coveted his new toy. Geurus was attended by Tavindre when Leo entered. Casinius was nowhere to be found, which was perfectly fine as far as he was concerned. Standing in front of the throne instead was Tarus Gardstar. Leonidas struggled to keep his face neutral as he beheld the Widower Prince. Since the fateful wedding day, Leonidas had avoided Tarus whenever possible. For his part, the prince didn't make this difficult, only pulling a horribly concealed face of consternation when the knight passed. Tarus scrambled to the side, bowing hastily to his father, and the knight in turn.

"Sir Leonidas," Geurus drawled. "I apologize. I was having a conference with my son. This couldn't wait, could it?"

"I'll only take a moment of your time, m'lord. I know you are an exceedingly busy man."

Geurus snorted. "Just get on with it, man. I have no need for pleasantries. I'd rather you just spit out what you came to say, so I can decide what to do with the information."

"Very well, m'lord." Leonidas cleared his throat. "I only came here to tell you I'm leaving—today, shortly after we are done here. I fear I no longer have any purpose here in the castle. I would hate to impose upon you without good reason, and would like to look in on my family." He stared defiantly at the usurper king, daring Geurus to challenge his right to leave.

But to his surprise, Lord Gardstar did nothing of the sort. In fact, the king laughed mirthfully. "Oh yes, Sir Leonidas, you have been imposing on us! And I'm sure that escaping the ghosts of your past is no small part of your desire to escape," Leo grimaced, taking deep breaths to keep from lashing out. "It only makes sense that we would allow you to leave." He leaned down, lowering his voice to a cruel whisper. "What use do I have for a knight who cannot even protect his own princess, after all?" Leonidas knew that the last bit was meant to hurt, but with the satisfaction at the successful completion of the first part of his plan, no harsh words could reach his heart, let alone harm it.

"As you say, milord. I shall be out of your hair as soon as I possibly can." As he withdrew, Leonidas caught a look of fear in Tarus's face. He cocked an eyebrow but didn't question it any further. It didn't concern him what Tarus Gardstar felt.

Besides, he was too pleased to care. He had talked his way out from Geurus' watchful eye, where he could act out his revenge through indirect, and therefore more effective methods. All in all, Leonidas was more than just content. For the first time since Emery's death, his heart felt free.

CAITRIAL

HEARTACHE BRINGS NEW DEVOTION

Her arms ached like hellfire, but Caitrial felt alive. Ever since she'd been promoted to an equal shareholder of the Sunwright Artisans company, Caitrial had found endless enjoyment in her days. She would get up early in the morning and head over to the smithy, usually to find Thraedan fast asleep at his planning desk, head bent over his chest, and a scroll in dwarvish or elvish text in his lap. Smiling, Caitrial would extract the parchment from his hands, to ensure it wasn't damaged when he awoke. Then, until Briskelthiar arrived, she would organize and get the day's projects in order at each of their stations. The two master smiths had been very proud that the eldest Rainclaw had taken this task entirely on her own initiative; no prodding needed. After Briskelthiar showed up and woke Thraedan, the three would get to work on filling the requests for nails, horseshoes, and other building supplies. Then one of the masters would go off to deliver the pieces to their proper destinations personally, while the other schooled Caitrial in the more advanced smithing techniques. Much to Thraedan and Briskelthiar's pleasure, if not surprise, Caitrial was a quick hand with picking up these new skills, and it wasn't long before they had her moving on to more intricate projects and rarer metals. In the evening, after the smithy closed down, Caitrial would return home to find Reyna and Arcadia waiting for her, the former having cooked dinner already.

And to Caitrial and Reyna's joy, Leonidas and Grayson often showed up shortly after they'd eaten. Caitrial and Leonidas would talk for hours about any variety of subjects, her job, her sisters, weapons, fighting. And sometimes, when Caitrial's arms were feeling up to it, and occasionally when they weren't, the two warriors would spar. She was quickly improving at swordplay under Leonidas's skilled instruction. There would be days where the two would hammer relentlessly at each other's defenses, matching strikes and parries without ever getting through, until at last, they collapsed on the floor, soaked in sweat and laughing. Caitrial came to anticipate these meetings, finding herself thinking about them during idle moments at work. It had been quite some time since all three sisters had been so happy together. Even dour Arcadia seemed affected by the jovial mood, even if just a little bit.

The last meeting came as a shock to her.

Caitrial was sitting on the couch that had become her bed, belly full with breakfast made of mutton pie, which Leonidas had pilfered from the kitchens when the knock came at the door. This alone told the smith that something was up. She'd told Leonidas to just come right in, so he wouldn't be left on the step were she not around. He'd arrived unusually early, but it was the Day of Sun's Zenith, the holy day, meaning the smithy and herb shop were closed. They'd be able to spend the whole day together, perhaps even take a couple of horses out on the trails just outside city limits, all five of them. An auspicious number, and a beautiful day for a picnic; truly, Yamaria smiled upon them today.

Crinkling her brow, Caitrial stood and crossed to the door. She knew immediately as she opened it that something was different.

First of all, Leonidas was wearing his armor again, the set she'd crafted by hand. Plates of steel and silver glinted in the sunlight. During his visits after the first, the knight had only worn chain mail underneath a surcoat, allowing them to spar. There was a look of mingled sadness and excitement in his eyes. Looking down at Caitrial, he managed a small smile. "Fare thee well, Lady Rainclaw?"

"As well as can be said, Sir Leonidas," Caitrial answered dutifully. That had become their customary greeting. "Please, come in."

But Leonidas shook his head. "I'm afraid I cannot. If I want to make it to Ridgeset by midday, I'd best leave soon.

Ridgeset! But that's the first of the settlements on the Sunne Steps! What business does Leonidas have there?

Without being verbally prompted, perhaps spurred on by something in her eyes, Leonidas continued. "I'm leaving, Caitrial. You told me to find a project worth devoting myself to and that I have done. But to fulfill this request, I must go and not return for some time, if at all."

"Divines," Caitrial said, stunned. At that moment, a gust of wind could have toppled the smith. She was keenly aware of Reyna and Arcadia behind her, keeping a safe distance back from the two friends as they spoke. "I don't know what to say."

"All there is left is to say farewell to you, Caitrial. I wish I could tell you more about my plans, but suffice it to say that I am doing what's right."

"I don't doubt it." Caitrial then opened her arms, and Leonidas gratefully came forward into the smith's embrace. Leo had been worried that Caitrial might take his sudden decision to leave badly. He gladly accepted the prolonged hug from the remarkable woman who had not only forged him physical armor but helped him rebuild his spiritual armor, which had rusted apart after Emery's fall.

After many long moments, Leonidas broke off the embrace and held Caitrial at arm's length. "I know it must be challenging to have the people you care for disappearing one by one. I cannot reassure you that we will see each other again, but know this: I will attempt to return once my task is complete. Stay strong, Caitrial Rainclaw, for, whether or not they know it, this city needs people like you, Thraedan, and Briskelthiar to serve as a bulwark against whatever Geurus throws down next. Allow me to give you a little hope in the meantime. Do you recall the wedding at which we danced?" Caitrial nodded wordlessly. "I mentioned that I'd seen some incredible things, and asked if you believed in the Divines. I've told you before that it was my dwarf friend Dalphamair with a Water Caller gnome who freed me. But those weren't the only ones. I only didn't tell you before because I thought you'd think me insane. I, for one, wouldn't have believed it without firsthand experience. There in the desert, I found Alaric Honeytone, and a Fyroxi named Amaru Sunbrand. Amaru claimed to be the daughter of Yamaria herself. And I believe her, for she commanded healing magic. That magic was the only reason I could return from my ordeal as swiftly as I did. Without her aid, I may not have even been here to see my Princess's fall."

Caitrial's mouth hung open in near disbelief, but she didn't dare think Leonidas was playing her false. It had been an enigma how the knight had arrived at the castle so shortly after being released from capture. Caitrial had been willing to chalk up a point for the Water Callers, and their mysterious herb craft. But, as crazy as this was, it made a strange sort of sense. "An actual magical healer, for the first time since the Eclipse. And even at that turbulent time, their powers were on the wane. But now, you claim another has shown up with divine blood in her veins. With that and..." she glanced outside hastily to make sure nobody else was listening in, "and my sisters, it would seem that the Divines are preparing us for some sort of great battle, unlike anything we've seen since the Eclipse." She shuddered. "A horrifying thought that soon we might need all of it, but it's good to know Yamaria hasn't abandoned us."

"Indeed it is," Leonidas agreed. "And I'm glad that I'm not the only one who sees the dire omens in these happenings. Though I can only blame myself for not trusting, you and I have long been of the same mind. Now, I beg you, remain hopeful, and keep strong, as you always do. I certainly hope that Yamaria will grant us the chance to see each other again someday." With all due formality, Leonidas Braveheart took her hand in his, bowed down, and kissed the back of it. Then, he flashed her one more smile, swept his chin-length brown hair behind his ears, and mounted the roan stallion behind him. With a quick press of his heels into the horses' flank, the knight trotted down the road.

As Caitrial Rainclaw watched him depart, an unfamiliar, dull ache began inside of her. She couldn't put a name to it, nor could she tear her eyes away from her retreating friend. The smith stood there until Leonidas was nowhere to be seen, and it took Reyna grabbing her hand and leading her from the door to move her away. Caitrial sat heavily on the sofa, staring blankly ahead for a few more moments, before turning to her sisters. "You heard what he said, right? The Divines have sent us a healer, and two mages, which means you two may have a part to play in all of this soon. We need to begin training your magic immediately."

Reyna and Arcadia gulped, their faces seeming to pale. Then, they turned to each other, and nodded simultaneously, gaining strength from one another. They understood perfectly.

From that day forward, any time Caitrial would normally have spent with Leonidas, she devoted to Arcadia and Reyna. They would meet in the alley behind Berdur's shop. The secluded area, with high walls and a plaza practically invisible to the people of the city, provided the perfect place for the three to hide the Khindre sisters' magic. Berdur, who'd lived many long years before the Eclipse, had no grudge against magic, and so, as before, he allowed the two to practice behind the Shield and Pestle. "As long as you don't scorch up the back of my shop or nothin', I don't mind. Not that I'd be able to tell if you did!"

Whether or not the blind old dwarf would be able to discern any damages done to his shop, the herbalist was in luck. Neither Reyna nor Arcadia had much in the way of elemental magic in their repertoire. Neither could cast so much as a flame, or conjure a droplet of water from the air. For her part, Caitrial was glad for that. Magic that called the elements to do the caster's bidding had a reputation for being fickle on the best days and utterly unpredictable on the worst. Berdur Longshield recounted many tales from the days of his prime concerning magic to help the twins in their practice.

"I was quite young, for a dwarf, at least, when I decided to leave my hammer behind for the herb pouch and bandage." After so many years above the ground and living with humans, most traces of the dwarven accent had fled Berdur's speech. Only by listening very carefully could one hear the whisper-quiet lisp beneath his gravelly voice. "Because of that, I had many years of healing wounded men and women when magic was still around. There were years I thought to myself, 'Are you daft, Berdur? You could have had a quiet life hammering iron by the forge, yet you subject yourself to these peoples' screams day in and day out!' But despite my own misgivings, I knew I was doing the right thing. Healers were needed desperately at that time. I can't tell you just how many times I went out to the aftermath of the battle to find people with burns so serious nothing I could do would bring them back, but still, they clung to life." The old dwarf's voice became thick with emotion. "And the worst part of it was hearing their stories. One time, I went into a tower, and on the top floor, there was a mound of charred bodies. In the center was a young wizard, not as severely burned as the rest of them, thanks in part to his enchanted robes. As I cleaned the exposed wounds, he told me what had happened. He'd been assigned to that tower with a good-sized force of men, tasked with holding it until a more powerful wizard could be rerouted to set up an arcane barrier and stop the Lunari army. But the crafty generals sent men with some nasty weapons that disabled the sentries at the gates. When they broke through, the wizard started his casting. It was supposed to be a wave of flame, starting in front of his allies, killing only enemies. Had it worked the way he'd hoped, those bastards from Moonwatch wouldn't have stood a chance. But though he pronounced every arcane word precisely as he had in school, and did all the proper gestures, the flames, always hungry things, had their own ideas. Besides that wizard, nobody in that tower during the explosion left there alive."

Yes, Caitrial was very glad that her sisters couldn't command the elements.

Reyna's magic, for the most part, seemed to be what Berdur called "Basic fare." The simple arcane spells that most wizards could learn with practice, and the most common of the sorcery Gifts. Not much in the way of magic that could hurt people directly, but still very useful. Caitrial always got a laugh out of watching her sisters practice. There would be points during the mock combat when Arcadia would be in the middle of casting some spell, and Reyna would mutter something under her breath. Arcadia would find herself standing quite still, stuck in whatever ridiculous gesture she'd been doing at that moment. Or with a word, Reyna would cause her sister to trip, breaking her concentration.

In the heat of the moment, Caitrial would see the frustration and anger flash in Arcadia's mismatched pink and purple eyes. But no matter what happened in the battle, Reyna would always go over to her twin and lift her from the ground, and the two would embrace, repairing their friendship and sisterhood. Caitrial knew that this was stressful for both of them. They spent every free moment practicing, and Caitrial, fearing that the Gardstars might move at any time, was a hard taskmaster. Many times, the smith expected their relationship to shatter like an overheated ingot. Given its tenuous beginning, Caitrial was pleasantly surprised to see their bond grow.

Reyna had been the first to show arcane talent as a child. Caitrial remembered watching her sisters as they ran around the yard. Being Khindre, set apart by their appearance, the two had very few other friends. They had each other, and they had Emery. The princess had met them one day in the city when her father stopped at Cynderstone for a drink, and the three had connected almost instantly. The grassy lot of Sardan's bar became the three's special meeting place. Though Godfrey reluctantly allowed Emery to play with the Khindre, he never let them into the castle walls. That was likely for the best, for it was a day when Emery was with them that Reyna first cast a spell. Had they been in the castle, there might have been trouble. Caitrial snorted derisively at the understatement. More accurately, Reyna would have been executed on the spot.

It was a slow day at Cynderstone, so Sardan had been watching the children himself, rather than one of the servants. Her father recounted to Caitrial the absolute shock of seeing the friends sitting together, playing some game with their hands, when suddenly, orbs of colorful light had popped up around Reyna's. The girls had all begun to bat at them, laughing as they bobbed through the air. But Sardan, being one of the traditionalists of the new age, knew this for what it was. He immediately smothered the girls' laughter. Emery, perhaps having some prior knowledge of the Eclipse from her tutoring, understood instantly, and clammed up about the affair. But try as Sardan and Cos might, they couldn't smother the magic in their daughter's blood. So instead, they urged them to keep it discreet.

Then came the day that Arcadia had her own magic show up. Sardan and Cos had expected their other daughter to display as well, and were pleasantly surprised when it never blossomed naturally.

Though Reyna and Arcadia were not allowed inside the castle gates, the plaza outside was still fair game. Emery invited them to play there, with Leonidas, her new guardian, to watch over them. Sardan and Cos had both met Leonidas and trusted him, so they allowed their daughters to go out.

Surrounding the castle was a moat spanned by a bridge, otherwise only separated from the street by small embankments. It was enough because everyone who lived in Searstar knew the story of that moat. One of the many creations of Qrakzt the Mad Mage, the circular waterway seemed only to be a rapidly running river, but like everything Qrakzt left behind, it was far, far more than that. Many rumors flew through the marketplace of its power. Very few knew the truth of that moat, but few were willing to try it out, given the ancient tales of utter decimation of would-be assassins or thieves. Reputedly, no bodies were ever found.

Thus, when during play, an unexpected, unrestrained burst of magic from Reyna knocked Arcadia into that moat. The Khindre girl should have died that day, but a frantic Leonidas, working together with Reyna and a few passing guards, managed to extract her using rope and canvas from a nearby stall. Arcadia was barely breathing and convulsing spastically. They wrapped her in clothes and Leo's cape, and the knight carried her back to her parents. Caitrial thanked Yamaria that Leo was the dependable sort, and not easily flustered, for he kept the secret of seeing Reyna's magic between those who already knew.

Though Arcadia recovered, the time she spent in the moat irrevocably changed her. From that day on, the Khindre was quiet and reserved, with a black mood more often than not. And something else within her was released when the Aethyr ran over her. Unlike Reyna, Arcadia's brand of magic was darker, like her newfound mood. She found herself with surprising control over shadows, which she'd used many times to disperse mobs, making the shadows take the forms of rats to trick and drive away protestors with a sharp nip or two. Caitrial wasn't sure just how far Arcadia could go with her magic, as her sister was secretive, but Caitrial got the sense while they trained that Arcadia was holding back. The smith worried about what might happen if the full force of her magic was released. What sort of power had the moat granted Arcadia, and how? Aethyr was viewed as a product of light, goodness even, yet the sorceress born from its influence had powers over darkness.

Peculiar, that's for certain.

TARUS

CHOOSING SIDES

The Widower Prince of Sun's Reach sat with his knees folded underneath him. His hands were folded in front of his bowed head. And Tarus Gardstar prayed. He prayed to Yamaria, the goddess that he'd been told since the day he was born, was evil, vile, cruel. But from everything Tarus had heard from the priests here—and he trusted them—Yamaria's mercy was legendary. Even in the histories, at the height of godly power, a period that the people of Moonwatch called the *Havoc*, there were few reports of Yamaria punishing her mortal subjects. The same couldn't be said for Gaarhowl. During the Havoc, several priests were found dead in the morning after evening mass, often with ugly gashes across their bodies, or missing throats and other parts. This had been a turbulent time for the Lunari; a revolt was the order of the day, and mutiny was a fun pastime. Nobody had accurate reports of how many people died in that year, but the tally was undeniably high. Savage creatures and tribes of barbarians ruled the tundra, held back only by the wizards that every wise Lord employed. Those unwise ones or those who couldn't afford the services of wizards? Well... they didn't keep their lordships, lands, or lives for long. Nothing of that magnitude happened in Sun's Reach. Sure, there were riots, rebellions, and wars between houses, especially after the Eclipse, but never once did Yamaria get involved, displaying her displeasure only through the edicts of priests.

So Tarus prayed to this merciful goddess that he might be granted some reprieve, that perhaps, treasonous though the thought might be, that King Geurus would be stopped from implementing his plans. For Geurus definitely had plans, though he was taking his time in putting them into motion. Tarus had been at the meetings when Geurus had shared these orders with the commanders of his Enforcers. Not only was his father using deception to trick people outside the walls into believing Godfrey Redwyn was still alive, but he was stamping out rebellion and rumors the only way he knew how: with force. The people of Searstar were already being cowed by their new ruler. Few people dared to speak openly about Geurus Gardstar, and those that did often found themselves in the castle dungeons, courtesy of their neighbors, and occasionally their own family.

Tarus had taken a discreet trip down to the dungeons on a mission from Father Vail, so many people confined in filthy cages, underfed and scared for their lives. He didn't blame them for cursing him and his whole family. They had no way of knowing that he was just as angry at Geurus Gardstar as them. Hell, Tarus didn't think even *Geurus* knew his son was going under his nose. Or if he did, the king had chosen to do nothing about it. True, nothing Tarus was doing was harmful to the Gardstars' plans, only spending more time in the church than anything else.

Tarus hadn't even seen his father besides at those meetings, and Cereos Gardstar, his mother, had left a week ago, shortly after Sir Leonidas proffered his resignation. The prince had been terrified when Leonidas announced his departure. Tarus had hoped he might work up the courage to speak with the knight. Leo had been the only living man on the balcony where the Redwyn family died not under Gardstar's influence. If Tarus had spoken to him, the prince might have received some much-needed closure. Father Vail helped as much as he could, but Emery hadn't spent all that much time at the temple, and the Patriarch didn't know her well enough to help him truly cope.

Tarus was still amazed that the Patriarch of Sun's Reach so much as spoke to him, not to mention answered his questions, even the stupid ones.

Once, when Tarus had arrived to meet with Vail, the priest had taken out the Holy Book and allowed Tarus to thumb through it. He'd flipped through until the painting of Yamaria had appeared before him. "It's surprising that, in a kingdom that so dislikes dark colors, your goddess has black hair." Yamaria was an extraordinarily beautiful woman, as most goddesses were portrayed to be. Tarus might even hazard to call her radiant, at risk of being droll. Fair-skinned, wearing a flowing robe of white silk trimmed with red, Yamaria was holding a staff in one hand, and the other painted so that the sun itself seemed to sit in her palm. The Sun Mother also sported large, fox-like ears and five glorious tails, white and tipped with red.

Father Vail chuckled. "Well, according to our teachings, Gaarhowl and Yamaria are sibling Divines. Understandably, they would have similar traits, or at least they would if Gaarhowl appeared in his original form." Vail flipped the page to show a picture that Tarus knew well, the werewolfesque figure wearing skulls braided onto strings hanging down his neck and back. Priests of Moonwatch said they were the skulls of evil devotees of Yamaria. "It is said that Yamaria's brother, once called the Divine Gaartenus, grew displeased with his domain, which he'd chosen earlier in life. Always the mischievous one, he changed his shape to one reminiscent of a favored animal, the wolf, and started to spread his dissenting ideals among the people of Celestiira, thus sparking the First Astral War. After a crushing defeat, Gaarhowl's people declared their cessation from the Solari people of Yamaria. This is how the two nations at odds, Moonwatch and Sun's Reach, were founded."

Tarus mulled that over for a bit. According to the mythos of Lunari lore, Gaartenus's transformation was brought about by Yamaria herself. There had once been a beautiful priest woman, Astalu, a devotee of both Sun and Moon. She loved both of the astral bodies equally, though being a creature of the day, couldn't spend as much time worshipping the moon, worshipping Gaartenus. In a clever compromise, Astalu would seclude herself in a dark room for a few hours each day to pray to her moon god. Yamaria was furious and jealous. How dare this woman use any of her precious sunlight to praise her brother! Yamaria had slain Astalu for her "treachery" and kidnapped the priest's spirit for her own. But Yamaria wouldn't stop there. She'd accused Gaartenus of corrupting Astalu and cursed him into his wolfish form as punishment.

When he told Vail as much, the priest shrugged. "There is no telling which one is the true story, or if either of them are. We mortals have little idea what goes on up in the Divine Realm, and that's probably for the best, my son."

Tarus thought about that on his way home that day. He was so deep in his own thoughts, he didn't even notice his sister until she delivered a none too gentle pat to his cheek from her soft hand. "Hello, brother," she said. "Long time no see. Have you spent *so* much time kneeling that you forgot how to walk straight?"

Tarus focused on his surroundings. He'd left the temple by the main path, but now he was somewhere around the courtyard. Off to the left, he could see the hedges that surrounded the palace gardens. Tarus shuddered involuntarily. Though much less frequent now, the horrible dreams still came to him occasionally, making him a wreck in the mornings. Those were the days that he went straight to the temple. His feet had wandered, taking him who knows where. "Sorry, Velara, I wasn't paying attention."

"That's plain enough to see. If I hadn't stopped you, you'd have plowed right into me! I just had this dress made too. If anything had happened to it, I might have had to kill you." The threat came out so casually that it took Tarus a moment to register it. Velara had always been that way, able to taunt anything without putting any telltale venom in her voice. She often left unsuspecting fools believing she'd complimented them. The prince looked at his sister, taking in the dress in question. It was made of a soft, pillowy material that contoured tightly to the upper half of her body. At the waist, the garment flowed out into a skirt, white with grey dapples, similar to the plumage of a snowy owl from home. The snowy owl had long been Velara's favorite animal, so unsuspecting, quiet, and yet deadly, like her own insults. Tarus wisely decided not to answer Velara, looking down at his own shabby clothing and thinking of all the scathing remarks his sister was just waiting to use. "Anyway," Velara said after the silence had stretched for just a moment too long, "How've your expeditions into the temple been going?"

"Well. I've gotten to know the Patriarch pretty well. He's been alive since the Eclipse."

"Ooh, now that *is* juicy." Velara giggled, covering her mouth with a hand like a proper lady. "I'm sure father will be glad to hear everything you've learned. He's *very* interested in the church, especially since the Enforcers can't get in there to scout it out. I'm sure they're hiding some revolutionaries somewhere there."

Tarus cursed himself quietly. He'd forgotten that little tidbit. The prince promised that he'd try to guard his tongue around his sister. Velara had always been their father's tool for gaining insight about allies and rivals both. Her beauty and lack of compunction for betrayal made her the perfect person for extracting critical information. The servants back home called Velara *Men's Bane* behind her back, a fitting moniker for the girl that Tarus could swear was half succubus. "I haven't seen anything of the like in my... er, investigations so far."

Velara gave a very unladylike snort. "Well, of course, you haven't! Do you actually think that the priests are going to trust *you* of all people? You might be worming your way towards their hearts, but you're still Geurus Gardstar's son." Tarus's sister looped her arm around his, "Come on, you. I've wanted to show you something for a while now, and we'll miss it if we aren't quick." Without waiting for a reply, Velara started across the courtyard, aiming for the gatehouse. She pulled him outside the gates and down the wide flagstone steps, over the bridge that spanned an impossibly fast-moving river. A droplet splashed up from the raging waterway onto his shoe, where it sizzled for a moment like acid before evaporating away. In its place, it bored a small hole, a reminder of the danger in Qrakzt's moat. Tarus did not know just how prophetic that display on the bridge would serve.

"Where are you taking me?" he asked as they passed Cynder-stone Brewery and Bar.

"Shush," Velara reprimanded. "You'll give us away. It's just down that alleyway." As his sister promised, when they reached the alley, Tarus started hearing voices. The tone was hushed, but it echoed through the area enough for the two to understand. Tarus suddenly noticed that this area was completely devoid of Enforcers. The noise grew louder, multiple voices trying to talk over each other, while still remaining quiet. Tarus asked Velara about that.

"Your devotion to the task is applaudable, but if you paid *any* attention to something outside of your temple, perhaps you'd know. Sardan and Cos Rainclaw convinced Father to pull the Enforcers from this area. Said the men were driving away paying customers. This tavern is their primary location, and Cynderstone helps the Crown with a lot of finances, so our king had good reason to grant their request."

Well, it seemed to Tarus that someone was taking advantage of Geurus's faith in the Rainclaw family.

Velara snuck forward, Tarus just on her heels, and the two crouched down close to the plaza opening. Within, a small horde of people were standing around an old, defunct fountain.

"You're out of your mind, boy," one gruff voice said. "We'll get ourselves killed! Think about our families."

"What do you think I'm doing, Jorjen, you daft fool! Are you going to sit around while Geurus takes advantage of your silence? What a great plan! Just wait, once he's had enough of slaying tradesmen from outside the city, or once the people out there wisen up enough to stop sending people inside our walls, take a guess at what will happen! Your family won't be safe for much longer if Geurus doesn't feel safe on the throne. He underestimates us, thinks that just because he sits in the Highsun Seat, he has power. And we've done nothing to discourage this belief. If we do nothing, the Five Cities will be smothered like underfed flames, leaving us subject to destruction. Jasqua, you've heard the reports, haven't you?" Tarus stared in disbelief at the person standing on the fountainhead above the crowd. Grayson Redwyn. The deposed prince was trying to stir up a rebellion!

Another voice answered Grayson, this one female. "Aye, sir. I have a direct word from the rangers. I trust that Geurus's rumors of monsters are no lie. Not only are there Chillfang running amok in the Scorched Waste, but there have been other reports too. Most notably of the filthy mutts in Fyrestone and goblins in Sulfaari."

"You see, everybody. The creatures of Moonwatch have

found a way to get across the Eclipse! I swear to you all when Qrakzt said that his plan would bring the Last Astral War; he was wrong. He underestimated the cruelty of the Lunari, their irrepressible drive to slay every last one of us. That's why we have Geurus here, and why the Chillfang have begun their invasion. He promised he would give us his mercy, but our new king can't be trusted." Tarus didn't miss the sudden thickness in the prince's voice, nor did anyone in the crowd. "I already know what it's like to lose my entire family. I'm trying to save all of you from that nightmare! You just need to listen and act before it's too late." Before the sobs could take over, Grayson stepped down from the fountain and walked through the crowd, which parted respectfully for him.

"Isn't that just adorable?" Velara sniggered. "He's going to inflame their hearts, and then they'll see just how far Geurus's *mercy* goes!"

"Velara, we can't tell father about this!" Tarus whispered harshly.

"And why not?" Tarus's sister looked at him queerly.

Tarus scrambled for an explanation. "Um, well uh. You know how Father is! He'll kill Grayson if he finds out about this."

"Yes, Tarus," she answered patiently. "He'll kill the traitor. It's unfortunate, the boy is decently handsome. I wouldn't have minded marrying him. But, oh well, Grayson denounced his right to the throne "

"With the executioner's blade to his throat! What else was he supposed to do?" Velara led him out of the alley, leaving him hanging until they were well out of earshot of the people in the plaza.

"What's wrong with you, Tarus? Have the past few months in the sun scrambled your brains, made you soft? I don't think I like the fact that you're sympathizing with the enemy. Or haven't you realized that? Just because you were supposed to marry Emery doesn't make her a saint. Let me spell it out for you. The Redwyn family and all the people still devoted to them are our E-N-E-M-I-E-S."

"N-no, it's not that," Tarus lied, hoping he sounded convincing enough to fool Velara. He knew full well these arguments would get nowhere with his father. "I'm thinking of the family. If Grayson is killed, especially after this speech, then we'll just be proving his point, and then we *will* have a revolt on our hands. They respect Grayson even when they think he's foolish and rash. It's easy to cover up the deaths of a few merchant families with stories of bandit attacks. But if Searstar revolts, even if by some unbelievable luck Geurus manages to survive, there is no way he'll be able to explain away the number of deaths necessary to quell a rebellion! Once word gets out, our already tenuous grasp on the throne is kaput."

Velara eyed Tarus suspiciously as he talked, but by the end, her face was screwed up in thought, and she was nodding. "Fine, I'll wait awhile, see how things develop. But if this goes too far, Father will hear about it." With that promise, she ran inside the gate. Tarus moved into a corner of the wall and sunk to his knees on the flagstone, silently sobbing in relief. He sent up a prayer of thanks to Yamaria for granting him this good luck.

Thinking for a moment, Tarus gulped. He'd just chosen to work actively against his family's plans. That made him a traitor, and if Geurus found out… Well, then he'd better figure out how not to get caught. His mind was made up; Tarus had always been on Emery's side, and she was on that of the people. He wanted the people of Sun's Reach to prosper, rather than eke out a pitiful existence like most in Moonwatch did. Geurus Gardstar would kill many, but as long as Tarus lived, he would do everything in his power to support the downtrodden. It's what Emery would have wanted.

PART II
SHADOWS OF THE LAND

LEONIDAS

A MOST ABSURD ALLY

Ridgeset, as the name implied, was a smallish village nestled in the nook below the Capstone, the plateau upon which Searstar was built. A crisp autumn breeze blew over the rocky shelf, sending dust flying in the air. Leonidas had to cover his face, but he was covering a smile. Just leaving the city lightened the knight's heart significantly. The duty of protecting the princess, being a royal knight, had been more an honor than Leo had ever expected to know. But, if he took a few moments to forget that he had a critical mission, he could believe this was just a jaunt through the country, as he'd enjoyed as a young boy. Being out here, he felt so much closer to home. Leonidas's heart yearned for Morndale. It would be wonderful to see his family again. It had been almost ten years, with the only correspondence being via letter. Leo missed his young sister, Melody, and his friends, who he'd once sparred with and played games of Mercenaries & Marauders.

Godfrey was, in part, to blame for keeping him away. Had the king allowed Emery to travel outside the gates, he could've visited. *The princess would have enjoyed that,* Leo thought with a sad smile. He knew, without a doubt, the people of Morndale would have loved her.

He shook his head to push the fond memories away. Now was not the time to be wistful; he had a job to complete. Leonidas glanced back one last time as he reached the downward curving path that would put him in line with the village that was his goal. With any luck, the people of Ridgeset would have some knowledge of the whereabouts of the Lightstriders, since one of them —he believed it was the dwarf, Raerizen—was on patrol here. The meticulously carved wall of Searstar was slipping out of sight now. With the sun sitting directly above and behind it, Searstar cast a shadow over the Capstone and only now was Leonidas coming out into the sunlight. *It's like Geurus, and his Enforcers are a shadow, and now I'm escaping his greatest influence by moving into the sunshine of the less political country.* The comparison was fitting, if chilling. "I'm sorry to leave you in that shadow, Caitrial. It's the last thing you deserve." But if Leo had escaped with the smith and her two Khindre sisters in tow, that might have drawn attention, which neither of them could afford. More reasons to finish this task with haste, then.

As Leonidas approached Ridgeset, it was just past midday, as he'd hoped. From here, Leonidas had a clear view of the village. With the plateau wall at its back and a cliff to the east side, Ridgeset was surprisingly defendable. It was said in ancient times that Ridgeset, like all the settlements on the Sunne Steps, was tasked with keeping watch for invading bands and reduce their numbers a bit. The buildings of the village were built with blocks of the same red stone upon which they sat, supported by solid beams of hardwood from Kindol. Every house was topped with a plank barricade meant for catching enemy arrows, protecting the archers stationed there. Besides a waist-high clay barricade and a few bored-looking guards, little stood in the way of outside defenses. Leonidas was secretly relieved to see it still standing. Old habits die hard, and the knight feared that the citizens might have tried attacking the Gardstar army as they trooped up towards the Capstone.

"Hail, citizen!" he called as he approached the wall. The guard jolted awake, his blade ripping from its scabbard with a ringing sound. Slowly, Leonidas raised his hands in a peaceful gesture. "I mean you no harm, good sir."

The man stared blankly for a moment, but then his face lit up in recognition. "Sir Leonidas!"

"You know me, sir?"

The guard nodded. "Why, of course!" he said. "Who wouldn't recognize Leonidas Braveheart! You're something of a legend on the Sunne Steps. This place is crawling with folk feeling inspired to find themselves a position in some lord's army, to do what's right for their country! I feel a fool for drawing a blade on you!"

Leonidas felt mightily pleased to hear that. He figured, if push came to shove, he would need to find as many of those good-hearted men and women as he could to help take on the Enforcers. Leonidas couldn't suppress a grin at those thoughts that would surely see him hanged. *Geurus will have to catch me first!*

"That aside, how can we help you, sir? Are you out on the princess's business? I'll be honest, I'm surprised she's letting you out again after your long excursion in the desert!" He chuckled, somewhat lewdly, Leonidas thought. He hadn't expected rumors of Emery's affections to fly outside the gates, though he really shouldn't be surprised. Grayson and the Lightstriders noticed the way she acted around him, so why not others? But more importantly, it set in on Leonidas that Galbraith had been correct. Nobody outside the gate knew that Geurus Gardstar sat on the throne. Nobody knew that Emery, Lysaria, and Godfrey were all dead. *Then that is my first duty. The people, who have heard tales of her mercy and kindness, must know of Geurus' betrayal, and Emery's fall.*

"I've come for two things. One, I shall ask now. The second, I will save for later. I have heard rumors that Lady Raerizen of the Lightstriders is around this area. Do you know where I could find her?"

The guard scratched his stubbly chin. "Raerizen? You just missed her, I think. If I recall the dwarf correctly, she said, *I'm sick o' standin' round here doing jack squat! Orders or no orders, I'm gittin' outa here!*" His approximation of a dwarvish accent was passing fair, at least. And that sounded like the sort of thing the fiery Raerizen would say.

"Do you know where she is now?" Leonidas asked again.

The guard nodded. "The crazy woman mumbled something about a bandit camp off a distance to the west, then went off on her lonesome to take care of it."

Leonidas once again could not resist the smile that stretched over his face. Bandits: traitorous men and women waiting for the executioner's blade. Leo would be glad to save them the trouble. *See me now, Emery? I can finally do as I have long desired. I wish this opportunity hadn't come at the expense of your life, but I've sworn to avenge you, and I shall do that in time. First, I have another score to settle. Tara, if you can hear my prayers, know that this is for you, your family, and our unborn child. I'll not fail you again.*

With the image of Tara convulsing, skin purpling, and mouth foaming as she died in his arms, Leonidas resolutely stood. These bandits would die, just as surely as if they were the same clan that sent his wife of five years to her death.

It took Leonidas less than half an hour to reach the copse of trees to the west where Raerizen waited. As he approached, he caught a glimpse of the telltale shade of red armor that all Lightstriders wore in some capacity. The knight approached, the dwarf sat with her back to him, entirely focused on something in front of her. Leonidas approached slowly, in a futile attempt not to startle Raerizen. Leonidas flinched at every noise his armor, clanking and crunching mid-autumn leaves, made. Though Leonidas thought he was making quite the racket, the stout dwarf never seemed to notice his approach. Or so he thought.

When he was perhaps ten feet behind her, Raerizen suddenly whipped about, and Leonidas just managed to duck in time as a spiked mace flew end over end, sticking and quivering in the tree right where Leonidas's head had been only moments earlier.

For the second time that day, Leonidas made a show of peace, lifting his hands, and smiling with a mixture of relief and nervousness. The dwarf woman stood, allowing Leonidas to get a good look at her.

Raerizen stood only a little over four feet tall, her helm just barely reaching Leo's chest. True to her titles, the dwarf's face bore no beard, surprisingly smooth as if it had never even born stubble, unusual, even for a dwarven woman. Her squat face was square-jawed and powerful, with close-set black eyes and a sharp, almost beakish nose. Stringy red-brown hair flew out in a wild shock as if the dwarf had been used as a lightning rod. A red cape, like Casinius's, flew from the pauldrons of her red half-plate armor. Swaths of shining chain and padded leather showed through the gaps. If he didn't know that most dwarves made their living by a hot forge, he would have wondered how she wasn't burning up in that suit. The wind hadn't yet lost its summer heat, and Leonidas was feeling a little uncomfortable in his new armor. *I'll get used to it soon enough. It's not that much different from my old armor, besides the beautiful, care-filled creation.*

In one hand, the dwarf held a filthy rag, saturated with oil, the other hand still outstretched in the follow-through of her throw.

"Eh? Yer no bandit-type!" the dwarf exclaimed in shock. "Or ye are an' ye managed t' kill one of th' knight-folk, a general by th' armor!" Raerizen scratched her beardless chin. "Aye, but 'is reflexes are better than' most I've seen round in th' bandit trade. Most wouldn'ta bin able t' dodge outa me mace's way!" She peered up into Leonidas's face, covering her eyes with one large hand, succeeding in wiping silvery polish on her forehead. "Oh wait jus' a morsel! I know who ye are! Yer tha' knight Galbraith used t' go on and on about! Supposed t' replace one o' us. Is it me then? I can't be sure about tha'! I'll fight ye fer it! May th' best warrior be Lightstrider! Ye'd hafta find some new armor though, mine wouldn't fit ye!" Leonidas chuckled. "What're ye laughin' bout. Ye're not seriously thinkin' ye can take me?"

"Never would I presume such strength of myself. I've been told that a castle knight could never stand up to a Lightstrider, and I won't test my luck. Especially not against Raerizen the Beardless!"

Raerizen looked like she was ready to bite Leonidas's head off, but then the dwarf seemed to absorb his words. "Humph. Wise choice." She strode over to the base of the tree and, with a short hop, grasped the handle of the mace. The dwarf hung there for a moment before the mace finally pulled free from the tree. A rivulet of sap dripped down as the spike was removed, slowly making its way down the tree to pool at the roots. "So, if y'aint here t' claim me title as Lightstrider, what're ye here fer?"

Leonidas shot her a sly smile, placing a hand on the long-handled hammer slung over his shoulder. "I heard you were hunting bandits," he said. "I hoped that you might accept an extra body to join you."

"No big fan o' the smelly bastards, are ye?"

"I suppose we have some grievances to sort out."

"Oi, then yer welcome t' take part in th' slayin'!" Raerizen pointed beyond the treeline, where a cave mouth was clearly visible, a wild grin taking over her face. "Th' bastards took over an ol' shrine t' Yamaria earlier this month. I bin watchin' them fer some time, seein' a fair number o' smaller figures escorted in. Methinks they have some children in there, an' I mean to do summat about it!"

"If they have children, then we must rescue them at once!" Leonidas exclaimed.

Raerizen's grin grew wider, if such a thing was possible, threatening to take in her ears. It was a frightful sight, combined with the fires of battle flaring up in the dwarf's eyes. From the ground, she lifted a long chain with a heavy steel ball at the end, studded with sharp spikes. In the hands of any other, the weapon would have been impossibly unwieldy, especially given the location of the bandit camp. But given that Raerizen was a Lightstrider, Leonidas wasn't the least bit surprised with how the dwarf weaved the flail through the air, missing the trees by mere inches. "Me thoughts exactly!"

The two dashed from the tree line, crossed the stony bluff, and entered the cave, Raerizen leading with her spinning flail, Leonidas shortly behind.

The bandits didn't stand a chance. As the two warriors charged inside, they took only a moment to view their surroundings. The sprawling cave must once have been used for large gatherings of devotions to Yamaria. A central dais raised above the floor, with an opening in the ceiling allowing sunlight to wash over the priests. Now, the skylight served to illuminate the bandits, maybe eight in all, whose faces twisted in shock. They might as well have been mirror images of the ones Leonidas had sworn vengeance against. The same scruffy beards, mismatched armor, furs, and stolen trinkets. All of Leo's instincts cried out for him to rush in, smiting those who would desecrate Yamaria's temple, but more importantly, who reminded him of his dead wife. But the castle trained knight, his anger sublimated by years of protecting sweet, caring Emery, wrangled his emotions down. "You have committed crimes against Yamaria and her people," he said evenly, ignoring Raerizen's incredulous glare as he tried to talk with their foes. "If you surrender yourselves to justice, and return all you have stolen, you will be granted mercy." In times past, Leonidas could have threatened the king's own justice, for the royal gallows were a place no man wanted to visit. *King Geurus would more likely take these men into his retinue, adding to his already considerable network.* He had no idea what he would do with these men, were they to choose peace, and thus mercy. Luckily—for Leonidas's sake anyway—these cutthroats had no intention of surrendering. To prove that very point, the man closest to Leonidas yelled in rage and charged, bringing a dagger to bear.

He didn't even get close. Leonidas let him close within a few feet, then jabbed out with his tall shield. The knife was summarily deflected, and the bandit, somehow not expecting the sudden strike, fell hard to his back.

"Yield," Leonidas ordered.

"Never to the likes of you!" the man spat, attempting to stand and jab with his knife once more. One blow from Leonidas's hammer ended the bandit's pitiful attempts.

His mouth creasing into a frown now, Leonidas regarded the rest of the outlaws. "I'll imagine the lot of you feel much the same?" Brandished weapons were the only answer the knight needed. "Very well." Raerizen, and any bandit who cared to look at Leo's face, saw a distinct change come over it, a warlike shift, of which the dwarf much approved. "For Tara!" Invoking the name of his beloved gave him strength. He and Raerizen rushed forward, the dwarf claiming the second kill of the day, launching the heavy flail out straight in front of her, laying a bandit low. With a marvelous pull and swing, the Lightstrider reversed the momentum, bringing the heavy ball slamming into his chest.

Leonidas found himself surrounded by three men, and said a

silent prayer of thanks for Caitrial, as the armor deflected the untrained men's clumsy blows. A low sweep blasted out the knee of one, who limped back, howling in pain. The second man managed to bring his shield to bear as Leonidas delivered a predictable diagonal uppercut, but the sheer force behind the attack left him staggering as well. The third took advantage of Leonidas's preoccupation, lining up what promised to be a devastating jab to the elbow joint of the knight's weapon arm. An excruciating flare of pain in his lower back caused him to whirl about, his plan totally forgotten. He turned just in time to see death spinning towards him in the shape of Raerizen's second morningstar.

Against the Lighstrider and a Royal Defender, the rest of the bandits were quick to fall.

Raerizen flashed a grin, beholding the battlefield. "Ye scared me there fer a minute! I thought ye's about t' let them off th' hook!"

"Violence isn't the answer to every solution," Leonidas said reprovingly. "I may have a grudge against bandits, but everyone has a reason for what they do. These men here had no remorse for their actions against the church or people and would have slain us had they been given a chance. Thus, they earned their death. Had they surrendered, they would earn a fair trial with the king's justice."

Raerizen scratched her beardless chin, face screwed up in thought. "Oi, ye're right 'bout tha' I suppose. An' Galbraith was right 'bout ye! Tha' aside, let's see what else's here! "The dwarf retrieved her two morning stars and slung the chain flail over her shoulder, crossing the cave.

Leonidas was unsurprised, though disheartened, to see the damage done to the altar, tapestries, and all other holy implements that once made this cave a wonderful source of inspiration to the folk of the Sunne Steps. He vowed vengeance against whoever was behind this, no matter how long it took to root them out.

Suddenly, from around the corner, there came a shout from his dwarven companion. "Rotten daughter of a bearded Elf !" Leo rushed to catch up to his partner and found her surrounded by a small horde of cloaked figures—the "children" Raerizen had seen being escorted into the cave. Leonidas could see now, as could the dwarf, that these were by no means children. Or rather, they weren't *human* children. The stunted figures were shorter than even the diminutive dwarf, with sickly greenish-yellow skin, which reminded Leo of phlegm. Wide mouths chock full of pointed teeth dripped with thick saliva. Their eyes were red-orange and beady, sitting right above protruding noses. Notched fanlike ears jutted from the sides of their leathery heads.

"Yamaria durned goblins!" Raerizen cried, drawing a return screech from the creatures.

Goblins? Leonidas remembered Geurus' words after he'd usurped the throne. He'd warned of monsters appearing in the Sulfaari Expanse, as the Chillfang had in the Scorched Waste. *More likely, Geurus only told us about the reinforcements he knew were coming.* What little Leonidas knew about goblins led him to believe they were creatures of Moonwatch. They had never been accustomed to sunlight and preferred cool shade, often living underground, coming out only to feed or raid villages, usually both at the same time. And, they hated gnomes and dwarves above all else.

Raerizen let fly with her chain mace, but the spiked ball only bounced harmlessly off the cave floor. Goblins were quick little things, Leonidas realized. If the dwarven Lightstrider, impossibly fast with her cumbersome weapon, couldn't hit one, he wouldn't have a chance with his hammer.

Leonidas set the hammer down on the floor and reached down to his hip, where a silver sword was sheathed. *I don't think*

I'll ever get out of Caitrial's debt for her work. Though the crown had paid the smith handsomely for armor commission, Leonidas felt Caitrial had rendered a service more than equal to the gold price. It was as if the eldest Rainclaw sibling had used some of her sisters' magic to see into the future and anticipate every situation. *Though, I suppose it's just common sense. There are places where swinging around a hammer is merely impractical. Either way, thank you, Caitrial Rainclaw.* Those were the thoughts in his head as he grasped the golden hilt of the silvery sword, feeling the bulge of the three rubies carved in the likeness of hearts under his fingers. It could have been a piece of art, but a deadly one.

The goblins, so distracted by the sight of their ancestral enemy, didn't even notice as Leo charged in and decapitated one with a single swing of his perfectly balanced, impossibly light sword. Usually, the knight liked his weapons to have some heft behind them, but he couldn't deny that Caitrial's blade felt like an extension of his own arm.

"Watch their mouths!" Raerizen warned, pulling out her morning-stars. "Them ugly bastards carry all sorts o' disease!"

Just in time, Leonidas twisted his arm, as one of the spry creatures leaped at him, needle-like teeth bared. The goblin clamped down hard on the sword blade. Braveheart imagined them jabbing through his mail and delivering a dose of foul-smelling saliva into his veins. Revulsion shuddering through him, the knight flicked the goblin into the wall. Moments later, the dazed creature righted itself and stared stupidly at the knight. Leonidas just managed to get his shield up in time as the little beast yipped, and in a flurry of motion, the other goblins swarmed Leonidas.

Goblins hadn't the slightest clue about tactics, but their shock and swarm strategy worked surprisingly well. Leonidas found himself on his toes, defending more than attacking. If it weren't for Raerizen, Leo doubted he could have held out against them.

The dwarf's mere presence distracted the goblins once their original frenzy had worn off. They seemed divided between killing the big knight with the shiny armor and weapons, or their smaller, though no less fierce, most hated foe. That distraction allowed the two warriors to diminish the horde significantly, without taking more than a few scratches and nicks from a wildly flying claw. When only a quarter of the goblins remained, the rest fled, leaving their dead and injured companions to rot.

"Peh!" Raerizen snorted. "I'm fer hatin' them goblins. A cowardly lot. Though suren, I'm not fer knowin' how they got here!"

Leonidas stared grimly as one goblin twitched with increasing slowness, the last of its vitality draining into a pool around it, not unlike the tree on the plateau. "I do."

CAITRIAL

AID FROM UNEXPECTED SOURCES

"That should be enough for today, Caitrial." Briskelthiar's voice broke the smith's concentration. She looked up to see the elf grinning. A similar expression beamed on her face as well. On the table in front of her sat a nearly perfect crescent made of a strange red metal called Kerazar steel. Kerazar was a scarce material, found only in the Scorched Waste. Briskelthiar had confided in his apprentice that any lesser smith would never have managed to prize a single ingot out of the Sun Elves of the Scorched Waste. It wasn't pride on his part that made him say this. No, Briskelthiar and Thraedan might be the Sunwright Artisans, laudable smiths, and undeniably wealthy, but they worked the forges for the sheer enjoyment of the constant challenge. A mindset which Caitrial shared. And so, though she felt some measure of pride when she looked down upon the single curve of Kerazar steel, it was overshadowed by a deep sense of relief and joy. It had been three weeks since her promotion, and even

Thraedan, never one to compliment lightly, was surprised at the speed of her improvement. She spent hours at the forge every day, practicing making different shapes with the metals she'd been introduced to. Much of Caitrial's free time was spent reading books about forging techniques and properties of the metals. She doubted she'd ever know even half of what her masters did, but for a human, her knowledge and dedication were impressive.

Caitrial picked up the dull crescent and held it up to the forge, marveling at how the light flame seemed to dance and refract through the translucent Kerazar. Though it hadn't yet been perfected or sharpened, Caitrial could tell the weapon would hold a miraculously fine edge.

"Sun elves aren't the only race that uses Kerazar steel," Briskelthiar remarked, drawing Caitrial's attention. Her elf tutor had a penchant for interrupting her work to deliver history lessons, something that Caitrial— who used to read everything she could find about Khindre for the sake of her sisters —greatly appreciated. "Or at the very least, they aren't the only ones who have used it in their time."

"I wouldn't expect the elves to be the type to sell or teach their secrets to others. Without due cause, of course," Caitrial amended, seeing Briskelthiar's reproving look. "It could be possible that the knowledge was stolen from them," she mused. "Are there other humans who work with Kerazar?"

Briskelthiar chuckled. "You are partially correct in your theories. The elves of the Scorched Waste are a secretive lot, spending most of their days in their massive pyramid fortresses. No, they wouldn't teach their smithing secrets to tribal barbarians. The strongest tribe's most elite army couldn't infiltrate one of their pyramids. That's why nobody frets over the fate of the Sun Elves. I'm sure were they inclined to leave their homes, no army, no matter their training, equipment, or leadership, could survive." Caitrial cocked her head, wondering why Briskelthiar had made that reference. The elf had no intention of answering that question. "But, I'm getting off-topic. Your assumption that Elves would never share that information is correct. Thraedan doesn't know the secrets of this metal any more than I know the proper workings of Dwaelthread. But the reason why they won't share it might come as a surprise. In fact, it's because the knowledge is not theirs to give. The elves did not discover Kerazar; instead, the Fyroxi, inspired by Yamaria, first mined and used it to create their legendary weapons. I wish I could show you one, but unfortunately, it seems that they were either lost to poachers or moved to Fyrestone for safe-keeping following the Last Astral War."

And Fyrestone was lost to Chillfang.

"It was those weapons, combined with their magic, that allowed the Fyroxi to push back the Chillfang in their countless wars and skirmishes, despite being horrendously outnumbered. Without their weapons or their magic, this rekindled battle against their most hated foes will be far more devastating than any other before it."

Something suddenly occurred to Caitrial. "Wait a moment, Briskelthiar. If the elves don't have the right to share the secrets of Kerazar steel, then why are you teaching me? Isn't that breaking a sacred trust?"

"The Sun Elves cannot share the information," Briskelthiar replied slyly. "But I can. Many years ago, I knew a few Fyroxi, and after my work alongside them, Durrigan gave me permission to teach my chosen apprentice. I think even back then, wise Durrigan knew that the peace wouldn't last, and wanted to ensure that the art of crafting Kerazar didn't die out."

"Durrigan is dead," Caitrial informed her tutor.

Briskelthiar took a moment to digest that. "How? And how did you learn of this before me?" He answered his own question a few moments later. "Leonidas told you, or I'm an oversized gnome."

Caitrial nodded in confirmation. "He expired from old age, with his adopted daughter, and his closest advisors and friends around him."

Briskelthiar sighed heavily. "I remember young Amaru. A pity it will be if this war takes that fragment of Yamaria's light from us."

Caitrial could only nod in agreement.

At the end of that week, another secret meeting was held near Cynderstone. Cos and Sardan were attending the King, and the bar was closed, leaving the perfect opportunity. Caitrial stood with her sisters on the edge of the mob. Grayson was standing on the fountain again. "....we won't stand a chance. Geurus banished most of my father's army from the city, on the pretense of sending them to the Scorched Waste. I don't know how many of them still live, whether Geurus allowed any of them to survive, or massacred them outside the gates some-where. But I have learned that a few regiments have found hiding spots in the multiple empty wings left by the sudden departure. Experienced generals and foot soldiers alike. All will be crucial in our plans if we are to go up against Geurus' Enforcers. He only brought a few thousand with him to the city. If we could only get word out to some of the Lords who allied with my father in the past, we might be able to bring in rein-forcements."

"And how do you propose to manage that?" Jasqua the ranger asked. "Geurus has got us bottled up, tighter than a rat in a mousehole. If armed soldiers started to come up to the gates, what do you think would happen?"

Grayson sighed. The ranger was right, of course. "Twas a pipe dream, nothing more. If we can't get people in, then we'll just have to fight them ourselves, which we discussed last time. We need to start studying these Enforcers of his. Back in his glory days, my father would say, 'The uninformed warrior gets skewered first.' Once we learn more about them, we can think about fighting them. The last issue I want to bring up is weaponry. Knowledge is great and all, but if we can't get steel into our friend's hands, we'll be slaughtered."

"Jorjen is tied down," Jasqua said. "Gueurus won't let him sell so much as a horseshoe to anyone outside his inner circle."

"Those Enforcers and soldiers keep me busier than ever. No respect for their weapons, I swear," the castle smith spat. "I still make enough gold, though I have to give a considerable discount to Enforcers on threat of disembowelment.

"If Jorjen can't help us, then perhaps the Sunwright Artisans..."

"No," Caitrial's voice cut through the air like a freshly-sharpened knife. A few murmurs started up, but a fierce glare from Caitrial shut them all down. "Trust me, Thraedan and Briskelthiar hate Geurus as much as the next man. But that doesn't mean they're willing to risk everything they've worked and lived for. They aren't idiots. Think about it. Briskelthiar asks the King to allow a large shipment of metals into the city for his business. Suspicious enough, but then they start hiring new hands, the forges fire incessantly, and weapons start appearing in commoners' hands. Geurus will trace it all back to them. Thraedan and Briskelthiar won't rat us out, but we can't speak for the other employees, especially if Geurus decides he needs to do some persuading. No, my tutors will not get involved in this, not unless the playing field is leveled a bit. We can't rush into a rebellion, Grayson. We'll just get ourselves killed. You know this, but anger is getting the better of you. Clear your mind and heart before you make plans. That's how you'll grow into an effective leader." That was true whether you led men as a king, the master of a forge, or even a band of adventurers.

Grayson clenched his fists until his knuckles turned white, breathing seething breaths between gritted teeth. Slowly, he released them and followed the smith's advice. He thought for a moment. "Even the playing field, hmm? So we have to hit them where it hurts."

"Yes," Jasqua agreed. "I think a hit to their line of succession would work. But we'd have to be careful, make it seem like an accident, and leave no unwitting witnesses. As Caitrial said, Geurus cannot be underestimated."

"We have time to plan," Grayson admitted. "Let the Gard-stars grow comfortable before we strike. Then we can wring Tarus Gardstar's neck, or stuff him with some untraceable poison. I'm sure Berdur knows something. Anything to pay Tarus back for what he's done."

At Grayson's threat, there came a yelp and the patter of scur-rying feet. As one, the group turned around to see a figure in a nondescript brown cloak and a bouncy mane of blond hair trying to escape down the alley. A couple people near the back started after Tarus, at Grayson's command, but the Widower Prince had too far of a lead. He would escape, it seemed. But then Arcadia growled, "You filthy rat!" Shadows coalesced on the tip of her finger, before darting off after the fleeing figure. The sizzling black bolt struck Tarus in the legs, and expanded, restraining his lower body, and sending the boy crashing to the flagstones.

Everything went quiet for a moment, and Caitrial put a hand on the hilt of her broadsword, prepared to pull it from her back and protect her sisters. The crowd's collective gaze seemed to switch between the fallen Tarus and Arcadia, who'd just used magic in plain sight.

It was Grayson who broke the tension. "Ladies and gentlemen, I introduce to you our first advantage over the Gardstars. Arcadia and Reyna Rainclaw, the first mages since the Eclipse!" The silence erupted into a great cheer, and people swarmed to surround the three sisters. The two Khindre found themselves lifted into the air by cheering rebels. Caitrial tried very hard to stifle a laugh at the look of sheer discomfort on Arcadia's face, such a contrast to the bright expression on Reyna's.

After a few moments, the two were placed gently on the ground, and the mob moved. As many as could fit found their way into the alley, moving to surround Tarus Gardstar.

The three Rainclaws pushed themselves to the front.

Arcadia leveled a finger at Tarus's head. "When you see your father in the afterlife, scum, you can tell him that your foolish actions brought his downfall."

The Widower Prince stared defiantly back, matching the Khindre's intense stare. "That I shall tell him," he growled. "But I plan to do so while I'm still alive."

That set Arcadia, perfectly ready to release her bolt of destructive energy, back on her heels. "Come again?"

"Gladly." Tarus seemed to sit up a little straighter. "You hate me, I know you all do."

"We won't deny it," Grayson said, pushing his way to the front. "Based on your actions since entering this city, we have every right to that hatred. Justified anger at the enemy of Sun's Reach."

"You do have that right," he admitted, again puzzling the crowd. "And I support you fully in your decisions. But I'm not your enemy. I was never your enemy."

"You killed my sister!"

"I loved your sister!" Tarus shouted. "I loved her with all of my heart," he said, more quietly this time. "When I was betrothed to her, I felt like I had all the world before me, a gift."

"Then why'd you throw her from the tower?" Reyna asked. Her fists were clenched tight, fingernails close to drawing blood in her palm. "If you loved her then why is she dead, and not wrapped in your arms?" The ordinarily gentle Khindre seemed on the verge of exploding.

"I wish I could tell you." All of the defiance fled Tarus's tone, tears choking him up instead. He'd done some soul searching during his time with Father Vail. "I don't know why it happened, but every trail of reasoning I've followed leads to Geurus Gardstar."

"Oh, what shocking news," Arcadia drawled. "Thinking about following your father's plan leads you to your father. I'm *so* glad you were here to tell us. We never could have figured it out ourselves."

"No! Not my father," Tarus said, stopping Arcadia in her tracks yet again. "Geurus Gardstar is many things, but not that. He may have sired and raised me, but that means nothing. In matters of the heart and soul, we are unrelated."

"What do you know of the soul?" Reyna queried.

"Much less than I should, but much more than I did when I came," Tarus answered. He searched the crowd. "You can ask Master Balvrich," he singled out the bald monk. "I have spoken with your patriarch, Vail, often over the past weeks. My goals in doing so have been entirely altruistic, as I'm sure Master Balvrich can attest."

Everyone turned to the monk, who rubbed his neck. "I can, though I don't like to admit it. I want to tell you that this man, Tarus Gardstar, infiltrates the chapel where his father's soldiers cannot, but that would be lying. He enters openly and retreats to the same room with the Patriarch, Yamaria bless his name, every time. Patriarch Vail seems to trust him and often alludes to Tarus's heavy guilt and his search for repentance."

"Do you want us to believe that you've come to see the error of your ways, Tarus Gardstar?" Caitrial asked in all seriousness. "That coming to Sun's Reach and seeing the woman you claim to have loved die by your hands has made you, who lived in Moonwatch beforehand, come around into the light?"

"Divines, but it sounds impossible when you say it that way!" Tarus cried. "But I don't blame you for being suspicious. I'm sure I'd feel the same in your place." He sighed and turned to Grayson. "Please, hear my words, my prince. I want to avenge Emery's wrongful slaughter, whatever that entails."

Grayson was at a loss. He looked to Caitrial for answers.

"I don't like this. It seems too convenient for my liking," the smith remarked. "How do we know a contingent of Enforcers isn't going to come storming down the alley to kill the lot of us?"

"Because I wasn't followed!" Tarus protested. "I made sure that none of my father's soldiers were anywhere around here. This time, I am the only Gardstar who knows what you've discussed."

"This time?" Caitrial regarded Tarus suspiciously. "Who else?"

"My sister, Velara," the prince answered honestly. "She saw your last meeting, but I convinced her not to tell our father. You don't have long to plan, but Geurus underestimates you, Grayson. Use that to your advantage. If you opt not to kill me, I can help you. However, if killing me is the only way to satisfy you, then I'll allow it."

"Like you have a choice in that matter," Arcadia reminded him sharply, raising her finger again, but she looked at Grayson. "Do we rid the world of this scum now, or does he get to breathe another day?"

Grayson made a gesture indicating Arcadia to cut off her

spell. "For now, the Widower Prince lives. In time, we'll discover the truth of his sincerity, but I think Emery would counsel me to be merciful." Tarus stretched out his arms as the shadow bonds slipped away. Grayson rounded suddenly on him. "But trust me," he threatened. "If I catch so much as a whiff of dishonesty from you, my sword will find your heart faster than you can beg to Yamaria for forgiveness."

TARUS

INFORMING ON THE STARS

The Widower Prince walked purposefully through the halls of the castle, his jaw set, and ears tuned in to every conversation. One way or another, he had to prove his worth to Grayson and the others. And right now, information was the best method. He was the rebel informant now, their inside man. The thought terrified him, but at the same time, it sent a thrill of excitement streaking down his spine.

Luck was with him, as he soon heard the first bit of valuable information from two conversing servants, who hadn't yet noticed his approach.

"Have you heard the news?" one asked. "They say Geurus is getting more comfortable. He sent off that arrogant Tavindre to follow his wife. He must think himself perfectly safe."

"Good reason to think that he does," the other argued. "He's still got that traitorous swine, Casinius on his side, plus all of those Enforcers."

"Aye," the first admitted. "That Casinius is worth any three Tavindres. Those Enforcers give me the creeps, too."

"I don't like how silent they are. Too obedient as well. I've never heard a single complaint from one of them, not even in the summer sun. Armor so dense and dark can't be comfortable here."

"I know. Damn Luneys." The servant spat into the courtyard below him. "I wish someone would give old Geurus something to fear. I've read enough books to know that once a villain like him gets a swelled head, it spells death for those unlucky folks beneath him who don't conform to their views."

"You know, I'd love to contradict you on the count of books not being real life. But I wouldn't be surprised. I still haven't seen Stervor since that day two weeks ago. He put too much cayenne in Lady Velara's soup, and she practically exploded. The way she reacted, you'd think he'd tried to poison the girl."

"Dungeons or a ditch, I'm sure, for poor Stervor," the man stood. "Speaking of the wretch, I've better go check on her. You know how she gets when someone's not waiting hand and foot on her." The man stood and straightened his outfit.

"It's a shame. she's such a pretty girl, but she'll never find a willing husband with her attitude. I don't want to see what she'd be like as a miserly mistress."

"Well, with our luck, and the current trend, none of us will live to see that day." They shared a bitter laugh and went their separate ways.

Tarus leaned back against the wall and sighed. "Father's starting his usual methods, killing whatever displeases him."

The servants had mentioned another interesting tidbit too. Tarus headed immediately towards Velara's room.

She wasn't there, but a quick inquiry led Tarus to Queen Lysaria's old chambers, where Velara was taking full advantage of the queen's spa. His sister stretched languidly as she heard footsteps and lifted a slice of green squash from her eye to peek over at the door. Leave it to Velara to recline and find luxury wherever she could. Their father had always pampered Velara, and in turn, she did his bidding, no matter what.

"Well, hello there, brother," she yawned. "To what do I owe this unexpected pleasure? I expected you to be at the temple by now."

"Normally, I would be," Tarus said. "But, I figured I'd wait until tonight to go." Since he already went to the temple daily, and Velara had accepted his explanations, the rebels had decided to make Master Balvrich his contact. The bald monk would deliver the news to Vail, and he to Grayson when the prince went to pray for his family's souls. "I wanted to get a sense of any other patrons that might...um...frequent the place during non-operating hours."

Velara tapped her perfectly smooth chin with a velvet finger. "Hmmm. You're smarter than I thought, Tarus. If I was a bunch of rebels, I'd want my information center somewhere the king's Enforcers couldn't reach.

Tarus was very glad Velara still had the fruits over her eyes. All of the blood drained from his face. Did his sister know? And if so, did Geurus know? Tarus suddenly saw an image of himself hanging from the gallows or lying in a ditch with a hole in his stomach, just like Emery.

"But, unfortunately for those rebels, the king has an agent inside their walls!" Tarus quietly let out his breath. He was safe for now. "If you do find anything, brother dearest, please let me know. I really want to keep up on my needlework!"

Tarus shivered. Velara kept sheaths of daggers hidden underneath her dress sleeves and liked to call the stilettos 'needles.' More than a few servants back home—and here as well, Tarus suspected, had seen his dangerous sister's handiwork. She'd learned from the best. "I'll do that, Velara," he promised, hoping she wouldn't detect the blatant lie or fear in his voice. "Anyway, I came here to ask about something I overheard some servants talking about."

Tarus could almost feel her eyebrow arch. "Oh, and just who were these servants?"

"I-I didn't catch their names," Tarus answered, truthfully this time, and glad he was for it. "But they mentioned that our good cousin Tavindre went off to join Mother. Did you hear where she went; father never told me."

"Wonder why not?" Velara mused. "He told me." She shrugged. "I don't see any harm in telling you, though. Even if the rebels do capture and torture the information out of you, it'll be too late for them to do anything about it. Not to mention too far out of their reach! Father's army of Enforcers has been working out in the Sulfaari Expanse. They started in the desert, but a squadron was found dead, so Father moved out for a time. Things in Sulfaari are going much better anyway. Before Geurus even arrived here, Fyrestone was already captured. Soon trade should reopen. I've always wanted a fox tail scarf, so I hope it's fast! Mother and Tavindre went to strengthen the presence in Redhawk, a smaller city to the East. Since it was Mother who made everything go so smoothly in Fyrestone and the Scorched Waste, I have hopes for the complete annihilation of our foes!"

"How many did they take?" Tarus asked, fishing for whatever information he could.

Velara sat up and peeled the squash off again, shooting her brother an incredulous look. Tarus felt a cold sweat run down his back. "Why does it matter to you?"

"Um...well... Well, since she's my mother, I have every reason to fear for her life."

Velara gave a very unladylike snort. "Do you forget who we're talking about here? No worthless rebel can hurt Cereos Gardstar, let alone kill her! If they try, Mother's magic will show them their folly."

All of Tarus's blood went cold. With the more important matters of Emery's death and his work with the rebels, he'd forgotten the truth of his mother's magic, gifted to her by some mysterious patron. He gulped, thinking suddenly about Sir Leonidas. If the knight heard that a member of the Gardstar's family, two even, were out in the Sulfaari Expanse, might he go after them? Then Leonidas would die. *Why does it matter to you?* A small voice inside him asked. *He threatened your life last time you spoke.*

But Tarus denied the voice; he had to deny it because the answer was simple. It had been important to Emery, and that made it matter to him.

Less than an hour later, his father came upon Tarus taking repast in the dining room. Unlike their last face-to-face meeting, Geurus seemed to be in a good mood. That worried Tarus, but to his credit, the prince kept those fears from his face. Instead, they manifested as that typical headache, the distracting pressure in his mind, which always came when dealing with Geurus. "Father," he said respectfully. Something—maybe it was Geurus's expression, though he didn't notice any distinct changes there— gave Tarus the idea that his father was displeased with that address. *Let him be,* Tarus dared to think. *It's long past time I stopped slinking back like a beaten puppy.* "To what do I owe this visit? I expected you to be busy with your planning or some such activity."

Geurus snorted. "Hardly, boy. Only worthless kings like Godfrey stay barricaded behind their walls. A good king does what he must to answer the needs of his community."

Emery answered the needs of her community, and yet you desired her slain. And I followed through, despite my love of those very traits. Tarus thought back to that fateful day, back to all of his meetings with Geurus. That day, though Geurus hadn't been on the balcony when Tarus had stabbed Emery, the boy had felt this same headache then. At the time, he'd passed it off as nerves. But was there something more to it?"

"Boy, are you even listening?" Geurus's voice broke the Widower Prince from his ruminations. The king shook his head, disgusted. "You're testing my patience, son. I've still not heard any useful information from you despite your near-constant visits to the church. You'd be wise to proffer something of worth soon, else I'll have no choice but to put Velara above you on the chain of succession." Tarus gave his best effort to pretend that mattered to him, and he thought he did quite well, given the unexpected nature of the claim. Geurus stared daggers at him, but apparently decided that it was pointless, and just sighed. "That aside, I didn't come here to ridicule you."

"Just a natural thing for you, then?" Tarus said under his breath. If Geurus heard him, he made no show of it. "What do you need of me, Father?"

"I'm sure you've heard the news about Tavindre leaving." Tarus nodded the affirmative. "Well, his departure leaves his position open. I figured that I would give you a chance to prove yourself. I have a meeting at Cynderstone today, with Cos and Sardan Rainclaw, and I'd like you to join me."

By looking at his father, Tarus could tell that Geurus meant to say, "You'll be joining me whether you want to or not." Putting on his most impassive face, Tarus excused himself to clean up. Now would come his most significant test to date. Could he keep Geurus Gardstar from learning about Grayson's rebels?

· · ·

Cos and Sardan were waiting for them at the tavern door when Geurus and Tarus arrived. Tarus had chosen an outfit similar to his father's, a black doublet with little crescent moons on it. It seemed that the entire city knew he was from Moonwatch now, so there was no point in hiding it from the residents. Not like they had any chance of leaving to spread that tidbit. They were flanked by only two Enforcers, and the people on the street gave them a wide berth. As many who could manage it bowed respectfully to their king. *Is it respect or fear?* Tarus wondered, scrutinizing their eyes. *Both,* he decided. *Some hold genuine respect for my father, but more obviously fear him, given the treatment any rebels have received thus far.* Geurus had made a point of permanently silencing any rebel groups he learned about. At their clandestine meetings at the broken fountain, Tarus had heard many laments for lost friends from other rebel outfits. *Will the same happen to Grayson if he is discovered?*

"My lord, we are pleased you could join with us today," Cos said, genuflecting beside her husband. "We have some information you might find pertinent."

"Wonderful," Geurus exclaimed. "But let us not talk about business quite yet. Let us have some drinks first."

Sardan nodded and went behind the bar to fetch their liquor, while Cos shooed away the only other patrons, two completely drunk men, one of which Tarus recognized from their group. The man, sloshed beyond reason, raised his glass in the air in salute before pouring the rest of the amber liquid down his throat. "My prince," he said. "An unexpected pleasure."

Tarus nodded stiffly, silently warning the man not to continue with a glare so cold the prince could almost feel the rebel shiver.

After a few minutes, Sardan returned, carrying four glasses and a pitcher filled with a drink that Tarus recognized as Shiverspine Reserve, or something close to it, by the icy blue color. Shiverspine was his father's favorite drink from Moonwatch.

"My lord," Sardan said, pouring the king's glass first, "After many attempts, and nearly as many failures, I do believe I have succeeded in mimicking this specialty liquor. It certainly wasn't easy, but I am proud to claim this triumph."

Geurus sampled a small sip of the drink, and a broad smile spread across his face. "Good Sardan, had you served this to me without telling me it was a facsimile, I'd not have guessed it. You've done your king proud this day!"

Sardan beamed and puffed out his chest. "There is nothing I wouldn't do for you, King Geurus."

"It does my heart good to hear this, good man. Mark my words, once I have finished purging Searstar's streets of this rebel menace, I will frequent your establishment, and encourage my soldiers to do the same."

Cos broke into the conversation. "My king, these insurgents are precisely the reason we've asked you to speak with us today." Tarus felt his chest tighten. *Please, Yamaria, if any of my prayers have gotten through to you in your Sunlit Halls, grant me one favor. Don't let Geurus know I'm involved in this. Not yet, at least, not until I've done something right in Emery's name.* "You recall that the last time you visited, we discussed our daughters."

"Yes, the two Khindre, if I remember correctly," Geurus leaned forward. "What more do you have to say about them?"

"I told you of our anger when those two wretched creatures came from my womb before, my king," Cos supplied. "Despite our best efforts, it seemed we could not curb Arcadia's chaotic tendencies. We thought we could do the city a favor by expelling her from the household. We'd hoped that with nowhere to go, Arcadia would be forced into Carrion Cove, where her kind belongs. But no, her fool of a sister, Caitrial took her in. That left Reyna, the more reasonable half of the pair. Or so we thought." Tarus thought it strange how sudden the disgust for her children, or at least for Reyna, had been conjured up. It seemed more a grab for Geurus's favor than any legitimate feelings. Tarus got the sense that his father had noticed the same, though he wasn't quite sure from where.

"Reyna recently moved in with her other sisters," Sardan explained. "I fear her previous connections might lead her astray from our teachings. Curse her...."

"Get to the explanation," Geurus said, cutting Sardan off. "And you can cut the slander. It only serves to delay your point."

"Apologies, my king." Sardan bowed obsequiously. "The information that concerns you is this: Reyna and Arcadia were very close to Emery Redwyn." Tarus didn't miss the momentary raw pain in the bar owner's voice at the mention of that name. Sardan cleared his throat before continuing. "I worry that your actions might have earned you their ire. No disrespect meant, of course, milord."

"Is that all?" Geurus drawled. "I don't fear children, no matter their race. What could these Khindre possibly have at their disposal that would make them any threat to me? You'd best have a good answer for me. I would hate to have my time wasted by the babblings of overreactive parents."

"Magic, my king," Cos mumbled.

"Speak up, woman!" Geurus demanded. Tarus's gut clenched, his stomach roiling with fear.

"I said magic, milord Geurus," Cos repeated. "Those two are more than just Khindre and more than mere girls; they're sorceresses. It's the first time there has been any magic displayed among the people of Sun's Reach in a very long time, and we figured..."

Geurus chuckled darkly. "I've heard enough, Sardan and Cos Rainclaw. I believe my son and I shall take our leave now. Thank you for everything."

Geurus stood and swept out of the tavern, Tarus on his heels. "I do believe you once told me that Grayson had a lover out in the city, Tarus," the King remarked on the way home. "That would be Reyna Rainclaw if I'm not mistaken. Let's see what our dear former prince can tell us about her, shall we? When you see Grayson at your church, do tell him I desire to see him in my personal chambers."

Tarus could only nod faintly. This would not end well.

164

LEONIDAS

A MASTER'S RETURN

"We cannot waste even a moment, for there is much work to be done if you wish to keep your families safe from the coming storm. In the capital, the darkness of Geurus Gardstar has already taken hold, but here, out in the Sulfaari Expanse, we still have our chance to stand firm. Join me, people of Cendrillion, join me in spirit, that the evil of Moonwatch does not wipe out the brightness of Sun's Reach! This I beg as your humble servant, and as the carrier of Emery's legacy, her torch, which once burned so brightly. Help me carry this torch, that we all may be free!"

Around him, the people cheered and chanted Emery's name. Leonidas could see the determination on their faces. These people, like all wise citizens of Sun's Reach, didn't want to be extinguished, and now Leonidas had come along to inflame their hearts, rekindle their passion. The knight reveled in their cheers, the support he was receiving from the major settlements of the kingdom. Cendrillion, a large town claimed to be in the very center of Sun's Reach, was only his most recent stop. He'd already forewarned many smaller villages, on his way from Ridgeset to here, giving much the same speech, about the downfall of House Redwyn, and the vile man who had cast them down, at every stop. He wouldn't let it be said that Leonidas Braveheart had squandered his chance to save lives. In his trek down the Sunne Steps, and around Kindol Woods, Emery's knight had taken it upon himself to clear out all the outlaws he could find. He then donated most of the bounty money back into the towns, so that they could finance defenses, rebuild walls, hire mercenaries to stand guard, and purchase weapons.

Certes in doing so, Leonidas had gained himself no small amount of fame, but that wasn't why he did it. Through his work, not only was he gaining his personal retribution, avenging his dear Tara, but he had also won the ear of influential leaders such as Ellep Bult, Gnommaster of Bellepon, and Faenith of the Plainstrider Elves. Both had heard only good things about Emery, and the burgeoning reputation of her primary guardian only elevated his message in their minds. It was no small matter that he traveled alongside one of the Lightstriders, either. Raerizen's presence only reinforced Leo's claim. He knew without a doubt that when the Chillfang and the Enforcers moved in force against the people of the Sulfaari Expanse, they would be ready.

In his original plan, Leonidas had not thought to visit the larger towns like Cendrillion, or any of the Five Cities. He'd feared the possibility of meeting any of Geurus's Enforcers, who might end his trek and, with it, his revolution. Leonidas wouldn't put it past Geurus to send an assassin or a troop of soldiers in his wake; in fact, he'd fully expected it. But Raerizen had requested that they come to Cendrillion specifically, and thus far, they'd not met with any trouble.

As the patrons began to file out of the bar, Leonidas searched for his short, eccentric friend. Not seeing Raerizen, he turned to the barkeep, Dorian Blusterbuck, who offered him a grateful wink. These past few days, the mute old man had more coin flowing in the door than ever before, and the knight's commanding presence had kept the patrons from getting rowdy. Without the need to pay for post barfight repairs, Dorian was happier than a pig in slop.

Seeing his questioning expression, the barkeep waved Leonidas's attention his way. Dorian held his arm at his waist and then made a walking gesture with two fingers from the other hand.

"Raerizen left?" Leonidas guessed. Dorian nodded, giving a grin. The knight had learned in his time here that the simple tavern owner always enjoyed these guessing games. Always one to please, Leo obliged him. "Was she alone?" Dorian crossed his arms in front of his chest. No, then. "Did you recognize the person she was with?"

Dorian curved his arms over his head and shrunk his neck back.

"He had a big head?"

The barkeep shook his head hard. He looked around the bar quickly, pointing to a leather helmet hanging on the wall, made a motion like putting it over his head, and then directed Leo's attention to the coatrack. The knight took a moment to figure it out.

"He was wearing a cloak, with its hood up, so you couldn't make out who it was?"

The mute man grinned and drew a tankard of ale from a cask behind him, offering it to Leonidas. He accepted the cup with a nod of thanks.

"Any defining features at all?" he asked between sips.

Dorian tapped his lips thoughtfully. Suddenly, a light of clarity came into his eyes, and he drummed his fingers repeatedly against the bar. Then he closed his hands except for one finger on each and rested them against his head, so the two straight fingers were protruding from his head.

"She left with a Khindre?"

Another violent shake of the head. He indicated for Leo to wait, and Dorian ran back behind the casks. He came out with a few leaves of basil in his hair. The odd man drew himself up so that he looked particularly pompous and replaced his fingers in their previous position. Forcing down his ale against a laugh, Leonidas said, "An elf, then?"

Dorian grinned triumphantly, the edges of his mouth nearly taking in his ears. Leonidas finished the tankard and thanked Dorian before heading out into the dim orange light of sunfall.

The flagstones of this part of Cendrillion were similar in design to Searstar's royal sector, a fact that didn't escape Leonidas as he scanned the streets for Raerizen. It was well known that Cendrillion had five wards, each one decorated in a facsimile of one of the Five Cities. Here was Searstar. To the south, tall tapering spires, like those in Mirshiall, the Elven city, reached towards the sun, high enough to rival the trees of Kindol. To the west, squat houses with whimsical designs, and numerous different paint jobs lined the streets, often clashing, and yet still fitting for the likeness of Bellepon. Beneath northern storefronts sat a shallow underground settlement, similar to Cystur, for those who wanted the "Dwarven experience." Reinforced wood, straw, and canvas houses, functional and easily defensible, were the eastern houses of Little Fyrestone, which contained the temple to Yamaria, as was a Fyroxi's right. Leonidas wished there were more Fyroxi to live in those houses. It still saddened the knight greatly to know that the wondrous race stood on the knife's edge of extinction.

But looking down at the flagstones, Leonidas felt a distinct pang of despair. He recalled his dearly departed princess, the brightly burning Emery Redwyn. Would that hole in his life ever be filled again? He doubted it; Emery, in fact, the whole Redwyn family had held a special place in his heart. Their effect on his life couldn't be, would never be replicated. *Maybe*, he thought, *once all of this Gardstar business is finished, I'll leave Sun's Reach behind and try to start a new chapter of my life.* Leo knew he'd always carry Emery's spirit with him. Perhaps he could fulfill one of the princess's greatest desires while mending the rift in his heart. But as he had that thought, another image filled his mind: Caitrial Rainclaw, laughing, her bronzed face alight and shining with sweat from their sparring session. A smile crept over Leonidas's own visage. *Cait, I hope you are doing well. I eagerly anticipate the day all of this is over, that we might see each other and spar once more.* He chuckled to himself. As much as Leonidas wanted to leave and posthumously satisfy Emery's dream, he knew he wouldn't go because of Caitrial. He'd hate to leave such an amazing and supportive friend behind, no matter who ended up becoming king, be it Grayson, or any of the Rothssters. Nestor Rothsster had been slated as the next man in line should the unthinkable happen, and the Redwyn family step down or be slain. Never once had Leonidas thought that this might come to pass, but now... "How different this world will be, no matter how this ends," he mused aloud. "If the Eclipse is indeed weakening, then we're likely to end up at war with Moonwatch once again. In that case, Caitrial, Briskelthiar, and Thraedan will be put to work making military stock weapons and instruments of war, instead of their wonderful artwork." That was something Leonidas didn't want to see.

At last, he spotted his quarry. Raerizen was indeed standing with a tall, slender figure, which could very well be an elf, as Dorian had claimed.

The two were talking in hushed tones, leaning against the alcove. It was a strange pair to see, the tall elf in contrast with the diminutive Raerizen. Leonidas could imagine the Lightstrider saying, "Suren, I'm not fer lookin' up t' folks, but bein' a dwarf means I ain't gotta choice in th' matter! One o' these days, I'll git me some taller boots, or mebbe a tall pony!" Leo couldn't resist a chuckle at the image.

Without ever taking his eyes off of the dwarf, the cloaked figure raised his voice, addressing the knight. "It's pleasing to know that even in the direst times, as Sun's Reach seems to face now, there are those willing to step up and take the burden of the folk onto their own shoulders." There was something about the voice that rang familiar in Leo's mind, brought him back to the time before Tara's death. He'd met many elves, though, and he kept thinking of Alaric Valyaara, who he'd met in the desert. Though they sounded little alike. Alaric's voice was melodious and rich, like a mug of fresh, sweet water running down the throat. This elf, though, his voice carried power and authority, with the elegant touch of one who had often dealt with lords and kings, "Though, of course, I would expect nothing less from my apprentice."

Though it had been many years since he'd heard the voice, Leo berated himself for not recognizing it. "Sir Vedalken, I didn't know that you would be in town!"

"Did Raerizen neglect to mention her rendezvous with me?" Vedalken shook his head. "So careless of you, Raerizen."

"Peh, elf, I kept ye a secret fer me own reasons, an' yer not t' turn down yer pretty nose at em! Ye know how humans can be like. If he knew we was fer rende... randy... Peh, whatever ye called it!"

"Rendezvous," Leonidas supplied.

"Tha' one. If he'd 'ave known. I'm fer guessing he might've beelined t' Cendrillion quicker'n ye could snap out one o' yer rapiers t' skewer one o' them filthy goblins!"

"I never figured Leonidas to be the impatient one," Vedalken, the eldest of the Lightstriders, and inarguably the strongest among them, laughed. "Such was a trait I usually attributed to one Raerizen the Beardless."

That rocked Raerizen back on her heels. "Aye, me? Ye suren 'bout tha', elf? Might it be ye've grown daft in yer old age?"

Vedalken nodded, as if considering that for a moment, stroking his chin thoughtfully. "It's not unthinkable that six hundred years would muddle my brain, but no. I recall clearly the glory days of the Beardless dwarf. How many times you begged me to enchant your boots that you might run ahead and make the first contact with the enemy. The one time I actually granted your wish, you heedlessly dashed into a goblinoid lair. Had Tinco Anar not made it in when he did, well, you might have been Raerizen the Fleshless!"

"No rot-fer-brains goblin could've laid me low on me worst day!" Raerizen protested.

Vedalken conceded that point. "One on one, or ten-on-one, my bet will always go to Raerizen. But three score to one? That's a different story."

Raerizen harrumphed and folded her arms across her barrel-like chest. "Suren there was more goblin blood than me own on th' cavern floor when ye arrived," she grumbled.

Vedalken sighed helplessly with a shrug and turned towards Leonidas. Master and apprentice shared a secret smile while the Lightstrider dwarf continued to fuss underneath her breath. It had been many years since Leonidas had looked upon the man who'd trained him, and yet, as were the ways of elves, he hadn't changed a bit. His hair was bluish black, an unusual color for people in Sun's Reach, whose hair tended towards the lighter hues, like Valyaara's wheat color. The Lightstrider's locks were neatly coiffed, sheared at the nape of his neck, where they curled up inexplicably, like a stiff, horsehair brush. His eyes were a deep violet, which seemed to swirl with white spots, which Vedalken called stars. As with most elves, Vedalken Nairvebyen was lithe and slender, his movements so graceful that it left folk wondering whether they'd just seen one of Yamaria's divine servants flitting by.

"Where is your distinctive armor, Lightstrider?" Leonidas asked. Though Vedalken took great pride in his position as a heroic warrior of Sun's Reach, the elf had long ago forgone the pleasure of walking through the cities in his armor, suffering the gawking of peasants, merchants, and nobles alike.

"I left it with Calimero, as usual," the elf replied. "He's up in the hills past Cendrillion. I'll meet up with him when we leave."

Leonidas nodded. It made sense that Vedalken hadn't left his distinctive mount anywhere in the city. Calimero's presence would be just as telling a sign that the Lightstrider was in town than if he'd strode through the streets in full regalia, throwing magic into the air. "You're leaving so soon? I had hoped we might have a chance to speak on the state of the Kingdom. I imagine, as Lightstriders, you two have pressing business to attend to, so I shouldn't be surprised."

But Vedalken was shaking his head. "If you wish to speak of the kingdom's affairs, that would be acceptable. We must do something to tamp down the boredom of the trail." The elf grinned at the visibly stunned expression on Leo's face. "I think it is long past time you and I traveled together again, especially since you have grown as a warrior now, by Raerizen's first-hand accounts, and I won't have to keep so sharp an eye on you. Besides, there is a matter that must be dealt with, which I believe you are best suited for. As soon as you are ready to move, we two make for Valais Battlehall."

"I've wanted to visit that place since I was a young man," Leonidas remarked, somewhat sadly. "I've heard tales of the splendor. Enough food, and festivity to rival even Searstar's best, they say!"

"Have you never been?" Vedalken asked incredulously.

Leo shook his head. "I almost did once. Tara and I planned for a grand celebration, following the conception of our child." He gritted his teeth, waiting for the wave of guilt to wash over him, as had always happened before, thinking about his lost wife. But strangely, the guilt didn't come. Instead, there came a feeling of warmth, contentment even, as if Tara's spirit had come to wrap his heart in a warm embrace. He wasn't sure what it meant, but certes Leonidas would spend some time this evening in reflection. "It would be a pleasure to join you there, Master Vedalken."

The elf looked up into the sky, where the sun wasn't yet halfway across its span. "Then get yourself to your chambers and clamber into your armor. I'll expect you on the east hill afore the hour wanes." Vedalken turned to Raerizen one last time. "Tinco Anar should be around Fyrestone by now, perhaps even nearing the Scorched Waste. Once you've gathered him, check with the people of Fontain, see if they've noticed anything suspicious from Fyrestone since the attack. After that, make your way to Kindol, where I will join you once Sir Leonidas and I are finished with our business. And by Yamaria, Raerizen, do nothing foolish. We need all the Lightstriders alive to accomplish our task."

"Eh, ye fret too much, durned elf. I won't go runnin' into Fyrestone, much as I wanna. Suren, I don't got a beard, but tha' don't mean me noggin ain't workin' proper!" Raerizen saluted them, turned on her heel, and marched off with an exaggerated soldier's step.

Leo stifled a chuckle. "I'm going to miss that one."

"We always do," Vedalken replied. Leonidas blinked, and suddenly, the elf was gone. The knight whirled around and saw him already fully down the street, sitting atop an old fish barrel at an abandoned market stall. "Now make haste, Sir Leonidas. The day ages fast!"

. . .

When Leonidas arrived atop the eastern hill, Vedalken was already there and in full armor to boot. The elf sat astride his mount, black hair hidden underneath his half-helm. His armor, dyed red like all Lightstriders, was of a much lighter variety, almost seemed form-fitting on the lithe elf. It was decorated with various designs, little suns, clouds, swirls of wind, and text inscribed in a script—he guessed it was elvish—that Leonidas couldn't read. Everything the elves did was a work of art, from Briskelthiar's armor and weaponry to the musical instruments that found their way into the Searstar market from time to time. But even more impressive than Vedalken's armor was his mount. Leonidas loved his horse, a sturdy roan charger he'd picked up on his way down off of the Sunne Steps, but comparing it and Calimero, well, the winner was clear for anyone to see. Smaller and leaner than most other equines, Calimero still managed to outclass even the fastest bred racing horse with his leaping stride, similar to the gazelles that wandered the dry savannas near the Scorched Waste. His coat was coppery red and seemed to glimmer in the sunlight as if it was beaded with moisture or braided with infinitesimal diamonds. His coat was even-trimmed and short, except for tufts around the ankles, mane, and tail, both intricately braided, and the small goatee hanging off of the steed's chin. Perhaps most impressive of all was Calimero's head. His eyes were pools of molten gold and silver, swirling and drawing in any who dared to stare deep within them. And from Calimero's forehead, rose a single, elegantly twisting horn, pure white erupting from a body the color of a dim.

"I told you he'd make it on time," the unicorn said reprovingly. "That means you owe me two honey-cakes."

"Fear not, Vedalken," Leonidas called out, "I recalled the nature of our friend here, and was wise enough to pick up a few sweets in the market."

Calimero swung his head to stare at his rider with one large eye, while Leonidas rummaged in his pack. "See, somebody pays attention to what I need! Perhaps I should make Leonidas Braveheart my rider."

"Perhaps you should!" Vedalken retorted. "But I warn you, when you break your back trying to leap around with all of that bulky armor and man-flesh atop you, don't come crying to me."

"I will not break my back under that load, and you know it. Honestly, just because I prefer towing light-boned faeries such as yourself, doesn't mean I can't handle heavier loads," Calimero lectured. "Back when my kind was more plentiful on Celestiira, we were ridden by menfolk of light and heavy cavalry alike."

"No need to give me a history lesson," Vedalken said dryly. "I was there. Do you forget already that I'm older than even you, oh magnificent unicorn?"

Calimero started to reply again, but Leonidas cut him off, thrusting a candied apple underneath his nose. The unicorn took a brief sniff, whinnied in approval, and bit off a huge chunk of the treat. As he chewed, Calimero tried in vain to respond, his mouth full of sticky honey, juicy apple, and crunchy nuts as it was.

Leo stood, brushed off his knees, and climbed once more into his saddle. "Make haste, you two," he said, pressing his feet into his horse's flank. "The day ages fast." Calimero laughed thickly at that, knowing it was one of Vedalken's favorite sayings, while the elf shrugged helplessly. Without any urging, the unicorn trotted forward, easily pacing the knight's charger. Chatting lightly, knight, unicorn, and Lightstrider struck out at once, heading east towards Valias Battlehall, and the mysterious task Vedalken had arranged for his former student.

CAITRIAL

HOPEFUL DREAMS AND A MARTYR MADE

Sweat dripped ponderously down her forehead, marking clear trails in the soot and grime caking her face. Caitrial stared intently into the flame of the forge, at the white-hot curve within, watching, waiting. Anticipating the precise moment... There! Caitrial snapped her tongs into the heart of the flame and snatched the glowing piece of metal back. Grabbing a small hammer from her belt, she struck at the part with an artisan's touch, until at last, she saw it was perfect. With a hiss of air, the glowing curve sizzled into the water trough beside her. When at last it was cooled and set, Caitrial took it out. The translucent, almost crystalline metal was carved into a flawless, gentle arch, a perfect match for the other made only a few days prior. A triumphant grin spread across her filthy face, and Briskelthiar, who'd been observing from a safe distance, came over and clapped her shoulder.

"Exquisite work, Caitrial Rainclaw. Far better than my first attempt with Kerazar, or even my hundredth." The smith felt a flush of pleasure at the high praise from the Elven smith. "Of course, elves are known for taking their time with these sorts of things."

"Aye, an' dwarves ain't too far off o' tha'!" Thraedan said, coming up behind his partner. "But, suren as th' sun sets, there's no time fer wastin'! Hope yer arms ain't hankerin' for a rest, 'cause there's no' one in sight!"

Eager Caitrial shook her head, subtly flexing the muscles in her arms, which had grown firmer in the weeks of fervent work. "I could keep going all day if need be."

Thraedan laughed. "Aye, tha's the spirit. Ye'll make a fine smith an' a better wife if ye're fer takin' a husband. Ye're like t' outclass 'im in keepin' th' house in good repair!"

Unsurprisingly, the dwarf's remark brought thoughts of Leonidas to Caitrial's mind, as she reminisced about the short but incredible time they'd had together. She vowed that if she ever saw him again, she'd ask him for another dance like they'd had at the Rothsster-Leygrain wedding.

As Caitrial returned from the reverie, she followed Briskelthiar and Thraedan, who were descending down a tunnel she'd never before seen. It was pitch black, but it sounded as if the other two were having no difficulty walking along. Keeping one arm securely around the two unfinished blades, Caitrial placed the other hand against the wall, using it to guide her. After several minutes of walking down a gently sloping path, they came to a room. Caitrial could tell by the airflow and the difference in the echo of their footsteps. A few moments later, she flinched, as Briskelthiar struck flint and steel, bringing light to a torch on the wall.

Now the room was unveiled, and Caitrial's mouth dropped open. The whole place was filled with display cases, and all the walls hung with racks. Each exhibited an item, work of art, or weapon, crafted over-time by the Sunwright Artisans. All were the epitome of beauty, and every weapon sharp and deadly. Spears, halberds, swords, even specialty weapons, like flails, disci, and a few Caitrial couldn't identify, forged from a wide variety of metals.

On one table sat a silver and gold diadem, the metals shaped into the likeness of twisting flames, each arc crested by a garnet phoenix. "That was meant as a gift for Queen Emery's coronation, had her father stepped down before his death," Briskelthiar explained. "I imagine that it will sit down here and gather dust for eternity."

"You forget about Grayson and the support he has now," Caitrial pointed out. "He could very well outlast the coming confrontation with Geurus Gardstar."

Thraedan snorted. "Yeh, mighten be he'll win. But 'e won't wear this dinky little thing! It'd be like askin' 'im to wear a dress in public! We'd have to make a whole new crown, with swords an' the like t' fit 'is masculinity." Caitrial couldn't help but chuckle at the mental image of dour Grayson wearing a tiara and dress. "But tha's not why we brought ye down 'ere." The dwarf snapped, and his elf partner brought a stepstool over to the other side of the room. Flanking an alcove in which twin worktables sat, were two objects, which the two elder Sunwright Artisans grabbed down. Thraedan's was a heater shield, riveted and crafted with sturdy steel. The business end was embossed with a detailed recreation of a dwarven face, mouth wide open in a battle snarl. Its bulbous proboscis protruded out from the front. In Briskelthiar's hands was the hilt of a weapon. Red-dyed leather, engraved with silver ribs for a better grip, was the least ornate thing about the piece. Its basket hand guard was intricately shaped into the forms of a dozen snakes. Every detail was perfect, down to the scales on their twisting bodies, and the tiny emerald eyes. Out from them was a fox-tail-shaped bar to block swipes at the side of her hand as well. The pommel stone was swirling gray hematite, carved into the horned head of a Khindre. But stranger than all that, the feature that caught Caitrial's attention most was on the disc-like top of the hilt, where the blade would be set. Or blades, in this case, for there were two slots set within, a few inches apart. And each slot seemed to be the perfect width for...

"Indeed, Caitrial," Briskelthiar said approvingly, noting her glance at the Kerazar blades in her hand, "this hilt and those blades belong together, as the resulting sword, Thraedan's shield, and the woman who will wield them belong together. But while there is still time in the workday, we will affix these blades, then we may speak of the past and the future."

Though the grooves were already cut in the handle, fastening the blades in them was still a painstaking project. It took Caitrial, with her master's guidance, the better part of two hours to align, set, and sharpen the weapon. At last, it was finished: a dual bladed sword of Kerazar steel, with a keen edge, and gravings of Caitrial's choosing. On the right-most blade, were the names of her sisters, Arcadia, and Reyna in Dwarvish runes. On the left, Emery and Leonidas in Elvish. Scrolled around the circular blade-plate was "In the Divines, we trust," just like her old broadsword, in both scripts.

As they drank cups of bitter coffee next to a hearth in the underground treasure chamber, Briskelthiar lectured Caitrial on their creation. "What you have now is based on an old diagram gifted to me by Ignis Duskwalker, the Secretkeeper. I know not where he acquired it, but it gave me chills to see a piece of the believed lost works of the Dusk Elves!"

"Dusk Elves, who are they?" Caitrial asked.

Not looking up from the weapon, Briskelthiar said, "Who *were* they, lass. The Dusk Elves, as was one of their more traditional titles, were an ancient subset of elves who were devoted to neither Yamaria nor Gaarhowl, neither the sun nor the moon."

"What happened to them?"

Briskelthiar shook his head. "Nobody knows, in truth. Some legends claim their disappearance happened during a cataclysmic period of history, called the Severance, which destroyed many different races and brought about the rise of several new ones, including the Fyroxi and the Chillfang. And of course, because historians cannot agree on anything, some say it was war or deliberate culling. Either way, as far as is known, no more Dusk Elves live to tell their tale."

He rotated the armament in his hands, his expressive eyes reflecting the light refracting through the Kerazar. "This is a weapon that they called a cythwarsai, or cythwai for short. Elegant yet deadly was always the way of the Children of Astral Passage. It was said that they embodied all of the best traits of the Sun and Moon Elves combined, which, if this cythwai is a proper representation of their handiwork, is a claim I will gladly second."

"Since their sudden disappearance, a few pieces o' lore 'ave been found, an' fewer designs, but when they do pop up, they're often the decidin' factors in a war. Accordin' t' th' histories, the trebuchets invented durin' one o' the early battles between Sun's Reach and Moonwatch was one o' them Dusk Elven designs, delivered to th' Solari general by 'is own Secretkeeper."

"And now," Caitrial supplied, "they've become an ordinary part of noble's battle strategies, like countless other things we take for granted these days. It's a tragedy that they're gone, but we're fortunate that their plans and inventions still find their way to us. As smiths of our particular talents, I believe we are uniquely suited to reintroducing their creations to the world."

"Aye," Thraedan said solemnly. "Tha's why ye're now the owner o' tha' cythwai."

"A fantastic weapon, and one I'm proud to wield, but I must wonder what use it will serve me in the city. Much as I'd like to stick two sharp blades through Geurus's heart, or disembowel a few Enforcers, I doubt it would turn out well for the rest of us."

"Well, it never hurts to be prepared," Briskelthiar put in. "This cythwai will be keener by far than your broadsword at its sharpest. I'm sure that Sir Leonidas taught you how to fight warriors in heavy armor during those sparring sessions you were always so excited for."

"If sparring was really wha' ye were doin', tha' is," Thraedan said under his breath, but in the confined cavern, the others were able to hear it just fine. Caitrial went bright red at the suggestion, and Briskelthiar rolled his eyes. The dwarf plowed on casually, seeming not to notice. "But either way, ye'd be best off to be armed with yer best."

"And I wholeheartedly believe that our ensemble could allow you to carve your mark in the minds of whatever foes you face."

"Why carve it in th' mind, when ye could carve it directly through th' brain?" Thraedan replied enthusiastically. "But seriously, if ye do find yerself in a pail o' hot water, use th' cythwai, an' then use this." He stomped on a wooden panel in the floor that Caitrial had noticed but refrained from asking about. If it was necessary, she trusted her one-time tutors to inform her. Noting her quizzical look, Thraedan was quick to answer, becoming gravely serious. "It's a bolthole girl. If ye need a quick way out o' the city, ye come 'ere. It'll dump ye out somewhere on th' Sunne Steps. But by Yamaria's bushy tail bits, girl, don't ye go bringing a swarm o' refugees down this way. Keep it a secret if ye can. If ye canno'... well, it'll be hard t' convince Geurus an' them rebel rabble tha' we're still neutral."

"That I won't do," Caitrial promised. "If I make use of your bolthole, it will just be Arcadia, Reyna, and myself."

"We expected as much of you," Briskelthiar said. "In the case you need it, we've placed three bags with food, water, and some essential supplies, enough to last until you arrive at a proper market. I hope you don't mind that we've taken the expenses out of your pay."

Caitrial nodded her acceptance. "I wouldn't want charity anyway. Survival should always come at the expense of she who strikes into danger."

"And that's why we like you, Caitrial," Briskelthiar replied with a smile. "And why we hope you never have to make use of the information we've just given you."

On a crisp, late fall day, Caitrial, Reyna, and Arcadia sat at the table, enjoying mugs of steaming hot chocolate, one of Reyna's favorite beverages. She'd been introduced to it by Emery when they were young. The princess, together with Leonidas, had snuck out three mugs of the sweet delicacy, to get around the fact Godfrey wouldn't allow Khindre into his sitting room. Cocoa was egregiously expensive, shipped in from some continent far away, and unknown to the simple smith. But given the times, and the money the family was bringing in, Caitrial figured it wouldn't hurt to treat themselves for once. And so, when a bag of it appeared at the market, Caitrial hastened to grab it up.

The three sisters sat mostly in silence, only the sounds of sipping and the clink of their mugs piercing the air. Though they'd done this many times before, enjoying each other's presence without the need for words, Caitrial felt that something was different today. There was a palpable tension in the air, which had appeared shortly after the delight from seeing the cocoa faded.

"What's wrong, Dreamer?" she asked Arcadia. The dark-skinned Khindre nodded subtly at her twin sister. "Rey? Is something the matter?"

Reyna nodded and set down her mug. Part of Caitrial wanted to laugh at the chocolate mustache that streaked across Reyna's brow, but she judged it wouldn't be prudent, given the look in her sister's eyes.

"I'm not sure how to preface this, so I'm just going to say it."

A million possibilities whirled through Caitrial's head. What was Reyna going to say? Had she done something with her magic, something she was ashamed of, like when she'd accidentally pushed Arcadia into the moat? Or, perhaps, she was pregnant with Grayson's child. They'd been spending plenty of intimate time together. Wouldn't that be a twist! The prince who lost his throne having a child with a Khindre sorceress. There would be objections, no doubt, but thinking long term, having that child might be beneficial to their cause. Especially if Grayson claimed the child as legitimate. Caitrial shook off the fanciful thoughts as Reyna started to speak, and it seemed like the former issue was closer to the truth.

"I-I've had strange dreams recently... though perhaps visions are a more accurate description; they're far too vivid to just be regular dreams," Reyna explained. "There have been several different ones, but some seem more important than others."

"Any you could describe for us now?" Caitrial remembered what Leonidas had said about her sister's magic. What if these were visions from Yamaria, sent to help them push back the darkness encroaching on their land? Leonidas had proven that Chillfang, the creatures of foul Gaarhowl, were causing havoc out in the kingdom, and Tarus, that surprising child, had held nothing back from the rebels, as far as they knew. The Gardstar family hailed from Moonwatch, though why they'd come over to Sun's Reach was still an enigma to the young Lord. Geurus had received a mission from King Xangrus, but Tarus didn't know more than that. There was something else at work here, and maybe, just maybe, Reyna could help to unravel that mystery.

. . .

Reyna nodded and closed her eyes for a moment, gathering her thoughts. "The first one I saw was of a hooded stranger in dark leathers pulling a cart across a field. I-it wasn't like anything I've heard of in Sun's Reach. The grass was grayish, and the sparse trees were dark and menacing. I didn't like the feel of the place. It felt almost like an antithesis of life."

"What was in the cart?" Caitrial wanted to know.

"I don't know. It was latched shut, and I couldn't control what I saw in the vision. I watched the figure enter a village, bleak and lifeless, and then next thing I knew, they were on the road again. In the distance, I saw a big castle, bigger than Emery's old home, even."

"That's disturbing, to say the least, but I'm as confused as you are, Rey," Caitrial said. "Have there been any more definitive visions?"

"Only one, and it's honestly more confusing than the rest. It was really brief, just a moment's flash of an image before I woke up." She went quiet, and tears splashed down from her golden eyes, streaking down her orange skin to plop down into her mug. Caitrial carefully pulled the forgotten cocoa away, so it wouldn't be tainted by tears or mucus. "I thought... I thought I saw Emery. She looked a bit different, but I could have sworn it was her, alive and breathing."

"Oh, dear," Caitrial hurriedly stood and rushed to her sister's side, firmly rubbing her back. The smith hated that she couldn't think of the right words to say.

"I know it can't be," Reyna sobbed. "But, I can't help myself from hoping that the image is more than just delusion. We all saw her fall to her death, and heard Leo's story, but what if she could have survived?"

"Even if she did," Arcadia put in, "even if somebody found

Emery and bound her wounds before she died, the sort of head trauma..."

Both of them knew it; they'd talked to Berdur about the possibility several times, drilling the old medic about any way she could have survived. The dwarf had assured them that best-case scenario, the fall would have conked the memories right out of poor Emery. If she survived that fall, she would likely never remember Reyna, or Arcadia, or even her beloved Leonidas. And given the amount of gore and brain matter found by the street-sweepers, that chance of survival was already slim. Besides, if somebody knew that Emery was alive, wouldn't either Geurus or one of the rebels have said something by now? No, Emery Redwyn was long gone.

"I just wish I could see her again," Reyna murmured.

Caitrial just squeezed her Khindre sister closer, whispering comforting words in her ear. Neither of them saw Arcadia, an intense look in her heterochromatic eyes, clench her fist and grimace.

The day was surprisingly busy at the market near the Castle Ward. Caitrial, Arcadia, and Reyna were spending the day walking about and viewing the new wares, just like old times. Geurus had allowed a caravan with new goods in a surprising act from the restricting king. Many people were gathered here, the buzz of the crowd drowning out the ever-present whistling of Qrakzt's moat, which everyone gave a wide berth.

Reyna wasn't paying much attention to the various trinkets in the stalls, often peeking at the castle, hoping to catch a glimpse of Grayson. Nobody had seen the prince in several days, and under-standably, his Khindre lover was growing worried. Caitrial was also concerned, though, for a different reason. Grayson was the cornerstone of the rebel movement. If something happened to him, would the rebellion survive?

The eldest Rainclaw sister saw Reyna's eyes light up a few

minutes later, and knew she'd spotted him. When the Khindre caught her breath and tensed, Caitrial followed her gaze. Instantly, she knew that something was wrong.

Grayson was walking jerkily down from the castle gatehouse, down towards the bridge. With his strained movements and the contorted expression on his face, it seemed like he was either fighting against something, or wracked by pain. Reyna started to rush over to him, but both Arcadia and Caitrial grasped at her arms, holding her back. All eyes were on Grayson now, his face pale and covered with a sheen of sweat. His lips twitched as if he couldn't maintain control of the muscles. Then the prince lifted an arm laboriously and crooked a finger in Reyna's direction. The crowd parted like grass in the wind, leaving a clear path between the sisters and Grayson. The last remaining Redwyn rooted himself on the bridge, taking a considerable measure of will to do so. Reyna looked pleadingly back at her sisters and then relaxed, seeming defeated. No sooner had Caitrial let down her guard, than Reyna burst forward in a sudden movement, tearing away from them.

Grayson's eyes widened. "N-no!" he cried. "Stay. Back. Reyna!" He spat out each word like it pained him to do so. "P-please, I beg of you. Come no closer!"

"What's wrong, Grayson? Please, my love, tell me. I can see that you're in pain!"

"I-it's G-G...." He doubled over as if he'd been punched in the stomach. His pained groan was all that Reyna could take. Heedless of his warnings, she ran over to her lover and helped him stand.

"Reyna, please, go back to your family. There's something... I can't explain it. The King, he was asking about your magic and now...Agh!"

The sunset-skinned Khindre threw herself quickly into spell-casting, waving her arms about and muttering under her breath.

Her golden eyes gave off a sky blue radiance, and her smooth brow furrowed in confusion. "Grayson...there's an aura of magic all over you. Menacing, dark magic."

Her eyes intent on his, Reyna didn't see Grayson's free hand inching towards his belt, but Caitrial did. The appendage seemed to fight for every inch, constantly twitching up and away.

"I can't fight it anymore, Reyna," Grayson quavered. "You know I love you more than anything?" he asked out of the blue.

Reyna nodded. "Of course, my prince. And you know I feel the same."

"You know I would never hurt you if I had the choice?"

Before Reyna could even get the answer out of her mouth, Grayson's hand won the battle. Sweaty fingers grasped the dagger sheathed there, a curved white blade with black stones around the pommel, ripped it free, and jabbed it deep into Reyna's stomach. There was a long moment of stunned silence from the audience, who stood stock-still, staring at the scene on the bridge.

"Reyna," Grayson could barely get the words from his mouth. "Reyna, please don't hate me. Please, please, please..."

"Shhh, Grayson," Reyna managed to say. "I_I can feel it, the magic. I know it's not you. You would never w-willingly harm me. The au-aura feels similar to...Tarus's, but it's not...It's not..."

"Geurus, then. As I should have suspected," Grayson decided, and it seemed that the prince found his voice at that moment. "Mark me well, people of Searstar," he said, pulling his beloved Reyna closer to him. The Khindre sorceress wrapped her arms around his shoulders, nestling her face weakly into his neck. "What you have witnessed today are the actions of an evil king, who cannot tolerate any threat to his stolen throne. We know that somehow Chillfang entered our borders to wreak havoc. And now, Geurus Gardstar, this fiend from Moonwatch, has used his foul powers, magic, I believe, to destroy our lives, not once, but twice! He's killed my family, he's killed the woman I love, but as Yamaria as my witness, he'll not have me at his mercy!" He kissed the dying Reyna once more, softly, and gave a final shout, "Down with Geurus Gardstar!" before, with great effort, the last remaining Redwyn rocked jerkily, appearing to fight a mile for every inch, until he built up enough momentum to haul his uncooperative body off the bridge, and into the moat. Reyna, a bright, loving smile on her face, followed him in. A resounding splash and subsequent tall plume of displaced water heralded their disappearance, and seemed to set the world off kilter. For just a moment, there was silence as the whistling torrent carried them under and away, never to be seen again.

That's when the screams started.

Caitrial, her tears a waterfall pouring out from her amber eyes, had to hold Arcadia back, just as she had with Reyna.

"I'll kill him! I swear it!" she growled. Arcadia leveled her hurting, hostile gaze on her sister. "Let me go, damn you! Geurus must die for what he did to Reyna!"

She tried to pull away, but Caitrial yanked her back and forced Arcadia to look at her. "What are you going to do, rush in there? Get the fool-headed notion out of your mind!"

"How can you be so heartless!" she screamed, and truly it rent Caitrial's heart. "Reyna is dead!"

"I'm not being heartless, I'm thinking rationally! If you storm into Geurus' throne room, hands ablaze with magic, you'll be killed. What good would you do Reyna then?"

The words were cruel, they hurt Caitrial to say, but Arcadia stopped straining against her arms. The smith pulled her sister into a tight hug, but they were rudely forced out of it by a sound from ahead. Metal boots clanking against flagstones; the Enforcers were coming, no doubt, to kill Arcadia. Caitrial had no intention of letting them do that. "Run," she whispered to the Khindre.

"Sis," Arcadia stirred but didn't move.

"Did I stutter?" she queried, a bit imperiously. "Run, now. Let me buy you some time."

Arcadia hesitated only a moment more, threw a quick hug around Caitrial, and said, "Don't die," before darting off through the crowd, some of which were scattering, while a few others raised blades to fight.

There were nearly half a dozen of them, girt in glistening black armaments studded with motes of white. All had their helmets on, and their pikes were drawn.

Caitrial gripped the leather and filigree hilt of the cythwai. Taking a steadying breath, she ripped the marvelous blade from its sheath with a flourish. Was it just her imagination, or did the Enforcers stall a little at the reveal of the weapon? A trick of the light or not, Caitrial realized she had little choice but to fight, as the Enforcers were already quelling the fighting spirit of the daring few rebels by dint of pike and short sword. Giving credence to her suspicion of fear, none of the Enforcers dared to approach her directly, swerving around to strike at other sword-bearers or chop at undefended fleeing legs. The smith pictured one of those blades cleaving through Arcadia's bony legs, felling the poor Khindre as she ran for Briskelthiar's bolt-hole. That image steeled the most hesitant of her nerves, and she stalked up behind an Enforcer, which was occupied with Jasqua's flashing blade. With practiced ease, the ranger woman's blade flashed left, right, and down, picking off two jabs and an attempted leg sweep. It was an impressive display, which sent a thrill of triumph through the smith. But when Jasqua glanced into Cait's eyes, there was a pleading there. She was tiring quickly, and despite the exertion the Enforcer *had* to be putting into its futile attacks, it showed no sign of slowing—let alone stopping—any time soon. Caitrial assuaged her worries with a silent nod, though honestly, she wasn't quite sure what to do.

While Jasqua defeated one attack after another, slowly shrinking backward, the smith did what a smith does best: examine armor. Unlike the armaments Caitrial was familiar with, this set was bereft of visible rivets, dents, seams, or distinctive features that might help her determine its components or weak points. Perhaps stranger than that, the armor seemed to swirl and shift like storm-clouds when viewed up close. *Or like Arcadia's shadow magic,* she thought. Yes, that was it! The armor resembled fused shadows, with little definition, and a fluidity that couldn't possibly provide a proper defense. Yet when Jasqua's sword slipped past the Enforcer's guard, it rang cleanly off with a shower of sparks. What material was this, and what other properties might it have? Questions for later. Right now, it was either attack or hesitate and let Jasqua and others besides be killed. Fully occupied by the ranger, the Enforcer didn't notice Caitrial until she struck, the dual Kerazar blades diving towards a concealed knee joint to disable. There was a momentary resistance before sharp edges sliced flesh. With a horrifying screech that sounded like several human voices crying out in pain at once, the Enforcer overbalanced and toppled. Ripping the blade out with a spray of dark—almost black—crimson blood, Cait slashed the sword in a long arc down across her body. The cythwai carved effortlessly through the Enforcer's armor, leaving two long gashes and a dead Enforcer in its wake.

"Nice sword you got there," Jasqua commented through labored breaths. "Wager making a trade?"

Caitrial managed a small smile, but then turned her attention to the matter at hand, and found that the remaining four Enforcers were all staring in her direction. The smith found time to swear before she and Jasqua stood back to back, enemies warily closing a ring around the pair. The Enforcers probed with their pikes, using the long handles to stay out of reach of the women's swinging swords.

"This may be where we die, Caitrial Rainclaw," Jasqua said. "If so, I want you to know it's been an honor working with you and your sisters. I pray to Yamaria that Arcadia escapes." She laughed mirthlessly. "I never thought I'd be hoping for a Khindre to survive, given my old job, slaying bandits and wretched folk from Carrion Cove."

Caitrial wanted to reassure Jasqua, say that they'd escape, but the prospects looked bleak, for sure. At any moment, the Enforcers could choose to charge. If Yamaria granted them luck, they might take down one before sharp, black steel ran them through. *Leonidas,* she thought, *Yamaria's favor upon your mission, whether or not we meet again.* The Gardstar warriors all stepped back with one foot, setting up for their disemboweling charge. Cait glanced down at the cythwai, thinking it was a shame that the weapon might end up in enemy hands. She considered trying to toss it into the moat so that, like Reyna and Grayson, it too would be lost to Geurus Gardstar. So focussed were they on their impending doom that neither Caitrial nor Jasqua noticed the shadows writhing like so many snakes around their feet. The Enforcers muttered something in a guttural tongue neither understood, but both assumed was the native dialect of Moon-watch. Pikes were pulled back, stances were set, and smith and ranger readied to strike and to die.

But before the Enforcers could charge, there came an explosion of gloom as the shadows curling about them expanded exponentially, becoming tentacles grasping at the Enforcers, but leaving the women alone.

While they stood there stunned, a somewhat raspy voice called out, "Take care of them and let's go!" Arcadia! Cait nodded, and she and Jasqua made quick work of the struggling, nearly immobile enforcers, ending their surprised screeching once and for all. They paused only long enough to give a quick nod of thanks to the purple-skinned Khindre before the three ran off to the Sunwright Artisans. Thanks to Arcadia, who'd sent a magical message to the two master smiths, the way was already prepared. After a few hasty farewells, Jasqua, Arcadia, and Caitrial exited the City of the Sun, without any clue whether they'd ever see it again.

TARUS

THE BEGINNING OF THE END

The corridor leading to the throne room was cold and dark, as the Widower Prince hesitantly shambled down it. He was stunned by what he'd just seen, and thoughts whirled in his mind, going a hundred leagues a minute. Grayson had been called into the throne room alone. Not even Casinius or Velara had been allowed inside, so neither knew what had happened. But Tarus, waiting outside, had seen Grayson come out, his chin lifted higher than Tarus had ever seen it, practically strutting down the hall, with only the occasional twitch in his hand. The prince had thought little of it at the time. Perhaps Father had delivered some particularly painful news to the deposed prince. Maybe Emery's body had been found, and now she was being used to torture Grayson's sensibilities. Tarus certainly wouldn't put that past cruel Geurus. He didn't have the chance to go in and ask, however, as a host of Enforcers emerged from the chamber next. Two of them barred the door with their spears, while the rest followed Grayson down the corridor. With few other options ahead of him Tarus chose to join the entourage. As Grayson moved further from the throne room, the twitches seemed to intensify. As one particularly violent sway forced the prince to throw his hip back to avoid tripping, Tarus noticed the glint of a familiar dagger hilt. A near-perfect match for the one with which he'd killed Emery. Curious, but if anything, it only provided further proof of his running theory. Grayson was being forced to wear the blade stained with his sister's blood as punishment. Grayson was muttering darkly, and Tarus could only catch snippets of what was being said. Calling out to him only caused the prince to turn and growl. "Back away, boy. I've no need for interruptions. I'll deal with you later." The sudden hostility surprised Tarus. Hadn't they grown past the blatant suspicion already? The prince had hoped that his efforts in the battle for Emery's throne —for in Tarus's eyes, the Highsun Seat belonged to her, whether she was alive or dead—would have helped mitigate the distrust between them.

The shocking events at the bridge revealed the truth of the matter and gave Tarus much to think about.

When Reyna had cast that spell, something had resonated within Tarus, and he'd felt that awfully familiar pressure. What did it mean? Then the damning evidence: "Geurus then. As I should have expected." Grayson, the prince having a difficult time controlling his body, proclaimed his love for the Khindre, before stabbing her. In the stomach. With a white dagger. Also, when Grayson had gone toppling into the moat, Tarus had felt a presence, like something attempting to breach his mind. Reeling, confused, and caught by surprise, Tarus had thrown up a wall, blocking the intrusion. Back in Moonwatch, Geurus had admitted to his son and daughter that piercing the stomach was his favorite mode of killing someone, while Tarus despised that torturous method. As far as he was concerned, if you had to kill someone—which he hoped to avoid at all costs—you were obligated to make it quick. Tarus felt a fool for not putting it all together. The sudden headaches, his father's uncanny knack for reading his mind, even the slaying of Emery. Had it all been Geurus from the beginning? The Widower Prince had to know, and so here he was. When he arrived at the throne room door, the Enforcers now standing rigidly to the side, almost as if frozen, he rapped thrice in quick succession, unconsciously reverting to his and Velara's secret code.

He heard her voice come from within. "Tarus? Is that you? Get in here. Now!" It was tinged with worry and fear.

Geurus Gardstar was flopped over, more out of the Highsun Seat than in it. His head was thrown back, and his hair, the same white-blonde as Tarus's, was streaked with saliva and a bit of blood from his nose. Casinius stood on one side, anchoring the king to the throne with all his might, while Velara remained by his head, trying to talk to their father.

"What happened?" he asked, dumbfounded by the uncharacteristic weakness Geurus was showing.

"I don't know!" Velara said, clearly annoyed. "I was strolling the gardens when suddenly, the Enforcers attending me froze, unresponsive as statues. They reacted to nothing, not even me sticking a dagger in their visor slits." Velara tossed her head, sending blonde curls bouncing. "As far as I saw on my way up here, none of the Enforcers outside the castle itself were affected. Only the ones here, so I came to ask Father about it and found him like this. I don't know where you were during all of this, but I swear, if someone, maybe those damned priests, found some way to spread their blessed zone outside their temple, and I hear you had anything to do with it..." She left the sentence hanging, unfinished, but the message was there all the same.

"Peace, sis, I'm just as confused as you are." *Probably more. Now I'll never get the answer to my question. Did Father take over my mind, like he tried to do with Grayson? Is that why I killed the woman I loved with all of my heart, just as the deposed prince did with the Khindre sorceress?* He figured now wouldn't be a good time to bring this up with Velara. Given the stress of the current circumstances, any attempt to explain himself—and his betrayal— would likely end with a knife driven into his *own* gut! "We need to figure out what to do, and quickly." He summarized the events at the bridge. "I doubt the grieving people are going to wait long to show their fangs. Especially now that there aren't any more Redwyns to assuage their anger."

"By Gaarhowl, Father." Velara brushed the hair back from Geurus's face in a surprising act of tenderness. "In most circumstances, I love your take-all mindset, but now look at what you've done. Mother's off in Redhawk with Tavindre, and we have a city about to riot. What are we supposed to do?"

"One thing and one thing only is clear," Casinius cut in. "This man is no longer fit to rule." The Lighstrider captain gave a rude snort. "Ironic how after cleansing the throne of the unworthy Godfrey Redwyn, Geurus Gardstar becomes just like his predecessor."

Velara turned a hateful gaze upon the aging warrior. "Current health afflictions aside, Geurus Gardstar is still king! You will show proper respect."

"Not my king," Casinius said derisively. "Just as Godfrey wasn't." Quick as a hare, Velara shook a stiletto from her sleeve and trained it at the man's face, but Casinius was faster. Before either Gardstar had a chance to blink, the Lightstrider's sword was in hand, and a breath later, the miraculous blade sheared the tip from Velara's weapon. "This is not a game you wish to play, upstart princess."

With the runes on the royal-slaying sword pulsing inches from her nose, Velara had no choice but to submit. She stepped back, dropped the useless stiletto to the ground, and Brightblade's sword snapped back into its sheath.

"In a way, his idiotic actions today have done you at least one favor," Casinius said, as if that exchange hadn't happened. "The people won't want to see your father, so his current...condition won't cause him further issues. You might even be better off keeping him in a dark hole far from prying eyes."

In an attempt to prove the warrior right, Geurus began to tremble violently. His pale lips flapped, spewing flecks of saliva and blood. The siblings couldn't hope to stop their father as he slid to the floor and began to convulse, flailing limbs slapping repeatedly against the dais and throne. After what seemed like an agonizing eternity, Geurus calmed at last. His mouth's movements became less wild, more rhythmic. It took several moments for Tarus and Velara to realize he was speaking. At first, his words were too garbled and feeble to make out, but they slowly grew in strength until the three in the room could make out. "All...must...die. T-the Lich Lords command it-t." He repeated this mantra over and over, occasionally punctuating it with a spasm.

"How quaint," Casinius said sardonically. "I wonder if..."

"We get it, Brightblade," Tarus cut him off. He was quickly growing tired of the Lightstrider Captain's mockery and superior attitude. "Your opinions are worthless to us at this moment, and I'd suggest you turn your back and leave. I've wondered why you even joined my father's endeavor to take the throne in the first place, given the disdain you show him now. Did you hope to claim the throne yourself?"

"You are more naive than I thought, Widower Prince. I am not a royal, nor have I ever wanted to be. I am a servant to the royal family of Sun's Reach."

"That didn't stop you from permanently separating the queen from her head," Velara pointed out.

"You understand naught. I *am* a servant, but only to a worthy ruler. When your devil of a father approached me, he appealed to that logic. He knew, even from his limited experience with Godfrey, that he was a failure as a king, as many people forced into poverty by his love for festivities and lack of care about his own people could attest. Lysaria Redwyn wouldn't have served much better, living as the glorified scribe of the kingdom." Casinius's voice grew steely and cold. "All I wanted was a competent ruler. Emery would have been a competent ruler."

"But she's dead," Tarus said, beginning to grow queasy. "My father killed her." He was more willing to believe that than the other possibility.

"No, Tarus," Velara reminded unhelpfully, "you killed her." Tarus turned a venomous glare upon his sister.

"A part of the plan I was not made aware of. For all Geurus told me, only Godfrey and Lysaria were to die. Emery was then to marry you, boy, and go on to rule the kingdom, ushering in an age of goodwill that Sun's Reach sorely craves. Had Geurus let on that Emery was to die, I'd have withdrawn my aid immediately; I bore the girl no ill will, only her rags to knighthood protector."

"Had you withdrawn your aid, Casinius, you would not be alive to speak such treasonous words," Velara explained smugly.

"Perhaps," Casinius shrugged. "But now, it seems that your father is the one standing at the threshold of whatever afterlife you lot believe in. But, I have said my piece. I've no more desire to stand in this throne room devoid of viable rulers. Besides, I do believe your king has just soiled his breeches. Best of luck with running a kingdom that hates you."

"I should imprison you, Casinius!" Velara screeched.

"You could do so. But unfortunately for you, there are other, more pressing matters to deal with, such as the rioting mob that will likely soon be at your gates. I'd not suggest locking up valuable resources." With that, Casinius strode resolutely out of the room, paying no heed to the hateful stares piercing into his back.

When at last he was gone, Tarus and Velara turned as one to their father, still sprawled on the floor.

"What are we supposed to do?" Velara asked, wringing her soft hands.

"I don't know," Tarus said, confused by the tumult of contradicting emotions within him. On one hand, his heart fluttered with fear, knowing that neither he nor Velara were prepared to take on the crown, especially not when their subjects wanted to tear it out of their hands and place it on.... Whose head? Grayson was gone, just like Lysaria, and Godfrey. And… Emery. His gut twisted again. There was the source of the confusing thrill. With Geurus out of the picture, Tarus wouldn't have to worry about having his mind probed again, if it had been his father doing that. He wouldn't have to fear making another mistake like Emery.

"Kind of you to put us in this situation, father," Tarus murmured.

But if Geurus Gardstar heard him, he gave no response besides a new reprisal of his favorite phrase. "Destroy all resistance and open the portal. The Lich Lords command it." As he finished speaking, the Enforcers jerked into movement again, departing the room as if they'd been given an order.

"And the plot thickens," Velara said into the tumult, and Tarus had to agree.

LEONIDAS

WHAT COULD HAVE BEEN

Even from the outside, Valias was a feast for the senses. It sprawled across the eastern side of the Sulfaari Expanse, nearly half as expansive as Searstar. Clusters of clashing tents, pavilions, and more permanent structures encompassed the Battlehall in all its glory. A colossal, translucent dome stood in the very center, gleaming and faceted. When Leonidas had apprenticed as a carpenter back home, one of the elders claimed that Valias Battlehall had been grown with a combination of druidic and arcane magic. The sand was raised from the earth and held aloft, to be melted by magical fire and shaped with telekinesis. It all sounded absurd to Leonidas, but as Vedalken was known to say: "The past matters only to historians, and those who lived it. You live in the present, take care to remember that."

Staggered around the dome were several coliseums and faux castles, where various events, from jousting to target breaking, and even mock battles took place. Even now, sounds of hooting and cheering could be heard flowing out from one or the other.

"A foreign murderer is running the kingdom, and war looms, yet the games still run." Leonidas shook his head in bewilderment.

"For that, you should be glad," Vedalken said, sidling Calimero up next to his horse. "Valias Battlehall was founded with the realm and ran through storm and siege, war and flux. It remains a backbone of sorts for the people of Sun's Reach, and a distraction from those tragic events. By doing so, they serve as a bastion against despair and hopelessness."

"And should some foolish tyrant try to cancel the games, that man will find no stouter foe than Valias Battlehall. Inside he'll find several hundred warriors with something to say about it, big enough walls to require siege engines, and well equipped enough to weather it all," Calimero put in.

"Several hundred warriors would go well to support our cause," Leo said, scratching his chin where a blanket of stubble had already begun to grow. "Mayhap we can incite their ire, with talk of Emery and Godfrey." Godfrey had been very fond of the games, he recalled. Many radiants had flowed into their coffers from the crown's treasury. "I daresay we'll need them."

The news they'd heard on the road was far from pleasant. A small horde of angry peasants notified them that Lord Phaser had claimed for Geurus. The men and women had been from vassal towns of Fyrestone, angered by their Fyroxi friends' massacre within the city. Two Fyroxi traveled with them, brothers that had just been returning from a hunt on that fateful day. They had heard the horns and the screams and went running, but by the time they arrived, it was far too late. The two brothers were able to confirm the sightings of Chillfang, the Fyroxi's ancestral enemy in the square. Leonidas wanted badly to give them the solace of knowing there was still hope, but he'd made an oath to Amaru, and if nothing else, the knight was good for keeping his vows. Though Leonidas had won over Ellep

Bult of the gnomes, Faenith, and Gage Fletcher, as well as Cendrillion and a few other smaller holdings, they would do little against the vast army of Enforcers. "We are but a small band of renegades, with naught but a martyr as a figurehead, and very little military strength behind us," Leonidas said. Vedalken had nodded but said nothing. No doubt the Lightstrider was thinking about the other rumors they'd heard. Two wandering singers had a tale on their lips of demons in Redhawk. As of yet, the proud city had sent nothing more than silence to Geurus Gardstar, but what that meant was unclear. If the tales were true, and demons did walk the streets of Redhawk, Vedalken was at an impasse. Since its founding days the order, the Lightstriders raised their weapons against all threats to the kingdom. Demons were a far greater threat than a murderer king, but something kept Vedalken with Leonidas. When he asked, the knight only got this in response, "Prepare yourself, my one-time apprentice. We walk into a den of warriors. If you wish to sway their hearts, you'll need more than a few words."

"Indeed, you'll need a big tankard of ale, and a loud blade to get their attention," Calimero quipped.

"Though not the way I'd have put it, my steed has the right of it," Vedalken nodded. "A rousing battle against one of their best ought to do it."

"I'm to walk in and declare a challenge against their best," Leonidas said disbelievingly.

"Precisely," Vedalken answered.

"I saw a big falcon flying up above us a while ago," Calimero said. "He had a musk of magic to him. Probably some druid's familiar. It's possible that the people within already know who comes. I'm sure they're all shaking in their greaves."

"Good," the elf answered. "That's what we want. A man with a reputation such as Sir Leonidas_."

"As well as such famous personages as us," Calimero broke in.

"Yes," Vedalken said, a mite wearily, "we might not have to do so much searching. When I used to frequent taverns to gather news, I heard many whispers of challengers who wished to try their luck against you. But seeing as you've never visited the Battlehall, you've left them all disappointed."

"Am I supposed to apologize?" Leo asked. "I had a princess to protect. I come to them in an hour of need. But if I needs must battle to give them reason to strike out against Geurus Gardstar, then in the names of Emery Redwyn and Yamaria, I shall do so."

"I don't see what other reason they need." The eye roll was evident in Calimero's voice. "Besides the fact that Geurus Gardstar is an icy-hearted prick! If they can't see that, they're blind!"

Vedalken switched the unicorn across the muzzle. "Watch your glib tongue, fool beast," he whispered harshly. "You said yourself we had eyes upon us, and with eyes come ears. Gladiators are a prickly lot, and if we wish their banners behind us, we can't throw caution to the wind."

Many eyes upon the three companions as they pushed through the throng. Leonidas could see men and women alike pointing and whispering. *As if the sights and smells weren't enough on their own, their stares weigh near as much as my armor.* Indeed, a few of the whispers were borne from that armor. Whispers abound of "He looks so regal!" or "I'd like to meet the smith who managed that work of art!"

"Aye, it's a handsome piece, but can it stop a sword?" Another voice retorted.

"Far better than your flimsy hand-me-downs could stop that hammer strapped across his back!"

Leonidas found it difficult to pretend not to listen to the whispers. He wanted to take in the sights and smells around him, but the press of the crowd gave the three no quarter. They hadn't since Leonidas had deposited his horse at the stables outside. It almost seemed that the people were leading them somewhere, as they followed the holes that opened in the crowd. When Leo brought that up to Vedalken, the elf chuckled and said only, "The watchful eyes have made their report."

"We'd best hope they have a favorable view of us," came Calimero's reply. If icy worms have already begun nibbling at their heart, we'll soon find ourselves clapped in irons."

"If that is the case, they will try," Vedalken answered confidently, touching his spear.

"You must be Leonidas Braveheart," came a soft but cutting voice from beside him. The knight blinked. He hadn't even noticed the man who now walked beside him. The mysterious man's blonde hair was so fair it was almost white, shorn short atop his angular face. Dark eyes sunk in their sockets over a sharp nose and a knowing smile. *Half-Elven, this one.* He wore a green surcoat over an enameled green breastplate with what looked like a dragon picked out in jade on it. The gauntlets on his hands bore curved talons of bone, to evoke the image of a dragon as well.

"That is the name the people of this kingdom have seen fit to give me," Leo answered modestly. He looked his new companion over. "What name have they granted you?"

"I am called the Green Dragon Lance," he answered flatly. "But it isn't my name that should concern you. We know what you've come for, and we've been preparing."

"I don't know whether to be flattered or worried."

"I'd suggest flattered would serve you better. We rarely treat visitors this way. But your opponent has wished to test your mettle for quite some time."

This was moving much faster than Leonidas had expected, but speed is what the renegades needed, so the knight had no choice but to accept it. "I would thank you for giving me the name of my opponent. I'm not fond of surprises on the battlefield."

"Given your reputation, and your aim, I'd wager the honor is mine!" Yet another new voice, this time from above and to Leo's right, called out. The voice was feminine, and as it echoed through the atrium, all other talking ceased. Leonidas looked towards the source just in time to see a lithe figure leap from a pedestal upon which a gargoyle might have once stood. She rolled in the air, once, twice, thrice, before landing with all the grace of a cat. A young woman stood before him, girt in sturdy boiled leathers held together with bright silver clasps. Long, fiery red hair bounced about her shoulders, bound in three braids. A net of silver studded with garnets weaved through them, the sun glinting off of them like sparks amid a fire. For just a moment, gazing upon this woman, Leonidas thought it was Emery, and tears threatened to flow from his eyes. But the woman's eyes were green, flecked with gold, rather than the warm, rich brown of Em's orbs. There was a sharpness to them and a lilt in her tone that suggested that she, too, had Elven blood running in her veins.

"My lady, it is a pleasure to meet you." Leonidas bowed. "Would you do me the honor of introducing yourself ? Your friend here seems fond of mysteries."

The woman laughed, a clarion chime, but one that spoke of confidence and power, rather far removed from the innocent notes in Emery's every laugh. "'It's been too long since I heard such courtly manners, Sir Lion! The folk 'round here boast a much rougher vernacular. Her bow did Leonidas to shame, a sweeping thing that bent her body into a near-perfect L. "Cynthia Flash-Strike at your service!" Cynthia flourished with a jeweled dagger that suddenly appeared in her hand. Leonidas hadn't even seen her hand go to her belt! "They say my strikes come so fast, my opponents never see them! I tend to agree with them!" With a casual flick of her wrist, the dagger flew through the air, straight and true. It carved the empty air right beside Leonidas's head and buried itself in the wooden pillar of a merchant's tent, which swallowed the blade straight to the cross guard. Before it had stopped quivering, people were clambering over each other to claim it for their own. Cynthia took a step towards Leo. "The gold-crazy fools never seem to realize that the gems are fakes. Until they go to sell it, that is."

Leo smiled. "I hope you fight as well as you boast, Lady Flash-Strike. I've been waiting for a good test of my strength since the Venomsting captured me. Outlaws rarely put up enough fight for both a knight and a Lightstrider."

Cynthia plucked an apple from the stall next to them, leaving a silver bright in its place. Brushing it on her leathers, she tossed it, caught it deftly in one hand, and took a large bite. "Choose your weapon, Braveheart, and I'll see you on the morrow's morning. West Wing Coliseum is where our battle shall be held!"

Never in his wildest dreams had Leonidas wished to fight for sport. He'd dreamed of carving out a life as a carpenter with Tara and their children. But Yamaria had decided that wasn't his niche. Instead, he fought for vengeance and, more importantly, for protecting those who couldn't fight for themselves.

Now, he stood across the sunbaked hardpack of West Wing, facing a woman-warrior that reminded him too much of his past. Cynthia Flash-Strike brought not only to mind the phantom of Emery, but her weapon prowess called upon the memories of Caitrial, whom Leo missed sorely. The smith had always loved traveling. The knight wished he could have brought her and her sisters along. It would have gone a long way to make him feel more comfortable. Leonidas banished those thoughts as soon as he saw another man enter the arena to stand between the two competitors. His name was Barker Yoggwin, and he had a voice to match his outfit, that is to say, loud. His shaved head was inked with a checked design in red and white, and a sky-blue dyed beard hung down from his chin. Even his eyes played along, each one being a different color; the right was icy blue, and the left a strange hazel-green mixture. Yoggwin wore a motley assortment of clothing stitched together from half a hundred different fabrics. When Leo asked about it, the Barker only smiled and said, "You'd best be winning, Sir Lion! I'm for wanting a swath o' Flash-Strike's clothing to add on!"

Back in the arena, Yoggwin motioned for silence, and the gaggle of excited fans hushed, their collective breath held near as tightly as the bags of coin in their hands. It was strange to imagine that people were betting on his match.

"Today," Yoggwin boomed, "We have for you, watchers, a special sort o' treat!" He boasted a tremulous accent that sounded so ridiculous that Leonidas doubted it could be real. "You all stand—or rather sit—as witnesses to a grand spectacle. "In the winner's circle, we have a woman who has only ever lost her title thrice, but each time won it back in only a week! Our very own daring, dashing darling: Cynthia Flash-Strike!" After each word, Yoggwin paused, and the crowd emitted a short but loud, "Hey!" Cynthia looked to be thriving off of it, each exultation widening the smile on her comely face until it seemed that her mouth would take in her pointed ears. She still had the silver net in her hair, and the garnets set within glittered dangerously together with the rubies on the pommels of her twin swords and stilettos. Cynthia juggled all four blades at once, smoothly turning them in the air so as not to cut herself, without needing to spare them so much as a glance.

Dual swords, light armor, Elven blood, it seems I fight a Breeze-Dancer. I'll need to be careful. Leo was glad he'd chosen his long-sword and a borrowed shield over his unwieldy hammer or weighty heater shield. Here, a particular swiftness would be required if he wanted to counter the blindingly fast strikes he knew he could expect from this foe.

After the calls for Cynthia had quelled, Yoggwin continued. "Her opponent is a maiden in the Battlehall! Hailing from the City on High herself, Searstar, he is a knight of the kingdom, and once the personal guardian of Princess Emery Redwyn, may Yamaria harbor her soul! I present to you, Leonidas Braveheart!" The knight was surprised at the number of cheers he received, though had they gone at the same time, Flash-Strike's raucous fans would have drowned out his with ease. If the half-elf could drum up excitement with a movement, perhaps he could do the same.

With a hiss of steel on leather, Leonidas ripped his fine blade from its sheath, letting the sun reflect off the golden lion's head and the three hearts on the hilt. Closing one lobstered gauntlet around the lion, he grounded the blade and beat a slow rhythm against the borrowed buckler on his arm. It was emblazoned with the Valias Battlehall coat of arms, a flaming fist with several broken swords beneath it on a field of bronze, silver, and gold.

"This is the ultimate battle," Yoggwin continued, "o' human versus half-elf, man versus woman, sturdy versus slippery! Who will come out on top?" The air buzzed with a cacophony of noise and excitement as each person in the stands called out their wagered choice. "It seems that nobody here has a definitive answer, so instead, let us turn to the Divines! Glorious Yamaria, we entreat thee! Shine thine glory upon your chosen victor!" Yoggwin glanced once at each combatant and spoke so that only they could hear. "Fight with skill, dignity, and at least a smidge of honor. Don't forget you have live steel in those hands o' yours. The prize money won't be enough to cover the blood debt!"

Both Leonidas Braveheart and Cynthia Flash-Strike nodded solemnly, and Yoggwin grinned a gap-toothed grin, showing several golden teeth. Then, the Barker vaulted backward into a handspring and landed atop a stone bunker reserved for other combatants. He raised a bejeweled horn to his lips and blew. *Aaaaaaaaoooooooooooooooooo!* Its reverberating cry filled the coliseum, and the battle was on.

"It isn't too late to withdraw, Braveheart," Cynthia called from across the stadium.

Leonidas laughed. "A bit early to be offering surrender, don't you think? We've yet to even exchange blows!

"Aye, we've not," Cynthia allowed. "But just give me a moment and..." She didn't deign to finish the sentence. Instead, she crossed and uncrossed her blades, which seemed to jump from her belt to her hands. Then the half-elf crouched and dashed forward. In the span it took Leo to blink twice, the girl was already across the field.

"Hello," she said casually. In a single fluid movement, she brought her twin swords flying up to ring against his, one after another in quick succession. Leo tried to batter her back with his buckler, but Flash-Strike leaped free, leaving the knight overbalanced. In an attempt to recover, his sword gave chase, glancing uselessly against suddenly crossed twin swords. By the end of the first exchange, neither had landed a hit, and the playing field was still level. Yoggwin was saying something in the background, but Leo had already tuned him out, and by the expression on Cynthia's face, she'd done much the same.

Before Leo could even catch his breath, Cynthia was back on the offensive. Surprised by how quickly he'd maneuvered his sword to stop her previous attacks, she aimed for his other side, to test his shield reflexes. Used to using a much heavier shield of iron and oak, rather than the leather and wood affair they'd provided him, Leonidas didn't disappoint. Her swords delivered a flurry of kisses to his buckler. Though the touches were light, the twin short swords were sharp and bit into the leather, scratching against the pinewood frame. The knight knew that too many of those would see his shield falling to pieces. He recalled Calimero saying that competitors in the Battlehall loved a bit of banter.

"Flash-Strike indeed!" he said. "You do the Breeze-Dancers proud."

If Cynthia was surprised that he knew about the secretive elite Elven warriors, she didn't show it. "The praise is appreciated, but you're so very wrong if you think you can soften my defenses with sweet words. I'll not be swayed by chivalry, Sir!"

"Were you, I might think you shallow and wanton. My praise was genuine, not born of any guile."

She nodded, a look of approval flashing in her gold-green eyes. Flash-Strike danced forward gracefully, jabbing both swords forward with a corkscrew motion. Leo swept his sword in a horizontal arc, blade pointing towards the floor. The sheer force behind the blow knocked the girl out of line, giving Leonidas time to bring his sword to bear. While his opponent regained her feet, Leo tapped the flat of the long sword against her side. "First strike is mine, Flash-Strike."

"Aye," she said with a mischievous grin. "I hope it was worth it. That may be the only one you get!"

Sister swords walked up the edge of his blade and back down again, playing the weapon like an instrument.

Cynthia followed by dancing backward. Leonidas dashed in pursuit, but the half-elf drew a knife from her belt, and launched it, pommel first, at his legs. Leo dodged the stiletto, quick as it was, but he landed wrong on one foot, thrown into a sudden tumble. His sword went skittering across the dirt, coming to a stop at Cynthia's feet. Leonidas half expected the girl to run up and claim her victory then and there, but to his surprise, she let him rise, and then kicked his sword back to him. "A fine weapon that is. Does it have a name?"

"Not as yet," he answered. "It was made for me by a friend. The same friend who made this armor. Perhaps I'll ask her to name it when next I see her." *If I ever see Caitrial again.*

"I can see in your eyes; you wonder why I haven't yet been crowned victor of this fight when the opportunity was open to me. Valias Battlehall is a place of honor," Cynthia explained. "As far as I'm concerned, there is no honor in striking an enemy who can't rightly defend themselves."

"There is honor in you," Leo said. "A pleasant surprise, since I've heard gladiators love their dirty tricks."

"Fighting dirty is for outlaws and assassins," Cynthia spat," and we have far too many of those about as it is."

"With that sentiment, I feel we can all agree. But come, the audience isn't here to see us participate in genial palaver. Let us conclude this fight."

Both warriors squared their feet again, and Leonidas once again moved to close the space between them. Cynthia flicked the other dagger, this time towards his head, but this time, Leo anticipated it, throwing himself into a forward roll. Flash-Strike jabbed one sword forward, but Leonidas thrust his shield forward to match it. For once, he was glad for the relative weakness of his buckler, as the blade bit deep into the material and stuck there. The knight brought his long sword to bear and halted her second attack before it began. Gently pivoting to lay the edge against Cynthia's neck, he said simply. "Yield."

"It would seem that you have me beat, Sir knight," Cynthia flashed a painfully dazzling smile, and Leo found the image of

Emery kissing him under the gazebo, forcing itself to the forefront. "I suppose I should just yield to you and accept my loss."

What game is she playing? Leo wondered, putting more pressure on his shield arm.

"Oh, don't you worry," she smirked. "That sword isn't going anywhere. This one, though..." Before Leonidas could hope to react, Cynthia Flash-Strike dropped her legs out from under her, leaving her sword jammed in his buckler. When she straightened out again, she stood inside the ring of his arms, and her second blade was pressed against his throat. "Yield," she said with a smirk. Then she leaned in and whispered something in the knight's ear.

Stunned, Leonidas couldn't answer for a moment. He felt a fat drop of blood roll down his neck, took a deep breath, stepped back, and dropped his sword.

Then Leonidas Braveheart laughed.

CAITRIAL

Caitrial Rainclaw felt empty. In the dark tunnel that led underneath Searstar, the three walked silently, unable to speak for the sake of their lives. Seeing Reyna die had been horrible enough, but now that the adrenaline from the battle was gone, she was left with nothing but her thoughts and memories. She cursed herself for ever relaxing her grip on Reyna. As if she could read minds, Arcadia suddenly slipped a bony hand into hers.

"It's not your fault, sis," she assured bitterly. "It's Geurus's."

Cait knew her sister couldn't see her nod, but the smith didn't trust herself not to break down if she opened her mouth. They had to keep walking.

The two sisters were too shell-shocked to eat, but Jasqua didn't let that excuse fly. "You two are going to eat if I have to shove the rations down your throats! Much as I want that sword of yours, Rainclaw, I didn't escape from that city with you to watch you curl up and die of grief so I can take it!" The ranger stumbled forward until she could pat the smith on the back. "This is our chance to get out and gather some more allies. Our first stop'll be the Kindol Woods. I can rally the Elven folk there; then we can decide where to go next. Gardstar will pay for what he's done today, and all the days before. You know, if we're lucky, we might even run into your Leonidas out there."

Caitrial recalled the warmth of Leonidas's embrace, the comfort and support encircling her that last day they'd seen each other. *I would kill for another hug like that. I think I already have.* That brought to mind the horrific scream those Enforcers had given out when struck. When she asked the ranger about it, she could almost hear Jasqua's brain working.

"Aye, it wasn't anything like any voice I've heard before. Even the Khindre I used to hunt didn't sound like no screaming demon! No offense meant, of course."

"None taken," Arcadia mumbled. "Maybe one of your long-lived elves will have an answer. The only thing longer than an elf's life is their memory."

"Maybe," Jasqua said. "Come, we'd best hasten our flight. Without the sun, I can't tell how long we've been walking, but I'd rather be long gone if Geurus has some foul tracking magic to complement his human domination spells." She let out a long breath. "Buggering magic. Makes me wonder if the slimy creature used some to make Godfrey love him so much. I mean, our old king wasn't the most sensible man, but I'd like to imagine he had enough wits about him to see the venom in the Luney's eyes."

"You're giving him too much credit," Arcadia said acidly. "Emery was the smart one. Emery didn't trust Geurus, but Godfrey loved the big army and the money Geurus claimed to have at his disposal, so the marriage, and the slaughter, went ahead."

Jasqua didn't have an answer to that, so the three went on in silence, their thoughts on those they'd lost. Reyna and Grayson, freshest and most painful of all, but Godfrey, Lysaria, and Emery present as well. The two twins also counted their parents among the number. Perhaps they weren't dead, but they'd switched allegiance to Geurus's side quick enough.

Caitrial couldn't help wondering whether Geurus would kill them now that Reyna was dead and their other two children escaped. Though Sardan and Cos had sold them out to the enemy, Caitrial dreaded and feared the thought. *They are still my parents, and Arcadia's too, much as they'd like to forget it.*

As Briskelthiar and Thraedan had promised, the tunnel deposited the refugees on the Sunne Steps. Jasqua knew within the hour where they were, and over dinner, made from a block o' stew the master smiths had placed in each pack, she plotted a course that would lead them to the Outskirts of Kindol Woods with only a few days of travel.

"I'm glad you aren't some armor-wearing hulk," Jasqua said approvingly, looking at Caitrial's leather armor and sturdy armorer's cloak. "No offense to Sir Leonidas, or your handiwork, but it's near impossible to keep a fully armored knight hidden. According to the villagers, goblins are thick as thieves around these parts. Much as I want to cut the head off of their little incursion, I'm not risking anything else right now. We've had more than enough death."

So it was that three days of hard travel later, they stood just outside the sentinel trees of Kindol Woods. The trunks stretched gray-brown and sheer above them. Jasqua pointed to the boughs. "Don't you doubt we're being watched even now." She squinted then cupped her hand alongside her mouth. "Porvahl, that you? Get down here, you sorry son of a ferret! It's Jasqua, with guests, claiming the Ranger's Right!"

Caitrial didn't see anyone, but for some reason, she wasn't surprised when a slender figure dressed in shades of gray and green appeared right next to them.

"Pipe down, Ranger Jasqua. Your volume is like to harm our fragile ears."

"Fragile? As if !" Jasqua snorted. "I often had to yell at you to get you down from those trees when I had a question."

"Yes, you did often yell," the one called Porvahl said in a voice that sounded flat and emotionless. But after working with an elf for so many years, Caitrial could hear a playful tone buried within. "But my failure to listen to you had nothing to do with my having damaged ears, merely my having no desire to listen to your drivel any longer."

"You're a real charmer, Porvahl," Jasqua drawled. "How is your wife doing? Have you managed to drive her away with that tongue of yours yet?"

"In fact, I haven't. We'll be having our second child before season's end."

Jasqua started to reply, but Caitrial cut her off.

"I apologize on behalf of the rudeness of my companion, and for the intrusion," she said in Elvish, "but we needs must take refuge in your forest. We have traveled quite a long way, and would appreciate any succor we could receive from you."

Porvahl turned to look at her and blinked slowly. "You see, Jasqua," he said, "this is how one addresses an elf properly: In their home-tongue and with respect. Your companion seems to have grasped some manner of courtesy, and should you wish to enter our forest, you might wish to follow her lead."

"Peh," was all Jasqua said.

"As much as I appreciate your courtesy, lady," Porvahl said, returning to Elvish to address her. "I haven't the authority to allow a traveler in and out. Seeing as you travel with such an unorthodox companion," Porvahl shifted his eyes over to Arcadia. "I doubt I can be of any assistance."

Caitrial felt a surge of anger. She hadn't come all this way and lost a sister just to be denied entry to Kindol Woods just because her sister was a Khindre!

A bitter reply was burning on her lips when another Elvish voice saved her. "Be not so wary, Porvahl of the Swinging Vine," it cried from the tree branches. "They are to be allowed in!"

"By whose orders? The Lord Valyaara would dare not give that sort of command, especially to one of the Hell-Blooded! You know this as I do, Cassius of the Fountain Town."

"You speak truly. The Lord has given no decrees of the sort; he hasn't left his abode since word came from Solgaele about his son. But there is another who sent word ahead. The *Lithire Beyrdensi* has vouched for them. We are to give them every comfort and protection until he arrives. It should be less than two weeks, he claims."

Caitrial didn't know who this *Lithire Beyrdensi* was, but hearing the name caused Porvahl to drop his chin into a hand. After a moment, he removed it and gave a barely perceptible nod. "It is I who should be apologizing for discourteousness. I have wronged you and your companion, and I hope you can see it in your heart of hearts to forgive a suspicious elf."

"Your transgression is already forgotten," Caitrial said kindly in the Elvish manner.

"The lady graces this one with her kindness." Porvahl once more returned to the common tongue. "I welcome you, Ranger Jasqua, and your guests to our leafy halls. May the Queen of Sunlight watch over you as you walk among our boughs."

They were led into the city through some form of druidic magic, cast by the one Porvahl had called Cassius. He spoke a few words and kissed a tree lightly. Moments later, they heard a soft giggle, and the trunk opened up like a mouth, the wood warping and folding back, and sharp splinters folding inward like an opening gate. A black tunnel stood in front of them, and Cassius, Porvahl, and Jasqua strode in without hesitation. Caitrial and Arcadia shared a look, and the Khindre shrugged. The two stepped forward as well. No sooner had their feet crossed the boundary of shadow than the sisters were gliding along at a shockingly fast rate. They were propelled along the root system, a twisting and dark path. After a few moments in darkness, though for Caitrial it seemed far longer, they sprung to a halt, and a light appeared, peeking through a crack at first, and then suddenly flooding over them, as another tree opened up to reveal Mirshiall.

At first, Caitrial saw nothing, just logs and a few piles of leaves, but once they stepped from the tree and allowed their minds to adjust to their new surroundings, everything changed. The two sisters watched in wonderment as the piles of leaves turned into houses, a deadfall tree shift and warp into a table, set for a feast, and what Caitrial had believed were giant bird nests in the canopy became the abodes of all the elves of Mirshiall, the Elven city.

As Cassius had claimed, they were given every comfort they could imagine during their short stay. Once they finished ogling at the sights, the half-elf, who wore the blue and green robes of the druids, led them to a natural spring where they could bathe and wash their clothes. He touched the water, said a few words, and before their eyes, a veil of steam rose from the pool.

"It should be warm enough for your pleasure, ladies," Cassius said with a bow. "Should you find you need anything, just give this bell," he handed Caitrial a bell made of bone, wood, and an acorn which inexplicably trilled like a bird when shaken, "a ring, and I shall come to your aid."

After sunfall, they supped with a host of humans, half-elves, and other druids at the table. Cassius was there to describe the myriad of dishes, all Elven in design. "*Pithri* is a river trout filet rolled in smoked acorns and fresh herbs from the treetop garden. In this bowl here, you will find *Mersiika* sauce, beware, the first taste may seem sweet, but let it rest on your tongue, and it will become as fiery as the *Keshel,* which the folk of the Scorched Waste enjoy." Caitrial didn't know what *Keshel* was, but Cassius hadn't lied about the spice. It felt as if someone had lit a fire on her tongue, and then poured leftover cooking grease on it, for an extra flare. She washed it down with a strange, mildly sweet blue drink Cassius called *Emidew* and several spherical pastry puffs, light and filled with honey and herb butter.

Though everything the sisters needed was provided to them on the forest floor, Caitrial was curious about what waited above them.

"That's somewhat you'll likely never see. Your courtesy and fluency in the elvish tongue won your way into Lower Mirshiall, but the Upper City is kept private for the elves and those they deem worthy."

"What about you? They seem to like you well enough," Arcadia wondered.

"I won my way into their hearts through magic and by association with my mother. However, I prefer to stay down here, on the floor. I was raised in a ground city, Fondaine, where few elves lived. So this style is more to my liking. Besides, humans are less likely to give a haughty sniff at a half-elf than full-blooded elves are."

Caitrial liked Cassius. He had a good look to him, kept himself clean. Good eyes too, honest eyes. He played the part of the gracious host with aplomb, allowing her and Arcadia to stay in the house he shared with his mother, a kindly Elven druid, and leaving them wanting for nothing.

But more important than anything, unlike all the other druids and forest folk, Cassius didn't avoid Arcadia. Since cursing Geurus in the tunnel, her Khindre sister hadn't spoken a single word, and Caitrial was growing worried. Though she wasn't privy to the content, she knew that Arcadia was conversing with the half-elf druid. And once, while working in the forge—shaping Suulsurr iron, which Briskelthiar had introduced to her a lifetime ago—she heard a strange sound shock through the forest. It was grating and rough, and yet still somewhat familiar. *Divines, that was Arcadia's laugh! That half-elf made her laugh; after all she's been through!* The smith couldn't believe it, but it was a pleased sort of disbelief.

At the end of the promised two weeks, Caitrial finally learned who *Lithire Beyrdensi* was. She was displaying the cythwai to Cassius and Arcadia at the time. "When I so much as nicked them with the blade, the Enforcers let out this goddessawful screech. It pierced their armor like it wasn't even there! I don't know why."

"Dark-bloods can't stand such a brilliant red color. Too much in contrast with their shadowy mantles," came an excited voice from behind them. They all turned to see Vedalken Nairvebyen and his rust-red unicorn mount, Calimero.

"What my friend means to say," Vedalken explained with a sigh, dismounting, "is that you wield a weapon made of Kerazar steel. The innate magic—Fyroxi claim the ore is blessed by Yamaria herself—within the material is lethal to demons."

"Demons?" Caitrial knew the stories about the days before the Black Dawn as well as anyone else. Of horrid monsters running rampant, spreading death and disease all over the world. But on the Black Dawn, powerful priests, with the aid of angels that supposedly resided in palaces above the clouds, repelled the demons from the world, trapping them in a faraway realm. Apparently, they could never return, not without outside aid.

When Caitrial said as much to Vedalken, he nodded gravely. "Though I can't claim to know how, it is clear that demons have made their way here to Sun's Reach. Mayhap it was Geurus, or else his arrival is a consequence. Or vise versa."

"Perhaps the priests and angels didn't do quite as good a job sealing the portals as they thought," Calimero remarked.

"Quiet." Vedalken crossed to the unicorn's side, removing a halberd head from a case hung there. It was made of the same translucent red steel as the cythwai. "Truthfully, Calimero could be correct," the Lightstrider admitted. "I have no evidence to deny such a claim, save that demons are not patient creatures. If something weren't withholding them, they'd have their claws and teeth embattled with our blades and spears even now. No, I believe that these demons—and the Enforcers are indeed demons—were led into this world, and then here to Sun's Reach. I've learned very little about this particular class of demons, but I can tell you one thing: they are a rather weak variety— demonic spirits bound to suits of armor rather than true demons."

"And you'd best be thankful for that!" Calimero exclaimed. "There aren't near enough Kerazar weapons or unicorns around to save Sun's Reach should true demons wake from their slumber!"

"But enough talk of fear for now. You hold an essential key in that cythwai. The Chillfang, under Geurus's command, took Fyrestone, where a vast arsenal of Kerazar weapons is stored. Only our armaments, one spear in the Scorched Waste, and a few other scattered pieces remain in public knowledge." Vedalken whistled, and two horses trotted from between the trees. "Wielding that weapon, and having sorcerer sisters, gives you a place in the saving of this kingdom alongside my fellow Lighstriders, a few hundred volunteers, and Leonidas Braveheart."

Caitrial felt a sudden rush of relief. Leo was still alive! "Any news of Sir Leonidas?" she asked

Vedalken smiled. "I just came from his side. He is alive and well, and just recently reconnected with a fair-sized contingent of Redwyn foot-soldiers and knights that will be crucial to our plans."

"Then, he is safe?" Cait wanted to know.

"Yes," Calimero scuffed the dirt with a hoof and tossed his mane vainly. "Don't tell him, but before we met up with our brave knight, we shadowed him. Our valiant friend had quite a few tails—the kind with sun-bronzed skin, scorpion tattoos, and poisoned knives."

"Quell your heart, dear smith," Vedalken said to allay her fears. "Leonidas never saw them. When you two are reunited, he should be fully equipped with hammer, sword, armor, and all the body parts you recall."

"If he can keep himself out of trouble without the fabled *Lithire Beyrdensi* around to protect him!" Calimero tossed his head vainly.

Vedalken, meanwhile, rubbed at his temples. "I abhor that name."

"What's it mean?" Arcadia asked.

"*Illustrious Sunsworn*," he replied. "It makes me sound like some sort of prophet or divine agent."

"Yes, he's *only* a hero of legendary proportions, undefeated for nigh on 500 years! We don't understand why you folk can't tell the difference," Calimero snorted sarcastically.

"But we've gone off track," Vedalken cut in. "We must get on the road. You and your sister are needed, Caitrial."

"Where are we going?" Caitrial wanted to know.

The elf put a foot in his stirrup and fluidly raised himself into the saddle. "You'll learn when we arrive. Half the fun of a journey is finding the destination. Now, make haste, afore the day grows too old."

As they rode, Caitrial grilled Vedalken on Leonidas. She wanted to know what had happened to her dear friend. At first, he was reluctant to speak, but after she hectored him enough, he finally cracked.

"You are near as stubborn as Thraedan, that bearded dog!" The Lightstrider barked. "Leonidas, as we have assured, is unharmed. I left him at the Valias Battlehall after receiving word from Cassius, who, in turn, heard from Jasqua that you and your sorceress sister had escaped Searstar. He is now preparing with one Lady Cynthia Galladiir, the daughter of the previous leader of Redhawk.

"Some three years ago, there came an attack on the city. The Lady and Lord Galadiir were slain by a man, Valtahl, the Blood Knight. Ilyana, the firstborn of the twin daughters, was forced to marry Valtahl, which stopped the bloodshed. At least it did for a time. Shortly after the Redwyn Massacre, the battle rekindled. The folk within fought bravely and honorably, but recently, Ilyana has sent reports that her folk are sorely contested. She claims to have come across smoking corpses and bodies flung and torn in a way no ordinary man can."

"Why hasn't Valtahl slain Ilyana?" Arcadia queried.

"Good question. I've wondered that myself," Vedalken rubbed his smooth, pointed chin. "Honestly, we can only hope that this is indeed the case that Valtahl isn't just using this as a ploy to draw us in. This Blood Knight is a cunning foe. I've been chasing a Khindre of this name for nigh on a century. Whether it is the same man, I could not tell you, but he almost always slips away afore my spear can find his heart. I once took him in the kidney and left him bleeding heavily from several other wounds. The combination should have proved fatal, but his body was never found. A year later, I heard reports that Valtahl had pillaged a string of villages too small to have names on the fringe of the Scorched Waste."

"You hope to slay him once and for all," Caitrial stated.

"I hope this battle will give me the chance to finish this centuries-long rivalry, yes. The Blood Knight and whatever forces he has within will be sorely pressed. Cynthia has gathered Redwyn men-at-arms led by knights—including Sir Geralm and Sir Espern, old compatriots of Leonidas's—whom Geurus tried to have slain, and would have succeeded had Tinco Anar not seen the column of Enforcers attempting to ambush and slay them. I think we have a chance to deal a great deal of damage to one of Geurus's allies with the men already inside, these warriors, Leonidas, and myself."

"And once we have Redhawk behind us, other settlements may rise against Geurus," Caitrial realized. "This may be just what we need to turn the tide against the usurper Gardstar. So, I ask again, where are we going?"

Vedalken chuckled. "To a vassal town of Redhawk," he answered cryptically and would say no more.

The next day, they finally arrived. Caitrial knew by the sign hanging on the wooden arch around the wall-less town. *Morndale, a community of farmers, fishers, and friends,* it read.

"This is Leo's hometown!" she exclaimed, ecstatic. She'd hoped to visit someday. Of course, she'd always imagined she'd be with Leonidas and both her sisters, rather than a Lightstrider, and with one sister at her eternal rest at the bottom of a magical moat, but it was exciting all the same. The area seemed removed from the greater struggle of Sun's Reach. No blood stained the walls, no trenches lined the ground, save the irrigation canals. The air was fresh, with a hint of smoke from a cookfire, carrying the aroma of mutton stew from a cauldron in the town square. Men and women alike were at work in the fields and with animals. As the three passed, the denizens of Morndale waved and smiled welcomingly. They trotted through the town until they reached a simple wooden house. A wagon wheel set on the door had a sign across it that read: The Wainwright family welcomes you!" She glanced back at Vedalken, who just nodded and pantomimed knocking.

Curiously, Caitrial walked to the door and knocked. A few moments later, the door swung open. The girl who answered the door couldn't have been more than fifteen. She wore a rough spun tunic that left her long legs and arms bare. Her face was freckled, and her wide smile shone just as brightly in her grey eyes as her white teeth. *Grey eyes just like...* Brown hair hung down to her shoulders, thick and wavy. *Her hair's the same color as...*

Caitrial could hardly find her voice. "Hello," she managed. "My name is Caitrial Rainclaw. I'm a friend of Leonidas."

"My brother isn't home right now to confirm that," the girl said, her smile diminishing a bit. "Hasn't been for years." *She's worried sick,* Caitrial realized. *I would be too, in her position. Still, even with that empathy, the smith couldn't help but be unnerved by the pressure of the Wainwright girl's gaze. She didn't have the information this girl craved, which was a painful realization. We're in the same boat, yet unable, or unwilling, to reach out to each other. Together, but alone.* That weight momentarily lifted from Caitrial's chest as those unnervingly familiar grey eyes migrated from her to the other members of the party. The girl's head cocked curiously to the side when those eyes encountered Arcadia. But her gaze wasn't full of judgment. It was heartening to see that Leo's lack of prejudice was shared by his sister. After ogling at Arcadia for several seconds, she moved on to Vedalken, and there a shift occurred. It started as a dull spark of recognition that quickly evolved into a simmer of low fear. "Usually when a man's commanding officer shows up at the door...it doesn't portend good tidings. Please," she begged, clasping her hands in front of her chest. "Please tell me you don't bring bad news, Lightstrider!"

Vedalken shook his head, Calimero mimicking the motion. "Put your worries to bed, dear girl. Though not all the news we carry is pleasant, none of the darkest tidings pertain to your brother." He smiled gently. "In fact, your brother is doing quite well for himself."

Leo's sister sighed in relief, and then bowed her head briefly. When she raised it again, a pretty smile had plastered itself to her face. "If that's the case, and the illustrious Lightstrider says it's alright, then I think I can trust you. Leo would probably scold me if I left his known mentor and alleged friend on the stoop, though I wish he'd come to introduce you himself !" She thrust out a hand, which Caitrial accepted gladly. "The name's Melody! Please, come in, and tell me all you can of my brother. I can put some tea on the fire, if that'll be to your liking."

As Caitrial and Melody walked through Morndale several days later, the air rang with a cacophony of sounds—the sounds that came with preparation for war. In the town square, where an enormous pot of mutton stew had simmered when Caitrial arrived, a less appealing scent wafted. Ranks of sweaty men, farmhands young and old, and any other with the desire and grit in their hearts, trained with spears under the watchful eyes of Vedalken and Calimero. Caitrial could hear the familiar sound of metal slamming against metal and the *whoosh* of bellows from the smithy, where the spearheads were being manufactured. Caitrial spent most of her time there, working whenever possible. As the smiths told her day in and day out, her experience was much appreciated. It was nice to work with basic iron again after practicing with exotic ores like Suulsurr and Kerazar for so long.

When not at the smithy or doing her own training with

Vedalken to master the cythwai, Caitrial talked with Melody. Leonidas's sister shared not only his eye and hair color but his innate sense of honor. She believed in doing what was right by folk and often delivered meals to the workers, or refilled their water buckets without being asked. "During times of need, people need to step up, you know," she said once while they fished for supper. "Tara taught me that—Leonidas's old wife. I was young when she died, but I miss her. I'll never forget the day it happened. Leonidas had always believed in drinking water from the river, rather than the wells. *You never know what can make its way down that hole.'* When he was young, he'd been drawing water, and pulled up a waterlogged opossum that must have fallen in and drowned. He ever mistrusted the well water after that."

Caitrial had to chuckle, thinking of Leonidas running to his parents holding the dripping, furry creature. "One day," Melody continued, "Leonidas was out at a build, an outpost shack, ironically enough. Bandits usually overlooked Morndale, but one evening, after sunfall, they must have decided to taste what little we had. They snuck in and poisoned the wells first. Tara had long followed Leonidas's lead in drinking from the river, but that day..." Caitrial put a supportive arm around Melody's shoulders, and she stifled a sob. The girl smiled sadly at her. "Tara was pregnant with Lee's baby, though she was only starting to show a bump. True to tradition, though, Tara kept working on the farm, adamant not to rest until it became dangerous for the baby or her health. Working the farm is thirsty work, and she didn't feel like walking to the river, so she snatched a drink from the well.

It happened the next day, around suppertime, I recall it keenly as my first kiss. She laughed at some lame joke Leonidas had made, but then her expression soured, and she put her hands to her tummy. Her face went pale, and by the calls for a healer ringing across the town, she wasn't the only one. She fell from her chair, and Lee ran to her. The poison took Tara and her little baby as my brother cradled her in his arms. Her last words were *'above all else, my love, know forgiveness, and don't deny yourself joy.'* Then, as the sun began to fall, the bandits came in to take advantage of the sickness they caused. I've never seen Lee grow so angry. After finally laying his dead wife down, he snatched the wood axe from the closet and gave them what for. From what I heard, he had the bandits routing before they could light any of the houses aflame, as they'd planned. Lee was never the same after that. He left the town shortly after." She pointed at a half-built house barely visible from their vantage point. "He'd been building that one there for their family. Couldn't bear the sight of it, I s'pose. Nobody's had the gall to knock it down or complete it, so it became a memorial of sorts." Melody was freely crying now, and Caitrial with her. She couldn't imagine being Leonidas in that scenario. To lose your wife and child, and then later the princess you swore to protect, it was worse than awful. The smith couldn't even find a fitting word to put to it.

One day, Caitrial and Melody were walking back from the river, the girl carrying a full bucket of water. She proudly asserted that she'd made the bucket herself. A shaggy old greyhound panted at her heels—Ronnet, the family pet. As they passed the edge of town, defined by a worn path in the dirt where the sentries walked, Ronnet perked up and turned back the way they had come.

"What's wrong, old boy?" The dog barked in reply. Melody squinted to get a better view. As Cait watched, the bucket fell to the ground, forgotten, the water spilling out to be absorbed by the earth. Before the woman could ask what she'd seen, Melody took off at a run. Cait jogged after her and came to a standstill to watch Melody throw herself into the arms of a man coming down the path. The man wore a huge smile as his sister buried her face in his gilded breastplate. "Lee!" she heard Melody cry.

Leonidas. Seeing the knight, still clad in her armor, Caitrial felt a surge of something in her chest. She couldn't quite define it, a warmth, and a sense of excitement, all at once. After a long moment, Leo let Melody down and turned back towards town to see her. His smile widened even more, and he strolled over. Caitrial numbly walked to meet him.

"Fare thee well, Lady Rainclaw?" he asked, as per tradition.

All at once, tears sprang into her eyes, and she began to shake. She stepped forward into the circle of the big knight's arms and rested her head on his shoulder. "I'm better now, Leonidas," she breathed into his neck. Leo tightened his embrace around her. She could feel a few dents and scratches she would need to repair, and wondered how he'd gotten them. *Fighting monsters and bandits, I don't doubt.*

"Divines, it's been so long," he said, running an ungauntleted hand through her cinnamon-colored hair. "I can't imagine what you've seen, to drive you all the way here."

"Doesn't matter," she answered. "You are here now. That makes things a bit better, at least. Now, be quiet. I just...just want to savor this, all right?" It was strange, but being enfolded in Leonidas's arms like this just felt...right. It was a natural, comforting feeling, like being back at the smithy with Briskelthiar and Thraedan, and yet better than that at the same time.

They stood like that for several long moments, though it could have been hours for all Caitrial was concerned. Finally, Leo pulled away and looked her in the eyes. "We have so much to catch up on and discuss. Allow me to get out of my armor and bathe; then we'll talk."

Caitrial let go of him and watched him walk back towards his old home. After a few moments, she was aware of Melody studying her. She cocked her head at the girl.

Melody took a deep breath and looked Caitrial directly in the eye. "Do you love my brother?"

The sudden question took Caitrial aback, but she knew in her heart of hearts there was only one answer. "Yes," she said simply.

Melody nodded, and Caitrial held her breath, wondering what Leo's sister would say. Much to her relief, Melody grinned.

"Good. I like you, Caitrial Rainclaw," she said. "I think you'd make a wonderful kin-sister."

ARCADIA

A POINT GAINED

The Khindre woke at the barest indication of a shake. Her heterochromatic eyes blinked open to see her sister leaning over her bed. Arcadia lifted an eyebrow in silent question, and Cait nodded. The day had come. Arcadia had known it wouldn't be long after Leonidas had returned. Her stomach was in knots, but the girl was damned if she'd let anyone know. She was their sorceress, and Vedalken said she'd have a critical job. *Lady Ilyana's found bodies damaged in a way that no conventional method could explain. Vedalken believed the deaths had something to do with magic, and I agree with him.* The Lightstrider had taught her a few useful spells during their stay in Morndale, all of which she'd need.

The sun still hadn't risen completely when she and Caitrial met Vedalken and Leonidas outside. *The bloody town isn't even awake, yet here we are.* Unbidden, a memory popped into her head. Shortly after Reyna's accident when they were young, the three sisters had sat up on the roof of Cynderstone Brewery, watching the sunrise. They'd all been yawning like they hadn't slept in days, but still, they managed to give the spectacle all the attention it deserved. The sky had been the same color as Reyna's skin for a time, and the glitter in her twin's eyes had put a smile on Arcadia's face. That had been the first smile she'd had since the incident, and it had felt strange.

Now she wore her customary frown, made deeper by the remembrance of her sister. Vedalken, striking and gallant upon his unicorn, spoke a few words. Arcadia's horse stirred underneath her, and all around, the horses did the same.

"We've not any time to waste," the elf explained. "Thus, I've taken the liberty of imbuing your mounts with the *zephyr's gift.*"

"Now, they can all run as fast as me!" Calimero exclaimed. "The last one to the rally point is a moldy orange!" He reared and bolted off, with the other three close on his tail. It almost didn't feel like they were riding off to battle, where any one of them could take a grievous wound, or die. *Don't think about Grayson or Reyna,* Arcadia told herself. *They need you to find out who's using magic in there. And they need you to kill Enforcers. It won't feel quite as good as giving it to Geurus will, but it'll be close enough.*

They arrived at Redhawk in record time, thanks entirely to the *zephyr's gift.* From the outside, it still looked like your average, run-of-the-mill city, with its walls, towers, and central castle. *Not even half the size of Emery's castle,* Arcadia thought.

They were met at the rally point by Cynthia Galladiir, dressed in battle-leathers, not unlike Caitrial's. Her sister's were studded with knuckle sized metal bolts, though, for added stability and defense. Cynthia also didn't have Caitrial's heavy leather cloak that protected her against arrows. *And all those bright colors sure make a tempting target.* Arcadia could see what Leonidas meant when he said the gladiator woman reminded him of Em. However, Arcadia thought that comparing Emery Redwyn to any flaunting scrapper like this half-elf was a grave insult.

They settled in a vast silo with a stone floor. The farmer who owned it had been forced to give all his grain to Valtahl to feed his people. The Khindre had only paid the man a pittance, and he was rightfully angry. Angry enough to hole up a few hundred enemies of the Blood Knight.

"Valtahl must have received our note of challenge," said the lance wielder with green dragon adornments, whom Cynthia identified as her husband, Lancallius. "And he reacted just as we should have expected from a cowardly bandit like the Blood Knight. The gates to Redhawk were closed, and our druids have seen his men lining the streets in their scouting flights." The people around Arcadia started murmuring to each other. She couldn't make out any particular words, but they all sounded worried. This Lancallius also must have heard the fear. He brought the lance spinning from his back and slammed the pommel on the ground, thrice in quick succession. *Crack! Crack! Crack!* "Quiet, you lot! We have no time for your hemming and hawing. We have planned our attack, and we will proceed as planned. I know many of you are men-at-arms, used to traditional battle, but our foe is fittingly not traditional either. Valtahl, the Blood Knight, has been menacing the populace of Sun's Reach for centuries, and he will be cunning. Doubtlessly, there will be traps and secrets waiting in that city. We need every advantage we can get. If we cannot draw him out to the field, we must take his army unawares." The white-blonde haired elf gestured, and several figures stepped out from behind them. "Myself, my wife, and Sirs Leonidas, Geralm, and Espern will serve as your commanders for this operation. You will follow our commands as in war-time protocol. Am I understood?" Half a thousand voices rang out their consent. "Good. Now, I turn you over to one of our druids, who will be detailing our plan for getting inside."

Arcadia sighed as the druid in question stepped out from the crowd. He had mousy brown hair, bright eyes of a similar hue, and a sparse beard sprouting from his chin. *Who invited him?* Arcadia was surprised at the negativity in her conscience's voice. She genuinely liked Cassius. *I can count the number of people I can define in that way on one hand and still have fingers to spare.* Maybe it wasn't that she didn't want to see the young man, but that she was worried and afraid. Friends had been dropping like flies recently, and she didn't want to learn that Cassius had charged into battle and gotten himself skewered on some Enforcer's spear.

"At great risk to herself," Cassius began, "Ilyana has informed us of several points of entry we could use to make our strike. My fellow druids and I have scouted several of them, and, much to our chagrin, the most secure route is through the sewers."

"Of course it is," Arcadia heard herself saying. "Why can it never be the butterfly gardens?"

Lancallius turned a sharp, baleful glare upon her as a wave of tense laughter rolled through the warriors. Cassius patted his shoulder. "Let them have their laughs. You ask them to run to their possible deaths at the hands of creatures from before the Black Dawn." He smiled at Arcadia, which reminded her of Reyna's radiant white grin. "It's only right that we try to drum up a bit of morale before the fight."

Lancallius grunted and motioned for Cassius to continue.

"Our resident sorceress speaks for all of us, I believe," he said. "Redhawk is possessed of a rather fabulous hedge maze, but Valtahl keeps it under heavy guard for some reason." Arcadia suddenly remembered a garden with sizeable hedges, then a flash of blue-white pain. *"Ilyana's found smoking corpses, and bodies flung in torn in a way no ordinary man could manage."* She shuddered. The image of that...thing talking to Geurus still haunted her dreams to this day. *"Hello, little sorceress."* It had known what powers she possessed, though she was still no closer to figuring out who or what Deadvoice was. Geurus had magic of some sort. Both

Grayson and Reyna had said so before their deaths, and Vedalken had confirmed that the Enforcers were demons. What if Deadvoice had something to do with it? Vedalken had even noted that Valtahl had been evading him for centuries. If it was the same man, not just several bandits taking his name and armor, there was something wrong. Save being murdered by evil kings, Khindre only lived a scant few years longer than humans. Arcadia had a horrible feeling in the pit of her stomach. *Don't jump to conclusions, fool girl.*

She realized Cassius wasn't talking anymore. Now it was Sir Geralm, an older knight, long past his athletic prime, possessed of thick, ropy whiskers hanging from just the very bottom of his chin. *I've never seen a beard so ridiculous.* "...Five groups," he was saying. "Lancallius and Cynthia will lead the first, taking a select group of men underneath the moat and to the castle. Valtahl has drained the waterway and filled it with spikes. Their goal will be to soften up the castle defenses and rescue Lady Ilyana from her tower. Sir Espern and myself will lead two groups, splitting the archers and druids amongst us, on either side of the city. We'll come in through the aqueducts and take as many of the Enforcers running for the castle as possible. Sir Leonidas will receive the remaining men and come up near the front of the city. They will take care of any stragglers, make sure nobody escapes, and then meet up with us to leave the Enforcers between a rock and a battalion of hard places."

"That's only four groups," Caitrial pointed out. "What about the last one?"

"Very astute, Caitrial," Vedalken said. "The last group has a very specific goal. It is better if fewer people know about it, in case the demons have some way of reading our thoughts, unlikely though that is. But you may ask your sister for more details."

Leonidas nodded at Cait to reassure her, then turned back to the rest of the group. "We have our orders and our enemy. Now is the time we begin the return of our kingdom from the hands of Geurus and his demonic compatriots. With me, everybody! Fight, in the name of Emery Redwyn, and for the glory of Yamaria, wonderful Sun Mother!"

The cry was nearly deafening, and Arcadia couldn't help but wonder if the Enforcers could hear it in Redhawk. *Let them feel it. Let them know that their doom is upon them.*

The next few hours went by in a blur for the young sorceress. She could feel her magic furling and curling within her, like a Scorched Waste viper, preparing to strike a fatal blow. At one point, Caitrial came over to comfort her, though it seemed the smith needed the reassurance more. "I'll be fine," she said. "If Cynthia and her husband do their jobs, I shouldn't encounter too many foes. Even if I do, I'll have Cassius and Vedalken with me. Worry about yourself. I didn't give you my blessing so that you could die before you told Leo how you feel." Arcadia allowed her sister to see one of her scarce smiles. During the final hour, she, Cassius, and Vedalken went over their plan. It seemed only a few minutes passed before Sir Leonidas appeared in the doorway to notify them that their time was up. As they headed for the long-abandoned tunnels that led to Redhawk's active sewer system, Arcadia dropped a lingering look upon the big knight. *My sister loves you,* she might have said. *Don't you dare die on her!* But instead, she only waved to the man who had braved Qrakzt's moat to save her life, all those years ago.

The sewers smelled awful. *No surprise there.* The ripe odor made the pieces of cork they'd shoved up their noses useless, leaching through every pore and conceivable space to taint their air. Her footsteps smacked wetly on the slimy stone floor of the dark tunnels. Arcadia glanced back at Cassius, who had his eyes half-lidded in concentration, holding his arms to the sides, palms facing the walls. It was thanks to the druid that they weren't all waist-deep in watered-down piss and other rubbish. Vedalken crept ahead of them, pausing at every noise, be it squeaking mouse, dripping water, or the scuffing of a leather boot from the streets above. Eventually, they reached a rounded area that looked like nothing quite so much as a pot. However, the contents were not anything Arcadia—or any sane person—would find palatable. At the noise of their approach, Arcadia faintly saw little phosphorescent white fish scatter, only moments before they were swept up in Cassius's wave. Pillars of—Arcadia didn't want to think about what it could be—white, brown, and grayish material were calcified to the ceiling, dripping filthy water to the ground. *Splish, splish, splish, splorsh.*

"This should be one of the maintenance entrances," Vedalken explained, pointing to the faint outline of rough stone steps on the outskirts of the room. "Which means we should be nearing the center of the city. Like as not, we are half-way there. The battle should begin at any moment."

As if on cue, the three heard the loud blast of a horn. *Braaaaaaaaaaaaaap! Braaaaaaaaaaaaaaap!* Above them, the clanking of boots signaled their enemies had gone on the move.

"As I expected, this way is a dead-end," Vedalken said after running his hands along the walls. "We'll need to go up and find the next entrance."

Cassius used the tumult from the street-side to release the water he was holding in thrall. Arcadia shivered as the settling torrent slapped at her ankles. She looked back at the half-elf, half out of annoyance, but also to make sure he was holding up. Cassius flashed a smile and a wink her way, only just visible in the light filtering in from the grate. The Khindre rolled her eyes and groaned quietly.

. . .

Topside, the smell was better, but the sound made up for the lack of sensory input. Steel clashed, and men moaned in pain, joined by the cries of those unwitting folk, and the alien howls of Enforcers. All of it bounced off of walls and buildings while Arcadia, Vedalken, and Cassius prowled through the streets and alleyways, following the map Lady Ilyana had sent to them. *She's a brave woman.* Cynthia had told them that her sister still lived in the castle with her vile husband. *Going against your liege lord and husband often ends with your head rolling, especially if your husband is someone as volatile as this Valtahl seems to be.*

The aqueduct where Sir Geralm had hidden was visible, and the entrance to the sewers for the noble population of Redhawk was within. As they neared it, a pimply-faced boy, probably no more than a squire by his worn leather armor and dented sword, stepped out, his eyes turning the size of chicken eggs upon seeing them. He started off, nearly as fast as his gangly little legs could take him. The squire rounded the corner with a slithering shadow following him. A moment later, they all heard the cry and the subsequent whimpering as he was dragged back down the street by his ankle. Terror had swelled his eyes to near the size of dinner plates.

"P-please, d-don't kill me," he wailed pitifully.

"You would have gone to the Enforcers, led them over here to kill us," Arcadia argued. "What reason do I have to let you live, knowing that?"

"I-I-I-um." The boy couldn't seem to choke out any words.

Shaking her head in disappointment, Arcadia leaned in, her mismatched eyes boring into his. "Tell me one thing before I decide what to do with you." The miserable cretin was shaking, and Arcadia could smell the telltale odor of piss wafting up from his breeches. *I came up here to get a break from that smell.* She nodded at the aqueduct building. "Are there any guards in the sewer?"

The boy looked confused. Apparently, he'd been too afraid to register the fact that they all smelled like excrement. "The sewers? W-why should there be?"

Arcadia didn't deign to answer, only placed a finger on the bridge of the boy's nose. His face was the same color as his pimples now. "P-please, I gave you your answer...I gave…." He slumped over, motionless, before he could finish his sentence. Arcadia heard a sharp intake of breath from behind her.

"Just sleeping," she explained to a perturbed Cassius. "We have maybe an hour before he wakes and runs to tell the guards about us." The shadow tendril around her captive dragged him to a corner and melted back to its kin. "Let's go."

The noble's sewer smelled much the same as the peasant's sewer. *Fitting, if ironic.* In the hollow, noisome darkness, the sounds from above took on a new, more sinister tone. Even Arcadia had to shiver when they walked under a grate and watched bright red blood leaking down to mingle with the wastewater in the canal below. As they observed, something else slapped wetly against the grill and slid through to the stone. A heart, still pumping feebly, blood expelling from torn tubes with every palpitation. After five or ten beats, it realized there was no more body to feed, and forlornly shuddered to a stop. Arcadia heard Cassius retching behind her and had half a mind to do the same.

Eventually, they arrived at an old wooden ladder, which smelled faintly of cloying herbs. *This will be the place.* Arcadia gestured her friends forward.

Climbing up the rotting ladder proved dangerous, and at one point, Cassius placed his foot on a rung, which broke and sent the half-elf falling into the filthy water below with a loud splash. He siphoned most of the water off of himself with his magic, but the stench remained.

Up the ladder, they went, and through a second and third trapdoor, none of which were locked, fortunately, before they emerged inside the castle walls, as Ilyana had promised.

Now Vedalken took the lead, following the prescribed path Cynthia had drawn from memory. Having lived in the castle for at least a score of years before Valtahl's takeover and her escape, the half-elf provided a reasonably accurate map. Despite their armor and weapons, the servants spared them nary more than a glance as they slipped through their quarters. Again, Ilyana's work. The servants of Redhawk were deathly afraid of Valtahl and would be glad to see him gone.

One mute little maid girl even pointed them in the right direction when they came to a double set of stairs, and Vedalken forgot the way. Given the battle without, the corridors were all empty and eerily silent. They reached the door to the council room without difficulty. A slight push of the door was all it took for Vedalken to tell that it was barred or barricaded. He unslung the halberd from his back, letting the torchlight refract through the magnificent Kerazar head. He pressed the spear tip into the door and gestured for the other two to be ready. He counted down from three on his fingers and whispered a spell. The door suddenly buckled inward on the grain where the halberd was placed, and with a shuddering *boom!* The bisected door and whatever served as a barricade went flying across the room.

No sooner had they seen the foes within than the others went into the throes of spellcasting. Arcadia proved the faster. Though a crossbow bolt skipped against the frame by her head, her concentration didn't falter, and eight hands of shadow rushed from the corners to snatch up a like number of well-dressed nobles.

"Sun's blessing to you, gents," Vedalken said. "I have an audience of sorts with your Lord and master, Valtahl. I would be greatly appreciative if you'd point us in the right direction; it seems I have a bevy of options open to me." Indeed, the round council room had a wealth of doors; all painted the same garish purple color and decorated with the Blood Knight's sigil: a fist squeezing a stone, which dripped blood on a black field. A thick covering of razor-vine stretched across the ceiling from Cassius's magic.

When nobody deigned to answer the Lightstrider, Arcadia gave them a little squeeze for encouragement. All eight hands pointed then, though not all in the same direction. Five hands pointed towards four separate doors, while three others, all currently suspended near each other, pointed towards one door.

Cassius, never one to let a good spell go to waste, maneuvered stinging vines with razor-edged leaves to snake down to each of the doors indicated by the men. The first four doors were trapped. One led to what looked like a bridge over a fathomless pit, and the others spat arrows, sizzling acid, and even fire from hidden slits above the frame.

Cassius nodded with a wry grin and sent a vine to open the last door. This one led to a well-lit corridor, not unlike the one they had come from. After poking around a bit, Cassius deemed it safe.

When Arcadia closed the door behind her, only three living men were left to stand within. *Five is a holy number. Yamaria, hope you like this sacrifice. Do with them what you will. Divines, if I keep this up, I'll sound like a religious zealot!*

Through the corridors and up several sets of stairs, they went, climbing up to the Nesting Tower. According to Ilyana, Valtahl had commandeered the room above the rookery, and nobody was allowed in. Once, when her lord was away on some trip, she'd tried to enter, but found the door locked. None of her attempts had caused the portal to so much as budge. Marcus Kermot, the Loftkeeper, had reported the ravens repeating strange words, but besides that, nobody knew what went on in the room behind the painted window of Firstqueen Solanya and two phoenixes, gold, and silver to represent her father and brother respectively.

The ravens quorked and shuffled within their cages, but naught else seemed to be in there. Arcadia peered out the painted window. Through tinted colors, she could just make out the swarms of people fighting below. She wondered where Caitrial was, and Leonidas. Were they fighting foes side by side now? She hoped they were. *Stay safe, you two.*

I've been a sewer crawler, religious zealot, and mother hen, all in the span of an hour. What excitement this is, this wearing of many hats. Be still my beating heart. They continued their survey of the room, coming up with nothing more than feathers and droppings. But then Arcadia walked underneath one of the larger raven cages. It was huge, large enough to hold five men within comfortably. The birds themselves were freakishly large as well, nearly the size of falcons. When Arcadia approached, one of the ravens—a large white specimen—hopped over.

"Open the portal," it squawked. "Open the portal and drink the sweet nectar within. Fool! Fool! So easily fooled!" Then the raven's speech collapsed into a strange, jumbled muttering. The other two came up beside her to see what she'd found. Arcadia began to explain, but before she got far, the raven turned its large dark eye upon her. When its mouth opened this time, it was not the squawking voice of the raven that came out, but something chillier and dark. "Hello, little sorceress."

Arcadia felt a distinct chill run down her spine. "You let me live; why?"

A bitter laugh emanated out from the raven's beak. "My dear little Khindre. Our plans are unfathomable to petty casters like yourself and your companions." Arcadia shuddered at another triggered memory. *I'm pleasantly surprised. My colleagues and I all expected another failed coup. No offense, of course, but the people of Moonwatch don't have the best record concerning this matter.*

The throaty croak coming from the raven was distinctly different from Deadvoice's, Arcadia realized now. "But, never-mind me, let's talk about you. Come, enter my chambers, and we can talk about why you've barged so rudely into my castle."

"You know why we've come, Valtahl," Vedalken spat. "We're here to slay you."

"Yes, yes, how droll. The heroic Lightstrider steps up to defeat the mercurial outlaw leader. Unfortunately, my doughty little foe, you flirt with matters you should have learned to stay away from." They heard a clanking sound and a cacophony of squawking and wings aflutter as the cage bottom flipped upwards, and a steel ladder came sliding down. In a rather ridiculous display, the white raven shunned its wings, picking its way up the ladder one taloned leg at a time. "Come, my guests, and see the fathoms of your folly."

Arcadia turned to the others when it had gone and disappeared into a dark hole in the ceiling. "I mislike this. From everything you've told me, and some things I've seen, I don't doubt his claims." Turning a suspicious eye upon the other ravens—just because they weren't paying any particular attention to their new guests, didn't mean they weren't listening—she briefly told them about her encounter with Deadvoice. "I'm not saying we shouldn't try to kill him. We must, else everything we've done here will be in vain." *Leonidas and Caitrial will die. Unlike the stories, I doubt they'll get the chance to do so in each other's arms, whispering their love as the lifeblood trickles down into the sewers to await the next rainstorm.*

"That being said..." Cassius said, leadingly when Arcadia went quiet.

"We shouldn't underestimate this Valtahl," the Khindre continued. "What if he is the same bandit you've been chasing for a century, and that's more significant than you think?"

"So we go in there and listen to what he has to say, but as soon as things start smelling fishy, we jump ship," Cassius reasoned. "It's been smooth sailing up to this point, but if the winds of chance turn afoul, and we are sent adrift, I want you two to know it has been a pleasure serving with you."

Arcadia rubbed the bridge of her nose, silently impressed at Cassius's morale. As for herself, Arcadia figured she had one foot in the grave and the other twitching to join it.

The room they climbed into was seated just underneath the roof, and Arcadia could see the concave point where the spire poked into the belly of the sky. Tapestries of dead kings, ancient battles, and heroes, new and old, decorated the walls. One circular section of the floor didn't match the rest of the room, made of an old brownstone, unlike the checkered tiles that covered most of the chambers in the castle. The stone slab was cut and inscribed with strange lines and runes. Valtahl lounged on the far side of the room, his crimson skin flashing dimly in the glowing lanterns set symmetrically around the room. His chair was piled high with more tapestries. The Khindre picked his white teeth with a splinter of bone that Arcadia desperately hoped wasn't from a humanoid. The Blood Knight wasn't just an idle name, according to rumor. Some said Valtahl drank the blood of significant foes he slew. *If he kills us, will he drink our blood, or just Vedalken's?*

Unlike the knights Arcadia knew, Valtahl preferred a set of studded brigantine, blood-red like his skin, the metal's polished white sheen sending flecks of light across the room when he moved. Curling horns, like tightly coiled snakes, tipped with iron stuck out from his shaved head. Tattoos of eyes, ravens, and snakes decorated his arms.

"You've changed your look," Vedalken commented, holding tight to his Kerazar halberd. "I almost didn't recognize you."

The Khindre outlaw rolled eyes of startlingly bright red. *Not the same blue flames as Deadvoice. Could I be wrong about Valtahl?* "No man should content himself with one style of garb for their whole life. It grows dull after a time. Take, for example, *Lithire*

Beyrdensi, yourself. You've worn the armor of the Lightstriders for nearly four centuries now if I know my history. Don't you ever wish for a change of pace?"

"I'll never tired of defending the realm from monsters such as yourself. That is the pledge of a true knight!" Vedalken retorted.

"A true knight, hmm?" Valtahl tapped his finger on his block-like chin. "It seems we have three untrue knights rising in fame— or infamy—in the kingdom."

"What lies do you speak, brigand?" Arcadia could tell that Vedalken was trying very hard to restrain his hands. He wanted Valtahl dead.

"Speak clearly," Arcadia said in warning tones. "We're here for your blood, not hot wind and spittle."

"The little sorceress thinks she's in any position to bargain!" he said to Vedalken. "When you travel with a fool, it's common courtesy to dress them in motley, so others don't mistake them."

Vedalken only gritted his teeth and pressed the tip of the halberd into Valtahl's chest. Arcadia could have sworn she saw a wisp of smoke float up from where the weapon contacted the brigand. "My fool companion and I happen to share a sentiment. Speak."

"The ability to die leads to impatience, and impatience leads to death, I've always said," Valtahl reprimanded. "But, very well. I shall tell you what I've promised. Clearly, you see me as a false knight."

"If you've ever truly been knighted, it was by some false lord," Vedalken agreed.

"But there are two other knights who had failed at their duty, or perhaps even three. One chopped the head off of his queen, and the others allowed their charges to die."

Casinius, Leonidas, and Vedalken are who he's talking about, Arcadia realized, and by the look in Vedalken's eyes, the Lightstrider understood it as well.

"Yes, Lightstrider. I know of your failure. The look in your eyes when you turned to find your king dead; it was priceless!"

"How?" Vedalken asked. "How do you know about that?"

"I have my ways." Valtahl turned his attention to Arcadia. "However, I've wasted far too many words on you. It is your sorceress I am interested in talking to." He pointed at Vedalken. "I'm going to walk away from you now. If you claim yourself a true knight, you'll not attack me, since I've done you no harm."

Vedalken growled, but when the Khindre crossed towards Arcadia, he stayed his hand.

"What interest do you have in me?" Arcadia demanded.

"You are the first sorceress born in over one hundred years. Any man with knowledge of the kingdom's past would be interested."

"My sister was the first one from the womb; you should talk to her instead."

"I would, had you brought her. Unfortunately, our new king is just as foolish as the old one. Geurus just has the cold heart and severity to keep people from noticing it, where Godfrey had only weakness.

"A woman such as yourself shouldn't have to deal with fools and weaklings. You're an anomaly, Arcadia Rainclaw. Great power lies at your disposal, but you never reach for it—such wasted potential. Let me show you," Valtahl reached one manicured finger towards Arcadia's forehead. Beside her, Cassius and Vedalken twitched, but she held out a hand to forestall them.

The finger pressed into her flesh, and a sharp pain lanced through her. Darkness filled her eyes for a moment before it finally cleared away. In place of the room above the rookery, she saw an ornate chamber, decorated with colors red and orange. A set of stone steps stretched up to a throne, and sitting in the throne...was her. The Arcadia on the throne was dressed in fine robes of black and purple silk, hues she'd never seen in her life. Her mouth was moving in silent speech and gesturing. Beside her, Reyna stood laughing at something. Arcadia beckoned to something again, and Geurus stumbled into view, walking as jerkily as Grayson had on the day he and Reyna died. She noticed shadowy tendrils squirming around his arms and legs. The king was holding a platter with tea and biscuits. Behind him came Prince Tarus and Princess Velara holding covered dishes, and behind them. Divines, her parents, supported by the same shadows, like puppets on their strings! They carried steaming towels that they laid over their two Khindre daughters' necks, fear in their eyes all the while.

No! Arcadia squeezed her eyes shut, blocking out the vision. She tried to cry out, but the sound only bounced about in her head. "I don't want that! Dominion is not what I crave."

"Then you'd rather this?" Valtahl's voice brought on a new wave of vision. She saw the city of Searstar, once beautiful, now crumbled, and razed. The sun failed to shine, and screams rang against the buildings. The image shifted, and she saw an Enforcer looming over Caitrial, with her stomach split open. Slimy red entrails twisted in one of its demonic hands. Bright lifeblood dripped from them, and she squirmed futilely against the binds around her wrist and legs. Caitrial's face was pure, silent agony as her whole body trembled. Once again, Arcadia closed her eyes, unable to bear the view worse than the last one. This time, with the image of dying Caitrial in her mind, she managed to make her vocal cords work. "Kill him!" she screamed. "End his foul life!"

Suddenly, her brain flared white-hot, and Valtahl's raw cry of pain tore through her.

Her vision swam before her, and the cries of startlement coming from her allies sounded miles and miles away. She felt strong, sure hands lifting her shoulders. Blearily, she recognized

Cassius. "Are you all right?" three voices asked. "Please, don't die on us!"

"Valtahl?" she asked, shaking the triplicity from her eyes and ears. Taking the half-elf's hand, she rose to watch Valtahl somersault backward. His brigandine jerkin was torn open, a gaping wound beneath it, but no blood flowed out, only smoke. Two white knives—like the one that had slain her sister—were clutched in his hands. Vedalken thrust forward with the spike of his halberd, but Valtahl rolled under it. Instinctively, Arcadia snarled out a clipped word, and a shadowy tendril coiled up around him.

"Ah, how good to see you use your magic, little sorceress!" the lich crowed. "But, I fear it won't do you any good." Valtahl sucked in his breath, and the shadows dissipated and disappeared down his throat. *He swallowed my spell!*

"Farewell, little sorceress. We will meet again!" White mist puffed out around him. Vedalken jabbed the halberd in, but it swished through harmlessly.

"Over there!" Cassius cried, pointing. Valtahl stood on the other side of the room before an oval-shaped doorway, alternating purple and black bands beyond its frame.

"Oh no, you don't," Arcadia sprinted towards the escaping outlaw as he waved and stepped inside. *At least this proves he's a mage like Deadvoice. Not that I know what Deadvoice was, but it's a start.*

Vedalken and Cassius were just on her tail, which skipped against the tile floor. The portal was closing, but the three managed to leap in just in time. It closed on the hem of Cassius's cloak, leaving a swath of fabric on the floor.

It was a bizarre feeling, floating through nothingness, held aloft, and propelled by some magical force. Valtahl was a ways ahead of them, and no matter how Arcadia tried to maneuver, she couldn't bring herself any closer. The Khindre's cackling laugh echoed through the distorted tunnel.

The three could only watch as the tunnel split into two, Valtahl swerving down one path while they were thrown down another. Their cries of anger attended them to the end.

Sunlight peeked out from ahead.

"Prepare to land and fight!" Vedalken called. "I don't know where this is going to put us, but I doubt it will be anywhere we want to be." Of course, the Lightstrider was correct. They tumbled back into Sun's Reach onto dirt ground, surrounded by hedges. At first, Arcadia thought they were back in Searstar. But glancing over her shoulder showed not Emery's castle, but the tall towers of Redhawk's fortress.

But the more interesting sight lay before them. For in the center of the clearing, stood a baffled Cereos Gardstar. Five Enforcers surrounded her, dark lances bristling and gleaming.

Arcadia stood and dusted herself off. " I was angry that everything we'd done today was for naught, but this makes up for all the disappointment."

"What is the meaning of this? How did you get here?" Cereos demanded, clearly seeking the exits. Cassius' magic closed off her retreat with a thick blanket of vines.

"I couldn't tell you, truthfully," Arcadia shrugged. "Perhaps you should ask your master, Valtahl. I'm sure he'd be happy to explain." The Khindre sorceress didn't give the woman any chance to think about that. Deadvoice had claimed that they'd trained the woman in magic. She didn't know what sort of tricks she could expect from the queen. Arcadia wasn't waiting to find out.

She reached for the tall shadows cast by the hedges and called to them. Spheres of darkness rose upwards and pelted the queen like stones hurled from a sling. Cereos snarled, now aware of the situation she was in.

The first Enforcer leaped forward to meet them and found Vedalken matching him stride for stride. The Enforcer went for a stab, but Vedalken sidestepped and brought the axe blade on his halberd, slamming down. Sparks flew. For a moment, the two were frozen in space, elf and demon muscles tensing. Then, with a horrendous screeching of metal, the Enforcer's lance was shorn in two. Quicker than anyone could react, the Lightstrider brought his weapon back to bear, leaped into the air, and brought it jabbing down again to crash into a black iron breastplate. This time, it was the Enforcer that screeched.

Everyone watched the quick but brutal display in shock, frozen for just a moment. The other Enforcers were the first to react, cocking arms and launching their own spears through the air, a deadly rain of sharp shafts.

As quick as Vedalken was, he was still recovering from his kill and couldn't get out of the way fast enough. He would have become a slim Elven pincushion, had Cassius not begun his spell while everyone stood in awe of the Lightstrider. He'd watched elves fight for years, and their speed never surprised him anymore. A gout of water burst from the ground, knocking the missiles out of line, and drenching elf and demons in foul-smelling liquid.

Vedalken yanked the halberd from the corpse and nimbly flipped into the fray. Arcadia turned to Cassius. "Go, keep him alive. Cereos is mine."

Cassius looked like he wanted to argue, but something he saw in her eyes must have dissuaded him.

So, now it was just Arcadia Rainclaw and Cereos Gardstar, facing each other, hands poised to begin spellcasting.

"My husband was supposed to slay the two of you."

"He failed."

"I can see that. Leave it to men to muck everything up," a brief smile flashed on her face.

"You won't distract me with words." She focused on the shadow of the fountain. Atop it was a statue of a swordsman wearing a feathered cloak. Silently, a dark replica of it rose behind the queen, thrusting its sword forward to run the queen through.

With nary a movement of her hands, the sword bounced off harmlessly, deflected by an arcane barrier. "Neither will you, Khindre." She jabbed a finger into the shadow and muttered something. It burst apart, and the shards turned to black glass floating around Cereos. The queen pushed her hands forward, and a hundred and one sharp missiles flew forward to cut Arcadia to ribbons. The Khindre threw herself to the ground, causing most of the shards to miss, except for the three that embedded themselves in her tail. Arcadia hissed in pain and glanced back to see the shards turning around for another pass. Now Cereos would be wise to her tricks; she wouldn't get away with the roll again, she knew. So instead, she recycled a different trick. This time, leaf-shaped motes of shadow roiled forward to meet the flying fragments. Wisps of shadow curled on the ground, the only remnants of the two spells.

"Impressive casting, girl," Cereos taunted. "But you are outclassed. Those drips of blood from your tail are only the first of a great flow to come."

"Words aren't worth a dim," Arcadia spat. "And blood...Berdur says our bodies never stop making it 'till the day our heart stops beating. I have plenty to spare." Black energy lashed up and around Cereos's legs and arms. Fearfully, the queen began to murmur and gesture. It was a familiar chant, though, and Arcadia was already rolling forward when the blue-white flames exploded behind her. The force of the explosion sent her sprawling, but she threw her hands into the air as she fell. The black binds stretched and twisted, lifting Cereos high into the air, extending to stop her hands from moving and casting more spells. Arcadia was angry now. The rage she'd sublimated when Emery and Reyna died, and rage directed at Valtahl for his torturous visions and hasty escape, all manifested into a black and red fist, large enough for Arcadia to lounge on. But fists weren't made for lounging. She couldn't resist the smile that crept across her face as Cereos sobbed in pain. The fist battered her over and over and over again. Arcadia lost count of how many times, but she was delighted when she heard the sickening crack of Cereos's nose splattering against her cheek, and finally let it rest. The hand snatched her up and tossed her roughly to the ground in front of the Khindre. The queen's once fine silver and purple robes were torn and filthy with blood and dirt. Her face had once been gorgeous, but now it was discolored, her nose crooked, one eye was swollen shut.

"That's for everything you and your husband have done." Arcadia leaned in, nearly touching foreheads with the vile queen. "What do you have to say for yourself ?" Not much, clearly, since she chose to spit a gobbet of blood, saliva, and a tooth into her face. Arcadia nodded and pursed her lips and let the hand grasp her leg. "Do you know what they say, my queen? Don't trifle with a devil. Few remain to describe their revenge." Despite her show of hardness, even Arcadia flinched at the banshee scream and the resounding crack, as the blonde woman's leg snapped.

Cereos was trembling, and tears welled in her icy blue eyes. She whimpered something unintelligible. "What was that?"

"Farewell, devil-spawn." A purple and black doorway opened underneath the queen.

"Like master, like dog," Arcadia sighed and jumped in after her, summoned fist just behind.

Like before, she floated in the arcane tunnel, but this time she reached out to the magic itself, as Reyna had taught her to do. She didn't recognize the destination that it was sending them to, but when the foundering Cereos began to chant, she apprehended the distortion that came upon the passageway. "Not this time!" she called out as the tunnel split in two. Cereos slowly floated towards the second shaft, but Arcadia wasn't going to let another enemy escape. Not when she had a perfectly capable hand, ready to scoop her up. Gardstar squawked like a raven when the hand closed around her, squeezing and dragging her back to Arcadia. "Sorry, but you should try not to copy your master if you want to live." She turned her attention back to the portal. "Now, let's see where you were going to send me!" She saw a brief glimpse of red sand—the Scorched Waste. "I think not." Straining her mind, and casting the disrupting spell Vedalken had taught her. She reached out with her conscience and redirected the flow towards a familiar anchoring point.

Arcadia sent a magical message speeding ahead of her and waited for the tunnel to eject them in her chosen destination.

CAITRIAL

WHEN THE FLAMES BURN HOT

When the swirling portal opened in the sky, everyone around her jolted in surprise. But they held their position as Leonidas had commanded. "Get everyone ready; I'm bringing a gift," Arcadia had said in her head. Caitrial was half expecting Arcadia to appear holding Valtahl's head. When her sister slipped out of a magic tunnel with a battered, bloody, but unmistakable Queen Gardstar, she was as surprised as the rest. Immediately, Leonidas barked an order, and two soldiers jumped into the cleared circle to grab her arms.

"Valtahl escaped, but this prize is richer, methinks," Arcadia answered Caitrial's questioning look. *Indeed, it is. I can't wait to hear the tale behind this one.*

The smith ran a hand through her hair. "I'm not surprised to see a Gardstar agent here, though I'm delighted to see that it's someone so great as the illustrious Blood Queen! Now the only question is: What do we do with her now that we have her?"

Several suggestions bubbled up from the crowd, but after a moment, Sir Geralm stepped forward. "My men and I are of one mind in this. We have won this battle, but the war is as of yet undecided. We need information badly. No better place to get it than her Highness's mouth."

"If she's not forthcoming with the information you desire, what will you do?" Caitrial queried. "Or, if she does talk, how do you be sure her information is true?"

"Oh, we have our methods," Geralm said darkly.

Leonidas stepped forward, in front of the queen. "No."

"What was that, boy?" The older knight narrowed his eyes.

"I said no," Leonidas repeated. "You won't torture her."

"And why not?" Sir Espern shouldered forward, placing a hand on his sword hilt. Not a direct threat, but the warning was there.

Leonidas took a deep breath and looked between the two captains, both with years more experience than him. "We fight against the atrocities committed by Geurus Gardstar and his family," he said. "I agree they deserve to be punished. But torture is far more than punishment. It is the willful inflicting of suffering upon someone without the means to make it stop." Now gaining momentum, Leonidas faced his superiors down, evening the playing field without actually seeming threatening. "As knights, we are called to appeal to the spirit of honor, and sometimes honor means that we must make difficult choices. We are faced with one such choice now. Do we take this captive queen and cause pain to extort information that may all be false." He shook his head to show what he thought of that. "Or do we do the right thing, and inflict upon Cereos Gardstar the proper punishment for the murder of royalty—beheading, if I recall correctly. I've a sharp blade in my sheath and would be more than glad to deliver the justice myself, in the name of Emery Redwyn."

· · ·

Sir Geralm and Sir Espern stood there for a stunned moment, allowing Leonidas's words to sink in. Geralm looked at his fellow captain. "What say you, Espern?"

"I need no further convincing," the balding captain said. "Young Leonidas is possessed of a certain degree of integrity that is rare in this day and age, even among knights. Unlike us, Geralm, it seems he remembers his troth. I wish there were more of his like. Besides, he's offered to do the dirty work himself."

"Very well, Leonidas," Geralm said. "You have proven yourself an able warrior, a keen commander, and a man of fidelity. You may have your wish."

Leonidas bowed respectfully, and then turned to Caitrial, searching for approval in her eyes. She gladly gave it to him, smiling warmly and nodding.

Lady Ilyana gave them rooms in Redhawk's castle for as long as they needed. Caitrial lay on her bed, a softer affair than any she'd slept on before. The sheets were cool silk, the pillows delicate lace. But despite all that, sleep eluded her. The smith tossed and turned, but her mind would give her no rest. She glanced over to the chest of drawers, where the castle servants had left clothing for her. They were Ilyana's old garments and were a snug fit, riding high on her thighs, but they would serve. After spending a long time before the mirror, examining herself from every angle, she took a deep breath and steeled her nerves, knowing what she had to do.

She hesitated outside her door for just a moment and took another breath to calm her pounding heart, as persistent as a hammer on hot, pliable metal. Then, she started down the unfamiliar hallways towards Leonidas's room. She'd found out from the servants where he'd been quartered. Caitrial couldn't help but wonder if they were watching her now. *They always say that castle walls hold no secrets.*

Cait stopped a moment at Arcadia's door, listening for her sister's quiet, even breathing. The sorceress had used a lot of magic in the battle, far more than she was used to. She'd sleep deeply tonight.

The stones were cold beneath her bare feet, but the sensation only served to prove that she was alive. It was no dream; Caitrial was doing this. She paused one final time before his door and then reached up and knocked softly. Doubt grasped her. *Mayhap he's already asleep. If so, I'll not bother him tonight.* Just as she was about to turn on her heel, the door swung open, and Leonidas stood there. "Leo..." she said, unable to get anything more out. His face was still scraped red from a recent shave, his long hair damp from washing sweat and blood from battle and execution, and his clothing equally ill-fitting, but the sight of him stopped Caitrial in her tracks all the same.

"Cait?" There was a question in his voice, and was Caitrial imagining it, or did she hear a smidge of relief buried there too?

Caitrial felt the sudden need to clear her throat. "I-I couldn't find rest," she said. "And I..." She froze up, unsure of what to say. She was no woman's poet, couldn't work a piece of prose to save her life. Direct and straightforward was her style in battle, so why not do the same here? Her creativity came out in her work, not her words. "I don't want to be alone tonight," she finally admitted.

Leo's breath caught in his throat, and he stirred just enough for Caitrial to see. She feared the knight might laugh and tell her to go back to bed. But Leonidas seemed to understand, and Caitrial dared to let herself hope that the same thoughts that raged in her mind had kept him up. "You'd best come in then," he said, moving aside so that she could walk through the door.

His chambers were just as lavish as her own, but Caitrial barely spared them a cursory glance. She turned around and faced Leonidas, the man she'd grown to love. The red flower in the lantern cast a shifting glow over his face. Through the thin clothing he wore, she could see powerful muscles flexing with every move. "I hate these silk garments," Leonidas said with a smile. "I much prefer mail and plate. Especially the suit you made me."

Caitrial felt a spark catch in her chest, an unfamiliar spark, starting a flame like no other she'd ever experienced before. Suddenly, the room seemed very warm, and the smith felt momentarily afraid of the heat. She'd never feared fire before, so it was a queer sensation. But, as scary as the fire might be, it was tempting too. Caitrial barely noticed herself stepping forward. She placed her hands—bronze, scarred, the sort of hands that had seen hard use in their time—on Leo's chest. He didn't pull away but came closer, and Caitrial was glad for it. Glad to know that perhaps she wasn't alone in her feelings. She dared to nestle even closer, acutely aware of the flames in her chest licking eagerly, *hungrily* upwards. One of his big hands rested on her back, while the other came up to stroke her cinnamon-colored hair.

"Leo," she whispered. "I love you."

She lifted her face to his—they were so close now, mere inches apart. Slowly, haltingly, she leaned in, and Leonidas did the same. Their lips touched, and the flames leaped higher, reaching for that passionate contact. The fire was hungry, though; it would not be satisfied with just a kiss or two. It wanted more, so much more, and it wasn't to go unsatisfied.

"While I traveled the kingdom, I oft found my mind turning to you," Leo said, his voice growing husky. "I'd be mad to deny that I love you, Caitrial Rainclaw."

She'd expected this much, deep in her heart; if she hadn't,

the smith wouldn't have convinced herself to come. But hearing it from the knight's lips sent a thrill through her body, a thrill like no other. Better than seeing a great project finished, better than battle adrenaline. Unlike Leonidas, Caitrial couldn't find her voice; words were the first things the fire had devoured. Instead, her only answer was to kiss him again and let her teeth run over his bottom lip. Her arms suddenly ached, her heart beating wildly in her chest, on fire with pure desire. Behind the roar of passion in her ear, Caitrial faintly registered a sense of giddy joy, and thought: *Imagine that; a knight and a tradeswoman, falling in love. Not the most unorthodox pairing.* But before her mind could take that thought any further, her borrowed garment whispered to the floor, sounding like distant bellows, fanning the fires of passion higher. Caitrial could almost see herself standing at the forge with some tremendous unfinished work in her hands, just waiting to be placed into that forge. All the trepidation fled from Caitrial's mind in that instant, and she thrust her heart fully into the flames.

The next morning, she woke to a knock on the door. Sleepily, she cracked open her eyelids to see Leonidas stirring beside her. Warmth filled her chest as she reminisced about the night prior. Before she could think any more about it, however, the knock came again, this time followed by a voice. "Sir Leonidas? Lady Caitrial?" Her half-awake brain managed a chuckle at that. *Truly, the castle walls have no secrets; it is proven.* "Once you have washed and dressed, there is a guest who wishes to meet with you," the servant said. "He claims he has something that you'll want to see. He gave the name Ignis Duskwalker." She slipped a piece of parchment under the door, scrawled with the same message.

They shared a curious glance. What did the Secretkeeper want with them? Leonidas kissed Cait again, and she slipped her hand into his. Whatever dire information Ignis was sure to bring, it didn't matter. They had each other, and in that simple truth, they had a little bit of surety.

"Shall we go see what awaits us, my love?"

"Of course."

INTERLUDE

Ignis had learned much in his time in the Lords' Keep. It was far more than he'd hoped, but still less than he wanted. The Lords allowed him to see a few things—the inner workings of the keep, the creatures they kept, even some of the spells they cast—but for the most part, they kept the Secretkeeper in the dark. He still didn't know why they wanted his gift, or what their "plans" were, but trained as he was in the art of Secretkeeping, he could sense that something big was coming. The Lords had big plans and meant to act on them soon. From what he'd heard, the Gardstars and the Chillfang were only phase two. That scared Ignis, who knew from listening in on reports that they had already done significant damage. *How many more phases will they have?*

From hours slinking around corners and eavesdropping on private conversations, he knew there was animosity between the Lords. Without that, he figured Sun's Reach wouldn't have had the hundred some-odd years of peace it was granted. The dwarf and elf were especially combative, and all the Lords looked down at the gnome, both literally and metaphorically. He wasn't surprised. Whatever dark entity had created the lich, they'd made sure it wasn't the sort that played nicely with others. They'd not share power well, and yet they insisted on working together. Perhaps the act that created them had bound them in some way. Ignis couldn't be sure about that, but magic was fickle. He'd not rule out any possibilities.

The air in the Keep was tense that morning, the entire palace still with anticipation. Ignis was determined not to miss anything. When Qrakzt and the gnome walked around the corner, he slipped into an alcove, hoping his dark clothing and slight frame would keep him from sight. The two Lords were so distracted that they didn't even spare the nook a glance.

"Are you sure this will work, Yurghaz?" the taller Lord asked.

"Well, um," the gnome scratched at his once smooth face, now flaky and dry. *Undeath has adverse effects on the skin,* Ignis noted dryly. "Do you want to hear me say yes, or is it the truth you crave?"

"The truth, you bumbling idiot!"

"Y-yes, Greatlord," the gnome gave a quick bow that put Ignis in mind of a particular gnomish envoy, Odala Wala, he'd traveled with not so long ago. "Well, it is very experimental magic, so I can't exactly promise that it will go as planned."

"You fool! You have convinced us to follow your lead in this! Just when were you planning to tell me about your *experimental magics*?" Qrakzt's rattling voice was angrier than Ignis had ever heard it.

"I figured that we've had several experiments go awry before..."

"You figured wrong, gnome!" the dead man said coldly. "You'd best have some information that will alleviate my mood. Else you can spend the rest of your eternal life taking care of the failed experiments you seem to be so fond of."

Yurghaz dropped to his knees in front of the taller Lord. "Maybe experimental wasn't the best way to describe it, m'lord," he stuttered. "I spent ample time researching this procedure, and it has been accomplished in the past, several times! There was one time in Afuldrax, where some minor demon switched his soul with that of a well-beloved hero. Nobody suspected anything until all the priestesses were dead, and the ancient artifact they were protecting corrupted."

"He switched his soul with the human's? What has that to do with our escapade?" Qrakzt bore down upon Yurghaz, not allowing him to rise from his supplicant position.

"Well, it's a very similar procedure, surprisingly, and this too has been done before," Yurghaz managed. "Once..."

"Spare me your stories; your prattling annoys me. Get on with the point." Qrakzt tapped a foot impatiently. It was bizarre to see a powerful lich such as the Mad Mage doing that. *Old habits die hard. Or not at all.*

"As you command, Greatlord. So long as there are no magical interferences, it should be a simple matter to bind a soul back to the body it belonged to, even with the tampering we've done."

"Very well, Yurghaz," the lich Lord said. "This had better work. I've decided that the dungeons of past experiments are too good for you."

"You were always the wisest of us, Greatlord Qrakzt," Yurghaz answered obsequiously. "If this fails, it shall be upon my head."

"Yes, indeed it will, little gnome."

Later that day, Ignis heard the long, shivering moan that meant the Lords were convening. He padded down the hallway, shadowing the liches. He saw them enter the room one at a time —First Qrakzt, then the elf, Erendreth. Behind him came Aurvari, the dwarf, and Kephire the Khindre recently returned from a mission, sporting a fresh scar. Finally, Yurghaz, the keystone to this next step of the plan.

The stone door ground shut behind them, and Ignis knew there would be wards on the door—to stop his entry or that of the mute servant, and to discourage any hopeful eavesdroppers. Unfortunately for the Lords, Ignis Duskwalker had a few tricks of his own up his sleeve. He pulled a glove over his hand, woven of enchanted spider silk. The tips of the pointer finger and thumb had small black crystals on them. An invention the Secretkeeper had made following instructions on ancient diagrams from a long lost civilization.

He sidled up to the door and clicked the fingers, feeling the satisfying hum as the spell jamming crystals began their work. Now, he could hear inside, and the Lords would be completely clueless.

"We have waited long enough," Aurvari was saying. "Gnome, get yerself to tha' pedestal an' start yer castin'!"

Ignis heard the clomp of boots against the stone floor, as Yurgahz did as he was bid. One by one, staves cracked down upon the daises Ignis knew lined the runic circle within. Then came a low hum, and voices rose as the chanting began.

The Lords chanted for a good long while, Erendreth's musical voice mingling with Aurvari's rumble and the sly rolling speech of Kephire. As they intoned their spell, the feeling of magic grew stronger. Then, all at once, the magic seemed to stop. The air held still and stagnant. Ignis couldn't help but wonder, had it been a success?

He got his answer a moment later, as Qrakzt cried out in pure rage. "You fool of a gnome, what have you done!"

"Nothing, Greatlord, you must believe me. This shouldn't be..."

"You are correct, Yurghaz. This shouldn't be happening. But it is. Do you recall what we said in the passageway?"

"F-failure w-would be on m-my head," the gnome said sheepishly.

"Correct again. Well done. Here's your reward!" A loud boom echoed through the halls, followed by an ear-splitting crack and a bright flash of white light. The sounds nearly drowned out Yurghaz's screams. Nearly. *And then there were four,* Ignis thought with amusement.

"When it awakens, carry it down to the dungeons. I will try to salvage Yurghaz's failure later. Consider it done and prepare to move on to Phase Four—our last chance, and now with no worthless gnomes to jeopardize our success."

Ignis was just about to fade back down the hallway when he heard something that stilled his feet.

It was a girl's agonized and terrified scream. A scream that sounded hauntingly familiar.

He knew what had to be done. Ignis Duskwalker dashed to his chambers where his raven was waiting upon the rafters. "Doom and gloom. Doom and gloom. The air smells sweet when cherries bloom," it sang. The bird was absurdly fond of that ditty. He whistled at it and tore a scrap of parchment from the bottom of a scroll. On it, he scrawled a single word—*Run*—tied it to the raven's leg, and sent it flying off towards his home. With only a moment's hesitation, he began to pack his sparse gear. This could well be the most dangerous smuggling job he ever attempted.

PART III
THE HEAT OF HEART AND HATE

AMARU

A LIZARD WITH WINGS

The desert sun beat relentlessly upon the sand, like a carpenter's hammer on his latest project. Like the humble carpenter, the sun shapes the world, its transformative heat breaking, and remolding all things in its domain. Amaru sighed silently, surveying the bare sands stretching endlessly before, behind, and around her. Only a single small village and a few formations of stone marred the empty vista.

Amaru, Alaric, Dalphamair, and Celwyn sat together atop one such mesa, all watching the desert for the anticipated signs of change in the field of sand.

Alaric stretched out his arms with a yawn. "How long do we plan to stay out here?"

"Until th' durned beast shows up, fool elf," Dalphamair responded tightly. Amaru looked at both of them admonishingly. The last thing they could afford to do was begin another argument. She hushed them with a gesture; they could allow no unplanned sounds. Unwarranted disturbances to the still air could either draw or drive away their quarry, and Amaru wasn't sure which would be worse. So they sat in the cleft on the mesa, thankful for the shelf of stone above them, guarding them against most of the sun's wrath.

Amaru took a silent moment to glance at her companions, the three she trusted to join her on an assignment of this caliber. Alaric's fingers ghosted over the strings of his lute, not trying to hide his fear. Amaru reached a hand out and twined her fingers in his. "You'll perform wonderfully, I know it," she mouthed. She took solace in his brilliant smile, knowing that the elf would not betray her trust.

Dalphamair, on the other hand, made a valiant attempt at appearing unconcerned. His broad face, which looked as if it could weather a sand squall, was scrunched up in concentration as he quietly scraped a whetstone along the edges of Cryptfiller, his double-bladed ax. To any other, the dwarf would appear the stern soldier idly preparing for contact with the enemy. But Amaru knew Dalphamair had been sharpening the ax, and his javelin, Retirement, since before breakfast. It was already as sharp as Dalph was like to get it. Alaric had pointed out earlier that the dwarf could probably shave his beard with the weapon, to which the surly dwarf had replied. "Aye. Were ye not a prissy elf without th' mettle t' grow a beard, I'd offer t' do yers! I s'pose yer ears would do."

Only Celwyn seemed oblivious to the tension of the moment. The little flaxen-haired gnome was taking full advantage of the mesa to get a new perspective on her sandy home. "Too bad I can't just stay up here," she'd said as they climbed the pitted side. "It's weird being a giant when you're used to the world towering over you, but I think I could get used to it."

Amaru herself was as tense as could be. Their target today was not something Amaru was looking forward to dealing with. Several years had passed since she'd seen it last, and she wasn't excited about their reunion. But she was, if nothing else, a woman of duty. The Water Callers, nay, all the people of Scorched Waste needed her now. Amaru Sunbrand had shirked responsibility once before. Despite the relief, her decision to leave the village that had been her home had left a sour taste in her mouth. Now her first chance at redemption had come, and Amaru would not turn away.

Just then, Celwyn scrambled down from the ledge, making the agreed-upon signal. *It's here.* Amaru grasped her spear, an ancient weapon passed down as a symbol of pride through the chieftain line of the Fire-Striders, *Helios, Sun's Searing Tongue,* Dalphamair had called it.

Since its removal from the hand of a carved statue of Yamaria, the weapon had tasted the blood of monstrous Chill-fang, Venomsting assassins, and demonic Chitinites. Today, it hungered for the viscera of a final creature that bedeviled Amaru's past. *Either our weapons shall slay it, or it shall slay us.* She sent a silent prayer of guidance and protection up to Yamaria, Goddess of the sun, and her mother.

Now she could see the beast circling through the air, seeking a place to land. It had grown in the years since Amaru had seen it last. Hot sunlight glinted off burnished scales, once the color of sand, but now carrying hints of copper. Large leathery wings were outstretched, allowing the wyvern to glide effortlessly on the wind, like the sails of great ships, which Alaric had conjured images of for her benefit. The only sea she knew was the one of sand and fire. A long, sinewy neck craned back and forth, blood-red beady eyes trying to make sense of the ramshackle village built so near to its lair.

Amaru saw movement among the houses as the disguised Water Callers within played their own part perfectly. The cries of terror, some of which were genuine, drew the sand wyvern's attention away from the mesa, where Amaru and her companions were beginning to make their descent. The wyvern's wings flapped now, allowing it to hover in place above the makeshift village. Craning its head back, the great beast let out an ear-piercing shriek. Then it dove, its war cry striking fear into the hearts of the Water Callers below. The sand wyvern bulled through the ramshackle houses, splintering wood and sending thatched roofs flying through the air. Most of the "villagers" remembered their part and used their druidic magic to disappear beneath the sand, but two were not so lucky. As the monster swooped down upon them, deadly talons outstretched, a two-pronged barbed tail preceded it. The spike dug deep into one woman's back, injecting her with virulent toxins. She was dead before the claws gripped either leg and tore her to bits.

With more gallant bravery than sense, another man tried to rally his group to stand against the horrifying beast, but he was left alone. The other Water Callers scurried down below to safety, calling for him to join them. This did not deter the man, who instead pointed a finger at the sand wyvern and cursed its exis-tence. The wyvern, more interested in live prey than dead, tossed the woman's torn remains to the side, folded its wings, and crashed down to the sand, throwing up a vast cloud of dust.

If anything could be said of the foolishly brave man, he gave Amaru and the others time to get into position.

When the screams subsided, and enough debris had fled the air to reveal the monster's outline, the dance of death began.

It started with the bleating of a goat, as Dalphamair, astride his precious Priscilla, led the charge, Retirement in hand. A horned head snapped around to greet the noise, a double row of needle-sharp teeth gleaming in the mid-morning light. Had it just been Dalphamair, the wyvern would have made an appetizer out of the valiant dwarf, but before the creature could snap out and take a bite, Amaru's spear lanced into the vulnerable spot in the fold of its knee. The monster whirled around, but Amaru had already retreated. Despite the pain, the beast was more annoyed than actually hurt. Using primitive logic, the only thinking power allowed it, the wyvern ignored whatever small thing had pricked it from behind, choosing to go for what it believed was the easier meal. Already tired from the days' patrol of territory, it at least had the sense to expend as little energy as possible.

But, when it turned around, it found itself face to point with Retirement. Instinct caused it to jerk its head up just in time, sustaining only a bruising strike on the neck's leathery skin, rather than a fatal blow to the eyes.

The sand wyvern snorted hot breath from salt-crusted nostrils and screeched again. This time, the shivering sound reached Priscilla, and the goat turned hoof and fled. The wyvern gave chase, teeth snapping, and getting a mouthful of goat tail. Dalph's mount, overcome by the fear and pain, bucked the dwarf and ran off into the desert. The wyvern glanced between the prone dwarf and the fleeing goat, wondering which would make a better meal. It decided on the dwarf, hairy as it was. Scraping its left leg against the hardened sand, it flicked a snake-like tongue in the air, getting an early taste of dinner. Sinuous neck craned back, ready to lunge forward and sink a mouthful of teeth into dwarf flesh. When it did attack, it experienced not the pleasure of hot, gushing blood, and sweet flesh. Its teeth crunched into something hard, cold. And it felt pain. The beast reared back, its mouth of shattered teeth spurting blood, and regarded the protrusion of rock that had ended its feast before it could begin.

And more interestingly, the gnome squatting atop it.

"Yoohoo! Hey, dragon! Over here!" Enraged, the monster went after her, but Celwyn extended her legs in a single, fluid movement, flipping off with an enhanced jump, leaping clear from the wyvern, and taking off with abandon. The sand wyvern gathered its wings about it, preparing to take off. It would come in from the air and destroy this little gnome, and then it would find whatever else was lurking here and devour it in an orgy of bloodshed and feasting, as reparation for all the pain it had already experienced today.

It stretched its wings, punctuating the air with another piercing scream.

Then, its side exploded in immense, searing pain, and all thoughts of flying fled from its mind.

Amaru watched the scuffle from her hiding place behind one of the trees. Just as she and Alaric had hoped, filling the fake town with Water Callers had created such a panoply of smells that the wyvern couldn't rely on scent to single them out. They needed every advantage they could get. This creature was even more fearsome than before. All those years ago, when this creature—Amaru knew it was the same one by the fact that one horn was shorter than the other; Leif had shorn it off in their desperate struggle—had attacked and nearly killed an entire gathering party. It had only topped four feet standing half as tall as a camel now, bristling with natural weapons and advantages against the puny land-walkers that it preyed upon. It was the apex among apex predators, but today, it was prey, and Amaru and her friends had to be the ones to put it in its place.

Black blood dripped from Helios' translucent head, falling to the sand, where it dried almost instantly. Two simultaneous flashbacks played in her head. The first was of that attack when Leif had lain near death, his eyes filled with a strange mixture of pride and pleading. The combined blood of wyvern and Fyroxi had been this same color, mixed in the sand and the tears falling from Leif's eyes. Since that day, she'd never once seen the warrior Fyroxi cry, not even in the aftermath of the Hundredth Sun Massacre. That second event, when Fyroxi blood had been drunk by parched desert soil, also played in Amaru's mind. She shook her head, taking the whole force of her will to sublimate the thoughts. Now she needed to focus more than ever. This sand wyvern had been terrorizing the desert for months now, and the High Servant, Rovinald of the Water Callers, had tasked them with ridding Sun's Reach of its nuisance. So far, most everything was going to plan. Nobody had sustained any serious injury or, Yamaria forfend, died. But they'd managed little more than wounding the wyvern's pride if the beast had such emotion.

Amaru was determined to change that. Cracking a few teeth would be no issue to this thing, which still had wings, talons, and a venom-filled tail, along with horns, and its own bulk to pit against them. They had to disable as many of those weapons as possible to gain some sort of foothold in this battle.

The daughter of Yamaria watched as the wyvern chased after Celwyn, and saw Dalphamair take advantage of its distraction, circling behind a building, where Amaru knew he would drop Retirement and prepare Cryptfiller. With Priscilla fled, Dalph's job as a distraction was finished. Now, the dwarf could join in the real fight.

She watched as, much to her relief, Celwyn escaped the creature's still deadly maw. Then a grimace crossed her face. The wyvern was preparing to fly. If it got an aerial view of the battlefield, their whole plan might fall apart. From the air, the wyvern had superiority; it could swoop down and pick them off, one by one, at its leisure.

Amaru had only one option, and it was a perilous one. With her friend's lives in danger, she didn't even consider that fact.

The monstrous sand wyvern stretched its wings wide. It reflexively rolled its sinewy muscles, causing the coat of scales to ripple and rattle—an instinctual scare tactic passed down for generations, meant to petrify prey, keeping it from escaping while the beast attacked.

It worked too, Celwyn's eyes were as wide as vulture eggs, and her taunts died on her lips. The little gnome had survived many things over the past years she hadn't expected to ever happen to her, but she knew that life could be over in that instant staring up into deadly gnashing teeth dripping with saliva and blood, vertically slit eyes, like a massive desert cobra. The cacophony of clattering scales filled her ears, and her mouth gaped open idiotically, awaiting the sure death that furrowed the ground under taloned feet.

Amaru used the noise to dart across the sand without drawing the creature's attention. Knuckles whitened around a dark wood handle. Her keen eyes caught every movement, each twitch of muscle as the sand wyvern prepared to take off. Four springing strides and she was beside the wyvern, able to feel the heat emanating off the scales. Blazing sunlight reflected mercilessly off metallic scales. Amaru refused to let that distract her.

Like all armor, the wyvern's body couldn't be covered entirely. There were spots on its body where the scales were smaller, the skin softer. She'd already struck it behind the knee, but there were three more of note: the eyes, throat—but, of course, no sane person would present themselves before a sand wyvern, opening themselves up to a bevy of nasty weapons—and the wing joints. Tensing her arm muscles, feeling them tighten and bulge beneath her robe, she drove the Kerazar tip deep into the flesh, tearing ligaments and sinuous fibers just as the wings came down for their first beat, spraying sand into her eyes. The creature hissed and screamed, an ode to terrible pain, as its wing flopped, worthless, to its side. Amaru tugged on Helios but found it stuck fast, caught between clenched muscle and wing bones. Cursing, Amaru leaped back, enacting her racial magic. Before she even hit the ground, her body shrank, and white fur sprouted. Her nose elongated into a snout full of sharp teeth, meant for piercing rather than grinding. She landed on all fours, flared her two white tails, and sped away, knowing the wyvern would be close behind. She agilely weaved in between houses and tents. Her pursuer chose a much more direct method, its rage leading it to burst through and knock aside obstacles rather than avoid them. Amaru didn't spare a glance behind her, afraid to give the creature even a moment's notice, for fear it might make a desperate leap for her if it could read the fear in her eyes. Her conical ears funneled the sounds from her surroundings to her brain. Dully, she realized the creature was wheezing, the pain finally overcoming seemingly dauntless power. Amaru wondered briefly if she'd pricked a lung with that strike. Snorting, she shook away the thoughts. Her sides beginning to lather with sweat, as she led the sand wyvern in circles, Amaru scanned the border of the town. She had to tire it out as much as possible so that the final phase of the plan would have the highest chance of success.

There! A flash of off-gold skin caught her eyes, and Amaru ran towards it, risking a glance backward to make sure her foe had seen the sudden turn. It had, and, growling, picked up the pace as best it could with an injured leg. Before her, outside the faux town's border, a stretch of sand was punctuated only by a single boulder, tall as a man, and twice as thick. An instant before her paw landed on that empty land, she wrenched to the side, throwing herself to the right. She rolled behind one of a few remaining huts and waited. Predictably, the vast wyvern bulled forward, unable to stop its momentum in time to follow her newest target. Skidding to a stop, it let loose a roar of frustration and clawed at the ground.

Right before that soil collapsed beneath its feet, the hiss of sliding sand coupled with the morale drenched shouts of Water Callers leaping from pre-made tunnels beneath the earth, chains in hand.

The creature tried to whirl and knock away the surprising new prey, but the heavy chains looped over it, hammered into the sand a moment later by Water Callers on the other side.

With sand as the only binding agent, the bindings would not

hold for long, not against a snarling, biting sand wyvern. Indeed, several Water callers were knocked back by its mad thrashings, Amaru hearing a few definitive cracks—bones broken by desperate flailing. It seemed destined to break free and finish the massacre it had started.

Then Alaric stepped out from behind the rock, lute in hand.

He spared only a cursory glance at the sand wyvern before launching into a song, one he'd written long ago.

Amaru had listened to much of Alaric's music on the road from Solgaele Monastery and Oasi Sanctus, but this sounded much different from anything she'd heard her Elven friend play before. The tune seemed simple, almost elementary, and when Alaric began to sing, it was all the Fyroxi could do to keep from laughing.

"Oh, what is a dragon but a lizard with wings? Both have scales and tails, what a beautiful thing! If a kid sees a lizard, he's down in the clay, but if he sees a dragon, he'll run far away!

Oh, the lizard tastes good boiled in a soup, but the dragon'll eat your whole chicken coop! One will hide under the rocks, but the other has fun hunting your flocks!

A dragon's just a lizard who grew two wings, a fancy for jewels, among other things. He won't listen while you play your flute, he'll burn down your flocks and steal your loot. You can yell, scream, whine, and hoot, but because he's jealous, your point is moot!

Oh, a dragon sure is a sight to see, an eyes greatest treasure to you and me, but if you touch his hoard, you'd best scurry, else woe betide, your soul is flying free!"

As the childish song's final chords reverberated through the desert air, they were met with stunned silence. It was the most beautiful sound Amaru had ever heard. The dragon was moving, but sluggishly, seeming as if nothing happening around it registered in its primitive mind, caught up by the invisible phantasms surrounding and trapping it within itself. Alaric hurriedly beckoned to his allies. Ever curious, Celwyn was the first one over, hopping in front of the beast's half-lidded eyes, amazed at the lack of recognition in its slackened face.

Amaru crossed in front of the beast as well, pushing Celwyn back. Alaric came up to join her, standing as close as he could get.

Then, Amaru saw Dalphamair make his appearance behind their foe, slapping the handle of Cryptfiller, his deadly honed axe against his hand.

"Remember," Alaric said tensely, "one clean blow. I've never tried this spell against a creature of this caliber, and we might not have as long as I hope."

"Yeh, yeh, no need t' tell me twice," Dalph grumped, patting the air. In true dwarf fashion, he squared his legs, thumped his chest with one meaty fist, raised Cryptfiller high above his head, and brought it whistling down with perfect accuracy. The over honed edge sliced through scale, skin, and bone-like wet paper, and the tip of the wyvern's tail went flying off, amid a spray of red blood and green-grey venom. That caused a stir in the dragon, the muscles pulsing, and its wings lifting into the air. Several Water Callers scrabbled away, squeezing eyes shut, as chains were ripped out of soft sand. Its tail whipped reflexively, the impact knocking the brave dwarf back several feet.

"Quickly, Amaru, finish it off." Alaric sounded truly worried, and Amaru couldn't blame him. She regarded the long dirk in her hand, and then the soft skin of the sand wyvern's throat. It would take a perfect stab to send this hellbeast back to the infernal planes in which it belonged.

Before she could draw her arm back, she heard a slight whistle and looked towards the sound just in time to catch Helios, which spun through the air, thrown by a grinning, blond-haired gnome.

Without a second thought, she discarded the dagger, and sent off a quick prayer to the Sun Mother, before taking the Sun's Searing Tongue and jabbing it up into the soft places in the monster's throat, approximately where the thyroid would be on a man.

That killing blow finally broke the spell on the sand wyvern, and it laid about with claws, blunt tail, and head in a final gambit. Alaric reacted first, pushing Amaru back and taking the brunt of the frontal attack, a painful bruising blow that knocked the breath from the not so sturdy elf.

But then, at long last, the beast that had menaced the Scorched Waste for many years succumbed to its wounds, lifeblood streaming out of numerous holes, both natural and inflicted.

Alaric offered Amaru his hand and pulled his dark-haired friend up. They watched in silence as the foul monster collapsed. Then, the elf squeezed the Fyroxi woman's shoulder.

"We've done it," he said. "I'm sure Ephraim would be proud."

"You say that as if he is dead," Amaru answered. "Do you know something that I don't?" She hoped not. Ephraim had been the pair's first salvation, the old Water Caller who had taken them into his tent, then departed in after sunfall without saying farewell, leaving them the tent and some food, which kept them alive whilst they sought Oasi Sanctus.

Alaric shook his head. "No, if the man survived the desert this long, he's likely as tough as a gnarled root. Nothing will kill him, at least not without a fight. Me, on the other hand, my lady, I fear I might die for lack of amelioration."

Amaru laughed, taking his hands in hers. "Oh, please, Alaric. No need to be so dramatic. 'Tis no more than a bruise and a few cracked ribs," she admonished. Still, she let the divine magic granted to her by shared blood with the Goddess, Yamaria, flow through her into Alaric, mending his wounds and any other damages he'd taken on his journey to reach the sand wyvern's territory.

She gave his hands a quick squeeze and then separated herself from her bardic friend. "Now, I must go, there are others who require my healing hands."

She strode off, finding herself humming Alaric's strange little ditty under her breath as she walked towards the throng of injured Water Callers.

Thus she didn't hear Alaric sigh heavily and say, "Aye, but none who need them quite so desperately as I."

REN

WATER FOR THE FOXES

Had somebody asked Rienzi Gyndalon earlier that year whether there was anything hotter than the Scorched Waste in late summer, he'd have scoffed and laughed off the foolish questions. Of course, until now, Ren hadn't been privy to the goings-on within the Elders' elk-skinned tent. He was quickly learning what Durrigan had known: for all the presentation of unity they showed to their people, the Elders of Clan Fire-Strider argued profusely and heatedly. Ren knew that all five of the wizened men and women had the best interest of the tribe in mind, but they seemed to have a hard time showing that during council meetings. Usually unshakeable, Yarena was having a hard time retaining control of her fellow Elders. Sigmund, the scarred veteran, trapped permanently in fox form, not unlike Weylin, from injuries earned in battle, gnarred and slavered, pawing at the ground to keep himself from springing atop Elder Silque. Silque, head of the crafting division of Fyroxi, had taken the most significant damage from the recent attacks of the Chillfang, their race's mortal enemy. To the great surprise and fear of the Fire-Striders, the monstrous wolf-folk had made their way through the supposedly impenetrable barrier called the Eclipse to renew their raids on their hated rival. Thus far, they'd been mostly successful, destroying the entirety of Clan Bush-Walker and dealing a grievous blow to the Fire-Striders.

"The way I see it, we have only a few options," Lady Silque said. "We can either tuck our tails between our legs and withdraw from the Scorched Waste, where our foe runs rampant, seal ourselves within the Temple of Yamaria for safety until our population outgrows what little food and water stores we have remaining, or present ourselves neck first to the Chillfang. Whichever road we take, we can't afford to tarry in our decision. As you well know, Sigmund, our attempts at scavenging have been fruitless."

"The damned Chillfang have carelessly over hunted this section of desert," the veteran replied. "They've no regard for the delicate balance that living in the Scorched Waste demands. They, too, must be growing weak. Not that I believe we would stand a chance in another direct battle. I agree with you, Silque, that the outlook seems bleak and hopeless, but that doesn't mean I condone either hiding away or surrendering."

"I tend to agree with Sigmund in this," Elder Purell, the Clan's prayer-leader, said. "Offering ourselves like sacrificial lambs to Gaarhowl's children would be the ultimate insult to Yamaria. Do you genuinely propose that we sequester ourselves within the holy temple until our inevitable deaths by privation? You must be daft, Silque; undoubtedly, one so knowledgeable as yourself should know how awful such utilization of consecrated ground is! The Sun Mother, given her proclivity towards tender disposition, has no issue with the sheltering of our children within her temple, but what you suggest...I cannot even fathom such a possibility."

Ren buried his face in his paws. The Elders had been arguing non-stop since the start of this meeting, and they showed no signs of quitting anytime soon. He'd been called here due to his invaluable contributions towards the survival of the Clan. Together with his mentor Copernicus, and Weylin, one of the last three Fyroxi of the Bush-Walker Clan from the Sulfaari Expanse, Ren had developed several defensive measures, keeping the Chillfang at bay while the Elders came to a consensus on their next steps. Or rather, Ren realized, argued endlessly. It was enough to drive the young Fyroxi mad. Yarena had stopped trying to rein in her fellow leader's anger long ago. *That's the problem with losing a chieftain, but keeping the rest of the Elders the same,* Ren thought. Silque, Sigmund, and Purell all have their own agendas and preconceived notions of what was best for the Fire-Striders. Yarena hadn't the experience nor the sway over the council that Durrigan had possessed; to the rest of the tribe, she was the leader, but here, Yarena was less than a member. Ren almost felt bad for her. But the newly elected Chieftess wasn't doing much to raise the others' opinions of her, save deciding to include Ren in their discussions. With Copernicus's help, he'd negotiated trade deals with several other tribes in the past months, garnering necessary shields and other supplies to provide better protection against the Chillfang. Since their last two full-scale assaults on the Fire-Striders had been devastating to them, Gaarhowl's children were far more hesitant in their recent raids. Ren's defenses had made them more so. In concert with Silque's crafters, he'd stationed large slingshots around the border, where the Fyroxi with the best aim were posted to take preemptive strikes at any conniving enemy scouts. His most effective and proudest invention by far, however, was the dummies—made of burlap sacks and stuffed with anything from spoiled and poisoned meat to spikes, had caused several casualties and served to make their foe far more hesitant in their advances. Observing the Chillfang revealed that they had poor vision in the harsh, relentless sunlight of the Scorched Waste, so all Ren had needed to do was make the faux Fyroxi look somewhat realistic. The hungry and angry Chillfang had been quick to attack, and those that did sealed their fates.

As Sigmund had pointed out, the Chillfang didn't understand the first thing about surviving the Scorched Waste. The lack of sightings and the emaciated look of those wolves that made an appearance left that abundantly clear. The Chillfang were starving; they were tired and perhaps even harbored a modicum of fear.

Not that it mattered. The Fyroxi were still at a disadvantage.

First, the Chillfang could roam the desert; they could range far and wide to find sustenance and had no compunction about eating sentient organisms. They could prey upon wandering tribes of humans and elves, drinking their blood and devouring their meat and other provisions. The Fire-Striders were trapped in the makeshift barriers they'd built around their settlement. Each time they sent out hunters, they were tossing the bones. Would the patrolmen return, or would they find their end in their rivals' stomachs?

Beyond that, the Chillfang were unified in their desire to destroy the Fyroxi. The Fire-Striders, however...

Ren had zoned out, letting the arguments pass over his ears unheard. Though Purell had sided with Sigmund earlier, it seemed they were now embroiled in a dispute of their own. Of the Elders, only Copernicus didn't seem intent on joining the row. He slumped in his seat, eyes glazed like those of his apprentice, clutching the letter that had come by messenger bird this morning. Chieftess Yarena tried breaking into their squabbles, but they dismissed the woman out of paw. Both Copernicus and Amaru had told Ren stories about Chieftain Durrigan. The late Fyroxi leader once persuaded some of his peers to join him on a daring mission to bring his people closer to their goddess. He'd led them through the thickest and thinnest of situations. Even when it seemed like their purpose was doomed to failure, like they were to founder in the severe and uncaring Scorched Waste, he'd bolstered their morale, earning the respect and trust of his hand-picked council and tribe.

After nearly half a millennium of service to the people he loved so well, Durrigan died peacefully in his bed. To Ren, it seemed the entire world went wrong after this. First came the Hundredth Sun Massacre, then Amaru's departure, and now this. Ren couldn't take it any longer. Slapping his tails against the ground, he stood, shifting as he did, eyes gleaming with annoyance. Though he was short, couldn't tower over the Elders if he wanted to, his presence was felt and acknowledged, in a manner that even Yarena wasn't. It felt queer to command more respect than the Chieftess, but Ren discarded the notion.

"As much as my Fyroxi pride rankles at the thought, Silque might not be entirely wrong about turning tail and fleeing," He interjected, speaking for the first time in the meeting. "Even starved, the Chillfang have a hatred that even abiding in the chilly lands they must come from—with pelts so thick, and their strange, icebound allies—could not freeze out. We Fyroxi, much to our ultimate shame, took comfort in our sudden freedom, and our need to swap our attention to the poachers that burrowed up from the woodworks following the Eclipse. We forgot the real enemies, even those of you who lived through the worst years of their cruel torment. Look what we've become. Let me stress this point, one that Amaru made absolutely clear before she left. In the whole of Sun's Reach, all over the Known World, there are no other Fyroxi! See the fear those who remain all carry, the weight of possible extinction in the eyes of your fellow people." Ren spoke with the weight of history, spurred on by the look of approval in Copernicus and Purell's eyes, letting the scornful glances from the other three slide off his back. "He who bears the bad news suffers the contempt for it, but you've left me no choice. If we insist on bickering amongst ourselves, we'd best use what money our coffers hold to purchase platters to serve ourselves up to the Chillfang on. If I recall my teachings from Sigmund correctly, all we stand to wage here is a war of attrition —one we have no chance of winning. I don't know how many Chillfang there are left, but that's not a practical lesson in warfare I care to take. Eventually, our supplies will wear thin. Whether we die from lengthy suffering at the hands of time, hunger, and thirst, or get jointed and devoured by Chillfang depends entirely on the mercy of the Sun Mother. The choice would be yours, which end you'd want to pray for." Ren's voice was growing shaky from stress, and tears welled in his eyes. He'd never talked back to Elders like this, and he certainly didn't enjoy it. He wasn't even sure what deep, dark place they came from. But his words seemed to be getting through, harsh though they were.

He took two deep breaths, trying to calm himself, and crossed the room to where Elder Copernicus sat. The youngest of the elders seemed to know what he wanted. He handed over the parchment, then glanced into Ren's eyes, tacitly asking permission to speak. Ren allowed it and then gave the letter another read.

"As far as I see it, we have two possible chances for salvation. Well, three, but one is nearly impossible with all we know," Copernicus took full advantage of Ren's imposed silence to get the points he'd been withholding across. "Chief Durrigan was once friendly with the King of Men. I know what you are all thinking since I've dueled with many of the same worries. Men have an inherently shorter lifespan, and memories shorter than even that. But, perhaps they still count us allies important enough to treat with. Especially if we display to them the direness of our situation. King Godfrey, long may he reign may grant us shelter behind his walls, may even aid us in retaking Fyrestone, if we prostrate ourselves. Right now, we need protection."

Sigmund nodded slowly. "It's not the worst suggestion you've made, stripling though you are." Ren glared at the veteran. They had no time for divisive comments. Sigmund made a gesture to show that his comment had been made lightly, in a thin facsimile of humor rather than malice. "That being said, it's still danger-ous. The most direct route into the Sulfaari Expanse will still leave us vulnerable to attack from behind. Even if we made it out of the Waste, what would we do? Many of the younger members of the tribe, yourself included, Rienzi, have never seen anything save the desert. There might be more bountiful resources, but only Weylin knows what is safe to eat. What happens when someone consumes something that is either poisonous or precious to the sentient inhabitants of The Expanse? Dismissing even the problems of scavenging for food in a land we don't know, we aren't safe. Weylin has admitted that he never ranged more than three days away from Fyrestone. He cannot lead us to Searstar, and given the destruction of the Bush-Walkers, including my own brother, we have no idea who we could trust. For all we know, we could ask someone for aid and be led right into the jaws of the beast!"

The rest of the Elders nodded, and Ren was glad to see that civil discourse had returned to the tent.

"You are correct, Sigmund," said Copernicus. "Besides, to whom would we turn if King Godfrey refused, or couldn't help us? Nothing should have the power to pass the Eclipse. Recall when it first came to be? Durrigan, fearing what has come to pass now, sent two people to examine the wall, the son of an accom-plished arcanist who hadn't the gift, but some sense of the arts magical, and a builder. When the builder returned, he said that the arcanist's son had tried to force his way through, but died screaming in the attempt."

"So this might be the herald of more significant conflict," Yarena proposed.

"It's possible, though we shouldn't jump to conclusions without more information," Copernicus gestured to the note in Ren's hands. "With retreating into the kingdom proper out of the question, that leaves the Water Callers as our only hope."

"You mentioned one further possibility, though you claim it cannot be achieved," Purell prodded. "By the grace of Yamaria, anything is possible. Speak this hope now; if the Sun Mother hears you, perhaps she can grant us the boon of this particular aid."

Copernicus rubbed the back of his head. "I know it was done for our sake, but... well, we had a means of salvation once, one that the Goddess herself prophesized. If we could find Amaru, perhaps she'd be able to point us in the right direction. But, unfortunately, nobody has seen her since she slipped away those months ago. We don't even know if she still lives! Like I said, it is an impossible wish."

"Perhaps not so impossible," Ren breathed, a grin creasing his face. He'd just finished reading the missive, an offer of help and refuge within Oasi Sanctus, and was staring at the signatures. Most of the Elders were so used to seeing the names that they just glossed over them, and apparently, Copernicus had fallen into the same habit. But Ren, having never seen them before, had read each, committing each signature to memory. *Rovinald, the High Servant. Tos Kamarr, Commander of the Sandwards. Erein Ralliphi, Head of Healers.* But there, on the very bottom, was a signature that Ren knew by heart already. One that changed everything; that added a glimmer of hope to the future:

Amaru Sunbrand, Leader of the Scions of the Rising Sun.

"Praise Yamaria," Copernicus gasped.

AL ARIC

As was so often the case, Alaric found himself watching Amaru as she went about her daily business around Oasi Sanctus. Never one to slack when there was work to be done, the Fyroxi woman spent her days alternatively working with the Healers, training with the Sandwards, and planning with Rovinald to ensure the protection of the denizens of the Scorched Waste. It was during one of these meetings that Rovinald had mentioned the sand wyvern.

"This monster has lurked in the shadows, evading capture and distraction for several years," he'd said. "What with the threat of the Chillfang and the Chitinites, it is a contemporaneous problem that we cannot afford. Our spies have found corpses of both Venomsting and Chillfang in its wake, meaning it is unlikely that the beast is working in concert with our enemies. However, there have been too many ravaged settlements and diminished tribes to remain idle. Some of our best have failed in combatting it, but that was because we foolishly rushed in without proper preparations, or allowed it to choose the battlefield."

"Then that we shan't allow again," Alaric had assured. He'd then presented his plan, a method of wearing it down physically and mentally, so that his bardic magic could incapacitate it. It was a daring plan, and one that relied heavily on luck, but sometimes chance was all you had when fighting a creature of such great proportions. And the fight had gone much better than even optimistic Alaric expected. Those who had lost their lives would be mourned, but the number was far lower than expected.

That evening, as they helped clean the scales and claws scavenged from the wyvern, Dalphamair had returned from recovering his precious Priscilla—the goat had been so spooked that she'd run nearly a mile into the open desert before stopping and wandering slowly back towards the village. The dwarf had intercepted his mount on the road and rode her back. At their triumphant return, the cheers and accolades had been nearly as deafening as that celebration following the sand wyvern's death. The Water Callers purported that without Dalph and his mount's distraction, the battle couldn't have been won. Never before had Alaric seen a goat puff up its chest, but at that moment, he would have sworn to anyone that Priscilla had done precisely that.

When Dalphamair, lathered with sweat and drenched in viscera, plopped down next to them, Alaric clapped him on the back. "Do you hear that, dwarf ? Have your ears ever received such a marvelous noise? Those are the warm welcomes that a hero deserves, and today, I'd say you fit the bill."

"What're ye gettin' at, elf ?" Dalphamair said, putting his belt knife to work alongside his companions'.

"'Twas a compliment, dear friend. I'd hope you'd have the capacity to understand that much, at least. Be that as it may, you are correct, I do have a point to make." Amaru had turned his way, giving Alaric her full attention. "You see, though the brightness of the sun might mislead you in this, it is easy enough to discern that the Scorched Waste is facing a dark time. In the past, when the dark times came, heroes rose to meet the challenge, swords and shields brought to bear. They carried the burden of the people's hopes upon their backs, returning a vestige of light to the darkest of plains. The Scorched Waste and all of its inhabitants are desperately wanting for a hero or four, perhaps now more than ever. The Water Callers bring all the succor they can, but even their greatest Sandwards have never faced anything more than an ornery desert lion until today. They need a team of willing men and women, strong, brave, daring, and perhaps a little foolhardy, for despite what the stories say, there is no such thing as a perfect hero."

"And just who do you suppose is fit to volunteer for such a task?" Amaru asked, though, by her tone, Alaric thought she had it all figured out already.

Alaric made a show of scratching his chin and pulling at an imaginary beard. "Well, we've certainly had enough time to receive word from the capital, if word is indeed coming. Methinks that either Leonidas succumbed to his exhaustion on the road, or that his pleas to his king were met with reticence. This means the Scorched Waste won't be seeing regiments of knights or a brigade of Lightstriders riding over the dunes to deliver us from the Chillfang and Chitinites."

"So any heroes that the Scorched Waste makes use of must come from within," Celwyn said. "Like Amaru, I also wish to know your suggestions. Come, come. We don't have long before the peccary finishes roasting. They found a stash of rare spices among the wyvern's hoard, so it'll be especially scrumptious tonight!"

Alaric smiled, looked at each of his companions in turn. "Why, us, of course!" Amaru nodded, her suspicions confirmed.

"Is that so, elf ?" Dalphamair queried. "What makes ye think we're deservin' o' such an honor?"

"I think Rovinald himself already put the role upon us, though not by official announcement. He's a wise man, and sly when he wants to be. He convinced us to stay here, that we might help protect and inspire the Water Callers in these trying times. The High Servant planted the seeds in our heads while we were busy fretting over Amaru's safety. But he wanted to see if we would take the burden upon our backs ourselves, rather than foist it upon us. He's waited for those seeds to sprout, and I see no reason not to spare them what water and fertile ground our minds can provide."

"If that just requires thinking about water and arable soil, then there are fields of the stuff in my head whenever I think about home," Celwyn said with a huge grin. "I'm sure I can lend it a plot or two!"

Alaric saw a momentary flash of deep pain scar Amaru's gorgeous brassy eyes, as Cely mentioned home. He wanted to reach out and comfort her, but before he could, the pain disappeared, replaced by a solemn mien.

"So, what do you say, my friends? Shall we step into the mantle of heroes, become that which this desert sorely craves?"

Amaru nodded. "I was always told by my...my father that Yamaria named me the salvation of my kind. I'm not sure if she meant just the Fyroxi or the desert people as a whole, but I choose to accept the broader definition. If rising to the occasion as heroes are the way to fulfill this role, then I'll not hesitate."

"Much as I love arguin' with you, elf, I canno' find fault with yer plan fer once," Dalph laughed. "I promised me friend Leonidas tha' I'd protect ye lass, so ye kin count me in!" Priscilla bleated. "Me girl's fer joinin' too!"

Celwyn bobbed her head. "I think my answer should be plenty clear. I'm a Water Caller, after all. If I didn't want to devote my life to helping the people of the desert, I made a pretty poor career choice! Since you brought up the matter, I'm going to assume that you're with us. So, that leaves only one more important decision!"

"An' what's tha', Celwyn?"

The gnome's eyes twinkled. "Why, we need a name. All companies of heroes have names, whether they be the illustrious Lightstriders or the commoner vigilante warriors we used to have around when the last Gnommaster was young, the Red Runners! It serves as a call sign, and once we prove ourselves, a moniker to put fear in our enemies' hearts. So we need something for ourselves. Something like...uhm....like..." Celwyn gave an abashed grin. "Nope, I'm fresh out of ideas!"

Alaric unfolded his legs from beneath him, gracefully rising into a bow. "Fret not, for I have already considered this matter extensively. I hope you don't mind that I presumed all of your answers would be just as they were. After several hours of deliberating with my center of inspiration, I came to an appellation that signifies all we need it to. If you all agree, we will call ourselves the Scions of the Rising Sun!

"It's a good a name as any, I s'pose," Dalphamair said, pulling at his thick beard."

"Oh, that's wonderful!" Celwyn cried, drawing a few eyes around the camp to her. "It's especially perfect, given that our leader is descended from the goddess of the Sun. She is quite literally a Scion of the Sun."

"L-leader, me?" Amaru asked, flattered, though confused as well.

"Who else would it be, m'lady?" Alaric had to ask. "Not only would your leadership of our group serve as a powerful signal, but you also know the most about life in the desert, given that you've spent a full fifth of your total possible lifespan here."

The elf crouched down next to her and placed a smooth off-gold hand on her shoulder. "I have met many men and women in my life thus far, young as I may be in the eyes of my people. And in the remaining six centuries I hope to live, I know I'll meet many more."

"Six centuries?" Celwyn scratched her head. "I thought elves lived for a thousand years?"

"Alas, that is but another white lie, told to make elves seem that much more superior. To a human who lives only a single century or even a dwarf that might see three, anything more would seem close to eternity. My people can't help but seize any opportunity to elevate themselves above the rest of the world. Few elves live actually live longer seven centuries, though some of the most remarkable specimens have seen another half-century longer than their brethren.

But that's neither here nor there. As I was saying, I cannot be sure how many people I may meet. But even if I were to be intro- duced to the famous Vedalken Nairvebyen, there would be nobody I'd be more willing to follow than you, my sensational Amaru Sunbrand."

Dalphamair snorted at the conspicuous gallantry, but the derisive sound was cut short by a gnomish kick to the side. The dwarf turned an ugly glare on Cely, but dropped the matter. If a few complimentary words from a schmoozing elf were what it took to secure Amaru as the leader of the Scions of the Rising Sun, then he could stand to watch the display this time.

Alaric watched Amaru's eyes, in which the bard could see several emotions battling, though she was so guarded he couldn't tell quite what they were. He wondered why she was so hesitant to accept power. There must be a well of grief associated with that, perhaps having something to do with something back in the home she still refused to speak about. Alaric held his tongue, knowing that saying more might trigger a flight response. If Amaru wanted to accept this responsibility, she would do so.

Alaric knew the moment she'd made her decision. Grabbing up Helios, she boosted herself to a standing position, bowed, and said, "I'm honored by the trust you three place in me. I can only aspire not to let you down."

Alaric clapped, a bright smile slashing through the uncertainty that had clouded it before. "The day you let me down, Amaru is the day I renounce my position as a bard."

"Don't joke about such things," the Fyroxi girl said earnestly. "Putting it on the wind gives a chance for Gaarhowl's underhanded minions to grab hold and make it come to fruition. We need your music here, Alaric, so don't think for a moment that you'll be able to rest on the laurels you've earned thus far."

Before Alaric could reply, someone dressed in the tattered gray robes of those in service to Rovinald. A folded piece of parchment was gripped in his hands, and he scanned the room quickly before rushing over to Amaru. "A letter for you, Lady Sunbrand."

"I've told you before, Derik, it's Amaru, not Lady Sunbrand. Regardless, I thank you. Do you know the contents of it?"

The young boy shook his head. "The High Servant said it was addressed directly to you, so you should be the first to read it."

Kind of him, Alaric thought dryly. *It's a good thing that Rovinald has a good conscience. I can imagine other leaders not respecting that sacred privacy, especially concerning someone of such import as Amaru. My father, for one. Talisin infiltrated my letters several times. Had I not had the sense to have a lover of mine collect them, I may have never had half of the opportunities that made me what I am now.*

Alaric heard Amaru's slight gasp and watched as she left the tent. *I hope it's not bad news.* He decided to give her a few moments of privacy, so he wouldn't come upon her unprepared. Alaric had noticed that the Fyroxi tended to hide her emotions, even from her close friends. And Alaric unequivocally considered himself one of those. Even though they had only known each other for a few months, he might have been wounded by the gesture. *It certainly feels like it's been far longer than that. A few months, undertaken in shared solitude, with nothing to distract us from each other save the constant threats to our lives in the form of Venomsting, Chillfang, and basic desert survival. Danger does have its way of extending time.*

Finally, not hearing any heart-breaking sobs, or other signs of emotion, he signaled to Celwyn, Dalphamair, and the High Servant's boy, and brushed through the leathern tent flaps. He emerged into the light of sunfall, the orange radiance spilling over the tops of distant mountains, turning the harsh day's breath into an embrace of warmth and comfort. Amaru stood there, bathed in enhancing radiance, staring past the tents to the desert beyond, the letter clutched to her chest.

"Is everything alright out here, my Sun Maiden?" Alaric made a mental note to save that nickname, as it spurred the creative center of his mind into action.

Amaru turned, a broad smile splitting her tanned face. Her eyes had their own luminosity, sparkling with burgeoning tears born of joy. "Yes, Alaric." She passed him the letter, and Alaric immediately looked at the signatures on the bottom. He didn't recognize any of them, but there was one upon which Amaru's tears had fallen, which read, *Rienzi Gyndalon, Hero of the Second Raid.* "It's my family," Amaru said. "They're coming here."

Alaric, sitting and watching Amaru hum as she went about her work, was experiencing mixed emotions. On the one hand, he reveled in her joy, but then again, when Amaru was reunited with her friends and family, would she still wish to spend time with him? Or would Alaric Valyaara just be thrown to the wayside, forgotten amid homecoming tides?

"You know," a voice broke into his thoughts, startling Alaric,

"I never expected a bard with such stunning, charming confidence to be a coward!" His chair, upset by the elf's sudden jump, toppled over, and Alaric had to roll to save his lute from being damaged. The elf glared balefully up at the top of the tent, where a small blonde gnome lay, barely containing a fit of giggles, her legs kicking in the air merrily.

"Must you startle me so, you vexatious little fiend?" he asked acidly.

"Ooh, little fiend, I haven't heard that one before! Better than imp, or pixie, that's for sure."

Alaric sighed and caught sight of Amaru. She'd noticed Alaric's fall, and cocked her head, tacitly asking after her friend's health. He waved her off and turned back to Celwyn. "Pixie is far too kind a descriptor to attribute to you." This time, Cely couldn't resist, and a rolling, snort-punctuated guffaw sprayed from her mouth. The little gnome's laugh had some sort of power, almost like Amaru's smile. He could never stay mad in its presence. "Now, you nettlesome character. Would you like to explain your comment?"

Celwyn bobbed her head, wavy blonde hair flopping over her bright eyes and pronounced nose. "Well," she began, shaking away the obstruction, "you always appear confident in your abilities, but when it comes to admitting the truth to a certain member of the Scions of the Rising Sun, you get a chunk of prickly pear in your craw."

Alaric huffed, having already figured out where this was going. "Go on," he prompted.

"There's no foretelling what we'll be facing in the coming months," Celwyn said. "Unless, of course, you have some divination magic up your sleeves, and have just been hiding it from us this whole time," She smiled at her own joke, but quickly settled back to seriousness again. "Dalph and I can see it clearer than a beacon fire on a sand dune, and we marvel at the fact that

Amaru hasn't seen it. But the two of us think you'd best get to telling her."

"Dalphamair said that?" Alaric asked, bewildered.

"Well, actually, what he said was more like, 'Tha' durned elf better not cause lingerin' tension among us. Tell 'im to either spew it or lose it, or just ye watch, I'll cut off that ponytail o' 'is 'ead when 'e sleeps!'" Celwyn's approximation of a dwarvish accent was absolutely ridiculous at best, but Alaric decided not to comment.

"Sounds like something he'd say."

Celwyn vaulted down from her perch and put a small hand on Alaric's shoulder. "Look, if you're in love with her, as your ceaseless stares indicate, do something about it. At best, Oasi Sanctus gains a happy couple in a time where comfort and happiness are *maxasi imparete,*" Celwyn stressed the fact in the gnomish language. "At the worst, we druids get to laugh at your embarrassment. So we win either way. Oh, and if you aren't actually in love, and you're just steeped in carnal longings, Dalph promises to pare off your bells and feed them to his goat!" she finished cheerfully.

"Thanks for the support," Alaric grumbled, but he took the words to heart. He promised himself that he would find the right time and the proper method to reveal his heart's truth to the woman he loved. In fact, the Elven bard already had an idea. Leaping up from his uncomfortable seat in the sand, Alaric dashed towards his tent. He had to start writing.

AMARU

DRACONIC MEASURES

From her vantage point on the sandy ridge where Oasi Sanctus was temporarily settled, the daughter of the goddess of the Sun could just make out a group of figures creeping slowly across the Scorched Waste. She knew who the shadows belonged to, even though they were little more than dots in the sky, Amaru could feel their approach like a sand squall rumbling through her soul. *My family.* She'd lived with the Fyroxi Clan Fire-Striders for her whole life, one hundred years, and would likely be there still, hunting for food and raising children, had it not been for the Chillfang attack after sunfall. That horrid event, named the Hundredth Sun Massacre, had changed Amaru's life forever.

That night, she'd been slated, as Yamaria's daughter, to match with a hunter in her same age group, one Leif Kalix. Possessed of bull-like strength and blinding speed, Leif was seen as part of the future of the Clan, primarily because he trained directly under Sigmund, the Elder with exceptional skill in fighting and strategy. One of her best friends, Ren, had commented on the unfairness that everyone except the Fyroxi who most deserved it, could choose their mates. Leif, who had long believed that Amaru owed him her life, and thus, by rights, should surrender to his advances, had been validated by that ruling.

She did not look forward to seeing Leif again. He'd tried before to take her by force, and had the spear Helios not been at hand that night, he might have succeeded. But she'd escaped Leif's clutches and beat a hasty retreat, led, she believed, by two parts fear, and one part divine guidance.

Now, though, she was overjoyed at the thought of seeing Ren and Xio again, Amaru feared what Leif might do.

At least, this time, she had support. The kind she knew she could count on. She glanced back at the Elven bard, reclined on a rock in the shade of a small tent. He beamed a reassuring smile.

"Don't worry, Amaru," he said. "If this Leif character is anything like you've told me, then my little plan will work. Oh, he'll be angry—furious—I fully expect, but he'll have no choice but accept it." The grin that Amaru took so much comfort in twisted into a wicked smirk. "If he doesn't, then we have several score Water Callers here. I'm sure they'll be able to subdue him. It's probably been a while since the druids held a prisoner, but they'll manage, for your sake."

Amaru shook her head and laughed. "Yamaria above, you're a rogue."

She sidled up next to her Elven friend, squeezed his shoulder. Together, they waited. They would meet Amaru's family, as they faced all situations, pleasant or otherwise. Together.

When the front of the Fyroxi line came within defining distance, the people at the very front noticed the waiting group. By this time, Celwyn and Dalph, and of course, Priscilla, had joined them, the full coterie of the Scions of the Rising Sun, backed by several score Water Callers. With an excited shout, two figures came running forward, and Amaru, who had waited patiently this entire time, couldn't withhold herself any longer. Tears leaping into her eyes, the girl shifted skin into fox form and barreled towards the two, coming to a stop, and shifting once more just in time to fly into and embrace her two oldest and dearest friends.

Amaru pulled both Ren and Xio close to her chest, then separated and went to each one personally. She first examined Ren. The brown Fyroxi had always been small, but since she left, it seemed that little Ren had grown significantly wirier. He was slimmer than when last she'd seen him, but his arms and legs both had grown noticeably, the sinew standing out against the fabric of his shirt when he moved.

"Someone's been training, hmm?" she said, hugging him firmly and kissing the side of his head. "I'm so glad to see you looking well. I feared what might befall you in my absence."

"Ah...well, you know, fighting for your life has that effect on people," Ren muttered.

Amaru, remembering Ren's long-standing attraction to her, gracefully withdrew and examined Xio. There, she also noticed something different. To the untrained eye, there would have been nothing to see. But with her clerical abilities, and her propensity to guide people towards comfort, she'd been a natural help to the midwives of the Fyroxi Clan.

There was a slight thickening of Xio's body that hadn't been present before the Massacre, and Amaru knew, from the letters she'd sent to the Clan, that their food situation had only grown worse. That meant Xio's weight gain was a product of something far more joyful.

"Xio, you're looking well," Amaru said after delivering her

blonde friend her dose of love. "But I recall you leaving before pairing off at the Hundredth Sun, something that surely saved your life, and I am thrilled for it. But, if I'm not mistaken, you're eating for two now."

Xio beamed, her pretty brown eyes brimming with joy, and excitement nodded giddily. Amaru raised one eyebrow in silent question and was not surprised by the subtle nod she returned in answer. "I'm delighted for you two. We all deserve some happiness in our life. Now, you'll have the chance to explore the wonders of child-rearing. I've heard that it's tough, especially here in the desert, but nothing equals the rapture."

Ren couldn't help but chuckle, and he directed a soft smile towards the woman who was to be mother to his children. "What about you, Amaru?" The brown-haired Fyroxi turned beet red, realizing how that had come out. "Erm, how have you been." Ren eyed her for a moment. "You look tired, but...happy."

"It was a long, exhausting road to get here, to Oasi Sanctus, but I wouldn't give up anything I experienced, not for the world."

"Do you hear that, friends?" Alaric queried, striding up behind the happy reunion. "She wouldn't give up any of it. Speak no falsehoods, Amaru. Is there really nothing you would rather forget? Not even traveling with an elf who lived in the Waste for five years and yet still didn't know the least thing about survival?"

"Never, Alaric, and you know it," Amaru said without turning. "Teaching you kept me sane, and the value of an extra pair of eyes in the desert can never be underestimated.

Ren, Xio, I would like you to meet my new allies, the Scions of the Rising Sun. We have Celwyn, a Water Caller who rescued us from entrapment in a Venomsting hideaway. Dalphamair Knollaxe was a companion of a knight of the Kingdom who we liberated from Venomsting stockades during which we learned that the Chillfang and Venomsting are working together." Amaru saw both of her friend's faces freeze. "I know, 'tis awful news, but with allies who know more about the Scorched Waste than the oldest Water Caller, we cannot be surprised at the suddenness of their attacks. But those are matters for later. I've still not introduced you to one of my companions. Were you to ask him, he would name himself the man of all-embracing import, an elvish bard, with delusions of grandeur and fame."

"They are hardly delusions, my dear Amaru," Alaric said, his voice suffused with feigned injuries. "But, if it pleases you that I be a humble musician, rather than a famous and beloved bard, then call me Alaric, the humblest of troubadours." He folded nearly in half at the waist, held himself in place there, and grinned at Amaru's two friends. "You must be Ren the Hero, and Amaru's confidant, Xio." Finally unbending, he swept up the blonde girl's hand and kissed the back of it. "I have heard in my travels that the Fire-Striders have all the beauty of Sulfaari Fyroxi, and infused with a strength born of faith and perseverance. I am pleased to see that this is indeed true."

Xio turned crimson with embarrassment, and with a grudging smile, Ren scooped up her hand and pulled it tight to his side. Amaru and Xio both chuckled, "Careful, he's a charmer by nature," Yamaria's child said.

"But fear not," Alaric said, hoping to becalm the worried Ren. "I know many things about love, and looking into your lady's eyes, I can tell it would take a great feat to steal her away from you." Amaru was cheered to see Xio, happier than ever, kiss Ren's cheek, and twine her two tails in his, forming a gold and brown braid. "Besides," Alaric finished, "I have my eye set on a higher ideal of love, so I would not steal your beloved, even if she is a hero's lover."

"He's harmless, truly," Amaru promised, "so long as you stay on his lute's good side. If not, well, you may find yourself in deep trouble."

"I can tell you are no lackwit, but an insult to me could land you without the wit to follow through!" The elf said with a devilish grin, miming plucking a string in the air.

The four all shared a laugh, an explosion of joy and relief born of their return to each other's sides.

"Amaru Sunbrand, you misbegotten cretin. Is this where you've been hiding?" A rude, abrasive voice yelled out, slicing the merriment to ribbons as surely as his dual scimitars could. Leif stormed up, his booted feet kicking up clouds of sand with each step. His tails, a grainy mix of light-brown, black and grey, lashed through the air, reminding Amaru of the wyvern. She forced her muscles, which had clenched in sheer terror at the sight of the tall, hirsute Fyroxi, thick of thew, and heir to a scathing aura of cold intimidation that coiled around him at all times, to unwind, unconsciously grasping for Alaric's hand. She felt his long, calloused fingers close around hers, and took comfort in the sensation. *Only Leif could turn the air in the Scorched Waste chilly,* she thought.

"Remember the plan, Amaru," Alaric whispered softly, gently stroking her palm with one finger. "I believe in you, wholeheartedly." Amaru steeled her nerves as the elf ever so gingerly pushed her forward.

"Leif. It's a pleasure to see you," she said, concealing the truth of her feelings. At her request, Alaric had schooled her in the most basic of thespian's tricks.

The Fyroxi man shared Xio's fairness of hair, but none of her sweetness of spirit. He snorted and leveled her with a superior glare that could have curdled the milk within a goat's udders. "What, did you trip during your flight and smash your head on a rock? You know what, I don't care. Whatever made you come to your senses, I'll accept the turn. I hope you are ready to repent for your sins!"

Oh, if anyone has transgressions to atone for, it's you, Leif Kalix. But, no, let these thoughts perish. I cannot allow honesty to leak through now.

Calm your soul, become as the oasis, hide your truth behind a veneer of stone, allow yourself to imitate the sturdiness of the aubade palm.

"I know I wronged you on the evening of the Hundredth Sun," Amaru said, trying not to chafe at the words. "If ever you can see it in your heart to forgive me, it would please me to make reparations."

Out of the corner of her eyes, Amaru could see Ren and Xio, flesh blanched white, and bodies held rigidly. She wished she could reassure them, but doing so would break the illusion she had fostered for Leif. And like half-priced goats at the flesh-market, the bitter Fyroxi was buying it.

A smile crept across his strong-jawed face. He turned about, scoping out the expressions on the other Fyroxi's faces. Few were pleasant, but that seemed to inspire Leif.

"I was driven to rage at Amaru's disappearance, but little did I know that it would be the best thing for myself and the Clan. You see, Yarena, now the tribe can have the children it so desperately needs to survive. Now, excuse me, but I'm going to take my prize now."

Amaru nodded enthusiastically. "Indeed. Ren, and Yarena, I hope we might confer with the High Servant later. But for now, you must all be exhausted from your long trek. Oasi Sanctus is open to you, and we have tents prepared, with food and water, harvested from a cactus grove discovered three days ago." She turned back to Leif and beckoned. "Now, shall we? My gift awaits you within this shelter here," she gestured towards a box canvas usually reserved for storage."

"Let's," Leif said, hungrily.

Amaru strode directly to the tent, fully aware that the Fire Striders hadn't yet moved, that they were confounded by this sudden change in the demure woman they thought they knew.

So she knew that when she threw open the tent flaps and lashed them to the framing poles, they all saw what was revealed. Inside was not a bedroll or a mat of woven dried grass. In fact, not a single piece of furniture or ornament of comfort filled the space. The only thing inside was a massive, heavy-featured reptilian head. Sharp teeth protruded from unmoving lips. Scales, as hard as steel-riveted boiled leather, overlapped each other, creating natural armor as strong as any knight's helm. That head was crowned with horns—or rather, one horn—worn hard and sharp by years of hunting among the sands, the other sheared by a scimitar years ago. The sand wyvern's decapitated skull sat, dried, desiccated, but unmistakable.

Amaru whirled around and leveled an irrefutably potent glare on the taller, stronger Fyroxi. "Do you like my gift, Leif ? Go ahead, feel it, if you are unconvinced. You will find that this is the head of the creature who caused the wound you've used to control me all these years. It's dead." She reached into the tent and produced Helios, Sun's Searing Tongue.

"This weapon, which I used to deny you when *you* tried to deny the sounds of our Clan being attacked in your incessant desire for me, struck the final blow, though slaying it was an effort accomplished by the work of many." She heard the gratifying collective gasps of the Fire-Striders at the accusation, which, though some would never admit it aloud, they believed to a one. "Ask any of the Water Callers around if you don't trust me

"I healed you that day, Leif Kalix. I don't regret doing that, not anymore, but I regret allowing you to reach phantom fingers into my viscera, giving you power over me you didn't deserve. Never again. With Yamaria's spear, I have shorn the mantle with which you've blinded your fellow Fyroxi. We need your skill in hunting, but your deception and fear-mongering are not welcome, not among the Water Callers, and I would hope, not among the Fire Striders."

Fuming, spluttering, the Fyroxi's face darkened. "Do you lot honestly believe this...this filth? She has you all charmed with her comely face."

"End your yapping, boy!" Sigmund, the scarred veteran, stepped from the crowd, his snout spraying spittle. "Answer me one question. Do the accusations that Amaru Sunbrand, rightful daughter of the Sun Mother, lays upon you hold any water? Did the thought of abandoning our tribe to possible death cross your mind, caught up in a rutting furor, and one that was unwanted at that? Fyroxi *are* allowed to opt-out of the mating ritual if their paws grow chill. This was covered time and time again during the priming gatherings. Or did you forget this detail? These are powerful allegations, and if you think to lie, may Yamaria strike you down!"

Leif growled at Sigmund.

"Answer me!"

The fair-haired Fyroxi just spat lividly on the ground before his mentor's feet, turned tail, and dashed out of the encampment.

Amaru looked on, awash with a strange combination of pure relief and abject dread. She returned to her friends. Alaric put his arm around her shoulder.

"Admirably done, my lady," he said.

"I have both rescued my Clan from a dangerous, hostile man, and drove away their most skilled hunter," she said distantly, indecisively.

"The Water Callers will help us in that regard. And the rest of us are no slouches either, Amaru." Yarena, the Fire-Striders' Chieftess, appeared, her face grim, sandy ears flattened against her head. "And, though I know it's too late, I am bound by rights to apologize to you. I thought your efforts to escape the yoke I placed upon you with Leif were attempts to shirk your duties, perhaps even subtle rebellion in the name of the late Chief Durrigan. Had I known the truth of Hunter Kalix—"

"Peace," Amaru said, holding up a hand. "He is gone. I know not where he will go, but it matters not so long as he's far from here. Nothing ill came from it; thus, I'll not blame you for past decisions."

Yarena swallowed, nodded gratefully, and then led her people —three score minus one—to their tents and their rest.

LEIF

A BLACKHEART'S DESIRE

Betrayal. The Fyroxi warrior felt almost nothing besides betrayal. Oh, and hatred too, that ran blood deep. His blood was on fire, boiling and bubbling through his veins as he raced across the vista of the Scorched Waste, heedless of the energy he was wasting in his mad dash, heedless of his hunger, his thirst, or the tiredness of his muscles. He didn't care. He supped on rage tonight, and it was an ample meal, if not a nourishing one. The flames radiating from the sky, which was a sweet relief for most, felt like prickling needles over the Fyroxi's raised hackles. He had no map, but four legs and a nose were enough for him. He could smell the sweet water of an oasis in the distance, but he didn't care. Water, though necessary for survival, could not quench the blazing fury deep within him. Fury at the people he once called his Clan, and the man he viewed as a mentor. A clan of weak-willed fools, and a mentor without the mettle to show disdain for them. But more visceral than those two lurked a primal rage, directed at a woman. Barely more than a girl, just come of age, as he was. A woman who belonged to him, but refused to accept it. She teased him relentlessly with her beauty and then presumed to remain just out of reach. Then, she dared to flee her fate to take him as a mate, refusing to bear his children. And when he finally caught up to her, the illegitimate cur of a fool goddess cast him in a mantle of shame! Thanks to Amaru Sunbrand, Leif Kalix could not return to the tribe where once he was respected and feared.

"May the Chillfang take them all! They don't deserve the lives they've been granted," he snarled into the uncaring air.

He cursed and spat and roamed for nearly an hour before better sense seized hold of him. Reluctantly, the Fyroxi turned towards the oasis the aroma of which he'd caught on the breeze. He padded towards it, exhaustion dragging at his legs like heavy steel chains. *Just a few more steps. One, two...three. Now do it again. Survive, you worthless mutt, or you'll never get the revenge you are due.*

He struggled on until the barren canvas was splashed with green and blue, amazed that he hadn't seen it sooner. Black spots floated in his vision, and he sought to dispel them, bounding towards the pool.

Upon arrival, he threw all caution to the wind and splashed his fur-covered head ear-deep. He drank lustily, wishing it were the blood of the runt Fyroxi, the rising fire-spark of the Clan, or better, the sweet fluids of the pretender who owed him her life.

His stomach roiled at the sudden introduction of water, but the Fyroxi didn't care. He would settle it with a hearty meal. Rage fell flat in his belly now, and the scent of warm flesh washed over his nostrils. Food. He snuffled for a moment until he located the source, a small, unobtrusive campsite, neat and orderly. A canvas tent was set up far enough from the shore of the pond to not cause disruption. On a smoldering campfire sat a pot of thick, meaty stew, balanced on two evenly spaced rocks, stained white with ash. The meal was cool enough to eat, and

Leif, still in fox form, tucked in with relish, slurping the stew and gnashing the potatoes and meat chunks into mush.

He didn't even notice the rustling in the tent behind him.

"I apologize; I was busy reading and doing my daily prayers and must not have heard you arrive, my guest. How rude of me,"

Leif didn't even spare the woman a glance, finishing the contents of the pot. He hadn't eaten this well in months. With spare hunting and dwindling supplies, daily rations were bland and just serviceable for survival. As a hunter and warrior, he was fed more than most, but it wasn't enough as far as Leif was concerned. This pot of stew was a start in the right direction.

"I'm, ah, I'm honored, of course, for the chance to share my food with a Fyroxi, though I wish you'd have notified me of your arrival, then I could have served you," the woman said. "'Tis Water Caller custom, after all."

That name caused Leif to look up from his meal. Water Callers, the too-generous wanderers, where his worthless erstwhile tribe turned for succor, leaving their pride as a race at the threshold.

"I'm Caller Asha; might I have your name?" she prompted. Leif growled at the druid, but examined her. It didn't take long before his anger flared up once more. Asha was pretty enough, clearly not from the desert, and likely a neophyte among her order. Her skin—flushed from the encounter's awkwardness—though tan carried highlights that suggested paleness, and a tendency to burn. She smelled of aloe, too. Asha dressed like most other Water Callers: blue-dyed robe, wooden platform sandals, and a supply pouch filled with herbs and other medicines. This one, however, added a bit of flair to her outfit. Ribbons of deeper green than Leif had ever seen streamed down around her frilled necktie. A large, puffy hat, mint green, rested upon her head, looking like nothing quite so much as an unbaked loaf of bread. And streaming down from underneath it was hair, black as the fabled night. Leif blinked slowly, seeing phantasms of another woman in her place. But no, this Water Caller had large, round eyes, only slightly lighter than her hair, her lips were thicker, her face rounder, neck longer and thinner, the muscles contracting in fear as the shifted Fyroxi leered at her. Despite all of that, Asha looked familiar enough to grind stones between his ears.

I'm still hungry.

Overcome with lingering rage from this afternoon, he leaped, the dark parts of his brain reveling in her barely noticed scream. Noise carried across the Scorched Waste, though. Without more than a second's hesitation, Leif clamped down on that long, soft throat. Sweet, red lifeblood coursed into his mouth. He would have grinned, except he didn't want to waste any precious, delicious viscera. With a swift, savage jerk, he ripped the throat out, leaving a bloody mess behind. As soon as he finished that morsel, he savaged the druid's face. There would be no reminders of that contemptible tramp, Leif would make sure of that.

He slept deep and warm then, his rest undisturbed by images of Amaru, Ren, Sigmund, or the weak-willed Water Callers, his stomach full for the first time in months.

He drowsed in the woman's own tent until awoken by a cold, steel blade against his throat.

Leif startled, and tried to jerk away, but was quickly restrained by an arm strong as an iron bar. His hands instinctively moved towards the hilts of his swords.

"Don't bother, fox, removing those was the first thing we did," whispered an icy voice, thin and dangerous. Maybe it was the dagger nearly drawing blood on his throat, or perhaps the fact that his rage had been sated with his wanton rampage the evening before, but Leif got the sense that fighting back now would be pointless. Strange, when he'd always been so quick to jump into battle. But Leif heard the implicit threat, and he believed it.

For when he looked at the dagger against his throat, he could see its curved shape, and the glistening, oily blackness on its tip; these were Venomsting.

"What do you want?" he asked bluntly, though trying to fake respectful deference.

"You are not one of us," the man said. "But, this one piece of advice, I'll give freely. One of the many codes of the Venomsting is, 'When life is claimed, a life must be offered in return.'"

"What are you talking about? Speak plainly. I don't have time for vagaries."

That drew a laugh from his captor. "You are at my mercy. The amount of time you have is entirely reliant on said mercy. Thickheadedness makes the oasis of charity grow dry."

Leif clamped his jaw shut, realizing that it might spare his life at this moment. It was incredibly humbling, this shift in power and control.

"It seems he has a brain after all," another voice, this one female, and rather shrill, chuckled. "But since he's obviously confused, you might as well explain the phrase, Zossttak. It's not like he'll be alive long enough to make use of it."

"As you say, Venhana." Leif detected a faint hint of a smile in the Venomsting's voice and buried the urge to swallow nervously. He knew that any movement could break the skin, leaving the poison on the dagger tip free to course into his veins. "You have claimed a life, one that was not yours to claim," the man called Zossttak explained. "The Water Caller you have slain and consumed was our mark, or, more specifically, Venhana's. Since you have stolen the woman's life, Venhana has permission to end yours."

"And it is a permission I plan to make good use of," Venhana said, coming around so that Leif could see her. The woman was a gnome, of *course;* it was a sun-cursed gnome, Leif thought. Her skin was brown as a nut, her curly brown hair shot through with deep red stripes. Beady black eyes shone with cold anticipation that spoke of her murderous desire. "Especially since that was my initiation rite." She smiled dangerously. "But, I think that Kol-D'tah will appreciate this gift even more." From her belt, Venhana removed two black handles, just handles, though Leif could see a small rivet at the ovoid top of each. With one motion Leif could only just barely follow, she flicked them upwards, and curved, sickle-like blades flipped out and locked into place, and Venhana replaced Zossttak's knife with one sickle. "Now, given your position as a child of the Sun, I'll give you one last honor. You can choose whether I practice one of my quick kill methods or the slow one. If you choose slow, I'll even give you something that'll make you go numb, because I'm friendly like that."

Before Leif could respond, a low, angry growl came from outside the tent.

"Hurrry this farrrce up. The day is warrrm, and we have no time forrr games with any Fyrrroxi!" a guttural voice said in a language that sounded surprisingly like Fyran. Chillfang! "Kill him now and let's get on with it."

Venhana shrugged. "Well, you heard the wolf. A quick death, it is. Sorry to steal your choice, but them's the coconuts!"

Chillfang working together with Venomsting, hmm? Leif was somewhat surprised that creatures so powerful would lower themselves down to ally with others. *Of course, they're at a disadvantage here in Sun's Reach. And the Venomsting are probably the best allies to have, with how deadly and feared they are on their own. It gives them a chance to live longer. And,* he realized, *it grants me an opportunity for survival. I'm not sure what god is behind this, but be it Gaarhowl or the Venomsting's Kol-D'tah, they have blessed me indeed. With the right words, I can save my own skin and get one step closer to my revenge.* Leif knew just the words that would work.

"Wait!" he called hoarsely as Venhana moved to slide the sharp sickle across his throat. "Chillfang. I'm not the Fyroxi you want."

"You don't say, weak foxling? But, yourrr blood will serrrrve forrr now," the wolf-beast responded. "Yourrr people's numberrrs dwindle. They'll not live long, and how sweet it will be to bathe in the blood of ourrr hated enemy at long last!"

Leif glanced sidelong at the gnome. "You said that for a life, a life must be paid."

"That I did!"

"My life would be worth nothing to you. As far as my Clan is concerned, and for all I care, I am not one of them. You would be slaying a useful ally."

The Chillfang bulled forward, knocking Venhana to the side. "You look strrrong, but we have many strrrong fighterrrs. You would just be one in a numberrr. Unless you have something to set you aparrrt, I see no rrreason to leave you alive. Something that would rrrival the taste of yourrr blood!"

"Trust me," Leif said, his confidence returning. "None of your other fighters know where the Sun Wench is." He used the title the Chillfang who had attacked that night he should have had his prize had filled the air with. He looked between the dark blue, intense eyes of the Chillfang, and the gnome woman's sparkling black eyes, now filled with amusement. "I do."

"Rrrelease him," the Chillfang said. "I will find you anotherrr drrruid to kill."

I'm coming for you, Amaru.

AMARU

SIMPLICITY, THY NAME'S FRIENDSHIP

It had been several long days of meeting, planning, and, for Amaru, healing. The journey through the desert hadn't been kind to the Fire-Striders, though thanks to Amaru and the other Healers' ministrations, none of the injuries proved mortal.

She'd had nary a moment of rest and was on her feet, bustling about almost non-stop. Usually, she wouldn't have it any other way. But today, the High Servant had ordered her to take a day off.

"You work yourself thin, day in, and day out. You bade your Clan come, and they came. Go cool your heels for a while. I've given young Ren and Xio a reprieve as well. Do not let obligations stand between you and personal relationships; that doesn't make a healthy healer."

Amaru thanked him in a choked voice, remembering how Chief Durrigan had oft said something similar to her. Ren and Xio were waiting for her, beneath an awning, sprawled out in fox form, Xio with little Jarrah, the young male from Fyrestone. His sister was nowhere in sight, though Amaru knew that Purell had taken the foreign girl as an apprentice to replace Vienna, dead these past few months.

Ren flagged his tails at her, and Amaru realized just how long it had been since she'd let herself slip skin purely for pleasure. There was a languid strength and pleasant connectivity with Yamaria that came with taking fox form. Recently, Amaru had taken to using the form only in battle or sometimes, rarely, in hunting. It was dangerous, given the presence of Chillfang searching for her. Right now, though, she was safe in the company of friends and family. Without breaking stride, the girl shifted, becoming the long, two-tailed white fox that was her birthright shape. She recalled being young, before her First Shift, Durrigan stroking her gently and lovingly. She banished the thoughts, refusing to be overcome with sadness. Her two best friends lay before her, and she brushed her snout against each of theirs affectionately. With a contented sigh, she plopped down beside them.

"It's only been a few months, but it felt like a lifetime," Amaru began in Fyran. "I'm glad to be back with you." She surveyed the surrounding camp, ecstatic to see how well the Fyroxi were being received by the Water Callers. She noticed several groups of mixed people talking, even laughing, despite the direness of their situation. Then, Amaru caught sight of another familiar face, and a surge of joy and hope pulsed through her. Lily, the half-breed girl, pleyed with several other children, while her parents looked on proudly and content, finally able to be together. Lily seemed to notice Amaru's gaze and waved enthusiastically, sending Amaru a bright, warm smile. Finally, the girl who'd been given so much trouble because of her mixed blood had found friends.

"I'm just happy you survived," Ren said, reaching out his tail to wrap around hers. "When we heard no news about you, we all feared the worst. We didn't want to say anything, because had the Water Callers heard of your disappearance, they likely would have searched for you."

"To have one group seeking me is to lead those of less scrupulous minds to my trail," Amaru said. "So, I appreciate your silence."

Xio shooed Jarrah away with her tail, urging the kit to join the other children so that the three friends could talk in peace. "He's getting bigger," she remarked as Jarrah ran off with a gleeful yip. "Before you left, I could hold him up with my tail. Now, I think he'd break it if I tried."

"It's good that he's growing so well, especially given the sudden change in lifestyle he must have had coming from the fertile Sulfaari Expanse," Amaru pointed out. "He's young, and thus, more adaptable, but we can't be surprised, not for him, Savannah, or Weylin. It's not like they had any other choice in the matter."

"That's true. Thank Yamaria they came, though. They impressed upon us the truth of the Chillfang, so they didn't catch us irreparably off guard," Ren said, sounding more the warrior than Amaru had ever heard him before. She was proud. "We could have never predicted that our enemies would attack during the Hundredth Sun celebration, but I think, and Sigmund agrees, that knowing they existed within our lands, that fear kept us from being overwhelmed and slaughtered on the spot."

Amaru nodded. "It may be the only reason, save Yamaria's grace, that there are threescore of us left, rather than only three."

They sat in solemn silence for a few minutes before Xio grinned as much of a toothy grin as a fox could, "Enough talk about such upsetting things. Save that for the council meetings.

We're reunited as friends once more, and I, for one, want to hear what you've been up to!"

"How did you survive? You told us it was a difficult road, but we need every detail," Ren prodded.

"Every detail you're willing to share, that is," Xio said slyly. "No need to embarrass yourself."

"There is naught in my tale that would embarrass me to say," Amaru said, using her free tail to swish across Xio's snout and causing her to sneeze, a cloud of sand puffing up from the loosely woven grass mat beneath them. "So, you're the only remaining member of our age group that still retains her desert flower? Surprising if you traveled with that elvish bard. I could have sworn by the way you called him a 'charmer' that you two were hiding something more heartfelt."

"Alaric is a friend," Amaru replied. "A friend I would entrust my life to, though we've not known each other long, but still nothing more than a friend."

"If you say so," Xio teased, not sounding convinced.

"Would you like to hear my story or not?" Amaru demanded, somewhat tiredly, though the easy joking between friends had been desperately missed since her departure. The two other Fyroxi bobbed their heads. Amaru regaled them with the tale, from finding Alaric and the attack at Solgaele Monastery to their trek through the unnatural sandstorm and the Venomsting hideout raid. She left out almost no detail; these were her best friends after all, so what did she have to hide?

When she was finished, her throat was parched from the clawing desert air, so she gave her friends a chance to speak. "How about your journey here? Did you find much difficulty? I was relieved to learn that the tribe didn't lose more members, though surprised. I'd expected a mass movement of Fyroxi to prompt Chillfang reaction."

"As did I," Ren admitted. "But, strangely, though our scouts saw the beasts occasionally, they never approached us. Methinks it has to do with the glaivewraith."

"The glaivewraith?" Amaru asked. She'd never heard of anyone called that before.

"That was what the others insisted on calling him—or her—I didn't get close enough to check. Not that my fingers would have survived had I done so."

"We saw the glaivewraith in the distance a few times, and once Ren and I actually saw it fighting a Chillfang. It was a fantastic show. The glaivewraith's every movement was efficient, silent, and passionless, and he fought with his hands and a long wooden shaft with two big, arched blades on either end. He wore drab gray clothing over leather armor and a strange black mask."

Efficient in every movement, quiet, like a stone statue, but loose and flexible as a sand viper. Could it be Sultan? Amaru vaguely remembered the boy, one of Alaric's fellow monks. A strange character, that one, almost the dynamic opposite of her Elven traveling companion. He fit the description. *If it is Sultan, I wonder what caused him to leave. I hope Solgaele is still standing. Gemna and the others were so welcoming, it would be a shame to lose them.* But Amaru didn't want to jump to conclusions. It could be Sultan, or it could be someone else entirely. *And an assumption isn't worth its weight in dims.* She made a mental note to pick Alaric's brain about it later.

"He certainly sounds mysterious," Amaru said. "Especially with people giving him the name 'glaivewraith!' Leave it to our Clan to give out titles!" Xio nudged Ren with a paw. "Tell me about it. They named this silly fox Ren the Hero because they found him sleeping in a puddle of wolf blood the morning after a battle."

"H-hey, I did more than that!" Ren protested. "You'll make me sound bad!"

"What's wrong, honey?" Xio asked, a little too sweetly. "Does the hero want to keep up a dashing reputation for his old swain?

I'll let you in on a little secret, Ren. You have a mate now, and I have the right to tease you mercilessly." She playfully rolled onto her back, showing Ren her belly. "You can't do anything about it, and you wouldn't if you could, love!"

The short, brown Fyroxi, unable to refute Xio's claim, just let out something akin to a sigh, though it was more of a low gurgling growl. "I liked you more when you just slept all the time."

Amaru couldn't resist a laugh at her friends' antics. "You two are a perfect match! I find much comfort in your finding of each other in my absence."

"I won't deny that your departure made our relationship possible, but I wish it didn't have to be," Xio admitted. "You would have been wonderful to have around. The moment you crossed out of Fire-Strider borders, I could feel the stress that overtook the community. Everyone was afraid of losing you for good. Even now, being with you, it feels like there is some distance between us." Amaru tried to deny it, but Xio waved her off. "No, listen. We're your family, aye, you keep saying that, but with you becoming the leader of the Scions of the Rising Sun, it feels as if Yamaria's destiny has found you and locked you here with restraining chains. If it's going to save the tribe and the desert, then, by all means, stay with them. Just...don't forget your family at home, okay?"

Amaru nestled closer to Xio. "I promise that I'll never forget you. How could I? My first friends, and my dearest, from my earliest days to my final ones."

"I like the sound of that." Amaru could hear drowsiness in her tone. *Only Xio could fall asleep in mid-conversation,* she thought. "But, Amaru, don't forget yourself, either. You need happiness just as much as Ren and I do." Xio yawned cavernously. "Matchmaker, matchmaker, make yourself a match," she slurred. Then, with no other warning, she dropped into a deep sleep. Amaru and Ren hooked their tails in a Fyran shrug and cuddled up next to their friend and mate. Someday, maybe even soon, Amaru would be called away for duty, but for now, they could just go back to the halcyon days of three friends, together on a grass mat, soaking in the radiance of the Sun Mother's smile.

AL ARIC

SUN MAIDEN'S SONG

I play for beautiful women regularly, Alaric thought against his nervousness. *One might even say I make a career out of it!* He laughed humorlessly to himself. "This should be no different," he said quietly enough that even his keen Elven ears could barely pick it up. But it would be different, and Alaric knew it. As the Elven bard mounted the stairs leading up to the makeshift stage constructed at his request several weeks prior, he felt a roiling in his stomach. It felt akin to a bunch of silkworms taking full advantage of the space, squirming and secreting their threads, making a general tangle of his insides. *So long as I keep my jitters directed inward, let nothing show through my composure; I shouldn't have an issue.* His long, off-gold fingers were constricted chokingly around his fiddle's neck, the knuckles blanching from the pressure. *Relax and release. No need to strangle your poor instrument; it has served you faithfully.*

Alaric had long considered himself a daring man, willing to take risks where others dared not. Take, for instance, becoming a bard. At home in Mirshiall, he'd had all the creature comforts one could aspire to, save the respect of his father. But Taliesin Valyaara was notoriously difficult to please, so Alaric didn't feel so guilty about that. All of it had been tossed to the wayside—all except the parental disapproval—for a chance at the life of the humble wandering troubadour. *Well, perhaps not humble, but a wandering troubadour nonetheless.* He devoted himself to keeping history while subsequently making his mark upon it. And it had turned out well, remarkably so, even! He hadn't wanted for anything in his rambling life. Well, that wasn't necessarily true, but those things he lacked, Alaric had only viewed as trifling nuisances.

Until he'd met Amaru Sunbrand.

Being wrangled into a monastery in the Scorched Waste had seemed a cruel and unusual punishment. Clearly, his father had meant it as a slight, and Alaric had chafed at the injustice of it.

But Amaru had explained to him that he'd gone astray.

She'd come into his life as an unwilling traveler, drawn by sorely missed strains of music. Now, she was the subject of his sweetest songs. Amaru Sunbrand gave meaning to strumming that had once been nugatory.

The mood about Oasi Sanctus had grown undeniably dour. For the past several weeks it had been, now that the initial joy of welcoming the Fyroxi had worn thin. Following the defeat of the sand wyvern, spirits had been lofty. With the arrival of the last remaining members of Yamaria's signature race, these spirits had come crashing down and now hung around the encampment like a nebulous pall. Plans were still solidifying, and the reignition of Chillfang and Chitinite attacks added a killer punctuation to their world's sentence.

The crowd of onlookers, Water Caller and Fyroxi both,

sought an escape from. By Yamaria, Alaric had been called, and now, he would serve.

The elf's uniquely shaped green eyes scanned the throng. Standing to the left under the rearranged awnings were the Water Callers, Dalphamair, and Celwyn sitting with them. They stood apart from the Fyroxi, not out of fear or disrespect. The Fyroxi had been perfect guests thus far, not demanding nor taxing to their hosts' sanity. *The Fire-Striders couldn't have gotten far without learning to accept their load of work, so I'm not surprised to see them rise to the occasion. They are Amaru's people, after all.*

Among the Fyroxi side, Alaric first located Ren and Xio, the two lovers with their hands and tails entwined. He appreciated those two, the best friends of the woman who, to him, was the most precious jewel in the world. Leif Kalix hadn't deigned to make a reappearance, and Alaric was relieved. He wasn't sure how that Fyroxi with raging soul and possessive mind would have taken what Alaric knew he had to do today.

Finally, he sought out Amaru, gorgeous, sun-bright Amaru. She stood directly at the dividing line of the two groups, as radiant as the morning sun after a Sulfaari rainstorm, declaring herself as both a part of each group and separate, all at the same time. Alaric wondered whether that was deliberate? Whether it was or not, the symbolism made Alaric's heart flutter like a tent in a sand squall.

Alaric reached the top of the steps, bowed silently to his audience, and brought his fiddle around to the front, forcing himself to relax. These people loved hearing his idle music, and when the idea of Alaric holding a concert of sorts had been pitched, the answer had resounded with pure positivity. *Would you look at me now, father! I've even made a barren desert into an enclave of fans.*

As he had for Amaru's first solo concert, all that time ago, when he'd just been a reluctant monk, and she a beautiful stranger, the elf started small, picking off vocal and instrumental lead-ins, curtain raisers, of a sort. He had no curtain to reveal him now. And part of him wished he did, so he would have something to hide behind if this didn't go as planned. *Quiet thyself, cynical thoughts. My mind hasn't the vacancy to sustain you! You will pull this off with aplomb. The Water Callers and Fyroxi will cheer, and Amaru will see the truth.*

With a smile, he shared with everyone but felt private to each recipient; he launched into the true performance. Alaric led the enthralled crowd through an enchanting symphony, channeling bardic magic he'd mastered long ago to provide the instruments he couldn't, floating spectral implements appearing and dancing around the stage while they played. Alaric mixed songs of his own with beloved favorites of both desert dwellers and denizens of the Green Pastures, as some Callers preferred to label the Kingdom proper, weaving them together into an audile tapestry, like the world's most musically talented loom. He stopped but once to take a drink of water, graciously provided to him by Rovinald—an extra ration for his good deed. *I suppose I should thank my good graces that the High Servant doesn't see the selfishness behind my desire to perform;* he chuckled to himself. Alaric took a deep breath after whetting his throat and flexed his long, dextrous fingers in preparation for his most impressive piece, one that few bards had ever really mastered.

Volmund's String Burning.

The entire throng of Scorched Waste denizens stared in rapt awe and wonderment as he sawed his bow across the fiddle, generating heat from the instrument and conjuring spurts of illusory fire behind him. He relegated a tiny sliver of his concentration to making the plumes sway and twist, twining like lovers embracing and leaping in time with the pounding of Alaric's heart.

When at last he was finished, the audience was stunned, statues frozen in time, like the gallery of a possessive medusa.

Alaric should have stopped there. But he had one last piece, a capstone of sorts.

As men and women began to shuffle and turn away, Alaric cleared his throat, gathered his courage, and spoke, using magic to carry his whisper to every ear. "Ladies and gentlemen, my performance is not yet concluded." Behind him was a canvas draped stool, which the elf reached under to produce his lute. He perched upon the seat and bent over the instrument.

Alaric's final song was entirely sovereign, needing neither illusions nor magical amplification, and yet it held more latent power than any of his previous tunes.

"Once winter left a man alone to shiver, torn apart. The chill of night, like icy maw devouring his heart. It snuck in with a frigid knife, a fatal message to impart. But when it struck, it found no gain, deflected by a shield of comfort-warm flame. A fiery wall, brought by a desperate call, to stay daggers in the dark.

Then spring came round, to erupt in joyful sound, sending passions soaring high. Love blossomed as the flower, music was the bee. It flourished and grew, nourished by the heart, and nurtured by honey-sweet time.

In summer, the sun's intense scowl showed no mercy! It melted winter love like ice, such impermanence couldn't stay. And spring's sweetest illusions under heated glare so too did fade away.

The heart, an empty husk, shriveled within its prison bod, could only wait for autumn. It hoped that with glorious giving, to its lap, true love might fall. For amid the flying leaves, one may find a heart that's not a fraud.

You found me in the height of summer, weathered its dissolving stare. From prison stone-cold sterile, you led me by the hand. And through days of endless hardship, you won my heart while holding the sun's sharp brand.

Those who know you not spread slander in the air, 'wench,' they call you, "false prophet,' too! But by Yamaria, I know these words aren't true. I've seen many wenches, false prophets, more than my fair share.

But none could compare to you, radiant Sun Maiden fair!"

The following silence differed from before, more contemplative than admiring, though there was a mix of praise in the glazed eyes, too. Alaric forced himself to look at Amaru, afraid of what he'd see in her face.

With his sharp, Elven vision, he could make out every detail. The woman's arms were folded behind her back, her stance rigid. Her jaw was locked, and even skilled Alaric couldn't read her expression. Only her ears moved, twitching in a way that the elf knew telegraphed that she was mighty uncomfortable. Alaric's heart dropped as if the pedestal that held it up had crumbled. He lost track of everything at that moment. He wasn't even sure if his outward repose had lasted or whether the stage face had melted away to be replaced with the mask of anguish he felt so keenly in his heart.

Amaru recovered from the magicless spell before anyone else. She spared Alaric a single, fleeting glance before turning on her heel and retreating away from the stage and the crowd.

What did you expect? asked the cynical voice within him, cold, harsh, and uncaring. *Did you think she was going to mount the stage and throw her arms around you?*

No, he might have dreamed of that outcome, but he'd never dare expect it. But that wasn't the thing that broke him. He recognized the softness in Amaru's eyes in that last glance.

Alaric might very well be able to run and catch up to Yamaria's child, break down at her feet, and beg for forgiveness. If he asked for a kiss, he might even get it, but it wouldn't be delivered of love.

Alaric thought it would taste like pity.

. . .

Two weeks later, Alaric sat in his tent; most of his funk evaporated like so much water on the sands. He sipped reverently from the stone decanter beside him, one of the first lessons Amaru had taught him. Then, he returned to the paper before him, determined not to allow thoughts of his sweet Fyroxi cleric to subsume him. He was busy wracking his brain and writing. 'Twas not another song, nor an apology to Amaru, whom he hadn't spoken to since the concert fiasco. His slated task was arguably more difficult than either of those.

The attacks of the Chillfang had only increased in intensity, a renewed vigor coming over them. In the post-sunfall hours, the air would often be filled with their cries of "Sun Wench," or "Gaarhowl will devour your flesh," among other gruesome promises.

But, much to Rovinald's pride, and the Chillfang's dismay, the allies hadn't folded. In fact, led by the Scions of the Rising Sun, they had prospered. Sure, there had been many losses among the ranks of the Water Callers, but Dalphamair was fond of saying, "A war without losses ain't a war at all!"

Each member of the Scions rushed into battle, intrepid and infused with valor, and showed no restraint, not even Amaru, who they sought to capture. Now that they seemed to know she was here, the woman saw no reason to hide, and on the battle-field, she was a force to be reckoned with. Her deep faith in Yamaria was rewarded with fiery shields and devastating blows that crippled her foes and warmed her observers' hearts—Alaric's most of all. One of these days, he figured, he'd have to approach her. He needed to apologize before the estrangement between them festered.

I'll do it just as soon as I finish this letter, he vowed. But what a demanding task that was! He'd chosen to work alongside Elder Copernicus, drafting proposals for alliance between the Water Callers and the various tribes that roamed the desert. Many had answered in the affirmative, for the Chillfang scourge ranged far and wide across the Scorched Waste. Unfortunately, the tribe Alaric had been saddled with wooing now, the Water Callers knew the least about.

Apparently, the Drakenblood prided themselves on battle prowess, a sensible skill, since they ranged along the salt flats between the borders of the Goldbasket and the deepest part of the Scorched Waste, where few humans had the constitution to survive—the Desolation.

It was rumored that the black, volcanic sands of the Desolation could tear apart a man's feet if the monsters didn't get to them first. Alaric had never believed the tales of beasts, but in his travels with Amaru thus far, seeing the Chitinite and the massive wyvern first hand, those presuppositions had been shattered. He wondered if the tales of goblins and trolls in the kingdom proper were accurate as well.

If these Drakenblood fought these monsters as they trekked their arduous path, they could be a perfect ally in this war. That was why High Servant Rovinald wouldn't get off his back, demanding that he write to this chieftain that nobody knew, Gherkhill, and ask for his aid.

Alaric was puzzling over what words and promises might sway this mystery chieftain when a knock came at the front flap.

Alaric dropped his quill and ran an ink-stained hand through his long, wheat-colored tresses, leaving black streaks.

"No, I have come no closer to writing a decent proposal. If you insist on these interruptions, I fear I will never finish your damned letter!" Alaric growled tiredly.

A muffled laugh chimed through the tent flap, and Alaric recognized his mistake instantly. "It's just me, Alaric," the honeyed voice that haunted his dreams said. "I wished to speak with you, but seeing as you are so busy, I will return another time."

Alaric bolted upright so fast that he upended the water jug all over his attempts at letters. The Elven bard cringed for a moment, but only a moment, rushing over to the threshold and throwing open the flaps before the woman could escape from him once more. "Amaru, I'm sorry. I hadn't a clue." He'd committed the cadence of her steps to memory long ago and berated himself for not discerning it. "Please, my lady, come in."

Alaric winced at the desperation in his voice. *Come on, buck up! This woman is a warrior; she doesn't want to see you snivel.*

Amaru entered, and her gaze immediately went to the spilled water. She shook her head, but Alaric thought he caught a hint of a smile on her lips. Then she turned to study him, and Alaric didn't bother to put up any walls. He was weary, and he allowed Amaru to see it. Silence stretched long and awkward before Amaru came forward and took his hand. The nexus of their connection glowed warmly, and Alaric felt healing energy flow through his body.

"When you are wounded, common sense dictates you visit a healer," she scolded.

"I apologize, Amaru," Alaric said warily. "I didn't think it was so serious." *Nor did I think you'd seen.* In the last battle, he and Dalph had squared up against a Chitinite, and one of its crab-like claws had closed in around Alaric's arm. It had hurt like the devil, but it certainly wasn't anything life-threatening.

"Any wound can be serious if not properly taken care of," Amaru said. She paused for a moment, then locked her gaze on his. "You've been avoiding me," she accused.

"I—ah—aye, my lady," he confessed. "That I have,"

"Why?"

By Yamaria, how could Alaric explain? *I feared my words had driven you away. I don't think I could have survived had I bared my soul to you in private, and you rejected me. For that reason, I did you a grievous wrong. I couldn't bear to see your disdain, so I forced myself to stay away, though surely my heart and soul withered for it.* "I—apologize for the, um, th-the song," he choked out through a tightening throat. *Divines, elf, you sound like a wordless clod!*

"Oh, that," Amaru said. Alaric realized she was still holding his hand. She dragged him over to the woven grass mat that served as a bed and pointed to it. "Sit."

Alaric did, and Amaru settled down next to him. "What are you...?" Alaric asked.

"Shhh," Amaru placed a finger on his lips to hush him. "I don't want you worrying about the song," she said, peering into his soul with her enchanting brass orbs. "It was a wonderful piece."

"But you didn't like it," Alaric prompted.

Amaru laughed, and the sound pierced the elf's heart as wholly as her spear ever could. But, to his surprise, it wasn't derision that flowed from her mouth. "For someone who read me like a book when I first arrived at Solgaele, you are having surprising difficulty in rendering the truth now," she said gently, soothingly.

"What are you saying?" Alaric asked, perplexed.

Amaru shook her head and squeezed the elf's hand. "Alaric Valyaara, I loved your song," she declared, seeing that subtlety wasn't penetrating the fog around his heart. "I'll admit, it was...embarrassing in the moment, but it was a genuine and thoughtful lay. You told me once that you'd write a tune for me, and I am pleased with the result."

Alaric could feel the drumbeat of his heart in his ears, as blood rushed merrily throughout his body. "Amaru..."

"Actually, I've come here today to repay you for the honor."

"No payment necessary, my lady," Alaric insisted. "I am a seeker of beauty, and in you, I found a reservoir, both in your face, and, more importantly, in your heart. You inspire me every day, and I could only hope that my song could portray a pittance of that truth." Well, there it was. A confession, as shrouded in pretty words as though it was. He wondered what Amaru would make of it.

"Thank you, Alaric. Your words are appreciated, as they always will be to my ears." Those ears twitched a bit, and her two tails whooshed through the air, a flagging motion that Alaric recognized as Amaru being happy.

Ah, I've no idea whether she apprehended the declaration, or if she's merely playing coy. This is what you get for being indirect, fool elf. But, sooth, now you must wait. You don't wish to drive her away, after all.

Amaru reached into her cloak's breast pocket and pulled something out, quickly closing her hand around it. All Alaric got the chance to see was a leather cord and the glint of something shiny at the end.

Amaru reached out and placed her slender hand back into Alaric's. She opened her fingers, and something heavy plopped into the elf's palm. He withdrew his hand to look at it. The leather necklace had five small beads where it would rest against the nape of his neck; Alaric imagined that they represented both the lucky number of Yamaria and the Scions of the Rising Sun. The cord was plain leather, but the pendant on the end was anything but. Carved out of a chunk of translucent red material, like Helios's tip, was an emblem of the sun, with five perfectly chiseled rays of light radiating from the faceted center. It was gorgeous to behold, but the most impressive part about the craft was the small flickering flame burning eternally in the gem's center. Alaric didn't see any holes in the construct and wondered how it could remain burning without any visible fuel.

"It is the combination of Xio's craftmanship and my prayers to Yamaria. I figured you would appreciate it."

"It's beautiful, Amaru," Alaric said, "but what is it?"

Amaru smiled and grabbed the wrist of his free hand, guiding it up to her throat, where an identical pendant rested in the soft hollow at its base. A flame flickered in that one, too.

"What you hold in your hand is as precious a gift as someone can give. That flame, Alaric Valyaara, is a piece of my soul, as this spark about my neck is a piece of yours. You'll forgive me if I didn't ask outright. I prayed to Yamaria, and she said you would likely agree. I didn't want to ruin the surprise. You can take it back if you'd like."

Alaric was barely even listening. *Amaru gave me a portion of her soul, and I have given her a fragment of mine long ago, though it is only now visible.* "Never, Amaru. If you would treasure my soul as I will cherish yours, I will never take it away from you."

Amaru breathed a sigh that sounded like relief. "Now, if we are ever separated by our duties, we can each take comfort in knowing the other is safe."

"And, if the flame ever goes out?" Alaric asked, afraid to hear the answer.

"If that spark is ever snuffed, then the link to the soul has been broken. If the piece is gone, then the whole has likely slipped away as well."

Alaric felt tears leap to his eyes. "Promise me, Amaru Sunbrand. Promise me that the flame I hold will never go out. I don't think I could keep living if it did."

"Only the Divines know what lies in store for us. But, I will try with all I have not to let it extinguish." Amaru wrapped an arm around her friend's shoulder. "Now, don't cry; you'll waste the water," she whispered into his ear.

REN

THE FIFTH MEMBER

The Fyroxi Elders were already waiting with Rovinald, Tos, and Erein when they arrived. Only Rovinald's expression was dark enough to match the approximation of a scowl on Weylin's face, who looked as sour as a fox could. Had the Fyrestone refugee's tails still been present, Ren imagined that they'd be swishing agitatedly through the dry air. Rovinald hasn't told the others what news he has yet. Ren's training with Copernicus gave him further insight into the High Servant's expression. Whatever he has to say, it's not something he wanted to relay more than once.

Rovinald barely gave the Scions, Ren, and Xio a chance to sit and gather their thoughts before he launched into speaking.

"Dire news has recently come to us, information that might fare even worse than we could have ever feared," he began. Rovinald gestured tersely at Ren and Xio. "You two might recall that upon the melding of your tribe with the Water Callers, we surveyed for useful skills to better build ourselves up. Your friend from the pillaged city of Fyrestone has helped to rekindle Water Caller communications with places outside the Scorched Waste, something we practically lost after Godfrey Redwyn invalidated most of the desert as outskirts territory. The only part he cares about is the Goldbasket, where most of the precious gems that decked his fingers and lined the rim of his bathtub are derived from."

"Hold just one moment," Ren interjected, at the same time as Alaric. "You said 'lined.'" The elf's approving nod told Ren he'd noticed the same thing.

Rovinald cleared his throat solemnly. "While I'm sure the gems are still set in the bathtub, there is now a different man lounging within it. Godfrey Redwyn, along with his wife and daughter, has been slain."

"Goddess," Alaric breathed. "How?"

"It seems that Chillfang aren't the only things to come out of Moonwatch," Weylin growled. "Prevailing theory is that Geurus Gardstar hails from beyond the Eclipse. He and his tow-headed children certainly have the complexion for it."

"Alright, so th' king and 'is progeny are dead. I didn't hear ye mention the prince, but if Geurus's a smart usurper, Grayson Redwyn will find 'is own unmarked grave soon enough." Dalphamair pulled at his beard. "Me first question, ye hear anything about Sir Lion? Second question, what're we t' do about it?"

Weylin flicked his ears. "The only knight of any importance in my reports is Sir Casinius, and the lady Galbraith was also mentioned, though their level of involvement is practically unknown. Apparently, Galbraith was standing next to Geurus when Grayson was forced to abdicate the throne. But I think our focus is better off directed elsewhere. Our knowledge is outdated since my informant fled the city after the murder, but before Searstar was locked down."

"As for what we're going to do about it, I'm sure that's what we're here to figure out. I, for one, have a few suggestions." Tos Kamarr broke in, his voice gruff and gritty, like the sand squalls he and his soldiers had weathered for many years. "If we've got a Luney on the Highsun Seat, then we have to be quick about forming our alliances. No offense, Erein, as I know, you are fond of your letters, but we need direct action."

The Head of Healers shook her head. "You are correct."

Alaric lifted a finger. "Don't be so quick to toss words to the wayside. Thanks to my efforts, Elder Copernicus's, and our splendid cadre of messengers, we have affirmative answers from all but one tribe. The Drakenblood have responded, but their reply was less than I hoped for." The elf produced a thin, rolled scroll from his sleeves, unraveled it, and began reading. "'The Drakenblood pride strength above all else. We'll not join a war of attrition with allies who can't measure up. Send us the heart of the Water Caller's strength—not their strength of heart—and you will have your answer.' Then, there is one more thing that puzzles me. The document is signed by a Chieftain Gawain rather than Gherkhill."

"That name doesn't ring any bells," Rovinald said.

"None here, either," Tos admitted, scratching at his sparsely bearded chin, coaxing out a trickle of sand grains and dried salt. "But living in the Scorched Waste, especially in Drakenblood territory, is a precarious existence. To my ultimate shame, we haven't been keeping tabs on Gherkhill's people as we should have."

"We were all seduced by the peace of our lives," Ren mumbled. "That multiplied the severity of the Chillfang threat greatly. Durrigan and the other elders learned that lesson after the Hundredth Sun Massacre, and it seems now we all have." Sigmund, Copernicus, Silque, Purell, and Yarena all nodded mutely. Because of an untimely loss of vigilance, their tribe had suffered; it was not a mistake they were liable to make again. "So, he wants us to send proof of our strength?"

"Yes," Erein said, looking squarely at the Scions of the Rising Sun. "This Gawain knows of our prodigious generosity; that isn't the sort of assurance he is seeking. Right now, though I'm loath to send them away, the Scions are the best representation of our strength."

Tos concurred. "I'm sure that their chieftain has heard of our resident heroes and wishes to evaluate them for himself. Enclosed in that letter will be a destination for where he wants to meet you. It won't be an effortless journey, especially once you get to the salt flats, where almost no plants grow and few animals dare to wander. I'd say I know the warrior type well enough, so this will be a test of your endurance, and when you arrive, there will be a trial of sorts waiting for you."

"What will this trial entail?" Ren wondered.

"That's a good question. You should go ask Gawain yourself. Maybe he'll tell you before it starts."

"Maybe I will," the brown Fyroxi replied almost indignantly. Xio's eyes went wide, and everyone around the table stared at him."

"No offense, boy," Sigmund said, "we're sending the Scions with Amaru to them, not you."

With a tacit apology to Xio, he stood and addressed Amaru, his long-time friend. "With the openness of the desert, stealth will be almost entirely out of the question. If the Venomsting or the Chillfang come up against you, having an extra body along can only benefit you. I can carry more supplies, and even though I'm not as skilled a fighter as, say, Leif, or even you, Amaru, I'm quick. The tricks I have at my disposal could come in handy. But, more importantly, and I think my elders will support me on this, I think you should have another Fyroxi with you. I mean no offense to the allies you have traveled with, but I know my burden would be that much lighter as your friend if you had another pair of vulpine eyes watching your back. Finally, I don't mean to be too presumptuous, but your group...I count only four people. If you are working in the name of Yamaria, shouldn't you at least appeal to her divine numerology?"

A look of honest consideration filled Amaru's eyes, and now the weight of the room was all on her. His dear friend glanced first at Xio, delegating the responsibility to his mate. Ren felt a surge of hope; if Amaru was turning to Xio, that could only mean...

"I have the support of so many healers around me and several friends as well. If you insist on leaving me, Rienzi, just promise you'll come back in time to see our baby."

"You know I wouldn't miss their birth for anything, Xio," Ren said, a promise in his eyes. "It pains me to leave your side, but this feels like the right thing to do. It's like I have a voice in the back of my mind, urging me to not allow this opportunity to go to ruin."

"Oh, why didn't you say you have voices in your head?" Celwyn interjected. "If you have any mental hangers-on, your count might be off just a wee bit. Though if we're including semi-conscious voices, we might as well list Priscilla, and perhaps Yamaria, since she sometimes talks in Amaru's head." The gnome scratched her long nose. A bright smile took over her face, following the light of newfound understanding. "Unless the two voices are one and the same, Ren's and Amaru's." Just as quickly as it had appeared, the smile dropped back into a thoughtful frown. "But, even so, that leaves us at seven with the goat."

"Ye fool gnome. We're not fer countin' no goddess or me goat! Tha's not t' say Priscilla ain't more o' a member than this scrawny fox, no offense t' ye, Ren." Dalphamair paused, his stream of cohesive thought going dry. "Bah, ye confused me, gnome!"

"Not a hard thing to do," Cely taunted gaily. "Not a hard thing at all!"

"Why you, I oughta..." Dalphamair shook his fist at the small woman.

"You oughta what?" the blonde gnome asked. "Watch your words, or I just might make the next well we come upon have just enough water for either you or the goat."

Dalphamair eyed his friend skeptically. "Ye can't do tha'!" he turned up to Alaric. "She can't do tha' right?"

Alaric shrugged, an innocent expression of uncertainty covering his handsome features.

"Bah!" Dalphamair stormed over to the tent flaps and lifted one over his head. "Welcome t' th' team, lad. Now, I'm fer leavin', th' sooner th' better!

Amaru held out a hand to Ren, and he took it for a firm handshake. "You heard the dwarf. Welcome to the Scions of the Rising Sun, Rienzi Gyndalon.

"I'm looking forward to seeing how far you've come in the time I missed." She knelt in front of Xio. "I want to see your kit born as well."

"Well, I'll be sure to keep that in mind when I choose to give birth to them." Xio rolled her eyes sardonically. "Now, please, take my mate away, before I have the chance to think about what I've just agreed to. Because, trust me, if he doesn't leave now, he never will." Amaru nodded and led her team to their tents to gather supplies.

Ren followed them to the door but turned at the cusp of leaving, ran back to Xio, and kissed her tenderly. "I love you, and I can't wait until I'm back at your side."

Xio's eyes crinkled, and she pointed towards the sunlight. "Out. I love you but, get out, my Trinket." Ren hastened to obey, already thinking about what he'd stock his pouches with.

AL ARIC

A DESERT STROLL

Ah, to see Amaru back in her natural habitat was a stunning sight, and Alaric found it nigh impossible to keep his eyes off of her. Of course, watching Amaru in her deepest mode of concentration as she took care of an ailing patient was beautiful. Still, there was something about being out in the desert, combining her natural sense of her homeland with Celwyn's knowledge to guide them unerringly through the vast desert, from well to oasis, to stray Water Caller camp, that made her marvelous. Alaric fondled the Kerazar pendant and smiled, never once forgetting the significance of the gift. Save the Lightstriders, nobody, not even King Godfrey, when he still drew breath, not born of Fyroxi or Sun-Elven blood owned a weapon or bauble made of Kerazar steel. It was a genuinely singular contribution, only made more special because it contained a sliver of the soul of the woman he loved. He kept that pendant hanging by his heart always, feeling it resonate with his pulse, as Amaru would be with his against her own chest.

I will have to write more songs for her, at some point, he realized. *Though I'll keep them a bit more private. They don't even need to be about her, come to think of it. She likes my music well enough; she has no fondness for being the center of attention, and my display made her just that. So long as I don't repeat those fatal errors, I may yet redeem and glorify myself in her eyes. Nay, not glorify, for it is she who deserves worship, not I.*

"Alaric, are you hungry?"

The elf turned downwards to see Amaru's small, brown-furred friend, Ren. He had an oblong purple object in his hand, leaking staining juices from its shaved ends. It looked like a large potato with little star-shaped brown spots, similar to the afore-mentioned tuber's eyes. "Before I answer, I'd like to know what I might or might not be eating. I'm assuming you wouldn't try to poison me."

"Huh?" Ren looked genuinely perplexed. "N-no, why would I do that?"

"Well, if I wasn't around, that would be one less mouth to feed," Alaric pointed out. "Did that dwarf put you up to this?"

"Not at all. It's something people in the desert eat all the time," Ren promised, thoroughly flustered. "Trust me, Alaric, I like you, and more importantly, Amaru cherishes you. If I did anything to hurt you, she might skewer me with that spear."

"Ah, but if she cherishes me, she adores you. I doubt she could bring herself to bring harm upon your lean frame."

"If you don't trust me, then I'll eat this one, and you can have the next one Amaru finds." Ren brought the potato-shaped object up to his mouth, flicking his eyes back and forth from the food to Alaric.

"I was having fun with you, lad. Please, don't fault an elf for his tricks. It's nearly all I have to fall back on. Feel free to laugh." Ren did, albeit nervously. "Now, tell me what delicacy you have prepared for me."

"I wouldn't call it a delicacy. Actually, the taste is pretty bland, but prickly pear is a staple around these parts of the desert, where cacti grow." Alaric had noted the prevalence of the stocky, barrel-shaped plants.

Upon seeing them for the first time, Celwyn had said, "Now, I know from afar they look a bit like people, especially the two armed kinds."

"I don't know any other kinds of people," Ren had replied with mock innocence, earning him a laugh from the other Scions.

"Anyway, you don't want to hug them. Trust me, I have it on good authority that an embrace will not make them give up any of their liquids." The gnome cracked a grin. "You, however, will be drained of some of your vital ones. So, definitely not recommended."

"With how prohibitive their spikes are, I can't imagine wanting to prey upon a cactus," Alaric commented.

"You speak truth, elf," Ren sighed. "But, if you have your way around that issue, say, a particular spear made of a slightly magical metal that probably can't rust, the rewards are worthwhile. Especially when it comes to the nopales and pads of the prickly pear. The fruit is sweet if a bit starchy, and the pads have a great deal of water. When I paid visits to this area with elder Copernicus, we would always gather up as much of these as we could salvage and bring it as a peace offering to the villagers."

"Using a godsent spear to pick fruit seems a bit lowbrow, don't you think?"

"It may be, Alaric," Amaru chimed in from the front. "But I have full confidence if I use the weapon in a way that displeases Yamaria, she will smite me with all due swiftness. If you'd rather, we can sharpen the end of your flute and use it instead?" Amaru flicked her ears and winked in his direction.

"For that matter, why not use Dalph's Retirement?" Alaric mused.

"Because me javelin is more useful t' our cause than yer dinky little instrument, durned elf," the dwarf returned.

"I don't know," Ren said, "can your Retirement do magic?"

"Bah, I don't need no stinkin' spellcraft. Me magic comes from makin' me enemies' lifeblood disappear."

"Sigmund always said that was a useful strategy."

"Yer elder Sigmund is a real dwarf's Fyroxi if ye get me drift. 'E's a respectable one. Same wit' th' crippled feller from Fyrestone. Any man who thinks about fightin' after losin' a leg is th' kinda feller we dwarves can get behind."

Ren nodded. "He saved my life during the Hundredth Sun Massacre, but he might not have had the chance if Amaru hadn't healed him. He struggled to stand, and the wounds were close to infection when he stumbled into our home. But Amaru's skills allowed him to keep living."

"He has repaid the favor more than enough already. It wasn't even that impressive of a feat," Amaru said modestly, embarrassment creeping into her voice. "The healers at Oasi Sanctus could have done the same thing, given a couple weeks and the right materials."

"But ye didn't need no advanced medicines or long recovery times," Dalphamair protested. "Much as I love 'em, I'd rather have one o' ye than half a hundred Water Callers fussin' over me!"

Alaric could see Amaru growing increasingly flustered, and she was quickening her pace, trying to distance herself from the group. He stepped in behind her and stretched out his arms almost protectively.

"All right, my uncouth friends, that's enough. We don't need to dredge up these memories for our outstanding leader. Can't you see she's growing uncomfortable?"

Amaru flashed a grateful smile his way, and Alaric's heart warmed. Just then, the elf had an epiphany. *No wonder my song drove her away! I was deifying her in front of a whole gaggle of Water Callers. Every time she's been given praise or honor, she's deflected it, for she's as humble as I relish pretending to be. If my presumptions hold even a vestige of the truth, then I've been going about courting Amaru all wrong! She's the daughter of the goddess Yamaria, that much is true, but she craves to be treated like any normal Fyroxi. By the Divines! For someone who claims to be skilled at reading others, that was incredibly thick of me not to realize sooner! I must be more cautious and far more gracious. Don't praise as much; rather, amaze her with extremely fair treatment. And by all means, try to be more patient. I'm a young elf with a full stock of years ahead of me, after all. If it takes three or four to see Amaru sweet on me, then it will be worth it.* Alaric grinned to himself and glanced up at the sun, which was showing signs of moving from its mountain nest to bring on the scorching heat of the day.

"It's almost time for us to stop for the day," Amaru called out. Due to the cactus and other small vegetation around here, we should find some animals and have a proper meal tonight. Unfortunately, we're a bit far from any oases, but there ought to be enough water in our skins to last us until tomorrow."

Celwyn nodded enthusiastically. "Well, I guess that means we aren't taking a bath tonight. Pity, I'm starting to smell like Priscilla!"

The goat bleated and stamped its foot as if it had understood the slight.

The gnome ignored her and pointed up a dune in front of them, where Alaric could see a pair of distant, small boar-like animals. "I don't know about you lot," she said, "but I could really go for some bacon right about now!"

Amaru nodded, and before anyone could say anything, the Fyroxi handed her spear to Alaric and began to slip skin. With a fluid beauty, the likes of which Alaric had never seen the equal to, Amaru turned from her human-esque shape to that of a large, two-tailed white fox. She panted for a moment, then flicked her tails and began quick-stepping up the dune, treading so lightly she barely disturbed the sand. Prowling low up the sandy bluff, she came upon the beasts without them noticing she was there. Then, with a quick pounce and a perfectly aimed bite, the first one was dead. Amaru's jaw locked around its throat. She tossed it to the side and sighted the second one. Alaric watched her bound over the dune's crest and out of sight, amazed at the celerity with which she had sighted and hunted her prey in an open desert.

Then, all of a sudden, amazement shifted to utter horror, as a shape rolled over the front of the dune, and as a one, the Scions of the Rising Sun realized it wasn't the peccary careening down the hill. It was Amaru, and she was trying desperately to escape from something.

AMARU

A FOX IN WOLF'S CLOTHING

Swift and silent, as she had been taught, Amaru swept up the dune, sand flying out wherever her paws struck. The peccary was fully absorbed in attempting to eat the cactus standing at a strange angle on a hill that it didn't even snort in fear before it was felled. She tossed the pig-like animal to the side and cast her gaze around for the other one.

Then she saw it squirming in the mouth of another creature, larger than her and much more thickly built. Coarse grey fur covered its body, glistening with a thin layer of frost despite the desert sun. The great wolf shook its head once violently, breaking the peccary's neck and ending its helpless squealing. It stared directly at her as it dropped her potential meal on the desert sand, allowing all of its dark red blood to leach into the grains. Amaru's memory instantly flashed back to the red mess of the ground after the Hundredth Sun Massacre.

"Grrreedy little Sun Wench, arrrren't you," the Chillfang

growled teasingly. "Do you rrreally need two pigs to satiate yourrr hungerrr?"

Amaru locked her neck to keep from glancing back at her friends. "What do you desire from me, Chillfang?" she spat in the Fyran tongue, positioning herself to either pounce or spring away, whichever option seemed more sensible when the choice arose.

"I'm afrrraid that's morrre inforrrmation than you arrre allowed to take. Enough to say you'rrre mine, Sun Wench, or rrrather Garrrhowl's! You arrre Yamarrrria's get, arrre you not?"

Amaru knew the wolf was giving her a chance to betray the others in her Clan, her family. But, even if she knew it would save her life. Amaru wouldn't inform on them. So she nodded.

The Chillfang licked his lips, causing drops of water to spray down onto the peccary corpse below him. "It gives me pleasurrre to know that my sourrrce of inforrrmation didn't betrrray me." He flicked his thick, brushlike tail, and four more figures crested the ridge. On the far side of the group was another Chillfang, this one leaner and a bit smaller, likely female. The two wolves flanked three more humanoid figures, all cloaked. Amaru couldn't make out much from them, except that one was smaller than the others. By their size and gait, Amaru guessed they were a gnome like Celwyn.

"Greetings, Amaru," the central figure snarled in a bold voice, his tone tinged with ice not befitting his desert heritage as he slid two all too familiar scimitars from their sheaths. "I feared we'd never have the chance to meet again after you so rudely chased me out. I have missed that sleek white fur of yours."

"Leif Kalix, what in the name of Yamaria do you think you are doing?"

Leif sighed in mock annoyance. "I always regarded you as someone so smart, especially given your godly heritage, but it seems your brain is just as dull as little Trinket's!"

"Ren is more intelligent than you will ever be, Leif," Amaru rejoindered. "He was in love with me long before lust overtook your mind and livelihood, but when I rebuffed his attention, he did not flee and take up with our sworn enemy!"

The sizeable, muscular Fyroxi laughed abrasively. "Oh, yes! But you forget something crucial: Ren Gyndalon was not intended for you. I was. Yarena told you as much, I'm sure. Old Durrigan refused to tell you the truth; he was weak and doted on you. It was the design of the Clan that Amaru Sunbrand would belong to Leif Kalix."

"I would have rather mated with Ren than with you, by a significant margin."

Leif settled into a hunting stance, arms out to the side, and scimitars hooked inwards, a comfortable position for him. "Oh, trust me, Amaru. I will teach you to think differently about that soon enough. For now, though…." With no further warning, Leif leaped into the air, diving at her with swords extended.

Amaru had been expecting this. She had known, especially with the presence of Chillfang around him, that Leif would not be swayed with words save, "come and take me as you please, master Leif," a phrase which Amaru wouldn't have been caught dead with on her tongue. She held her breath until Leif was almost upon her and then released her prepared spell. With a flash of hot, white light, clinging tongues of retaliatory flame struck the larger male, sending him flying backward, yelping in pain. "Scumber!" he cried.

Amaru wasted no more time. The Chillfang were both ready to pounce, and she figured that whatever the other two figures were, they didn't mean her well either. Dinner wholly forgotten, she leaped backward and began rolling down the hill as fast as momentum could take her. Sand cascaded in a slide around her; half the face of the dune seemed to skitter about as she bumped and skidded down it. Her heart pounded as she assessed the situation at hand.

Then, from down below, she heard Alaric cry out her name. *Thank Yamaria! I'm not alone in his fight.* Gathering as much air into her lungs as she could, she roared something in Fyran and readied to steady herself when the slide ended.

She faintly heard Ren translate her phrase for everyone, "Enemies incoming, prepare to fight!" and smiled despite herself. They were the Scions of the Rising Sun. They had a mission and would prevail, one way or another. It didn't matter who stood in their path!

"Get herrr," she heard from the top of the dune.

"Amaru's mine. You lot, kill the rest!"

Another voice, this one painfully shrill, squeaked, "we don't take orders from you, Fyroxi. But, our goals align this time, so fine! If there's any Water Callers, I call dibs!"

Five figures stormed down the dune, and the five Scions stood resolutely below them. Amaru and Dalphamair stood in front, both snarling. Alaric and Celwyn were behind, spells curled on their tongues. And Ren was sandwiched in the middle, frantically searching through his packs.

"Ren," Amaru warned without looking back. "Leif is with them."

The little brown Fyroxi gulped audibly and nodded. "We survived the Hundredth Sun Massacre; we can survive this."

Amaru just grunted and braced herself for the two forces to clash.

The two Chillfang led the pack, ready to end their targets' lives with a crushing bite. Unfortunately for the male, Dalphamair was prepared for him. With a toothy grin flashing through his thick beard, the dwarf cocked his arm and let fly with Retirement. The missile soared through the sky, all the force a dwarf could muster behind it. It cracked into the gigantic wolf's skull with an awful splintering sound, calving through a melting icy helmet, pelt, and bone alike. An abrupt yip heralded the end of its life.

"See tha', Elf ?" Dalphamair yelled over his shoulder. "Me javelin's plenty useful! Let's see yer holey little twig do the same."

Amaru heard Alaric chuckle, put his lips to the flute, and blow a sharp whistle, like a coffee kettle coming to a boil. The two assassins had their weapons in bare hands, something they must have regretted a moment later. Their weapons' metal handles began to glow white-hot, and the Venomsting operatives dropped them in shock, bubbling blisters already forming on their calloused flesh. The weapons remained on the ground for only a moment, as Venomsting training allowed their members to fight through such trivialities as pain, but a moment was long enough. Celwyn's casting caused the already precarious dune to collapse out from under them, drawing both into a hole several feet deep.

"I don't know the spell for filling the hole back in, so it'll only stop them for a little while!" the gnome called over the cussing of her two prisoners. "I should probably learn that. It would make covering up privy holes *so* much easier!"

Amaru turned away from them, and the second Chillfang, who was hurtling towards her death, which rode on a goat and had a small Fyroxi behind him. She needn't worry about anything else. Leif Kalix had all of her attention. The two Fyroxi circled around each other, one shifted, the other in humanoid form, swords extended loosely. *He thinks of this as a sparring game,* Amaru realized. *One that, if he wins, will grant him a sweet prize.* She knew she had to be careful here. If Leif shifted, he'd be much bigger and stronger than her. Her only advantage now was the enhanced quickness of the fox's form. Looking at his stance, she realized that Leif's fighting style had changed little from his years of training for the Trial of Blades. *I'll need to use what I learned from that to defeat him.* She paused for but a moment, leaving herself open. Like a half-starved hare, the tall Fyroxi took the bait, arms raised to trap her in place. Restraining foes with an immediate, surprising leap had always been a favorite strategy of his. He'd sampled victory several times by taking control of crucial pivot points and wrenching his opponent into submission. But this time, he tasted nothing but tail, as Amaru compacted herself as much as possible and drove her sleek body right through the loop of his arm.

"That strategy will not work on me, Leif," Amaru said. "Recall who watched all of your battles before you became embittered and obsessed. I know the moves you favor and all the methods that your opponents used to escape them. "

"You can turn words into swords all you like. They'll not pierce my shell!" Leif straightened and crossed his weapons in front of himself defensively.

"Do you see yourself as a scorpion now?" Amaru wondered. "Are you truly one of *them*?" She nodded towards the holes where the Venomsting man's hands were feeling about. The gnome had already freed herself and was chasing Celwyn around with a gleefully murderous expression writ large across her face.

"Once I return the heads of your friends presented next to you, conquered, your spirit broken, I will be!" A wicked grin played across his lips. He glanced behind him, where the rest of the skirmish was taking place. Ren was following through on a throw of a length of weighted rope, which wrapped around the remaining Chillfang's legs, sending her sprawling on the dune.

Dalphamair leaped from Priscilla's back, ready to crush its head with Cryptfiller, but a sharp note from Alaric's flute stole the kill.

"That's one for me, and one for you," the elf said with a grin. "Three enemies to go, and we have three allies who haven't drawn blood. Would you like to call it a truce here?"

"Bah, I'll not concede t' ye!" Dalph stumped over to the hole, opting to mash the Venomsting's fingers with his weapon. The man crumpled back into the hole with a curse.

"And, it would seem, that as a sign of favor, you've even brought me a Trinket to play with. "That's an offering I'll gladly accept." Leif grinned again, this time with a much more playful aspect as if they were children once more, playing a game of dash tag.

"Your battle is with me, Leif," Amaru warned.

Heedlessly, the stronger Fyroxi streaked off across the small arena of disturbed sand, Amaru's fox form following shortly behind. Amaru should have been faster, could have pounced and dug her claws deep into his flesh, forcing him to refocus his attention on her rather than Ren. But a moment's hesitation stalled her enough to make Amaru too late. Though all of Leif's actions had been designed to hurt thus far, she couldn't bring herself to retaliate. He was still Fyroxi, and despite the many times she'd claimed to hate him, she couldn't forget the years when they were younger. They'd been so close until the sand wyvern and his pride tore them apart. Subconsciously, she realized that was why she'd been fighting defensively, at least partly. Amaru knew she had to appeal to him, try to pull him back from the hateful path he was running down, full tilt. The Fire Striders still had a place for him, if only Leif could deflate his ego enough to fit within it.

Ren was too focused to notice the snarling man bearing down upon him. Amaru shouted to gain her friend's attention. The smaller Fyroxi whirled in shock, throwing his arm up just in time as one of Leif's blades came down, the sharp edge digging deeply into the flesh and scraping against bone. Ren screamed and drew back, giving Leif the perfect opportunity to strafe around and take a tight hold. Ren whimpered, looking pleadingly at Amaru as Leif's second sword rested against his throat.

The entire battlefield went still, even Celwyn and Venhana

pausing to catch their breath and watch the spectacle. The only sounds were the wind sending skittering grains of sand across the dunes and the combined ragged breathing and whimpering of all gathered.

"What do you have to say, Amaru?" Leif asked, repositioning the blade so that it pressed into Ren's throat, causing a line of blood to trickle down his sweat-slicked neck.

Amaru tried to speak, but the words caught in her throat. She was terrified for the life of her dear friend, the chosen mate of her best friend. If she failed to save Ren here, how could she ever face Xio again? The silence stretched painfully long, and Amaru could feel herself start to tremble, fear running down her spine and through her tail. Then, she became aware of Alaric, his eyes seeking her own. She recognized the expression within them. She'd seen it once before when it was she in the grasp of a man intent on murder. He had a plan, but looked to her for guidance. There didn't seem to be another option, so, as subtly as she could, she nodded her foxlike head.

Alaric took a deep breath and stepped forward. "Leif Kalix wasn't it? Greetings, my name is Alaric Valyaara. We've met once before, and I daresay that even then, you didn't favor me."

"I remember you, scumber breath," Leif growled.

Alaric feigned displeasure. "I daresay my breath is quite sweet, enough to make the heart flutter in affection, rather than fear though, if I may be blunt, my guess is that's what makes you dislike me."

"Amaru was my promised, foul bard, not your plaything, and I'd appreciate it if you ended your meddling in our affairs."

"And I would appreciate it if you stopped treating our fair lady as a possession. In case you haven't noticed, she is a woman and, more importantly, one who understands what pleases her and what doesn't. If either of us is treating Amaru as a plaything, it's you. All you seem to wish is to have her squirming and squealing under your bulk so that you can feel validated in your quote-unquote accomplishments. It's frankly disgusting."

"Why you little..." Ren, who had passed out from fright, slumped down to the sand as Leif forgot entirely about his captive.

"There are always stories of those women who don't mind watching a man posture and preen to make themselves seem superior," Alaric said, his mouth twisting into a sad grimace. "But, I believe them to be myths. If they do exist, then they make up a small percentage of people, indeed. Intelligent women, a group that Amaru most certainly is a member of, require, nay, deserve to be treated with fairness and regard for their emotions." The elf gave a wicked grin. "If you don't believe me, then perhaps you could ask my fans." Alaric raised his flute to his mouth and blew a series of notes. All of a sudden, half a hundred spectral hands materialized in the air behind and around Leif. They grasped at his clothing as the brutish Fyroxi stirred angrily. When the hands began to pull him away from Alaric, he attempted to strike at Ren, but Amaru was already there, shielding her friend with her body.

Alaric's "fans" dragged Leif down to the ground. Venhana, snapped out of her stupor from watching the standoff, tried to react, but clever Celwyn had the foresight not to allow that. With a snap of the Water Caller's finger, a tongue of rock lashed out from the sand, battering Venhana and sending her flying to land near her prone companion.

Amaru shifted back to her humanoid form, passed Alaric with a grateful smile, and scooped her spear back into her hands. She stormed over and pressed the tip against the blonde man's exposed neck.

"Listen to me, Leif." Her old friend glared up at her balefully, a growl already forming on his lips. "I have you at my mercy, and it would be a matter of ease to slay you now." She gritted her teeth and momentarily pressed her advantage. Leif exhaled sharply as the tip ground into his skin, not hard enough to penetrate, but Helios made its presence known. Just as quickly, she pulled the weapon away. "I'm not going to, though."

"Why not?" Leif managed tauntingly. "Is your so-called 'mercy' holding you back once more? You're only proving your weakness."

Amaru's sandaled foot came down with crushing pressure on his hand. "Unless you are looking to bleed your last at the base of this dune, I'd suggest you temper your tongue. No, I am not slaying you today because that outcome benefits nobody. Call it mercy, but I doubt you'll believe that overlong." She nodded at Ren, his left sleeve drenched in blood. "Though I choose not to accept them, I understand your grievances against me. However, you had no reason to turn your anger on others of the Fire Striders, *your* Clan."

"My Clan no longer," Leif spat.

"If that is what you choose, then so be it." She sought Leif's eyes with her striking brass orbs. "But, in that case, you will never find family elsewhere."

"Says who?"

"As the voice of Yamaria and the kin-daughter of Durrigan, I know this much to be true. Our people are the last remnants of the Fyroxi race. You may leave today, and find other allies, be they among the Venomsting, or the Chillfang, who you've always claimed to respect the strength of. But no matter what, you will be a sheep wearing wolf's clothing, ever out of place. And, perhaps worse, if the other Fyroxi hear what you've done to Ren, no woman will take you as her mate." Her eyes going metallic and cold, Amaru returned Leif's glare. "You will never father a Fyroxi child. And I know how much you despise half-breeds."

The rage vanished from Leif's eyes as Amaru's words sunk in.

The Fyroxi woman gestured for Alaric to end the spell, and moments later, the spectral hands disappeared from Leif's body.

Amaru turned her back on Leif, moving directly to Ren, intent on healing and tending to her dear friend. Her defeated foe pulled himself to a kneeling position and slipped skin. "You are a dealer of cruel truths, Amaru Sunbrand," he said in the Fyran tongue.

"The desert offers no charity," she replied in the common language without turning around from her work. Though she didn't spare Leif another glance, she could hear the padding of his feet and the dragging of his tails as he retreated.

"Spit me out, you foxy bastard!" Venhana shrilled. "Where are you taking me? They are all still alive, in case you hadn't noticed."

"We're done here," Leif said from around the wild gnome's cloak. "And I might need a snack for the road."

The Scions of the Rising Sun all gathered around their fallen member, while Amaru laid a hand on Ren's wound and released a pulse of divine healing energy into it. They watched intently as the flesh and skin stitched back together, and Ren began to stir, his soft eyes flickering. "Amaru? Did you give Leif what for?"

"Yes, Ren, we did," the daughter of Yamaria let out a breath she hadn't known she was holding. "He shouldn't be a threat to us any longer."

The small, brown-haired Fyroxi chuckled weakly. "Pretty poor showing for my first battle, huh?"

Celwyn shook her head vigorously. "Phooey to that! Without your support, that might have turned out *far* worse. Besides, you slowed down your friend long enough for Alaric to catch him. You ought to be proud!"

Dalphamair reached down to pat Ren's shoulder. "Th' only thing ye lack is experience. An' if today's any indicator, you'll get plenty o' tha' truckin' with us!"

"It was only the stress and worry that got to you," Amaru promised. "You'll never get used to it, but over time, it will get somewhat easier to deal with." She squeezed his knee. "Now, dinner is waiting at the top of that dune, and we all deserve a rest."

"Just one question," Ren said, as he allowed Amaru to pull him to his feet. "What are we going to do with that one?" He waved his tails towards the hole in the ground, where once again, a set of fingers had appeared. Ever methodical Dalphamair stumped over and smashed his boot down on them, allowing Celwyn to come over and investigate.

As she stared, a more wicked smile grew than any that had crossed her features before. "I'd recognize that man anywhere." She said coldly. "He was part of the group that kidnapped me. And, if I remember correctly, that rotten bugger's the one who did in my partner. I guess we must've missed him in our little rock-trap!"

Amaru nodded and looked down at Celwyn. "Given that you have the most experience with this man, I delegate the responsibility of deciding his fate to you."

Cely's eyes lit up. "Let's go eat dinner!"

"What's tha' got t' do with anything?" Dalph wondered aloud.

"Simple," the blonde gnome crowed proudly, setting her arms akimbo. "Whatever we have for leftovers, we drop down this hole for him to eat. If his friends come looking for him, he'll be fine. If

not..." Celwyn concentrated for a moment, and the sand around the pit suddenly hardened into smooth stone. "Then I guess Yamaria's decided he's not worthy of any mercy!"

AL ARIC

MEETING THE GL AIVEWRAITH

That evening, at dinner, Amaru was quieter than usual, which, in a way, was an accomplishment, given her typical stoicism. She'd had only token participation in mealtime conversation, and not even Alaric's silly songs had pierced the veil of her somber mood.

Celwyn and Dalphamair were off delivering food and taunts to their captive Venomsting, and Ren had already retired to his tent to recover. That left Alaric practically alone in camp with Amaru. The woman he loved was staring into the fire, which had burned down to little more than glowing coals. The elf sighed and approached.

"The daughter of Sun shouldn't have such dark shadows dancing in her eyes," he said lightly, settling down on the sand next to her. "They do not become her."

Amaru looked up at him and gave a small smile but didn't make any further reply. She just returned her gaze to the flame, so Alaric took the initiative, sighed, and spoke. "I thought it was customary, even to you quiet desert folk, to proffer explanations when given probing questions," the elf said, earning Amaru's attention at last.

"You aren't going to leave me to my thoughts, are you, Alaric?"

"Well, of course not. Dark thoughts have no place in a mind so bright as yours." Amaru fixed her gaze on him at last. Alaric wondered what she was thinking about him at this moment. *Probably that I'm a terrible nuisance. But hopefully, she's glimpsed my lovable side enough to grow fond of it.*

Amaru remained silent for a few moments more, but eventually, she spoke up. "I know not if I made the right decision," she admitted at last.

The Elven bard slid as close to her as he dared, reaching one long arm over to grip Amaru's knee. "You showed mercy and restraint by not outright slaying that man. Though, in my humble opinion, a slow death would have been just right for him."

"Alaric!" Amaru gaped at him, her tone fully admonishing.

Embarrassed, the elf rubbed the back of his head, dislodging sand grains from his ponytail. "Sorry, my lady. I suppose when it comes to you, I get fiercely protective." He chuckled as he saw Amaru roll her eyes. "I'm serious. I refuse to be culpable in anything that causes you pain. I barely know him, and that Leif fellow causes *me* pain. I can't imagine living with him for well over a hundred years."

"He didn't always ascribe to such an abrasive manner." Alaric listened patiently while she described her youth alongside Leif, their friendship that might have blossomed into more, storing as much information as he could in the archives of his brain.

Alaric filed as much important information as he could, then considered the most key part of her story he'd latched onto. "You fear that you're at fault for his change, is that so?"

"He didn't show any obvious signs of that behavior until after I brought him back from death's door."

"Utterly preposterous," Alaric stated simply.

"What do you mean?" Amaru wasn't angry, thankfully, since he *had* minorly insulted her belief.

"I mean, that no magic of yours would be capable of taking a perfectly good man and turning them into the bag of cactus needles Leif seems to be. The face that has come free now was merely hiding underneath the veneer, and the near-death experience let the ugly side show," the elf explained. "Most people, at least, the sensible ones, learn to hide those dislikable faces, but others embrace them, like Leif did, letting the nasty truth in their heart speak for them. Throughout your story, I heard several warning signs that, to me, screamed that Leif wasn't all he was made out to be. But, that was only my experience in reading people talking, so you cannot be blamed for missing them. Honestly, I think it is rather faithless of you to blame Yamaria's granted magic of doing something so terribly heinous. You ought to apologize to her before turning in."

Amaru had never thought about it like that; Alaric could see that in her eyes. She would likely spend a fair deal of tonight in prayer, begging for forgiveness and the insight to never make that mistake again.

"Either way," Alaric continued. I would counsel you not to fret over what decisions you've made until they come to nip you in the tail. You cannot change the past, no matter how much you ruminate on it, and worrying about the future will only sap your strength and the determination to go on. Besides," the handsome bard quirked a smile, "if you ask me, I'd say you handled that situation with aplomb." He allowed Amaru to soak in everything he'd just said.

"Thank you, Alaric," she said sincerely, after a moment. "That means quite a bit, coming from you."

"Do you find me that lacking in the praise department?" Alaric asked with mock incredulity. "I thought you might find me effusive in that regard, and I wouldn't contradict you if so!"

"That's not what I mean, and you know it!" Amaru said, punching her friend's shoulder.

Alaric had to suppress the foolish grin that threatened to split his face in twain while rubbing away the sting of the Fyroxi's strong right jab. "I think I do," he confessed. The elf lay back, knowing that his hair was going to be full of grit but not minding. It wasn't like he'd be finding some place to take a bath anytime soon. He stared up at the vibrant orange sky with one eye, the other watching the calm sweeping of Amaru's tails. *I think I've found a woman that would make even Father proud. Though wooing her has proven like climbing a dune during a sand squall. It's a damned good thing I relish a challenge.*

He realized then that Amaru wasn't done talking and quickly focused back on her. "...they expect me to lead; they trained me specifically for that purpose. The Elders ensured I knew a little bit of everything, so I could have the skills to understand any situation at a base level."

"You fear you aren't skilled enough to shoulder that responsibility," Alaric interjected sagely. "After the trial that was today's encounter, your pretty head stews with worry that you'll fumble the next decision and lead your people to ruin."

Astonished, Amaru nodded along and laughed helplessly. "There you go, reading me like a book again." Her tails twitched through the air.

"Given my father's absolute disappointment in me, I've never seen far into the candor within the glitz and glamour of rulership," he confided in his dear friend.

"I knew you to be a bard of renown, but son to a Lord? Never would I have guessed it."

Alaric grinned. "You have no idea how much those words

please me, Amaru. But, believe it or don't, my blood is based in the noble heart of the Kindol Woods, that expanse of trees I showed you when I knew only Amber. The Elf-lord there, Taliesin, bears the regal last name of Valyaara. He did me the great honor of placing me in your path, so I hate him much less than I used to. More on him later, though; I'm still busy convincing the daughter of the Goddess that she's incredible. I can let you in on two little secrets, which your Elders won't say outright because they think you should learn these things yourself through trial and error. I love the idea, but devil to making you stress! First, you may have lived for over a century, but by both elf standards and Fyroxi, you are but a child. Given the unique circumstances of your birth, your Elders filled your lap with many responsibilities. While I understand the desire to fill your 'salvation's' head with all the knowledge you possess, that is the easiest way to ensure they become worn and burned out! Step back, try to milk some enjoyment out of life, and learn as you go. Right now, that might not be the easiest thing to accomplish, but we'll find a way, trust me. Once the world gives you a chance to reflect, you'll analyze the decisions you've made, understand your mistakes, and develop a working knowledge of your skills and the flaws that come with them.

"Second, you're human...or mortal rather. Yamaria's daughter or not, you'll never be perfect. Anyone who expects that of you ought to be slapped. Even the greatest rulers have people behind them, serving as advisors and providing them the necessary feedback to help them improve. No matter where you go, you can be sure I'll be behind you." The elf produced the sun-shaped charm from beneath his shirt. "You'll forgive a young elf for his romantic and courtly ideals, I pray. But, when I see this gift, I think only one thing. This signifies that we're meant to stick together. If ever you find a dune you cannot surmount, my hand shall be at your back to help you crest it. Or, if you find yourself at a crossroads and know not where to turn, allow me to be your guide. My compass, both navigational and moral, may not always be correct, but with any luck, they should guide you towards happiness, and I think that is the most treasured goal anyone could set their sights upon."

Amaru nodded mutely, and the elf thought that his power to peer into the soul was showing him some delightful developments. In the Fyroxi woman's eyes, those most glorious windows, there shone a light of relief and appreciation, as if for the first time, somebody had understood her. "Thank you for being my support, Alaric," she said after several quiet moments. "If I'd not had you, I fear I may have given up on this journey long ago." Then, to Alaric's ultimate surprise, the Fyroxi woman leaned in and pecked his cheek. She stood and made her way back to the tent, Alaric wishing she would invite him to join her. "Write me another song, would you? Make it one that could be sung to me and me alone," she requested before ducking inside her canvas shelter and depriving the elf of the beauty of her presence.

The salt flats passed underfoot those next several days, and the Scions knew they were close. As they'd been warned, animals became rather scarce, even more so than before, and it was only through the combined skill of Ren, Amaru, and Celwyn that they kept themselves fed and watered. Ren prepared traps, which most mornings were found empty, until Celwyn used her magic to lure them closer, and Amaru chased them within. The method wasn't flawless, but it brought in more food than not doing so, even if those animals were spare and skeletal.

Celwyn admitted many times that she felt guilty using her druidic powers to end the lives of these pathetic animals, and Amaru, who seemed to understand better than anyone else, would aid her in repentance as the sun set. And, when the sun rested, Alaric would play them a calming tune to lull them off to sleep.

Every day of travel, they were greeted by an eerie silence, as if they were being watched, and in the distance, they caught sight of Chitinites, those demonic creatures ranging the dunes. They hid, as they hadn't any antidote, and couldn't afford any extra time or energy that might be spent waging battle. It was for fear of these beings that they slept when the sun was low. It seemed even demon bugs needed rest, and few creatures were sturdy or foolish enough to sleep when the light was bright and the sun most like the deadly blade. But thanks to these precautions, they arrived on the Drakenblood doorstep without expiring on the sand.

The tribe was stationed in a yawning canyon of stone baked red and tan. An approach, proportionally thin as a bottle of fine wine, was marked by two wooden spears jabbed forcefully through the skulls of young sand wyverns. As the five companions made their way through the passage, the morning air was broken by a warhorn's fanfare, and three figures approached them from further down the way. Alaric held out a hand, signaling the others to stop. 'Twas not wise to encroach further upon a tribe leader's hospitality than verbally directed, after all. They all stood tensely, wondering what was going to happen. Alaric's sharp eye caught the gleam of bows leveled down at the five from the top of the rocky shelf. This Gawain was not messing around, it seemed. He did not hasten his pace upon seeing them halt, continuing forward as if measuring their mettle with each slow step he took. The Scions, for their part, stood tall, straight, and stoic, as if they were no strangers to the formalities necessary when dealing with such an impressive figure. Even Priscilla remained utterly silent. And impressive this man was, indeed! His garb immediately gave him away as the leader they sought. Gawain was girt in leather armor dyed red, yellow, and orange, loose folds of material shifting as the dragon's flame. His dark skin peeked through at a few points, showing a small but powerful figure, with wiry bands of muscle coalescing around his arms and legs. The outfit was topped with an intricate headdress, complete with a mask wrought to look like a rampant dragon and another skull securing it to his shaved head. *I wonder if he slew that himself? That's usually the way of these primal tribes. You wear only the tokens you've earned in contest, be it battle or the sparring of words.* Various tokens made of bone ornamented Gawain's neck and shoulders, rattling as he moved towards them. To Alaric's sharp eyes, every step seemed a study in grace and precision. Not a movement was wasted, and every twitch of muscle seemed controlled and deliberate.

Gawain stopped before them, his two warrior escorts, one male and of similar dusky skin tone as he, and the other female, with a deeply tanned complexion, took their places behind their Chief.

He regarded them all silently, gaze traveling over them as if stripping the flesh from their bones to view the truths of their innards with his very gaze. Only Gawain's eyes were visible through his mask, and they were black as coal, holding the severity of the sand squall.

After several long moments, Gawain fixed a glare upon Amaru and said, "You are the leader of this menagerie of heroes, though I'm unsure of their worthiness quite yet. You lead them, and yet you stand to the side and let this elvish fop represent you." His voice betrayed no emotion, yet imparted grave severity and weight to every word.

"It was he who contacted you through letter, and we thought it only appropriate that he be the first face to greet you, as custom normally demands," Amaru replied without hesitation, not in the least unnerved by this man.

"A good answer, conjured without fear, but is it a true one?"

"What do you mean?"

Gawain snagged a round, orange-gold crystal from one of his bracelets. "A girl, trapped in amber, it seems, refusing to let her true strength show when it would make her a figure worthy of great reverence. The Drakenblood does not consort with deceivers, Amaru Sunbrand.

"Neither do Fyroxi, Gawain of the Drakenblood," the goddess's daughter replied cooly. Alaric's poor heart was pounding. This wasn't going according to plan. Of course, he hadn't planned to confront accusations before even making it to the village. He could accept being called a fop; his father had labeled him with worse titles. But, any insult to Amaru was an insult to his very honor and that he couldn't allow to pass unpunished. He puffed up his chest and protested, but Amaru held up a finger, deflating him before he could begin.

"Many people wear masks, Gawain," Amaru continued. "Some are physical, like the one you sport now, while others are false personas we wear to hide from the truths of our past, lest our enemies find us and bring us to ruin. It may not be the most honorable strategy, but we are mortals, prone to lapses in moral nature. It is what makes us subject to Yamaria. We Fyroxi crave that position at her feet, for to aspire to more would be reaching above our station. And, when we hide, we buy ourselves the necessary time to grow stronger while protecting those we care most about. I believe you understand that well, Gawain Drakenblood."

After listening to Amaru's speech and putting the clan leader under more intense scrutiny, Alaric saw similarities to another dark-skinned warrior he'd known not that long ago. So it was that as Amaru finished with "Or should I say," the two said the boy's old name together, "Sultan."

Gawain nodded. "You are sharp, Amaru Sunbrand. My people report your claws are equally keen, as evidenced by the battle you waged against that Fyroxi and his Venomsting compatriots."

"I hope that we have shown enough strength that you'll consider our proposition."

Gawain nodded regally. "I had no intention of turning down your offer. You will have your alliance, as it is necessary for the continuation of our bloodlines and our livelihood."

"Wait, so you made us trek out all this way for nothing?" Ren wondered aloud.

"Not for nothing, Fyroxi," Gawain said. "Nothing I do is ever pointless, which is more than can be said for your elvish companion. I wonder why you still keep him around."

Alaric's heart leaped as Amaru shrugged and replied. "Alaric has his uses, some of which would be extremely difficult to replace in this land seen as forbidding to most Kingdom residents."

"Very well," Gawain turned on his heel and led them deeper into the canyon. "If you wish to know why you have been called, then follow me. There is much for you to learn and not nearly enough time for you to do so."

AMARU

A DAUGHTER'S PURPOSE

"We were a nomadic tribe as well," Gawain explained as he led them through the passage, which he called Stony Gullet. "But, much like your people, Amaru, recent events have sent us away from the life we knew as normal. However, whereas the Fyroxi had to leave their ancestral home, we of the Drakenblood have returned to ours."

"Where did you learn of our move?" Amaru wondered. "I don't recall having Alaric mention that in any of our correspondence." She glanced at the elf, who shrugged and shook his head.

"We don't need direct notification to learn things, Amaru," Gawain replied cryptically. "Don't you find it curious that such a large mass of moving people didn't invite the wrath of the Venomsting or the Chitinites, as you seem content to call them? An overly simplistic name, if I do say so myself, but the tongue of demons is harsh on most mouths."

Ren perked up. "I do recall hearing reports of figures on the outskirts of our march. Do you mean to say those were you?"

"Not me, but my kinsmen and women. They fought the creatures who attempted to forestall your journey and send your race into extinction."

"You have the Fyroxi's gratitude, then," Amaru said. "Many of our most skilled warriors were felled in the Chillfang attacks. You saved the lives of many women and children."

"Had they not made it there safely, you would have made regrettable decisions in their interest, thereby overextending the limited timeframe with which the Sun Mother has enabled us to act."

"Limited timetable? Speak plainly, Gawain. We haven't the time for words that wend like the adder."

Amaru didn't receive an answer immediately as the group exited the Stony Gullet and arrived in the Drakenblood ancestral home. It was a village built into the flanks of the Sunforge Gorge; the houses carved directly from the stone itself, subtle and yet powerful, not unlike their leader. Massive sets of stairs were carved into the walls, allowing access to the lower terraces, where Amaru could see a sizeable tented market square, roofless square structures with surprisingly lush gardens within, and an oasis larger than any she'd seen to date. Men and women marched purposefully through the streets, some in armor like Gawain, and others wearing the Water Callers' signature robes.

"I'm surprised such abundance can exist in a place that is otherwise so barren," Amaru remarked. "How did you manage it."

Without looking at her, Gawain pointed to the north. "Do you know what lies that way, child of the goddess?"

Amaru didn't, but Alaric and Ren had both done their research and answered in tandem, "the Eclipse."

The tall, emotionally reserved chieftain grunted his approval. "If you recall the story of the Mad Mage, it may become apparent why the druidic magic we've borrowed has such a powerful effect here."

Ren thought for a moment. "After the battle, Qrakzt and his fellows stole nearly all the magic from the people of Sun's Reach, and presumably Moonwatch. Then, they disappeared and left that wall in their place." The small Fyroxi's eyes widened. "That wall has to be overflowing with magic!"

"Precisely." Gawain nodded, and Amaru favored her friend with a smile, which caused Ren to blush. "Whatever he hoped to accomplish, it is our belief that the Mad Mage found himself with more magical energy than even he anticipated. It was how he froze the sun in the sky and created the Eclipse. For what reason, we know not, but it seems the magical nature of the wall is starting to fray, and the wellspring of power amplifies any and all magic cast near it. There are other effects, such as the corruption of nearby creatures without the willpower to resist."

"That's where the Chitinites come from," Amaru realized. "I was wondering how such vile creatures made it into Sun's Reach."

"Sharp, just as I'd expect from the daughter of the Goddess. I'm pleased to know you won't disappoint." Gawain gestured sharply towards a grand columned palace up on a higher terrace.

"Follow me. You will all be fed, watered, and given a reprieve from the heat. Once we are comfortable, we shall discuss the future and what I and the world require from you, Scions of the Rising Sun."

Amaru and Alaric shared a glance, but the elf shrugged, so Amaru followed the dark-skinned warrior, who had already begun the climb.

"Ahem," Dalphamair growled. "I'm not much o' a climber, an' me goat is less than tha'! What're we s'pposed t' do?"

Gawain clicked his tongue audibly, and suddenly one of his attendants appeared next to the dwarf, hands extended. "My man will see that your goat is handled properly. We have a woman in our stables who sees all animals brought into her care groomed, fed, and massaged."

"Ooh, your Priscilla's a lucky girl," Celwyn groaned. "I could kill for a massage right about now."

"Ye're not jokin'," Dalph added. "Me back's seen better days, tha's fer sure!"

"That can be arranged as well," Gawain said. "Any comfort we can provide is available to you. Trust me, you'll wish to indulge. I doubt that the directive I have for you will be pleasurable in the least."

"That's ominous," Alaric said. "What say you, Amaru?"

"I can't say for sure, but I get a good impression from this place, and I feel as if Yamaria herself is urging me to follow. Besides, I'm already climbing, so I see no reason to stop." The Fyroxi girl was hanging off the stone rung of a ladder built into the cliffside by one arm, her cloak twirling about her ankles. The muscles in her arm flexed as she hung, and she offered the clearly impressed elf a smile, much like she'd given Ren. Though Alaric was better at hiding his pleasure than her brown-haired friend, Amaru could see the boundless affection and respect in his eyes. Her mind recalled a conversation long ago with Ren and Xio about her duty to the Fire-Striders to mate and bear children. And just a few sunfalls ago, Alaric had said that the Kerazar amulets fit them as two parts of the same whole, something never to be separated. The charm was warm on her chest. Before she could recognize it, a thought slipped into the forefront of her mind. *I could do far worse than taking Alaric as my mate. He has proven his worth repeatedly, and his skill with the quill is something nobody can deny. Besides, choosing him would strengthen my argument that we should replenish the Fyroxi stock from without.* Amaru shook her head and finished the climb, allowing the others to come up behind her. *What am I thinking? Yamaria has saddled us with a duty, and there is another to come if Gawain speaks true. There will be time to consider pleasure once that has come to a close.* Amaru smiled to herself. "Then I can allow my soulmate to be my heart's match."

"Did you say something, Amaru?" Ren wondered, brushing his tails against hers.

"Nothing of import," Amaru lied. "Never you mind it." *Have I truly fallen for this flamboyant elf's conjured charms? I suppose I'll have to discuss with you on this subject at some point, Ren, as you've felt the needling arrow of love twice now.* Amaru let out a sigh and a chuckle. *He is rubbing off on me.*

An hour later, they were sitting in a tiled room; the walls splashed with murals of great stretches of beach and the glittering turquoise ocean beyond it. Depictions of animals the likes of which Amaru had never seen before dotted the floor. One was greenish-gray with a giant shell and feet more like a fish's fins than a functional paw or hoof. Others were clearly fish but wrought with more color and vibrancy than Amaru had ever dared to expect. The far wall, against which the woman saw a pair of ornate chairs, thrones, she imagined. *For the chieftain?* She wondered, or was there something more."

Ren noticed her interest and piped up. "I read somewhere that long ago, the Scorched Waste and the lands beyond had their own kings and queens. Great settlements once dotted this place, and powerful men would carve out pieces of the sandy expanse to claim as their own. Many of these kingdoms were founded and sustained on blood and lust, so they were quick to fall, but reports say that they served a buffer against the Most famous was *Valikharn's Retreat*, now known as the Swallowed City. It was set near the sea." Ren pointed to the thrones' mural, which depicted a substantial serpent-like creature whose head suggested some relation to the sand wyverns. Its scales were dyed various shades of blue and purple, and long whiskers flowed forth from its formidable face. "Rumors say that it was ruled by a sea dragon."

"Do you actually believe that?" Amaru wanted to know.

"Amaru, I've seen demons, murderous talking wolves, and healing magic sent from the heavens in my life. A story about an intelligent dragon ruling a city really doesn't sound so far-fetched anymore." He shrugged. "Whether this apparent jewel is carved from embellished rumors or if there is a core of truth to it, I suppose we'll never know. It was lost beneath waves of sand hundreds of years ago. Some of the rumors say that early Fyroxi mages and sailor elves that could breathe both water and air lived together in that city, underneath Valikharn's rule, though. You have to wonder what sort of relics and weapons one could find in such a settlement! Sun's Reach isn't known for its navy, but maybe, once in the distant past, it was, but the only evidence was consumed by the desert. It's pretty amazing to think about!" Amaru could see the sparkle in Ren's eyes, which always appeared when talking about history, or things that could have been. She ruffled his ears lovingly and brought her friend in for a hug.

"Never change, Ren. Promise me that,"

The shorter Fyroxi leaned in. "We still don't know what we're going to face ahead, so that's a promise I can't make in earnest, my friend."

"If not for me, then for Xio. She lives life at a slower pace than most of us, so significant differences from her status quo give her whiplash, I fear."

"Well, when you put it that way, I still can't foresee what will come to pass. But for her, you, and the rest of the Scions, I'll put my best paw forward. Now, come on," he urged. "I think Dalphamair is done grumbling about the fact that goat's on the menu, and Gawain isn't a man I want to keep waiting for long."

When they sat at the squat, pentagonal table, Amaru was

reminded of the dinners they'd shared at the Solgaele Monastery. The seating arrangement was much the same, though with a few added members. She was placed directly across from Alaric, with Gawain on the adjacent side, just like he had been in the guise of Sultan. Ren sat where Gemna would have, with Celwyn and Dalph sharing a side. The gnome lightly ribbing the dwarf, who, despite his protests, seemed to be immensely enjoying the fire-roasted and exquisitely seasoned rack of goat.

"Bah, but I wish I could stuff Priscilla's tail down yer gullet!"

"If you did, I might just try to take a bite of her haunches," Celwyn rejoindered.

"Only if ye liked the flavor o' goat hoof, an' ye wanted t' only eat food that's been all mushed up, fer th' rest o' yer long gnome life!"

"I guess that would make things a bit difficult. Hows about we wait on that until I get myself a husband to spoonfeed me."

"I dunno, girl. Methinks losing tha' impetuous smile might aid ye in yer quest."

"Ah, bugger off, ye fool dwarf," Celwyn said, waving Dalphamair off. "Like ye'd know anything about finding a wife."

"Would ye care t' repeat tha'?"

"Repeat what?" Celwyn asked innocently. "Did I say something wrong?"

"I'm no good at figuring out nothin' about love!" Dalph yelled.

"I mean, you said it, not me!" Celwyn said with mock surprise. "Brave of you to admit it, though!"

"Ngah! No, tha's what ye said before... Bah, damnable woman!"

The flaxen-haired gnome punched a fist into the air victoriously. "Did you see that? I out argued a surly dwarf."

"Ye did no such thing!" Dalph protested.

"I don't know, Dalph," Alaric butted in. "From my perspective, it looks like Celwyn defeated you quite handily."

"Bah, what d'you know?"

"As a bard, I'd say I'm quite proficient in the language of conversation," Alaric explained. "Both in forms civil and not. You allowed her to coax you into saying precisely what she wanted, embarrassing yourself in the process. Quite ingenious of her, if I do say. And I do."

"Whose side are ye on?"

"Last I recall, we had a rivalry! If that stops when we step off the battlefield, then I never got the memo. Doesn't sound like the dwarf way, either, truth be told."

By this point, Ren and Celwyn were in stitches from laughter, and Amaru was shaking her head in amusement. Only Gawain seemed unaffected by the merry atmosphere. "If you are quite done with your japery, we have more pressing matters to attend to." His sharp voice cut right through the joy like one blade of his signature dual-sided glaive cleaving through the brains of a foe.

Several long minutes of silence stretched while the group partook in the food provided to them, which besides the goat, consisted of succulent grapes, freshly baked bread, and a cool white spread that tasted faintly of limes. A pretty servant wearing loose-fitting, almost see-through garbs of mist-linen poured water infused with oranges for everyone. Amaru found herself pleasantly surprised to see that Alaric wasn't making eyes at the woman. At one point, he caught her staring and, in typical Alaric fashion, winked charmingly at her. She rolled her eyes outwardly, but on the inside, she was all smiles.

Amaru wasn't sure how much time passed, but eventually, Gawain dabbed his mouth primly and began to speak. "I have seen the question burning in your eyes since the moment you've arrived, Alaric. I know you are wondering when I left the Monastery."

"You are correct. You've taken command of your people and

assert your rule so quickly. Your people all respect you, almost to the point of reverence, despite your youth. And, if I'm not mistaken, it seems you have many plans and systems already at work behind the scenes, especially if you could get people out to save the Fyroxi from demonic harassment."

"Before the week was out following your own departure with Amber, as she was called then, I too was called to duty. I knew it would be so before the woman you so gaily pranced after even arrived at the monastery, though our reasons for departing are similar."

"How could they be? I'd not met you, nor any of your family beforehand?"

"Must people meet for their goals to be aligned? No, especially not where the Sun Mother is involved. Two months before you flashed the smile that roped in Alaric's desperate heart, Yamaria sent me visions pertaining to your arrival. I told Gemna to expect a special guest, which is why you were accepted so quickly and not questioned too heavily. Once I saw your face in the flesh, the visions came more frequently, guiding me back to the Drakenbloods. Five days before I arrived, my father was slain, raiding against the demonic forces, which had begun to boil out of their territory in the Desolation. I returned to take up the mantle I had been deemed worthy of long ago."

"How were you deemed worthy as just a child?" Alaric asked. "You were at the monastery before me, I thought?"

"When dealing with Yamaria, nothing is ever as it seems. That is a lesson I hoped you would have learned, dealing with Her daughter."

"You speak with such wisdom," Amaru said. "With no intention of discrediting your worth, I must wonder why She would grant you, of anyone, these visions. Why you over a Fyroxi, for example. You also speak as if you are familiar with my mother. As She is a goddess, I never expected anyone, even myself as her mortal daughter, to understand Yamaria's whims. From whence does your knowledge come."

"You see, Alaric, she asks the questions that matter. She doesn't mince words. You could learn much from this woman if you would only allow her lessons to pass through your absurdly thick skull."

"I don't appreciate all of these insults you fling my way, Sultan," the elf protested, using his old name for emphasis. "I've half a mind to ask you to stop."

Gawain ignored him. "Though your questions are astute, Child of Yamaria, I shan't answer them in full just yet. You will learn all you need in due time. For now, I will only say that I serve the Sun Mother much as you do. I am Her eyes, Her ears, and a weapon for Her to wield as she sees fit. And, in my most recent visions, I have seen where your spear is to be pointed next. Yamaria has entrusted me to deliver you to where you must go, to make sure that Sun's Reach keeps shining."

Amaru scrutinized the chieftain's impassive face, clean-shaven from head to chin. Somehow, though Amaru couldn't figure how, if asked, she got an impression of honesty from his noble visage. "You have saved the lives of my people, and thanks to your machinations, my journey was properly started. I cannot thank you enough, Gawain, and thus I shall trust you to deliver to words of Yamaria to me."

"This makes good hearing. She will be pleased to know that I have conducted myself accordingly. Already, your little band has taken down a few somewhat troublesome foes, but the time for trifles is over."

"Where should Helios be aimed, then?" Amaru asked.

"The Eclipse."

"The wall?" Ren wondered, confusedly. "I apologize, but as useful as that spear is, I don't think it can be used to take down a wall, especially not one with so much magic within it."

"Aye, me ax is called Cryptfiller, not Cryptbreaker!" Dalphamair slammed his fists together. "Though it could be an interesting challenge, were we not at war!"

"You garner information far more effectively when you choose to listen, rather than making your own assumptions," Gawain reprimanded. "Yes, the Eclipse is a wall. But, what few people seem to realize, is that more lies beyond that wall."

"Moonwatch lies there," Alaric said, furrowing his off-gold brow. "You cannot be insinuating that we are to cross the Eclipse into Moonwatch. If even a quarter of the legends spread about that place are true, we will die for sure!"

Gawain glanced at Amaru and blinked. "Your friends take great pleasure in ignoring the advice given to them, don't they?"

"It would seem so," Amaru admitted, twitching her tails through the air. "But, I love them all the same."

"That is good, for you shall need them to survive this coming ordeal. Yes, you will be crossing the Eclipse, as the Chillfang have, but you will not be entering Moonwatch directly. Alaric is correct in his supposition that your death would come quickly were you to step unprepared into that land ruled by Gaarhowl. Yours especially, Amaru, as the moment that frigid god noticed your presence, his servants would dog your every step. Nay, Yamaria loves you too well to send you on such a suicide mission. My visions have not been clear as I would have liked, so I don't have as much information as I'd like, but this much I can say. Most seem to have forgotten this, whether by sheer ignorance or magical design, but the line made by the Eclipse does not mark the end of the desert. Nor does it lie directly upon the border between the two kingdoms. Far from it, in fact. There is more land past the Eclipse, and it is Yamaria's belief that the threat upon your homeland stems from this place."

"So, it is my mother's will to see the Scions of the Rising Sun, who act in her name, investigate this land, find the source of this spreading corruption, and if our powers can prove strong enough, stop it?"

"That is what I have been led to believe, yes," Gawain said, finishing his glass of water and standing. "You may take a few days to recuperate at my pleasure and to prepare yourselves. As soon as you are ready, though, we strike through the Desolation. And I warn you now, that cursed land has its name for a reason. We will have to fight our way to reach the wall and then keep ourselves safe while we find the breaching point that the Chill-fang used to come through. The journey, though much shorter, shall make the trek from Oasi Sanctus to here feel like a leisurely stroll." With his piece said, Gawain turned on his heel once more and left the five companions to their food and thoughts.

"I don't like the sound of this," Alaric admitted. "But I know that look in your eyes, Amaru. You will not take no for an answer."

"Ren, do you recall the conversation about our fates?"

The short, brown-haired Fyroxi nodded. "You were always searching for some higher purpose."

"And I believe I've finally found it. This kingdom may not consider us in their rulings, but it is still *my* home, where *my* mother is worshiped. The Fyroxi that remain, the dwarves, elves, gnomes, humans, and Khindre too. They are all my people. Something has come to put them at risk and that I will not stand for. If Yamaria wishes for me to wipe out this scourge, then I will not back down from my duty."

"Well, you already know what I'm going to say," Alaric crossed the room and braced his hands on her slender but strong shoulders. "I'm behind you always. Partially because you are beholden to radiant beauty, I'll never be worthy of, but mostly because I am your friend, and we need each other to be at our best."

"I promised Sir Lion that I'd protect ye until things with the kingdom were cleared up. Seeing as th' royals have been over-thrown, methinks it's still pretty messy, so I'm at yer command." Dalphamair crushed his fist into his palm, splattering grease from his goat over his clothing and the table.

"Don't you dare forget me! As I gnome, I happen to love magic, and if you are going to travel to and through a giant magical wall, you can bet Dalph's iron-hard buttocks I'll be coming along!" Celwyn cheered.

Amaru looked finally towards Ren. "You are the newest member, and you have a pregnant wife back home, Ren. Don't feel pressured..."

She didn't even have the chance to finish before Ren was standing and shaking his head. "You are right, of course. I have a pregnant wife who would kill me if I returned home and told her I let her best friend go off to an unknown land across some magical barrier. I will pen a letter to her. I know Xio will under-stand. Besides, as someone who was in love with you once, I'm not just going to let you go off with a lovestruck elf I barely know, no matter how good of an impression he's made on me."

Amaru laughed and turned a coy smirk towards the elf. "Yes, I suppose it would be nice to have someone along to make sure Alaric's not doing anything untoward."

"Who, me?" Alaric asked innocently. "I would never." He joined his friends in their laugh. "But, in all honesty, I will be glad to have you along, Ren, but only if you're willing to help me bounce ideas off of you for wooing your dear friend."

Ren smiled slyly. "Who says I'll give you honest feedback. It might be more fun to watch you flounder through your attempts."

Amaru spun away from Alaric and eyed him evenly. "Who said you need his feedback to gain what you seek, anyway?" Before the suave elf could reply, she swept down the hall, off to prepare for the next leg of her fated journey.

EPILOGUE

LOOMS THE DARK

The sun's divine light, passing through the great window atop the Temple of Yamaria, glittered over the city. It covered every building and street in a blanket of peace, bringing radiance, a soothing balm for the open wounds it had sustained. It was as if Yamaria was looking down with sorrow at the ruin left upon her capital. Nearly every street was soaked in blood, many stains old, left by the brutal, tyrannical rule of one Geurus Gardstar. But, there, too, were a great number of pools that hadn't fully dried, the product of riots city-wide, as people demonstrated against the senseless murder of Prince Grayson and his commoner love, Reyna. The Enforcers struck without hesitation, showing no mercy to any man, woman, or child who dared to show their faces in the street, whether or not they wielded a weapon. This display of violence and depravity only deepened the passionate hatred Searstar held for the Gardstar family. One day, they vowed, they would make it inside the castle, and they would cut out the festering tumor that had inserted itself into their lives. They knew not what would come after, who would rule in Redwyn's absence, but there was no point questioning that while the tyrant still stood. Yamaria herself had designated the castle as a bastion of corruption, and any who bothered to look saw that the palace didn't shine as brightly as perhaps it once had. Geurus Gardstar had extinguished the flame in the phoenix statue atop the Roost, unknowingly kindling raging sparks in the bellies of those who knew the city's history. While the phoenix was a more recent addition, having been added some forty years ago, a similar fire had burned since antiquity, showing the never-ceasing spirit of the denizens of Sun's Reach. In slaying the royals and dousing that historic fire, Geurus had brought about his family's downfall.

In a surprising show of unity, businesses all across the city had come together to make a more unified whole. Barnio Boome, who had once made a fabulous dress for a princess to die in, worked with other tailors to sew garments emblazoned with the symbol the people had chosen. The white and yellow robes were adorned with a flaming bird curled about a red fist. The host called themselves the Phoenix Pugilists, and they went out in teams, working together to slay the demonic Enforcers before they could do harm. Bakeries and restaurants worked to keep the multitude of hungry people fed, hosting soup kitchens while inns allowed the homeless and grieving in. With commerce halted, everyone was strapped for silver, and with their city turned to a hellscape, only the corrupt and the foolish would try to turn a profit.

Inside the castle, which was shut and barricaded, tensions were nearly as high as without. Geurus spent his days tied and bolted to his throne, two loyal guards on him at all times, to ensure none of the servants got any funny ideas. His convulsions had died down in the weeks since Grayson's death, and he'd spoken more as well. But whatever came from his mouth seemed naught more than an incoherent jumble.

Velara Gardstar angrily rapped on her brother's door.

"Tarus, for Gaarhowl's sake, open the damned door!"

"What do you want?" came the muffled voice from within.

"In case you haven't noticed, our city is on fire! We need to decide what to do about it."

"Why are you asking me?" Tarus wondered, still not making any attempt to move towards the door. "We both know you won't like my input."

"Yes, Tarus, you're a bleating milk drinker, without the guts to step up and take up Father's helm! He never named an official heir, and since we are twins, it means we have to work together to complete his dream!"

A shuffling sound emanated from within, and a few moments later, the door opened to show a haggard Tarus, his hair frazzled and face streaked red by tears. "Hasn't there been enough death already?"

"Are you actually crying for them?" Velara asked incredulously. "We are Moonwatch; they are Sun's Reach. They are our foes and must be slain accordingly!"

"But they're just people, Velara. I'm beyond tired of killing innocent people." Tarus closed the door on his sister's face, which twisted in an awful, frightening rage.

"You are worthless, Tarus, do you know that?" she fumed, tapping her foot impatiently. "In case you were wondering, more news has come in. Redhawk is captured, Tarus. The rebels are building up an army, and they took control of one of our cities! Mother is dead, Tarus!" The only answer she received was the clicking of the door lock. Velara, fully taken by her rage, flipped out her knife and unleashed a flurry of deadly blows, each of which aimed to pierce her good-for-nothing brother's heart. Chips of wood flecked off with every stab, but the door was thick, and it would have taken hours to get through. "You aren't worth any further dulling of my blade," she hissed before turning away and storming down the hall. Sometimes Velara wondered if she and Tarus were truly related. They looked alike, but that was where the similarities ended. Tarus had neither their father's ruthless efficiency nor their mother's penchant for guile. He was a lamb—a lamb who had fallen in love with the woman he was supposed to kill.

Geurus must have seen this, for he'd told Velara she might need to take Grayson if something went wrong, and she had been ready. Had Father but said the word, Velara would have turned on her legendary charm, seduced the angry prince, and manipulated him, turning him against the rest of his family. But she'd never been called upon—a shame, really. Wrecking a happy home was just so much fun.

Velara wasn't surprised, though. Like always, Father had everything well in hand. Everything that had happened thus far reeked of Geurus's input, including Emery's death. Velara wasn't sure how he'd managed it, but there was no doubt in her mind that Tarus had too much milk in his bones to slay a woman who had him enthralled. Geurus had swept in and saved the day, like always. It was no wonder to Velara that he had been chosen by King Xangrus personally to tackle this mission. But now, some-how, the usurper king had reached too far. Something related to the death of Grayson and his pet Khindre witch had driven Father witless. Soon, they were going to have to put him in the dungeon, and one of them, probably her, would have to take up the throne in his stead. Velara had trained endlessly for the duties of a noblewoman, as one day, she knew she'd end up leading her house. In the savage political battlefield that was Moonwatch, Tarus would have found himself dead in the trenches, while

Velara stood proud as queen of the hill. But, now, everything was going wrong. After Geurus's incident, the Enforcers had gone out of control and wreaked havoc across the city. That, in and of itself, wasn't an issue. They were keeping the ravening citizens at bay at the very least. But Velara had to figure out how to control them. Now, the demonic creatures were doing damage, but it was disorganized and not as effective. If Velara could helm their attacks, they'd break the knaves' resistance in no time. It would be beautiful, a perfect symphony of destruction—just the way Mother would want to be avenged.

You are worthy. Suddenly a voice intruded into Velara's thoughts. It was cold and powerful, with the faintest hint of a death rattle behind its resonance.

"Of course I am," she replied almost instantly. "I'm me, after all."

A creaking door sound followed the ethereal voice's chuckle. The Dread Princess hadn't even realized where she was, but her feet had unconsciously carried her in front of the only tower she hadn't explored in the castle courtyard. It looked older than the rest, and the squeal of the hinges told of a building left in disuse for a very long time. A few rats scurried out as the probing fingers of Sunfall reached into the gloomy darkness.

"Who are you?" she asked the disembodied voice, taking a few cautious steps towards the door. She couldn't see anything inside, no visible force that might have caused this door to open. Velara couldn't remember the last time she'd been frightened of anything, and today was no different. There had to be secrets within this tower, if it had been shut never to be opened again. Secrets, perhaps, that might be able to rescue this situation.

Your father is a lost cause, his soul devoured by the Aethyr, and your mother is slain. We need a new agent to do our work in this land. You are worthy. If you would have more power than you could ever dream of, then come forward and join us. The Lich Lords move upon Sun's Reach very soon, and unprepared as they are, they will be crushed under our feet. What say you, Velara Dyrdra Gardstar?

"I say we have some fun." Velara crossed the threshold, her ambitions soaring high as they ever had.

END